Contents

Preamble

The first April day had been fine and sunny. It was one of those days that brought out the best of Paris. Couples strolled about arm in arm; men in smart suites, women in gauzy dresses holding twirling parasols over their shoulders. Trees wore new leaves and birds flitted around between them. Street cafés were full of people taking coffee, or wine, or snacks, or patisseries; even people going about their business seemed to do so without hurrying. It had been an idyllic Paris spring day and now it was a calm, warm spring night. It was also late; well past midnight. The great river was low and it ran sluggishly through the city from where it had entered at Ivry in the south and took a long curving turn to the west before starting on its journey out to the Atlantic Ocean at Le Havre and Honfleur. It had been around this long, gradual curve that the city had been built. As with many great cities, the river was its beating heart. It was a source of its trade and commerce, of its water and of its fish. It was also the destination of all the city's sewage. Thus the flotsam that made its sedate way down the river, passing either side of the *Île Saint-Louis* and the *Île de la Cité*, was a mixture of the natural and the unnatural. Small branches mixed with sodden rubbish, with shadowy ducks trying to pick something interesting as the clumps passed.

The slow river created eddies from time to time and where the river re-joined itself at the west end of the *Île St. Louis*, part of the flow paused in its downstream journey and bent back towards the gap between the two islands. The detritus that was caught by the small counter current followed and sometimes became caught on the narrow beach that bordered the *Quai de Bourbon*.

So it was with a slightly larger than usual such lump drifting downstream that slowly caught the eddy and was held against the shore, bobbing gently until a few curious gulls descended, attracted by the smell and started to peck at the eyes.

Chapter 1: Friday 1st April   Scene 1: The Journey to Work

The distance from his apartment on the north side of the *Place des Vosges* to his office on the *Île de la Cité* was little more than a couple of miles. He usually walked. As Chief Inspector of *La Sûreté,* as it was called, the criminal investigation branch of the Paris Police, he was entitled to a cab to take him to and from work and, indeed, this morning there were one or two of the regular cab drivers who had been available as usual to take him as and when he wanted. They had divided the days between them and one or another was always around at the time he usually left for work. Drangnet was a creature of habit and they knew him well enough to know when they might be required and when not. They also knew when the weather was bad enough to stop him walking and on those occasions one or another would wait outside no. 26 on the north east corner of the square for a few minutes from 6:30am to pick him up. If he knew he wanted them in advance, then he would open a curtain in his first-floor window slightly as a signal. It was a loose sort of arrangement, but it seemed to work more often than not. If, for some reason, it didn't, then most of the time he could hail a cab in the street. It didn't happen often. His regular cab drivers were somewhat possessive and seldom left him completely to his own devices. The same could be said of most of his work colleagues. They showed their loyalty too in a myriad of different ways, few of which he was ever conscious of. He was that sort of man. He would have been astonished to have been told of the high esteem in which he was held by the people who worked around him. Most of the time, however, he just enjoyed the walk.

Today it was a bright spring day but still early. The sun was out brightly but, as yet, without any real heat in it. Drangnet wore a good tweed coat and a pair of light calfskin gloves and Homburg hat. A gentleman's walking cane completed the ensemble. As usual he carried no briefcase. Long ago he had trained himself not to bring papers home from work. He usually stayed long enough at the Quai each day to deal with most of it. He almost never brought his work home with him, save, perhaps, in his mind.

There was a limited variation in his route to work and he didn't particularly make a point of thinking about that either. The most direct route took him out of the southern gate of the *Place des Vosges* and down the *Rue Royale* towards the river and through a series of small streets until he reached the *Caserne des Celestins*. The barracks for cavalry detachments of Republican Guard had been created out of the old Celestin Monastery after it had been abandoned in 1779. He would then turn west along the river past the famous *Bibliothèque de l'Arsenal* until he reached one of the bridges, *Le Pont au Change*, from the right bank that connected with the *Île de la Cité*. It had originally been home to the goldsmiths and money changers of Paris. His office was on the island in the north side of the *Palais de Justice* that now occupied most of the western end of the *Île* at number 7, *Quai de l'Horloge*. Occasionally when the weather was good, or he wasn't pressed for time, there were a number of variations to his route that didn't add too much to the overall distance he had to walk but served to keep him interested.

He enjoyed passing the many landmarks that had become so familiar to him over the years. He enjoyed too the easy familiarity with which he was greeted by the shop keepers and early restaurant staff along the way; some early customers too, regular travellers to work like himself. Ones who were also creatures of routine and habit who would smile or raise a hand as he passed. If he was early some would possibly expect him to stop for the pleasure of a cup of coffee or an easy word. More often he would just hurry by with a smile and cheerful wave. A lot of people tried to catch his eye. Many of them knew who he was; an important man, a man they liked but were happy avoid, professionally at least. Today, as usual, the streets were already quite busy; pedestrians heading in all directions; cabs as well. There was a constant line of carts heading west along the *Rue Saint Antoine* laden with produce towards the great market of *Les Halles*. The daily hubbub that always accompanied day-time Paris had risen a little too as the great city he served woke up and again set about its business and its streets began to fill with the sounds of horses and people.

His path took him westwards opposite to the length of the two islands in the river. He had always been amused by the rapid changes in street names as he walked. Starting with the *Quai les Celestines*,

4

the simple road along the riverbank became the *Quai Saint Paul,* the *Quai des Orpies,* the *Quai de la Grève,* the *Quai de Port au Blé,* the *Quai Pelletier* and finally the *Quai de Gevres* all in the space of a few hundred yards. Finally, he arrived at the *Pont au Change* across onto the island. Stretching out in front of him on the north side of the island along the *Quai de l'Horlorges* were the four great towers of the *Palais de Justice* that took up most of the western end of the *Île de la Cité.*

One way or another he had been in or near the Palais de Justice all his working life as a policeman; some twenty-five or so years. And for all of that time and more, it had been a building site. For centuries the west end of the *Île de la Cité* had been home to many bits of the administration of civic Paris. The *Palais de Justice* itself had originally been the residence of the Kings of France from the sixth century onwards and was also the site of their royal chapel, *Sainte Chapelle.* Then it became the home of the Paris Parliament, the Judiciary and the Treasury from the fourteenth century until the revolution of 1789. The west end of the island also was home to the *Concièrge,* the jail, the municipal barracks, *La Caserne Municipale,* and a hospital. By the beginning of the nineteenth century many of these buildings were in need of repair and restoration and the building work had started. Then in the mid-century the huge programme of reconstruction was started under the aegis of Georges-Eugène Haussmann who almost completely remodelled the centre of Paris. He built a new *Préfecture de Police* and a *Tribunal de Commerce* and a vastly expanded *Hôtel-Dieu* hospital in the space between the Palais and the great cathedral of *Notre Dame* that still dominated the eastern end of the island. Haussmann also extended the *Palais* across the full width of the island from the *Rue de Harlay* to the new and widened *Boulevard du Palais* to the east and west and from the original northern façade along the *Quai de l'Horloge.* This now reached all the way across to the southern edge to the *Quai des Orfèvfe.*

Throughout all this time the business of the *Palais de Justice* had to continue, of course, and the many departments and offices that were housed in the building were continually being relocated from one inconvenient place to another. Thus, it was often difficult for visitors and staff alike to find the current offices of the *Préfet de Police* and his large staff, the parquet of the judiciary and their clerks, as well as

5

the many of the other departments as they were regularly relocated to some obscure corner to make way for yet another phase of the building programme. Drangnet was often amused by the fact that sometimes his fellow detectives' first detection job of the day was to find their own offices. In reality the *Sûreté*, as his department was called, had been more fortunate than most. Almost since its inception during the early eighteen thirties and the days of its first chief, the infamous criminal-turned-policeman, Eugène-Francois Vidocq, it had been housed at *7 Quai de l'Horloge*, on the north western corner of the Palais just along from the rather grand main entrance to the *Cour de Cessation*, the major Court Rooms of France.

Much of the projected building work had been complete by 1870 then the war with Germany had intervened and Paris had been besieged by Bismarck's troops. France's subsequent defeat had led to the brief but violent takeover of power by the Communards. At the end of those few terrible months many buildings had been destroyed by shelling or by arson. Some, like the great Palais des Tuileries, were almost completely destroyed and, possibly because of their symbolism as the imperial palaces of France, hadn't been rebuilt. Others like the *Hôtel de Ville* had been. Many of the new buildings on the *Île* too were attacked with fire although were less severely damaged. So, after the Government had bloodily suppressed the uprising, the building work had started yet again, and Dragnet's life resumed in the habitual ocean of rubble and dust. His department had been fortunate than most. The fire damage was much less on his corner of the Palais and, more or less, they could resume their work without too much interruption.

As he walked he felt, as he always did, a growing sense of anticipation the nearer he got to his office. Much of his day was already set with the business that had been in train when he left the previous evening. One way or another these matters had occupied his mind overnight. No matter what he did of an evening, there were always things that pushed in on his thoughts; especially when he just spent the evening at home with a book and a little music. But the anticipation he felt each morning on his journey to work came from the unknown; the business that he didn't yet know about; the business that had arisen without his knowledge during the previous night as he ate, read and finally slept. He relished the moment when his morning walk ended. He had passed the four great towers of the *Palais de Justice* and he entered the great building, made his way to his office on the third floor, sat at his desk and reached for the inevitable pile of papers that had mysteriously grown from nothing overnight.

For a man of his senior rank, his office was almost austere; more of an academic study than the centre of activities of one of the most influential policemen in Paris. The walls were lined with bookshelves containing the department's collection of legal and administrative reference books. The furniture was good quality and dignified in style; a far cry from the over-decorated interiors of many of his senior colleagues. A few surprisingly modern paintings also graced the walls, but the main decoration was supplied by the three long windows that looked out over the river back across to the right bank. It was a quiet and business-like room. The only alien note was struck by the new and extremely ugly machine that had been recently installed and which hung malevolently on the wall beside the door. The new invention of the telephone had recently come to Paris and a condition of the contract that awarded a licence to the newly established *Société Génerale du Téléphone* to create a network in central Paris was that it should include connections to the more important administrative offices. The SGT was not particularly happy with the arrangement as they could charge the City considerably less for their new service that they could the affluent businesses and families for whom the service was originally intended. However, many of the police stations in the centre of town now had a telephone service and bit by bit police telephone boxes were beginning to appear on the streets too. Drangnet had found the actual service was of limited use as it was both unreliable and, for the moment at least, so unfamiliar that people tended not to use it. However, there is was; the future, he knew, but still an alien presence in his dignified office.

He turned to the pile of papers on his desk. They were arranged in chronological order, the most recent page on top. They were all the same; a standard report form that ordered the events they described in an organised and controlled way starting with the time and the location, then proceeding to a description of events, a list of the people involved, the origin of the information and a list of the men who had dealt with the matter during the night. All the events of the previous night were listed here in spite of not all being his immediate concern. It was a system of reporting that he had started years ago when he got his current job. Even if many of the events, most, in fact, were immediately handed on to other departments, he wanted to have a feel for everything that had happened overnight in his beloved Paris.

He quickly ran down the pile, pencil in hand; twenty pieces of paper, drawing each page from the pile one at a time, sliding it in front of him and scanning the contents with a practiced eye. Each page got only a few seconds before being marked in the last space at the bottom of the form with his squiggled initial and a small mark to say where the business of the page should go to in his organisation. Sometimes he added a short remark or instruction. Very few of the pages remained on his desk for long for he and his colleagues to add to their already considerable workload. Today it was just one.

The process was soon finished and at eight o'clock exactly he took the remaining form in hand, left his office, crossed the small landing at the top of the stairs and entered a well-equipped and comfortable conference room. It was time for the daily briefing with his senior staff. A large rectangular table was surrounded by eight rather formal chairs; one at either end and three on either side. Not for the first time he thought it looked more like a dining room than a briefing room. As usual the full team was already assembled. It was a standing joke between them. Knowing how much he disliked any form of ceremony or fuss; they made a point of arriving early so he would be forced to make what amounted to a grand entry to their daily meeting. Originally, they had even risen as he entered the room. He was after all the boss. He had played the game for a while, arriving progressively earlier to try to get there first but they had defeated him by arriving earlier still. In the end, good-humouredly, he gave up. At least he managed to stop them getting up. So as usual he sat down at the head of the table; Roger Gant, his deputy, at the opposite end and the rest of the group on either side, all looking at him expectantly. That was hardly surprising. He was the man in charge. He was Louis Drangnet, *Chef Inspecteur du Service de la Police de la Sûreté de la Ville de Paris* and these were his investigators.

'Good morning, gentlemen. Let's get down to it. Roger could you bring up us to date with things, please.'

Roger Gant, Inspector in the department, nodded and did precisely that. It wasn't a long report. Most of the crime that was current in their area of central Paris was relatively minor and had already been handed over to the uniform departments who had probably discovered it in the first place. It was Drangnet's policy to deal with most petty crime, especially amongst the young, with a light hand believing rightly that a stern talking to by a large man in a police uniform would prevent many young pick pockets and petty thieves from doing it again – for the moment, at least. A short stay in one of Paris's numerous and thoroughly squalid prison cells was as much a deterrent as anything. Drunken brawls and street disturbances were not their concern unless something serious or violent transpired.

'We arrested a Monsieur Peruzzi, the thief who had robbed the house of the Comte de Billancourt,' Gant continued. 'As you knew we had a good description from a passer-by who actually recognised the man as he was leaving through the back window. We visited him at home to find him and his wife sorting the loot on their kitchen table. That has been handed over to the prosecutors. The other cases on our books at the moment are still being investigated but very little progress in being made. So very little to report that's new,' he concluded looking down the length of the table.

Gant knew his Chief's penchant for short meetings and he certainly didn't like going over old ground when there was little to report.

'Good,' Drangnet said briskly waving the incident report in his hand slightly. 'That's just as well as we seem to have something more important on our plates this morning. We have a dead prostitute at *Rue de Hanovre* in the *deuxième*. Roger, you'll come with me. The rest of you please get on with your current investigations. We should have enough information for a more general briefing either this evening or as usual tomorrow morning. Jean?' he nodded towards one of the new members of his group, 'Please go around to the *Préfecture* and notify them. They'll need to assign a *juge d'instruction* to the case. Thank you.'

With that he got up from the table and went to collect his hat and coat. Gant did the same.

Chapter 1: Friday 1st April Scene 2: The First Prostitute Murder

By the time they arrived at *6, Rue de Hanovre* it was almost mid-morning. The death had been reported to the local police precinct on the *Rue du Croissant*, during the night. A pair of uniformed *gardians de la paix* had been dispatched to make a preliminary investigation and the news had been telegraphed in to the *Sûreté*. It was a quiet looking house in a terrace of similar ones on one of the narrow roads that ran east to west just off the *Boulevard des Capucines* near the newly built opera house, the *Palais Garnier*. A small crowd had already gathered outside the house, and the two uniformed members of the *Police Municipal* now stationed at the doorway were looking flustered as they tried to hold people back from entering. Unfortunately, these included someone who had a right to be there; Dr Xavier Dankovich, the Deputy Director of the Paris Faculty of Medicine and Professor of Forensic Medicine. He also acted as a medical examiner. Irascible at the best of times, he was positively fuming as Drangnet and Gant arrived.

'*Chef de la Sûreté*. Perhaps you would inform this numbskull that I have business here?'

Drangnet nodded the man through, then followed him, giving the offending constable a quick wink as he passed. There was a small crowd inside the house comprised mostly of the ladies who would normally have their business there. An older, rather matronly woman came up to them and offered the barest of bobbed curtsies.

'Second floor back, Chef.'

'Thank you, Madame Vierne.' Drangnet replied with a slight smile. 'I'm very sorry to see this. I hope the girls are all right?'

They had met before.

'Thank you, Chef. I'll have them all in the parlour down here when you want to speak to them.'

Drangnet smiled his thanks as he moved further into the house. Dankovich took his arm as they went up the narrow stairs together. He was by no means in his first youth and had remained in his post at the School of Medicine long after his possible retirement. Now in his eighties he was still one of the most widely respected medical teachers and authorities on the new science of forensic medicine. The two had worked together often in the past and were good friends. They shared many interests including music and playing chess. They were also two of the very few people in the French police service to have a deep suspicion of the new science of anthropometrics; the use of body dimensions to identify criminal suspects that was beginning to become popular in other parts of the police force. Dankovich was an old-fashioned medical man and Drangnet trusted that.

'As usual, I suppose you want to look first, my friend?' said Dankovich.

'Yes please, Xavier. Don't worry. I won't touch anything.' Drangnet replied. 'Just give me a minute or two.'

Leaving Gant to keep the good doctor company for a while, he stepped into the room. Dragnet usually wanted to have a few moments alone on the crime scene if he could. Often, when he arrived it was a crowded place with many people milling around most of whom had little reason to be there, if any at all. From time to time he left word with the local precinct brigadiers around the city that he wanted the scene of the crime kept private. The local uniformed police were usually the first to be called to a violent crime and if they could keep the scene free of voyeurs and reporters for a while at least, then it made his job a lot easier. This message had obviously got through this time for on the way in he saw at least three newspaper reporters in the crowd outside getting outraged because the policeman on the door wouldn't let them in.

At first glance the room looked undisturbed. The heavy maroon damask curtains were still drawn and the gas lamps at the walls were still alight. The room was comfortably furnished and there was no evidence of a struggle of any sort. The bed was relatively undisturbed and the furniture was still in place. The victim lay on her bed as if she were no more than asleep. She was dressed in a long white chemise, having left her day dress draped over a small sofa at the foot of the bed. It was only the staring look in her eyes that betrayed any signs of distress. Her eyes were bulging out and there

12

was a thin line of saliva trickling down from the edge of her open mouth. A large lace pillow lay to one side of her head.

Drangnet stood quietly at the doorway and slowly took in the scene, committing it to memory. It was a typical room of a middle rank prostitute. This was not one of the Grand Dames of their trade, surrounded by luxury and rich suitors. It was no *Chabanais* or *La Fleur Blanche*. But nor was it a *maison d'abattage* or a back-street whore's room, dark, squalid and unhealthy. It was a typical *maison close*; bourgeois and comfortable and, above all from his point of view, legally licenced and regulated.

It only took a moment or two. All he wanted was an initial impression. Later he would be back for a more detailed examination but for now, having quickly glanced around, he stood aside and let Dankovich into the room. He paused for a moment at the top of the stairs while he addressed his deputy.

'Roger. I'll have a preliminary chat with the ladies. After that I'll want to get statements from them all but you should wait until they are on their own. Perhaps we could both do that to save time. I don't want to haul them down to the office. It would be all rather unsettling and draw much too much publicity. But before that, please could you just look around the house? Look for any entrances other than the front door or any evidence of a forced entry through the windows. It is slightly too easy to assume that the poor girl's last client was her killer. It may be someone completely different. Try to find out if there's anyone else other than the clients who regularly comes here; deliveries or even social callers.'

Gant just nodded as Drangnet turned down the staircase. He didn't make any objection to the instructions that were in fact completely unnecessary. He had done this sort of thing many times before. But he knew that his boss was just going through his own mental checklist. No offense was intended. He went into the front parlour where a group of six young ladies and the house manager were waiting. They all looked worried, but Madame Vierne had done a good job of calming them all down. They were all modestly dressed in their church best and looked, to his eyes at least, impossibly young and innocent; pretty too.

13

This was Drangnet at his most avuncular. He had long since gone beyond having any reservations about Paris and its large population of prostitutes. To him they were citizens like any under his care. He felt responsible for their welfare, perhaps more than with others. They were more vulnerable than most of his other charges. He felt a paternal instinct and the young women looked on this middle-aged policeman in a similar way. They knew him and would have no secrets from him. It was Madame Vierne who started.

'Chief Inspector. I've talked to my girls. Other than the usual clients there were no strangers here last night. We must assume that Lisette was killed by her last client.'

Drangnet saw no reason to point out that this was only one of a number of possibilities.

'Did you see who that was, Madame?'

She shook her head a little sadly.

'No, monsieur. There was quite a lot of coming and going last night with clients throughout the evening. I recognised a few of them but not all, I'm afraid.'

Drangnet thought for a moment. He knew that the girls would be reluctant to speak out while they were all together. But he also knew that Madame Vierne would talk to each of them quietly and that he would get some good information later. He did, however, offer one thought.

'Tell me, ladies. Did any of you have new clients yesterday; anyone that you haven't seen before?'

He felt instinctively that a regular client would be much less likely to do something like this, if indeed it was a client at all. He was disappointed to see all six girls nod their heads. Unfortunately, there were many visitors to the city at the moment and that would inevitably increase the business for Madame Vierne and her colleagues. He was still pretty sure that they wouldn't talk freely whilst they were all together.

'I'm truly sorry that this has happened, and I assure you that I'll do everything I can to catch the person responsible. I'll want either Inspector Gant or myself to talk to each of you individually to see if you can remember anything. I'll also talk to Madame Vierne about how we can possibly make thing a little safer here for you. I know that many of your clients won't want to be recognised, in public at least, but we have to think of something.'

He then turned to Madame.

'I also think it would be better if you closed for a day or two while we finish our examinations. In any case, I'm not sure how many clients will want to come when they see police all over the place.'

'Of course, Monsieur,' she replied and turned to the girls. 'Please go to your rooms now, ladies. I'll call you to come and talk to Chief Inspector Dragnet or his colleague when they're ready.'

There was a general rustling of long skirts and petticoats and they all got up and made their way out of the room, each offering a small bobbed curtsey and a charming smile to Drangnet as they went. As soon as they were alone, Drangnet continued.

'Tell me, Madame, what records do you keep? I know you must keep some as you have to pay your taxes to the city.'

Actually, he knew that the laws that now governed the operation of *maisons closes* within the city boundaries were quite strict. Houses were required to keep sufficient records to enable them pay income tax to the city and to withstand the occasional audit. They were also required to register the girls and make sure that they received regular medical checks and had places to sleep when they weren't working. The *maison* usually supplied food and lodging when they were not at work and assistance with their costumes but all that was usually voluntary.

'Well, I think you know most of them already, Monsieur. There are the records that we have to keep. Apart from those we don't really keep track of our clients at all. Most of them wouldn't like to be on some sort of list or have to sign in or some such. I see most of them, of course, when they arrive. I have to collect the fee and obviously, I get to know the regulars even if I actually don't know their names or who they are. We do try to respect their privacy.'

'Do you ever reject someone; someone who you don't know, perhaps?'

She drew herself up a little.

'Well yes. Sometimes I don't allow someone in if they don't look right; if they're badly dressed or if they start arguing about the fees. But not many. We have a certain reputation and, of course, we are not cheap. That, in itself, seems to keep a lot of the riff-raff out.'

The next question was a little more difficult and he didn't know whether to be embarrassed or proud. It all depended on one's point of view, he thought.

'Madame, perhaps you could tell be what actually happens when client comes here, especially one that you don't know.'

Her light smile bore witness to her understanding of his predicament. He was actually admitting to having to investigate a crime in a brothel without ever have been a customer of one.

'Well, they all have to see me, of course. I decide who goes to which of my girls. Some of the regular have their preferences and we try to accommodate those. I collect the fees. If the girl is available, she will be in this sitting room. If she isn't, we show the client in here and they'll wait. The girls who aren't occupied will chat to them, get them some tea or a glass of something.'

'I don't suppose you keep records of the names of your clients?'

'No, Chief Inspector. I don't think that our clients would like that very much.'

Dragnet was all too well aware that while he was talking about the clients there were other possible people who might have done the killing; the six girls and their matron in front of him to name but seven. There was also the possibility of someone totally different who managed to get in without anyone knowing.

'And you didn't see anything out of the ordinary yesterday; no strangers hanging around outside or visitors that were unusual?'

'No, monsieur.'

Drangnet sighed. He wasn't entirely sure whether Madame Vierne was being truthful with him, but he didn't think it would be useful to press her further. One final question remained.

'Do all the girls stay here all night or do they have somewhere else where they sleep – their own apartment or some such?

'Some of the girls have an apartment or a room away from here. If they do, they mostly share with each other, of course. They don't make enough money to afford anything special. Some stay here, especially the newer ones before they have settled in.'

'Tell me, Madame,' he asked almost embarrassedly, 'do any of them go home for the night - with their clients, as it were?'

She again smiled at his embarrassment.

'I try to dissuade them from any such action, of course. But from time to time a regular client might strike up something more than, shall we say, a strictly professional relationship with one of my girls so I have been known to make the occasional exception. As long as the man is a reliable sort and I know him and where he lives, and he pays what he should then there is not usually much danger in it. But at the moment, I have no one with such an arrangement.'

He felt there was little more he would get from Madame Vierne. He just thanked her and went out into the hall to catch up with Gant and to start the individual interviews.

'Is Dankovich still here?'

'No, Boss. He's already left and taken the body to the morgue as usual. Can't think there is much to be learned there though. She was obviously suffocated with her own pillow. But you know what an old woman Dankovich can be; still wants to dot the i's and cross all the t's.'

Drangnet nodded.

17

'What about the judge. Has anyone turned up yet?'

Gant shook his head.

'No. I hardly think that the simple murder of a prostitute would interest him or his department. We'll hopefully be left on our own for this one.'

'You're probably right, Roger. So much the better. But I'll make sure they've been informed in any case when I get back to the office. No harm in covering our backs.'

Drangnet knew that while, in theory at least, all his investigations fell under the remit of the office of the *Juge d'Instruction* and his examining magistrates, they often tended not to get involved in lesser cases. They seemed increasingly to take an interest only in the higher profile cases; the ones where their reputations could be enhanced. There was clearly little value to these high-ranking lawyers of a simple prostitute murder. For himself, Drangnet was perfectly happy with this. The appointed judge usually tended to interfere more than he helped. However, Drangnet would send a report to get lost in the files of the Palais de Justice just to be on the safe side.

'All right. I think I've got as much as I can out of Madame Vierne for the moment, so I suggest we split the girls between us and get their statements. Then whatever time we finish individually, we could meet up again at the office later this afternoon and put the thing together. On your way back, could you call into the station on the *Rue du Croissant* and make sure that they have a couple of men on patrol outside the house for the next day or so? It just a gesture obviously and I don't think that Madame Vierne will be very happy about it. But at least it'll demonstrate to passers-by and to the press that we are taking this seriously. In any case I've asked for the place to be closed for the next two days. Let's meet up again at 3pm.'

'All right, Sir,' replied Gant with a slight smile. He knew full well that it was lunch that was Dragnet's priority now.

Having finished two of the six interviews and leaving the rest to his deputy, Drangnet started to walk back towards the *Sûreté* at a brisk pace. The day was still bright and sunny, and the streets were now teeming with people. Had anyone been observing, they would indeed have thought that this policeman's route took him more or less straight towards the *Île de la Cité*. He walked down the length of the *Rue St. Augustin* until he reached the *Rue Montmartre* and turned south along it. He walked through the great market halls of *Les Halles* and continued south. The same observer would, by now, be convinced that Drangnet was headed directly to the *Quai de l'Horlorge* that lay only a few hundred metres further on. But just as he entered the *Rue des Halles* to take him there he turned sharply to his right into a little alley called the *Rue de Decaux* and dived into one of his favourite restaurants, the *Café du Marché*. His destination had been lunch all along. He was a regular visitor there and was greeted with the easy familiarity of a regular customer but equally with a slight reserve as he was also a well-known policeman and the company that made up most of his fellow diners was not at its most relaxed sharing their tables with an officer of the law; especially one with a reputation of being the best thief-catcher in Paris. It was a fair guess that most of them were thieves in one form or another for they mostly came from the huge market close by. It was a favourite place for Drangnet because the food was good, solidly and traditionally cooked. Produce came directly from the market and always had a freshness that made the simple cooking worth tasting. It was also very reasonably priced and a policeman, even one as senior as Drangnet, was not paid an excessive salary.

It was a noisy place with harassed waiters taking trays-full of food around, threading their way between customers who were constantly coming and going between the tables. He nodded at the owner and sat to settled into his usual lunch, the plat du jour and a carafe of simple red wine.

Most of the regulars left him to eat his lunch in peace. One of the problems he had learned to live with was being recognised in many of the cafés and restaurants within reach of the *Sûreté* offices. It wasn't usually a matter of celebrity at all, but many people thought that seeing the policeman eating alone was a good opportunity to interrupt him and talk. Drangnet couldn't really discourage this too much in spite of it regularly getting in the way of his meal. From time to time some useful titbit of information would come his way. But more often it was a pet grouse or a complaint or a request for a favour.

Today's daily menu was a lamb stew made with small onions and carrots and a good white wine. Dauphinoise potatoes were the vegetables. As usual it was completely satisfying, and the large plateful was quickly finished. Usually he didn't eat a pudding but on this occasion the pear tart looked particularly irresistible. So, having savoured the last morsel of that, he began to look around for the waiter to settle up and leave for his meeting with Gant. Unusually Serge Blanco, the café owner, arrived at his table and sat down opposite him pushing a small glass of Marc across to his customer. Drangnet was surprised. Blanco was not one of those owners who mixed with the customers too often. He had started life transporting oysters and other shellfish from the Cancale and Quiberon Bays in Brittany to the *Les Halles* market but after a while he got tired of the long hours looking at his horse's rump and set up his restaurant cooking and selling what he had been transporting. Business had been slow in the beginning with the locals initially being suspicious of someone who came from the depths of the primitive countryside, but things had taken a turn for the better after Blanco had taken up with the daughter of one of the main market stallholders. The woman was not only a charming hostess and a considerable beauty but also had her father's head for running a business. That the café was full today was due primarily to her elegant presence on show running the bar and keeping accounts.

'Bad business last night,' was his opening comment. Monsieur Blanco was not a man for long sentences. If fact, Drangnet could hardly recall the man making conversation of any length before. He remained silent wondering what would follow.

'Her father works here in the market. Her brother too. Family. Any idea who did it?'

Drangnet just shook his head.

'Not yet.'

'Nice girl.' The man continued. 'Hadn't an enemy in the world.'

Drangnet didn't feel the need to remark that she certainly had at least one. He was much more interested in why Blanco was having this conversation with him at all. Up until now, and he had been a regular customer for a number of years, the most he had got from the man had been an occasional curt nod of recognition when he came in. He decided to join in.

'She was a local girl, then?'

It was the man's turn to nod.

'Many of the local working girls have family around here,' he replied. 'Some even work in the market from time to time when someone's short-handed. It's a big family around here and Madame takes care of them.'

'Madame?' Drangnet was immediately interested. Blanco looked a little embarrassed and immediately changed the subject.

'Have you got a suspect yet?'

'No, not yet.'

Dragnet instinctively knew that this was not the time or place to press the man further. He just filed the remark away and made a mental note to come back to it as he continued:

'Any thoughts about it around the market today?'

'Want us to do your job for you, Inspector?'

'No, Monsieur Blanco. But help from concerned citizens is always welcome. Perhaps you can ask around. I'm sure people would be more prepared to talk to you than to me.'

His companion just grunted. But as Drangnet reached into his pocket to find some money, he held up his hand.

'Today, Inspector, you are my guest. Now just push off and catch the bastard who killed little Lisette.'

Drangnet was surprised. This was most unexpected. He hadn't immediately made any connection with the Les Halles community, but something was clearly going on.

He left and walked the short remaining distance to the Quai. Gant was nowhere to be seen. Drangnet sat at his desk and started the usual administration that accompanied any new investigation. He checked that the message had in fact been sent through to the *Palais de Justice* next door, informing the office of the *Juge d'instruction* of what had happened. He hoped that the judge would continue to keep out of it as life was always much simpler if he didn't insist on taking charge of the investigation. It was the judge's decision as to the extent to which he would get involved in any of Drangnet's current cases. But the official papers had to be filed in any case. He also sent a young constable to Dr.Dankovich's mortuary in the forensic medicine department of the *L'hôpital de la Pitié-Salpêtrière* up the river in the 13th to wait for his report. He began to write up the interviews he had carried out earlier and make some personal notes as well. It was all the necessary paperwork that was increasingly part of running a large modern police department. Much to Drangnet's amusement, when Gant finally arrived, he had the grace to appear a little flustered.

'Ah,' smiled Drangnet. 'A combination of pretty girls to interview and a good lunch, perhaps?'

Gant just shrugged. These two had worked together for too long for any offence to be intended or taken.

'Right. What do we have?

Gant's impressions were very similar to his own. None of the people he interviewed could remember anything particularly unusual from last night's activities. Some of the clients had been new but all had passed Madame Vierne casual examination. Each of the six girls had spent the night in the house, and none had heard anything unusual.

'What about getting into the house? Could a stranger have got in at some stage?'

'Well, the place is pretty busy while it's open. There would usually be someone around although it must be admitted that it's not unusual for strangers to be in the house obviously and even Madame Vierne could hardly be expected to keep track of all the comings and goings. She can't be everywhere at once. There's also no real reason for any of the girls to know whether someone they see or even talk to is anything more than just a client. So no, I'd say it would be pretty easy for someone to get in and out even during the day, let alone after the house is closed at about midnight. Someone could have got in during the working day, hide perhaps, kill the girl and get out again. There are enough windows front and back and, given that Madame's bedroom is in the basement at the back, they could probably just open the front door and walk out when they felt like it.'

Drangnet sighed.

'Motive?'

'Could be anything, Boss, from a dissatisfied customer, something personal with the girl that has nothing to do with the house, or just some passing madman. All are possible and we've no way of finding out that I can see.'

Drangnet remembered his recent lunch conversation.

'We may be able to get something from *Les Halles*. I got the impression from Blanco, the owner of the *Café du Marché*, that the girl was known to them or at least had some family connection of some sort. Maybe tomorrow, I can go and start asking around. Perhaps you can organise some of the gendarmerie so ask around the neighbourhood. Until then there seems little we can to but file the paperwork and wait for the medical report, although I wouldn't hope for any great surprises there. It seemed obvious to me that Mademoiselle Flandrette was just suffocated with her own pillow and we are unlikely to find who did it. Let's start tomorrow with some questions around the neighbourhood and unless we haven't made any real progress by this time tomorrow, I suspect that something else more important will arrive on our desks.'

'Humph,' exclaimed Gant as he got up. 'I'm surprised you got anything out of the miscrable old sod, Blanco. He never talks to me. God knows what goes on in that place, though. In any case he definitely doesn't like me very much. I did him for selling illegal liquor a year or two back and I'm sure he spits in my food whenever I eat there. You better follow that up, Boss. Not me.'

He paused as he was halfway out of the door and looked back.

'I assume there will be no *juge d'instruction* on this. Not important enough for that lot.'

Drangnet smiled. It was often Gant who had to deal with the Juge's interference in the investigation rather that he. There wasn't much love lost there.

'Probably not. But I've notified them in any case.'

Gant left and Drangnet sat silently at his desk. He had had all too many of this sort of case during his career. Without a reliable eyewitness cases of this sort was always difficult. Paris could be a violent place and killings were a regular occurrence and often remained unsolved. Higher profile killings could often be solved as they were usually reasons for them; motives that could be discovered by talking to people. Street killings were often motiveless, spur of the moment events and there was usually precious little evidence to work with. Nor did people seem to care very much. All of a sudden Gant's head reappeared around the door.

'Oh, by the way, Boss, your friend the President sent a message to say that your tennis game will be an hour later than arranged. Some daft excuse about affairs of state or some such malarkey.'

'Thank you, Roger.' Gant replied smilingly. It was an old joke.

Chapter 1: Friday 1st April   Scene 3: A Game of Tennis

He stayed on an extra hour or so in his office before setting out to walk to the recently constructed pair of tennis courts that now graced the western end of the Tuileries Gardens on the edge of the *Place de la Concorde*. It was still light, but a slight chill had set in. It was still very early spring, and the day was cooling rapidly. He kept up a brisk walking pace.

Drangnet had been playing tennis for most of his life. As a child he had played the popular game of Long Tennis joining in with groups of friends who got together to play in local parks wherever he was living. It was a game easily set up and was open to variable numbers on people on either side. It needed no net and sometimes was played with a racquet and sometime just with the hand. The young Drangnet had a good eye and was fast over the ground and was much in demand when sides were drawn up. He was also adept at judging the chase, the crucial measure of where the ball landed. The decision of whether to play the ball or not was the key to success and Drangnet was skilled at making the decisions whether to play the ball or to leave it. The game was still played outdoors in the public parks and gardens of Paris.

But it was the more complex variation of the game, short tennis, the *Jeu de Paume*, where the game was played indoors in specially constructed courts and back and forth over a net with the ball directed at high speed against walls and buttresses and into side galleries that had become his passion.

He had been introduced to the game in his early teens by his father at the court just along the Seine on the *Île St. Louis* and over the years had become a very good player and like most people who play, he was an addict. He never ceased to take pleasure in the subtleties of the game, in the almost infinite variety of its tactics and strategies. He took pleasure in the fact that as he got older, he became a better player for it was a game that rewarded thought rather than strength. The skills and talents required to win at *Jeu de Paume* were to be found in the head much more than in the legs. Also, the game of doubles at which he specialised was a very different game to singles in many ways and good doubles partnerships took a long time to develop. He had been playing with Jules Ferry for nearly thirty years. The young lawyer from the Voges had been called to the Paris bar at about the same time as Dragnet had graduated from the military academy of St. Cyr and their paths often crossed during the early years of Dragnet's career in the army and then as a Paris policeman. The fact they came from opposite edges of France might have been the reason they got on so well and they soon formed a strong friendship. Dragnet had gained rapid promotions while Ferry's career had outstripped even that. His doubles partner had risen to currently Head of State or to give him his full title '*Ministre de l'Instruction publique et des Beaux Arts et Président du Conseil.*' Gant's remark was actually true. The man did usually concern himself with "affairs of state". He was effectively President of France's combined parliament.

This evening's match was a game doubles. It was a few days before the annual club doubles competition and Drangnet and Ferry were the current holders. Although they were both in their forties, tennis was a game that rewarded skill and tactics over strength and fitness and their long time playing together has given them a wealth of experience with each other's games that made them very hard to beat. But it was always necessary to practice, especially against younger players who tended to have a more energetic and thus more erratic style of play.

The match was with a pair of much younger men who hit the ball hard and ran around a lot. They went regularly for the few outright winners that are available in the game of *Jeu de Paume*, while the older pairing adopted a more defensive approach that relied on keeping the ball in play and waiting for their opponents to make the mistakes. Their retrieving was more reliable, and their chases were all much better and closer to the back wall than those of their opponents. This more conservative approach also meant that they retained the service end for longer with the winning gallery, tambour and the grille, all winning targets, available to them. Their defence against the forces by their opponents to the dedans from the hazard end was almost faultless with Drangnet, whose normal position was defending the side galleries, automatically falling back in defence when it was safe to do so. It was a game of attrition and subtlety much appreciated by the viewing crowd that was, like the players themselves, slightly older and appreciated an old fashioned game.

Their opponents were intending to stay on court for a singles game between each other so, having shaken hands over the net on a convincing victory that left their opponents more baffled than tired, the two older men headed for the changing room and a pair of weak whisky and sodas that had been put there by a member of the club staff.

'Good game, Louis.' said Ferry. 'I thought we played a very nice controlled game.'

'Well,' Drangnet laughed. 'It was certainly good enough to annoy the hell out of our young opponents. They seem to think that the solution to making mistakes by hitting the ball too hard was to hit it even harder. I know it took me a long time to learn to play this game properly but I'm sure I never played like that.

His companion took a long pull at his whisky.

'No, my friend, in our day when we were learning nobody played like that. In fact, it would have been thought of as rather impolite to try to knock your opponent's head off if he was standing close to the net. However, at least we offer a more restrained example to these young men.'

'I gather we're favourites for the cup again this year, Jules. A lot of people will have money riding on us. As usual Biboche is making a book.'

Ferry grimaced. 'I really don't like that very much, Louis. I do wish he would desist. I know that people make bets on most of the games whether they're in a tournament or not, but it really isn't the sort of thing I should be associated with.'

Drangnet gave his friend an affectionate punch on the arm.

'Don't be silly, Jules. Betting of matches is as old as the game itself and well you know it. It is normal that some people will be putting a lot of money on it. But they are people who can afford to lose and, in any case, our much-loved *Maître Paumier* takes his ten percent of the book. It is a nice little bonus for him. He really isn't paid very much, as you know.'

Ferry just grunted and got on with changing. Drangnet asked: 'Do you have time for dinner, Jules?'

The older man shook his head.

'Unfortunately I don't, Louis. I'm sorry. It's back to work for me, I'm afraid. You? What does the rest of your evening comprise?'

'Well if the weather is still good, I might walk back via *Les Halles* and take some supper in one of the cafés. I'm chasing a rather elusive lead in a case.'

They paused while the club waiter brought a new pair of full tumblers of whisky. It was their habit to drink two, excusing themselves the indulgence with the claim that they were made very weak. As soon as the man left, Ferry continued.

'What case is that?'

'Oh, a young prostitute was murdered last night rather unusually in her bed and no-one in the rest of a very full house seems to have seen anything. Or, at least, they aren't admitting anything. But I picked up a rather intriguing hint at lunchtime in the *Café du Marché* and thought I might do a bit of sniffing around as it is on my way home.

'Oh dear. I'm very sorry to hear that. Where was the murder?'

'In a *maison close* on the *Rue du Hanovre* in the second.'

Ferry nodded just slightly, enough not to offer recognition.

'And what is your elusive clue, my friend?'

'Well the murdered girl seems to have had some connection with the *Les Halles* markets or at least she was well known around there. When Blanco, the owner of the café, was talking to me he dropped a hint, by mistake I think, that there seems to be some sort of connection between the market community and some of the local prostitutes.'

'Well,' he said gathering up his tennis kit. 'That sounds like an excellently Parisian approach to a murder investigation – though good food and prostitution. Paris at its best, I feel.'

Drangnet laughed. They both finished their drinks and left the beautiful tennis court building and went their separate ways; Drangnet on foot back through the Tuileries gardens towards the Marais, Ferry into a waiting cab across the *Pont de la Concorde* on a much shorter journey back to his office in the *Palais de Luxembourg*. Unusually for a building containing a pair of tennis courts this once had been built with the courts end-to-end. The plot of ground that had been made available by Napoleon III was long and narrow being at the corner between the *Place de la Concorde* and the *Rue de Rivoli*. It was an arrangement that made for an extremely elegant, slim building some eighty metres long with each side consisting of an arcade of long, arched windows that illuminated the courts.

Chapter 2: Saturday 2ⁿᵈ April   Scene 1: Autopsy at the *Hôpital Salpêtrière*

The following morning Gant followed his boss back into his office after the early meeting. As it was the weekend there were fewer people than usual but Drangnet had passed the word that he wanted at least some of his team to work over the weekend.

'So, it doesn't seem that we've had much luck overnight. None of the local police picked up anything worth reporting. The house on the *Rue de Hanovre* was shut for business, of course. We had a couple of officers outside most of the night, but I don't think that did any good. No-one came near the place, so they didn't get any information from passers-by primarily because there weren't any. In fact, far from feeling protected by them, Madame Vierne spent most of the evening complaining that they should go away as she was losing money. Bit of a waste of time if you want my view.'

'Yes, I suppose you're right, Roger.' Drangnet sighed. 'I didn't pick up anything more when I had dinner in the Café Conrad last night. I picked it as it was another place near the market, but everyone seems to have decided to keep silent; at least when I was around.'

'Well,' the deputy replied. 'At least you got a decent meal.'

Drangnet was just about to reply good humouredly to this little jibe when both men were startled by a loud and completely alien noise. They both first looked out of the window. Drangnet usually had at least one of them slightly open. Unless it was particularly cold, he liked to hear the sounds of the river traffic. It reminded him of the city outside; the city he was paid to protect. But the dreadful noise came from inside the room. It was Gant who identified it first.

'Your telephone, Boss.'

It was indeed the large and obtrusive wood and metal box that hung on the wall by his office door. It had a pair of shiny brass bells on top and they were making a dreadful racket.

'What!' Drangnet snapped, looking confused. 'Why is the bloody thing making that infernal noise?'

'Er, I think someone wants to speak to you, Boss.'

'And…?'

'Well perhaps you should answer it, Boss.'

Drangnet scowled fiercely at the thing.

'You mean I have to get up from my desk, walk all the way over to that infernal machine and use it to try to speak to someone without knowing who it might be and whether or not I particularly want to speak to them?'

'Er, yes, sir.' replied an increasingly nervous Inspector. He knew what was coming.

'And what happens, pray, if I don't want to speak to whoever it is?'

'Then you just don't answer it, Boss.'

'Am how, pray, can I decide whether or not I want to speak to whoever is using that thing, if I don't know who it is?'

'I don't know, sir.' Gant was getting a bit rattled now.

'And how do I stop it making that infernal noise?' asked Drangnet, changing the direction of his attack slightly.

'Er, you answer it, Boss.'

'This conversation is becoming annoyingly circular, Gant. You answer it.'

'But Sir, what happens if they don't want to talk to me?'

'Inspector Gant.' Drangnet's voice was becoming dangerously sharp. He was not a man who often lost his temper but having experienced the odd rare eruption in the past, Gant felt it better to stop teasing his boss who was very clearly not at all amused. So, he got up and went to the machine.

'Hello?'

After a few moments he put down the earpiece and returned to his seat.

'Well?' snapped Drangnet. 'Who was it and what did they want?'

'It was Sergeant Clement and he..'

'Who?'

'Sergeant Clement, sir.'

'Our own Sergeant Clement?'

'Er, yes.'

'The one who works here in this office?'

'Yes, boss.' Gant had a terrible premonition of where this conversation was leading as Drangnet continued relentlessly.

'You mean the Sergeant Clement who is the senior desk sergeant in charge of the administration of this whole office?'

'Yes, sir.'

'The Sergeant Clement who has an office two floors down and almost directly below the one in which we are presently sitting?'

'Yes, sir.'

There was a pregnant silence before Drangnet said in a very dangerous low tone of voice.

'Then perhaps, Inspector Gant, you might like to use this internal machine of yours and request that the said Sergeant Clement gets his backside up to this office as fast as his short stubby legs can carry him and before I can remember where I can lay my hands on the forms required to dismiss someone from the police force with immediate effect.'

Gant positively flew to the machine to pass on the message and then stood by the open door while the sound of a very large policeman in a great hurry could be heard climbing the staircase as rapidly as his generous corporation would allow. It was a thoroughly flustered officer that stood to attention in front of his Chief Inspector's desk panting like a nervous spaniel. Another even more pregnant pause followed before Drangnet addressed the nervous policemen in a level tone that was as hard as steel and just as menacing.

'Sergeant Clement. How long have you been in the police force?'

'Er, about thirty years, sir.'

Drangnet nodded

'And how long have you been attached to the *Sûreté* and worked in this particular office?

'About eleven years, sir.'

'And when do you intend to retire, Sergeant?'

'In about ten years time. sir.'

Again, Drangnet just nodded and repeated the words 'ten years' just loud enough for them to hear, before continuing.

'And how long do you imagine I have worked in the office?'

'Er, I'm not sure, sir.'

By this time, he was terrified of saying the wrong thing.

'Well Sergeant, let me enlighten you. I have worked here for some eleven as well. In fact, if you remember, we arrived on the same day when they opened this particular office.'

'Yes, sir.'

'And in all those years have we ever had difficulty speaking to each other?'

In spite of knowing full well where this conversation was going, he was powerless to stop it.

'No sir.'

'And if my memory serves, we have always stood or sat in each other's company and conversed in a calm and civilised matter.

We have never found the slightest difficulty in passing information to each other or in understanding each other?

'No sir.'

'Essentially what we have been doing is talking to each other.'

'Yes, sir.'

'And has this process ever caused either of us to misunderstand the other or caused any difficulty in our communicating with each other?'

'No, sir.'

'Hum,' he muttered with a deep frown on his face as another, much longer, silent pause ensued with Drangnet sat gently staring out of the window, nodding his head in the manner of someone contemplating deep thoughts or wrestling with some great imponderable. Both Clement and Gant were rooted to the spot. This was Drangnet at his most dangerous.

'Sergeant, pray do tell me now what you wanted to say to me just now before your infatuation with this modern device..' as he waved contemptuously at the offending machine '...made you forget how we have talked together for the last twenty-five years.'

'It was Professor Dankovich, sir.'

'Professor Dankovich?'

'Er, yes sir. Professor Dankovich.'

Drangnet frowned a little as if somewhat perplexed. Both Gant and Clement knew these signs as well and both stiffened even more as their boss's voice dropped to a dangerous low.

'You mean, Sergeant Clement, the same Professor Dankovich with whom I have had an excellent working relationship for almost as many years as I have had with you?'

'Yes sir,' came the nervous response.

'The same Professor Dankovich with whom I have also communicated freely and efficiently throughout the same number of years without finding any great hindrance that had obstructed our progressing on an investigation with the benefit of his excellent and almost infallibly accurate advice? That Professor Dankovich or was a new one with whom I have not met or ever talked?'

'No sir.' came the even more nervous response. 'It was the original one.'

'Ah. I see, Sergeant and what did the good Professor say, pray?'

'Er, he said he wanted to see you immediately?'

'Immediately Sergeant. Immediately. Did actually say that?'

Gant found himself praying that Clement said 'yes' to this question even if it was a lie. If it proved that it was Clement's own embellishment, then the man would be out of the building within the hour, ten years before his pension.

'Yes sir. He said it was quite urgent.'

Gant relaxed and his boss indulged in yet another pause. After a while he looked again at the sweating sergeant.

'Then my good Sergeant, I will do what I have done for the last quarter of a century and go and see him.'

'Yes, sir.'

'A good idea, *n'est ce pas*?

'Yes, sir. Very, sir.' The man agreed enthusiastically in the manner of someone emerging from a long, dark and terrifying underground tunnel.

Drangnet nodded with a smile of satisfaction broadening sunnily across his face as if some deep and complex mystery had just been solved and all was now as clear as day. He rose from his desk and made to put on his coat and hat. Both his companions silently sighed with relief that it seemed that they were to be spared one of Drangnet's rare but memorable tongue lashings. However, Drangnet was not quite done. He turned to his colleague.

'Tell me, Sergeant..'

'Yessir..?'

'Do you remember that rather pretty little painting of mine that used to hang on the wall by the door. You remember where that thing is now hanging?'

'Yes, sir.'

'It was removed without my permission, as I recall, during my absence on a short investigation in Reims, in order to make room, I was told, for that thing.' he said gesturing towards the machine.

'Yes, sir.'

'And do you remember where it was put for safe storage in order to make room for this essential piece of modern policing.'

'Yes, sir.'

A change in tone of voice indicated that this painful interview was reaching its conclusion.

'Right then, Sergeant Clement.; Drangnet said decisively, 'I will respond to Professor Dankovich's plea and go to see him. In the old-fashioned way, you understand, as I said. Face-to-face. So please can you get me a cab to take me to the *Hôpital Pitié-Salpêtrière*. I will probably be gone for most of the morning. When I return I will expect my pretty little painting of the River Seine by a new local artist called Camille Pissarro to be hanging once again in its proper place on my wall and for that….that….monstrosity to be removed and hung somewhere in Inspector Gant's office not in mine. Have I made myself quite clear, Sergeant?'

'Yes sir. Completely sir.'

Drangnet waved a dismissive hand.

'Off you go then. Remember, I want that cab in five minutes. And Sergeant…?'

'Yes, sir?'

'Please remember that I am always delighted to talk to any member of my staff, especially you who have been my companion for so very long, at any time. Fact-to-face, of course. It's usually the best way. I think you'll find.'

'Yes, sir.'

'Good. I'm pleased that we got all that sorted out. Now run along. I'm sure there are many others who want to talk with you.'

A highly relieved Clement couldn't get out of the office quickly enough. Gant had something of a frown on his face.

'I don't think that moving one of these things is as easy as all that, sir. I think they have to be installed by a specialist technician. There are wires and things to be moved and I don't think that anyone here understands much of it. Perhaps we should wait until we have got someone from the telephone company to come and do the work.'

Drangnet nodded understandingly. He got up from his desk and stood in front of the offending machine staring at it. He then reached up, grasped it by the top of its frame and pulled it off the wall with one powerful wrench. It fell to the ground with a resounding crash with both of the little brass bells becoming detached and rolling musically around the floor for a while. Drangnet watched them with a slightly amused smile until they finally came to rest. He then turned to his deputy.

'There you are. Pretty simple I would have thought. And by the way, you had better find a way silencing the bloody thing, at least from me. If I ever hear it again, it goes in the Seine.'

And with that he picked up his hat, coat and cane and swept out of the office heading briskly for the stairs. He instructed the cab driver to take the *Pont St Michel* onto the left bank and drive eastwards up the river. It was again a fine spring morning and Drangnet felt again the pleasure on getting out of the office especially as it seemed to be taken over by mad people and machinery. If fact, he wasn't so much against the new machinery as many might have thought. His opposition was a purely practical one. He felt there was little point if relying on these new-fangled ideas unless they worked properly, were reliable and, in the case of telephone, more than just a few people were connected to the system. He was all for many of these technological advances, especially in forensics, but he judged by results rather than intentions. He wasn't extreme in his views, but he adopted more of a wait and see attitude. He was, after all, responsible for the results of all this, not just its experimentation. More than anything he hated things that wasted his time.

Just as he passed the end of the island he saw that as usual there was a crowd of people waiting to get into the Paris Morgue to look at the most recent corpses on view. Ostensibly this rather macabre exhibition was in order to aid identification of the regular stream of dead bodies that was found in the city every week. Few of these were the business of the *Sûreté*. They were the usual collection of accidents, suicides, deaths by natural causes. The staff of the morgue were under instructions to notify his office only if they saw foul play or anything that might indicate a crime. If such a body came in it would be transferred to the *Hôpital Pitié-Salpêtrière* where one of Professor Dankovich's staff would decide whether there was, in fact, anything to investigate.

If that proved to be the case, the *Sûreté* would be informed and Dankovich would do an autopsy. If not, the body would be taken back to the morgue. It was a system that worked quite well most of the time. His route up the left bank of the river took him past some other Paris landmarks. The first was the small *Marché aux Veaux* followed quickly by the much larger and busier wine market, *Les Halles aux Vins*. Then past the botanical gardens, the *Jardin des Plantes* and finally to the great hospital nestling beside the *Gare d'Orleans*.

He found Dankovich sitting at his desk in his office reading a copy of the morning's *Le Temps*, the city's most serious newspaper. He seemed remarkably relaxed and cheerful for someone who had attempted to summoned his guest with an urgent morning telephone call.

'Ah, Louis. Nice to see you. Nice of you to drop in,' he offered with a welcoming smile. 'Always nice to get a visit from one of Paris's most senior policemen.'

Drangnet smelt a rat.

'All right, Xavier. What going on? What's all the flap about.'

'Flap?' the great man offered insouciantly. 'No flap at all. At least not apparently for you as you didn't bother to take my urgent telephone call earlier.'

'Oh, come on. I came as soon as I got your message. What more do you want?'

'You're a bit of a Luddite, you know, Louis. Sooner or later you're going to have to use the telephone whether you like it or not.'

'I'll use it when the bloody thing works and when, other than you, there is a decent number of people who can be bothered with it. Anyway, what's a Luddite?'

'It's a secret society in England under the leadership of someone apparently called Ned Lud made up of people who want to oppose mechanisation in the textile industry.'

'I'm not opposed to these new-fangled things at all. I'm just reluctant to waste time before the thing works properly. Otherwise I am very open to new methods and inventions especially in the field of forensics as you will know.'

'All right, all right. My guess is that rather that use the new machine to get my report on the unfortunate young woman who was killed yesterday morning, you took advantage to get out of your office and take a trip up the river in this nice spring sunshine.'

Drangnet just grunted. The man was, of course, completely right. The doctor continued.

'As it happens, I am quite pleased that you came in person because I have a complaint to make or rather a crime to report. But first the woman. Mademoiselle Lisette Sanier was twenty-six years old and lived, to all intents and purposes, at number 6 *Rue de Hanovre*. She was in excellent health and well-nourished. She was suffocated to death by person or persons unknown sometime during the night of Thursday the 31st.'

He leaned over to his desk, pulled a piece of paper from his typewriter, and handed it to Drangnet, separating the top page from two below it.

'Another of these new inventions that you hate so much. Now I can type a report for you, keep one copy for myself and file a third somewhere: although I'm not sure where yet. That's the progress you're so unhappy about, my friend.'

Drangnet didn't rise to the bait. He just folded the paper and put it into his inside jacket pocket.

'Thank you, Xavier. Now what about this complaint of yours?'

The professor slid his reading glassed down his nose and looked over them at his guest.

'Well to be frank, I'm not sure whether I'm making a complaint or reporting a crime or perhaps both. However, last night, sometime well after midnight, a body was apparently brought into the City morgue. I gather it was that of a youngish man that had been found washed up on the little beach at the west end of *Île St. Louis* just below the *Pont Louis Phillippe*. It had been discovered by a pair of lovers having a romantic midnight wander along the Seine. They reported it to the local gendarmerie and the body was brought into the morgue by the local gendarmes in the usual way. According to his records, the morgue technician who was on the night shift saw that the body had a garrotte around his neck and immediately told the gendarmes to bring the body here for examination as it clearly wasn't a natural death. This is normal procedure, of course. However, the problem is that the body never arrived.'

'Never arrived?' Drangnet was surprised.

'No.' Dankovich shook his head. 'It had vanished.'

'Have you made any enquiries?'

'No. I rather thought that was your job not mine. But was the reason I tried to speak to you earlier this morning.'

'Do you know what station the gendarmes came from.'

'No.'

'Hum. Very odd. I assume that nothing like this has happened before?'

'Not to my knowledge. Actually, I only found out about it because the Director of the morgue got in touch about some other matter and he mentioned that they had sent someone on to us last night. I checked and nothing had appeared here, I thought I'd better tell you about it.'

'Well, thank you my friend. I'll certainly look into it.'

With that he left the hospital and set off to walk to the *Commissariat de Police* on the *Boulevard Bourdon*. It was the *commissariat* closest to his office and he knew all the people working from there including its Commander, Philippe Papon. He would know what was going on if anyone did.

Papon listened to his unexpected guest with an exasperated expression on his face. As soon as Drangnet had finished the policeman offered an immediate and somewhat indignant explanation.

'It was those bloody politicos. I gather that two of our porters were taking it on a morgue cart down to the hospital as normal when they were intercepted by three men from our esteemed colleagues in the political division. They had no paperwork, no authority and only one of them actually identified himself. My men were about to make an issue of it when one of the politicals started waving a revolver around, so they thought better of it and just get them get on with it.'

'You mean they just took the body?'

'Yes.'

'How?'

'They used our cart. I want it back soon, too. I'm just writing a memo about it.'

'No explanation?'

'None whatsoever,'

'Very odd.'

'It certainly is. But with that lot you never know. They tend to make their own rules up as they go along.'

The political police were a relatively new group and, if truth be told, a highly unpopular one amongst both the general public and other members in the police department. They had grown out of the gendarmerie that had left Paris for the safety of Fontainebleau with Adolph Thiers and the national government eleven years before when the Germans got too close. Some of them had secretly gone back into Paris to spy on the Communards and their leadership. Theirs was a completely passive role. They weren't there to do anything specific other than observe what was going on, to see who the leaders of the attempted revolution were, the leaders at street level. They dressed like ordinary citizens and attended their many and interminable meetings and debates, silently taking notes.

Their job was to make lists; lists of people to be arrested and interrogated when *Maréchal MacMahon* and his army took over the city again. The army crushed the Commune with extreme violence. The secret police were also the people who later did many of the interrogations. As a consequence, they were much hated as these interrogations were often violent in the extreme and it was not uncommon for the victim not to survive. The ordinary people of Paris remembered this all to well. But these police had proven their worth to successive new administrations who found that they also needed spies to go amongst the local population to keep them informed of sedition or plotting against the new republic. From the time of the Commune onwards all new governments were afraid of the new anarchist tendencies that were beginning to be felt in France and a specialist police force was deemed necessary to control it. A necessary evil, some thought. Some five years previously they had been given official status. However, almost as if it was intended to separate them from the everyday police structure, they were put officially under the control of the Ministry of the Interior not the Prefect of Police.

Drangnet sighed. The very last thing he wanted to do was to get involved with that lot. But he also knew that there was also little more that Papon could do to help him. Clearly the man was less uninterested in taking the problem further than he was. He therefore thanked his colleague and left to walk back to his office. The City morgue was almost on his way back so he decided to drop in to see if he could get any more information. The director of the morgue was in his office but could only offer Drangnet a copy of the brief notes that were made by the attendant who was on duty last night when they bought in the body and they didn't help very much. A man in his thirties or forties, medium height and build, well dressed, with no obvious external wounds or marks seemed to have been strangled with a garotte. The morgue technician hadn't examined the body further as the garotte meant that it would immediately be one of those who were sent to the forensic department for examination. The night attendant wasn't there when Drangnet visited but the morgue director suggested that he would be able to add very little to the written record if he was interviewed personally.

Drangnet was pleased to see that his pretty little picture of the Seine was back hanging in its usual place when he got back to his office. No-one mentioned the infernal machine; not even Gant whose office was presumably being torn apart to give the thing its new home. He quickly informed his deputy about Dankovich's report on Lisette Sanier as well as the mysterious business of the missing murder victim. Gant seemed unsurprised by the former and uninterested in the latter.

'As usual, our good Professor doesn't really tell us much that we couldn't see for ourselves and, as for the missing body, I can't really see why we should try to get involved. If the politicos want to take it on and investigate then why not let them? It isn't that we haven't got enough work of our own.'

In a way, Drangnet had to agree. Although, in theory, the missing body was his concern, he understood what Gant was saying. Much as he disliked the political department, the matter was being investigated by the police even if it wasn't by him.

Chapter 3: Sunday 3rd April   Scene 1: The Second Prostitute Murder

The morning dawned brightly and Drangnet yet again enjoyed his brisk walk to work. April was his favourite month in Paris. The long winters in the city could be cold and wet while summers were often hot and the long tradition of the population, or those that could, leaving the city to escape the heat and the smell that still persisted. Everything now in April was new and fresh. The leaves on the trees of the Tuileries Gardens were young and bright green. Ladies walking in the street had shed their restrained winter plumage and were to be seen strolling the boulevards in floral prints and bonnets with a suggestion of an added swing to their hips and a twirling lacy parasols over their shoulders. Even sober-suited businessmen walking to work did so with a spring in their steps and a smile on their faces. The city felt reborn.

It was a Sunday, so the pace of the day was a little more relaxed. There was a morning Mass at *Saint Gervais Saint Protais* at 10 o'clock that should have demanded his attention. He was a long-time member of the famous choir there and would normally have sung for the morning mass but given that he had fresh murders on his books he had pleaded an absence from the choirmaster. There was no special music to be sung, just the usual responses during the service. No solo singing so he was let off. The *Sûreté* as a whole didn't always work on Sundays but he had asked some people to come in to get the investigation under way.

The morning meeting went off quickly and without difficulty. Nothing new of any significance had come in overnight. No more information had been found about the murder of the *Rue du Hanovre* and, as a consequence, the enquiry hadn't progressed much since the murder of Lisette Sanier. So, his mind was only half on his job and the pile of paperwork waiting for him, when his assistant knocked and came in. Inspector Gant was a small man, dark of hair and skin and also from the south of France, although in his case it was closer to Spain than his chief. The two got on well; well enough for jokes about working fully hand in glove tended to be common amongst their colleagues. The man wasted little time.

'We've got another one, Boss.'

Immediately Drangnet found himself sad and angry in almost equal measure. It was bad enough having one unsolved prostitute murder on his hands but a second in such a short space of time felt sinister.

'Where?'

'*Rue Lobineau*, just next to *St German* market, Sir. Behind St Sulpice. Number 7.'

Drangnet sighed. Wearily he levered himself up from his desk and its burden of papers and the two started out into the spring sunshine on the relatively short walk to the scene. They walked across the *Pont Neuf* and up the *Rue Dauphine* towards the *Boulevard St Germain* and the market beyond. As they walked, a thought occurred to him.

'What proportion of *maisons closes* are here south of the river, do you think?'

'Less than a third, I would think, sir; certainly of the better ones. The number of illegal brothels increases as you get further out into the suburbs of course but I suppose you could say the same whichever direction you took from the centre.'

Their arrival was greeted by an all-too-familiar scene. The street was directly behind the *marché St. Germain* and like all markets there were always a lot of people around both day and night. The house itself and a good distance on either side was cordoned off by a ring of uniformed police. There was again the inevitable crowd of onlookers.

Drangnet acknowledged the salute of the officer on the door.

'Second floor, sir.' the man said as he passed.

The scene that greeted him was very different from that at the previous night's killing. They again passed a line of beautiful but anxious young faces as the other residents of the house lined the stairs. But the room was obviously different. This time the girl was naked on the bed, a single stab wound to the chest. She lay in a sea of blood-stained, rumpled bed linen. He glanced around and took in the scene instantly and, having fixed the impression in his mind he left as the other investigators arrived. Actually, there was very little point in his being there. He knew what they'd find. So, he called the girls into an impromptu meeting on the ground floor sitting room that belonged to the concierge.

He saw that all the girls were again dressed in respectable day dresses. He also saw yet again that they were all young and quite beautiful in spite of wearing very little makeup. The older concierge was equally well-turned out albeit in a style more befitting her age and status. She was obviously there to look after the girls as well as the house and her expression showed this. All of them looked on him with a certain apprehension but again with none of the hostility with which potential witnesses to a murder usually greeted him.

'Ladies. Thank you for agreeing to see me. I am very sorry indeed that this has happened in your house and I can assure you that I will do my utmost to find who did this.'

Madame Bondine, the concierge, spoke for all of them.

'Chief Inspector. You are welcome here at any time, even on such a melancholy occasion as this. We will, of course, try to help you as much as we can. Mademoiselle Flandrette was a great favourite amongst her clients as well as being a charming and popular member of my household.'

He nodded to acknowledge the fact that the dead woman had been neatly identified for him.

'Obviously, I'd like to know if anyone saw any of Mademoiselle Flandrette's clients yesterday, especially the last one, of course.'

To give her credit Madame Bondine gave the assembled group a few slightly embarrassed moments before answering for them.

'Chief Inspector, you will understand why my girls are reluctant to be specific about their visitors. So, I will answer your question on their behalf. However, before I do, I need your assurance on something. Not only do I trust you; your reputation goes before you. I have also been told by others additionally that you are a reliable man. But please forgive me if I ask for your assurance that anything we say here will only be used on a general way and not used as evidence, as they say, when the judge comes to call.'

The policeman drew breath to reply but she held him by a slight hand gesture as she continued.

'Quite simply, Chief Inspector, I want your assurance that if I give you names, you will not disclose them to anyone.'

Dragnet thought for a moment.

'Unless they prove to have a material bearing on this case, Madame, you have my word. But if they are germane, then they and their identities will have to be part of the investigation.'

This seemed to satisfy her for she continued.

'A few weeks ago, I and some of my fellow concierges were asked to keep records of our visitors. This is the list from yesterday.'

Drangnet's immediate thought was to wonder who might have issued such an instruction but his questions was forestalled by Madame Bondin taking a piece of paper from her large bag that seem to contain a large variety of items, some of which were visible poking out of the top; newspapers, knitting needles, the end of a tasselled shawl. Drangnet made to rise but one of the girls beat him to it and delivered the paper to him with a slight courtesy and a little smile that made his heart leap a little. He glanced down quickly as the list of names. The girls had been busy. A comment came to mind, but he decided against making it almost immediately. He just asked the question for which he knew would get no answer.

'Madame, your girls are almost never seen on the streets. That means that there is some sort of booking systems' in place.' He waved the little paper slightly. 'Can you tell me how these, er, visitors, as you put, it know when to, er, visit?'

His conviction that his question wouldn't receive an answer was confirmed with a charming smile.

'Chief Inspector Dragnet I won't tell you that but from what I hear you have other places where you might find that information if it is thought appropriate that you have it.'

The irony of this lady refusing to answer the questions of Paris's most senior criminal policeman wasn't lost on him. He looked down at the list again.

'I see that Mam'selle Florette's last visitor was a Monsieur Funar. Can you describe him, Madame?'

She thought for a while.

'Very tall, more than six feet, dark hair, slim - almost thin -, a small goatee beard, well-dressed, well-polished black shoes. In his mid-thirties I would think. Very blue eyes, I remember.'

'Was he French?'

'No, monsieur. I always ask them who they are visiting before I let them in, and he definitely had an accent. If I had to guess I would say he was central European.'

'Was he carrying anything?'

'A small attaché case. Nothing more'

'And you saw him leave?'

'Yes, Monsieur. He seemed perfectly normal.'

'And he had the case with him still?'

'Yes Monsieur.'

There was very little more he could do. If Madame Bondine or her charges had heard anything they would probably have said so. The men upstairs were still working. There were uniformed police out in the street making enquiries about anyone who might have been seen entering the house last night but the list of names in his pocket suggested that no-one would admit to remembering much. He set Gant to do the interviews with the girls and he set off back to his office. There was a little line of chaste kisses to be experienced - endured was definitely the wrong word - from each of Madame's girls followed by a slightly longer encounter with Madame. She was not unattractive herself. He attempted to reassure her.

'I will do my best to catch this man, Madame. It may take some time, but I won't give up.'

She smiled back at him.

'I know that, Chief Inspector. But you'd better be quick.'

He thought to ask why but stopped himself. She wouldn't have told him. He had a habit of connecting things that would otherwise remain separate and Madam Bondine's remark had sparked a connection in his mind. It was entirely too much of a coincidence to hope for but as he walked back towards his office he couldn't but wonder whether there might not be another body floating down the Seine tonight. That would indeed make things interesting.

He already realised how difficult it was going to be to solve these crimes. So much of his work relied on witnesses; people who saw the comings and goings of the streets. People who might have overheard a conversation in a bar or café. The great sadness was that few people really cared much about prostitutes or if they did, they didn't want to admit publicly to it. These women were people of little value or consequence. To Drangnet they were much more. They were his people as much as anyone else in the city and they were under his protection as much as anyone else. That was why he felt these killings so keenly. If it was his responsibility to protect these women, then he was failing.

Two deaths in two days. The newspapers would get hold of it now and there would be pressure from above. Politicians were always sensitive to public opinion if it swung against them and the press, if not the general public immediately, would want results. All that pressure would end up on his desk before long.

The day meandered on until about teatime and, on a whim, he decided that he wanted to visit the scene of the first crime again. The house was presumably shut up but he thought that Madame Vierne might still be there and so it proved. He hadn't really formulated any particular questions for her. He just wanted to remind himself of the house and see if she had remembered anything else. However, when he arrived, he found her in a highly agitated state. She was sitting in the drawing room with two of her girls in attendance. She had clearly been crying. To Drangnet's eye there was a great deal of rather attractive fluttering around her as he crouched at the side her chair.

'Madame Vierne. Whatever is the matter? What's happened?'

'Oh, Chief Inspector. It was horrible. We were visited by three very rough and uncouth men who said they were policemen. They forced their way in in spite of my saying that you had ordered the house closed and when through the whole place. They took away some things from poor Lisette's room but didn't tell me what they were. The leader, a man called Tergia, I think he was called, interrogated me very harshly. My girls too. I told him that we had already talked to you and we couldn't remember anything else. But he took no notice. He was horrible.'

Drangnet was angry and horrified. He had heard of this man Tergia. He was an inspector in the political police. A very nasty piece of work indeed. He wasn't surprised that Madame Vierne was upset.

'Madame, I'm very sorry that this happened. This man unfortunately was indeed a policeman. I know him but he's not one of my men. He certainly had no right to come here without my permission. My suggestion is that we keep the house closed and you lock it up. Do you have somewhere else you can go to stay of a few days?'

'Oh, Chief Inspector. I'd rather stay here if you don't mind. I feel safer with my girls around me even if we aren't open for business. We have friends in the market too, and I can ask them to send some people to keep an eye on us. I should have done this before, perhaps.'

'So should I,' thought Drangnet grimly.

There was no point of asking any of the questions he had come for. She was much too upset. He could always come back another time. So left a recovering Madame Vierne in the hands of her girls and went to walk back home.

What on earth were the political police doing there? He had no idea. This was the second intervention in his business in two day by these people and he didn't like it at all. Some high-level protests would obviously have to start flying around pretty soon. But now he was more interested in why. By and large the politicals generally kept out of his way. In fact, he hadn't come across them for some months. The ordinary policing of the city was usually none of their business. They held themselves above all that. Yet here they were. Twice. Now, of course, he also had the second prostitute killing on his hands. He certainly ought to get Gant to arrange a guard on the house on the *Rue Lobineau* at the very least in spite of it being rather too late. He was just about to set course to walk back to the *Place des Vosges* when another rather random thought struck him. Perhaps this recent sequence of events was not all a coincidence, The political police seemed involved in both the disappearing body and the murder of Mademoiselle Flandrette. Instead of making his way home he hailed a cab and headed back to the office to find Gant.

'Roger,' he said as he slumped down into the chair at the side of Gant's office desk. 'Get some men down to the river tonight, just at the west end of the *Île St. Louis* just in case we get another of these bodies floating down. If we do, I want them to collect it and escort it to *Hôpital Salpêtrière*. Then I want it guarded until Dankovich gets to work in the morning. You can tell some of the local gendarmerie to do that.'

Gant frowned.

'That's an awful lot of people, Boss. Don't you think it's a bit of a long shot? There's very little reason to think that anything will happen again tonight.'

He told him of Madame Vierne's unwelcome guests.

'Yes. I admit it's a very long shot indeed. But just think what idiots we'd look if a second body did appear in the river and we missed this one as well. Make sure you take enough men and some of our beefier brethren too. It could get nasty.'

Gant just nodded and left to make the arrangements. He was well used to his boss going off in peculiar directions during an investigation and had learned his lesson a long time ago. The man wasn't often wrong.

Chapter 3: Sunday 3ʳᵈ April   Scene 2: The Second Body in the Seine

Drangnet's breakfast ritual on his way to work was well under way when, to his surprise, Roger Gant walked into the café. Before arriving at Drangnet's table he stopped off at the bar and ordered a coffee. Unusually he waited until they made it for him. Drangnet just looked on with amused interest and tried to work out what was happening. The coffee was produced somewhat grudgingly it should be admitted and Gant carried it across to the table followed by the scowls of various waiters whose noses were obviously put well out of joint by this behaviour. Gant only got away with it because they knew him to be police. As he sat, Drangnet realised what is happening and decided to demonstrate his detective skills.

'Good morning, Roger. You've obviously got some news for me that couldn't wait until I got to the office. However you also wanted a cup of coffee and you thought that the news you have is important enough to make me want to get up immediately and fly off to wherever your news comes from, thus denying you the chance to order your coffee in the usual manner, wait for it to be served at the table and to drink it in peace. So, you got your coffee first hoping that I would allow you at least the time to drink it in a civilised manner before insisting that we rush off. Well let me assure you that the consumption of your cup of coffee is safe. Now what is it?'

Gant grinned. His boss was right as usual.

'Well, I don't know how you did it but you called it right, sir. We fished a body out of the river last night at about midnight. Same place as before apparently. Also garrotted with a thin cord. There was what can only be described as a robust discussion between our men and a somewhat smaller number of the other lot which resulted in the corpse being delivered safe and sound to the *Hôpital Salpetrière* all ready for Dr Dankovich when he gets to work this morning. I left enough people guarding it. It looks like a police convention down there.'

Drangnet smiled. And as if to prove his deputy's fears unfounded, called the waiter over to take a further order.

'Roger do I gather that you've been out there most of the night?'

'Well, I wanted to make sure the job was done properly, sir.'

'Have you eaten anything yet today?'

'No, boss. Not yet.'

'Then you must have some breakfast before we do anything else. There's no hurry. Dankovich will take his time and if he knows we're waiting for him, he'll take even longer.'

Drangnet turned to the waiter.

'Please give my friend whatever he wants and bring me another coffee and a demi-ficelle with unsalted butter and apricot jam.'

Gant, delighted to have breakfast on the department, ordered a mushroom omelette and two croissants with all the trimmings. The waiter was still in a bad mood and turned away with a very bad grace only to be called back very sharply by an instantly angry Drangnet.

'Young man. I suggest that you find some manners from somewhere very quickly. I am Chief Inspector Drangnet of the *Paris Sûreté*. This gentleman is Inspector Gant also of the *Paris Sûreté*. He has been up all night doing his job defending unpleasant little pieces of shit like you from the forces of evil and he deserves your courtesy. I am personally acquainted with the owner of this establishment and unless you find a very different attitude immediately, I'll make sure that you are kicked out of here into the gutter before I have finished my coffee. Do I make myself understood?'

The man blanched and fled.

'Well sir. That was impressive.' said Gant. 'We don't often see you like that.'

Drangnet just grunted.

'Roger, my friend, as you know I have a great passion for this city of ours. I love many things about it. Even most of its idiosyncrasies too. But one thing I cannot abide it this tradition we seem to have developed for bloody-minded, offensive waiters in our cafés. I won't tolerate rudeness to anyone but especially to someone who has been up working all night. I wasn't joking. Unless you get an apology of some sort, I'll get the little sod dismissed.'

'It's OK boss. As long as I get my breakfast, I'll be happy.'

'You're too forgiving, Roger. Now anything more you can tell me about last night?'

'Well to be honest, apart from a few politicos making threats it was all pretty calm. They were outnumbered and knew it. Once we got to the hospital, they left us alone.'

'Who was in charge?'

'I'm not sure that anyone was actually in charge. They just seemed to be milling about like a mob. But I did spot that man Tergia. I gather he's an inspector now.'

'Nasty piece of work that, I seem to remember. He was the man who shot Raoul Rigault in the street at the end of the Commune. Just the sort of person who would find a new career with the political police.'

The waiter arrived with a tray full of breakfast that he distributed over their table. The order was complete, and he did look at Gant with the best possible grace and asked if there was anything else monsieur wished.

Gant acknowledged the gesture and let the man go.

'You're too soft, Roger. He'll never learn, you know.'

Their conversation drifted into more general topics, in including the two dead prostitutes but it was clear that they had come up with very little more in terms of leads. Until Dankovich got to work they were at a bit of a loose end. They both finished a leisurely breakfast and Drangnet signalled for the bill. It was the owner who came over to the table.

'Chief Inspector. I can only apologise for the attitude of the waiter earlier. He's new to the job and he still has to learn about our customers.'

'I would hope, Monsieur Paul, that he would behave correctly whoever the customers might be.'

'I agree, Chief, but he is new to the café and this is his first job. But I will get rid of him.'

Drangnet relented. Perhaps he had been a little hasty.

'No. Don't do that. If he is still learning the job, then give him the chance to show that he has learned a lesson.'

The man nodded and went back behind the bar having refused to give Drangnet a bill.

'Now see whose being soft, boss,' offered Gant as they rose and started the leisurely short walk to the *Quai de l'Horloge.*

Chapter 4: Monday 4th April   Scene 1: The Third Prostitute Murder

The call had come just after he concluded the morning meeting. Superintendent Dancart's secretary knocked politely on his door and waited. Drangnet was so unused to the courtesy that he temporarily forgot that he was supposed to answer. In any case he never liked shouting and it was a substantial oak door. He just waited, expecting the door to open and a recognisable head to poke itself around it. In the end he got up and opened it himself.

'Good morning, Suzette.' he said smilingly. 'How are you today?'

'Very well, thank you Chief Inspector. I hope you are too.'

'What time does he want me?'

The question was completely unnecessary.

'As soon as you can, sir. If you have a moment, of course.'

'Now's as good a time as any, madame. I'll follow you down.'

As befits the man who was the senior ranked officer of the *Sûreté*, Dancart's office was spacious and extremely formal. It was fitted with an elegant full suite of Louis Quinze furniture, all beautiful polished woods and ormolu decoration. It was rumoured to be all of a set by Charles Cressent and Drangnet who was no expert saw no reason to disagree. Heaven only knows how it escaped the attention of both the Prussians and the Communards, but it had and here it was, doing what it was supposed to do. It was in use and lived in rather than destined for the museum or auction house. The walls of the tall first floor room were pale green and blue and elegantly swagged floral silk curtains framed the five tall windows that looked out over the same view on the river at Drangnet's, but from a lower level.

Dancart got up from behind his writing table as Drangnet entered and escorted him to a pair of armchairs arranged on either side of an elaborate fireplace containing an extravagant arrangement of fresh flowers. Madame Dancart maintained this display throughout the spring and summer months to remind her husband of their origins in the Midi. Suzette appeared with coffee that she served and left on each man's table at his elbow.

Like Gant, Drangnet had been working with Dancart ever since the Commune. They were friends as well as colleagues. Dancart had often had to protect his protégé from outside pressure when he went off in one of his less orthodox directions during an investigation. It was support that Drangnet appreciated and he regularly rewarded his boss with enough famous successes to silence the most voluble of critics. The scene was more like two old friends having coffee together than a meeting between the Head of the *Sûreté* and his deputy.

'Well Louis. That's two in a couple of days and I've already got the Prefect wanting to see me. The press seems to have latched onto this very quickly as well.'

Drangnet just shrugged.

'As you yourself say it's only been a couple of days and our investigation is in it's very early days. We were notified of the first killing in Friday morning and the second yesterday. It's now Monday. Hardly any time at all. Why on earth is this pressure coming so quickly. Usually we get at least a week of peace. Who's making all the noise?'

This time it was Dancart's turn to shrug.

'It's coming from all over. From the Prefect, or at least his office, as well as both the *Palais de Luxembourg* and the *Palais Bourbon*. The *Hôtel de Ville* too. You name it.'

Drangnet just smiled broadly.

'Ah. Clients from all over Paris, eh?. Come on Émile. You know as well as I do that many of these people are just worried that their little peccadillos on the way home from work to their loving families every night might come up in our investigation. They don't care about the investigation at all.'

'Be that as it may, Louis, they're still asking some very difficult questions. Make sure you give this your highest priority.'

He did have the grace to look embarrassed as he said it. He was just passing along the message. He knew full well that Drangnet, irrespective of the occasionally idiosyncratic methods he employed from time to time, never gave anything but his best.

'Well,' he said rising to leave. 'I'll leave you to do what you do so much better than I and keep all these people happy while I get on with finding the murderers. The penalties of high rank, I'm afraid, sir.'

'It's nowhere near as easy as you often seem to think, Louis,' Dancart replied a touch grumpily.

'Ah, that's why you've got the big office and the pretty furniture, sir.'

'If you must know,' Dancart addressed to retreating back of his Chief Inspector, 'I inherited it from my grandparents.'

Drangnet knew, of course, but he also enjoyed teasing Dancart who was a little touchy on the subject.

He got back to his office and spent an hour or so going through Gant's reports of the interviews with the girls from *Rue Lobineau*. As before, there was nothing useful. There were a few reports from the local gendarmerie who had made some interviews with some of the locals but there was equally little of interest there. He sat back in his chair and again stared out over the river. He remained in that position when a knock on his door heralded Sergeant Clement holding a small brown paper packet.

'This just arrived from Dr. Dankovich, sir.'

It was just a heavy brown Manilla envelope closed with a seal bearing the hospital coat of arms. A note had been written on Dankovich's new typing machine and was therefore completely legible as opposed to the man's usual handwriting that was the usual indecipherable scrawl offered by most doctors. Perhaps there is some virtue in this new-fangled machine, Drangnet thought as he read the enclosed note.

I thought you might like to see this that came attached to the dead man's neck as a garrotte. I have examined it and in my opinion it is standard butcher's twine of the sort used for tying joints of meat together. Nothing else to say about it. As it came out of the river, I can't use it to help estimate a time of death. You'll get the full autopsy report later today or tomorrow morning. Just thought you might like this as some sort of a clue to get you started. XD.

Other than offering the possibility of a connection to a butcher he couldn't immediately see a connection. There were an large numbers in butchers in Paris. It was certainly an idiosyncratic type of garrotte but no more that any other type of string. He took it out and tested it. It was very thin and very strong. Ideal for purpose, he thought but it really didn't seem to get him any further along. He had to think of something that would give the investigation a severe kick up the backside. But his mind went back to the only lead of any sort he remembered getting and it was a pretty obscure one at that. Monsieur Blanco and his remark about the community surrounding *les Halles* and in particular the very passing reference to a certain unidentified lady. He thought he knew who this lady might be, by reputation at least, if not in actual fact. Perhaps that offered a way forward. There was certainly a large number of butchers working in *Les Halles*.

As he stared out of the window, he heard a sharp knock behind him and the sound of his door opening. His heart lurched at the words:

'We've got another one, sir.'

Drangnet found himself sad and angry in almost equal measure.

'Oh Christ. Where this time?'

'*Rue des Tournelles* in the *Marais*, sir. Number 34.'

Drangnet fell silent. This was very near where his lived, just behind his house in fact, near the Synagogue. Wearily he levered himself up from his desk and its burden of papers and the two started out again into the spring sunshine heading towards the scene.

As they walked together Drangnet was silent. He was beginning to become anxious about the way this was developing. There were now three dead prostitutes in as many days. No evidence, especially nothing from the streets. The *Sûreté* had a wide network of informants and usually whispers started almost immediately a crime of any magnitude was committed. Many people saw it as an opportunity to earn a little money. But this time there was nothing. Now with this third killing the newspapers would be all over the story by tomorrow and pressure would increase on Drangnet and his men.

Number 34 rather let the side down on the elegant *Rue des Tournelle*. Most of the road had been rebuilt or remodelled recently but number 34 remained a plain-fronted house containing a large number of pokey little apartments. Just immediately to the west, the more fashionable *Marais* district that included Drangnet's own *Place des Vosges* remained popular especially with the artistic set of writers, painters and so on. To the east of the *Rue des Tournelles*, the tone changed very quickly with the area around the *Bastille* and its reputation declined along with that. Drangnet's impression was that number 34 seemed to cling to the old rather than embrace the new.

That impression was born out by the woman who was the *concièrge* who met them on the doorstep. She was immediately both defensive and aggressive.

'I thought you people were supposed to be protecting us.'

Drangnet took a deep breath.

'Good morning, Madame. I'm sorry to hear this has happened. I'd like to come in and talk to you and some of your girls.'

The woman remained surly and reluctant.

'I've sent the girls home. There's no one here except me. Your people are swarming all over the place. I've already given a statement to some unformed policeman so I don't see why I should bother saying it all again to you just because you're wearing a suit.'

Normally Drangnet was even-tempered. He seldom got really upset, especially in public, but this third murder, coming so soon after the previous two finally got to him. He turned to Gant and spoke loudly enough for the some of the crowd and journalists to hear.

'Inspector Gant. Arrest this woman for obstruction of police business. Handcuff her and take her to the cells at the *Sûreté*. I'll interview her in due course. Close and seal this building when our people have finished with it and keep it locked and guarded until I say so. Arrest anyone trying to get in.'

With that he turned briskly away and left the house without saying anything more to anyone, leaving a scene somewhat close to chaos behind him.

'You can interview that bloody woman. I might end up attacking her if she keeps that attitude towards me. Get someone large and nasty to help you. Scare the hell out of her and see what happens.'

Gant was sitting in front of him back in the office. Drangnet had cooled off only a little and he was still fed up.

'So what's the story of this latest killing.'

'Very similar to the previous two, sir. I did manage to talk to some of the girls that Madame Sucart – she's the concierge, by the way - said she had sent home. They are well-known in the area and I sent some of the uniform boys to talk to them. Essentially the story in the same. No one heard anything unusual. Most of the clients were regulars. There were a couple of new ones, but I'll get their details from Madame when I talk to her. The girl was stabbed again. She was only discovered when they shut up shop for the night which presumably means that again it seems that she might have been killed by her last client of the day. I'll have more for you later after I've talked to this concierge woman.'

'Presumably we'll have another body in the Seine any moment now as well,' said Drangnet gloomily.

'Probably, sir.'

'We need to get to it again before the politicos do. I'm not losing this body either. I want Dankovich to have a good sight of this one too. If whoever it is who decides to kill the killers, as it were, if they're running true to form, we should indeed see another body in the Seine sometime tonight. Again I don't want any interference, so get enough people on the streets again to prevent that even if they had to continue to get rough with the political police.'

Gant just raised an eyebrow. They both knew how this idea could go wrong very easily.

'They might be better prepared this time, boss. After last night they may come mob-handed.'

However, given Drangnet's current mood he decided not to say anything and deal with any problems when and where they arose – much later that day and out on the night-time streets of Paris.

'All right, Roger. You get on and see what you can get from that bloody woman in the cells and set up our attempts to find the new body in the Seine before it gets too cold. Why don't we meet for a drink later on in the Café Galleon at six o'clock and try to take stock of all this. I'm going to take a good long walk.

Chapter 4: Monday 4th April   Scene 2: Conversation with Gant

Drangnet arrived before his colleague and sat in the late afternoon sun with a glass of red wine at his elbow. His thoughts wandered over a number of things with no particular structure. He often mulled over a case like this hoping, often correctly, that things would begin to connect each other in his mind without his forcing them. Now his mind was on the political police and why they might be taking such an interest in his case.

The political police were a relatively new group and, if truth be told, a highly unpopular one amongst both the general public and their fellow policemen. They had grown of the Imperial army's military police and the spies that were sent into Paris from the army to spy on the Communards and their leadership. Back then theirs was a completely passive role. They were not there to do anything other than observe what was going on and to identify the leaders of the attempted revolution, the leaders at street level. They dressed like ordinary citizens and attended their many and interminable meetings and debates. Their job was to make lists; lists of people to be arrested and interrogated when the forces of General MacMahon took over the city again to restore order. They were the people who later did the interrogations of communards. They were also the ones who gave evidence at the summary trials that had resulted in the execution of so many who had been arrested during *La Semaine sanglante* when the commune revolution was finally and bloodily supressed.

As a consequence, they were much hated in the town, but successive administrations had found their knowledge of opposition groups useful. Even now still needed spies to go amongst the local population and keep them informed of sedition or plotting. It was a group that pretty quickly came together and stayed together. But when they were finally organised into a proper department, they had been put officially under the control of the Ministry of Defence and not of the Prefect of Police. Drangnet understood that they were needed. Their knowledge of the trouble-making underworld was second to none. But he, like many who had survived the commune and the extremes that followed it, remained deeply suspicious.

All policemen have their contacts and informants and Drangnet was no exception. Over the years he had also accumulated a wide variety of people to whom he could go for information when required. Most lived in the gutter or pretty near to it. They heard things because the people talked thinking these men were of no consequence and for a few sous he could find out more than his men could themselves by official interrogations and arrests. But this time none of his colleagues reported anything from the streets and he had drawn a blank as well. He and his deputy sat in the local café at the junction of the *Pont Neuf* and the *Quai de l'Hôtel de Ville* taking a glass of wine at the end of another fruitless day of asking questions of people who either knew nothing or, more likely, were saying nothing.

'You know,' said Gant. 'it's almost as if someone has decided that everyone will keep their mouth shut. None of my snitches are saying a word even if I know they need the money.'

'Why, do you wonder? What are they afraid of?'

'It doesn't seem that they are afraid of anything in particular. It's just that, on this particular topic at least, they won't say anything. Normally we get a lot of information when we have this sort of crime. But now while they try to sell us all sorts of other titbits about every little crime under the sun as usual, on these dead prostitutes we get nothing. It's as if someone just told them to keep their mouths shut.'

Drangnet drained his glass and gestured towards the bar for a refill. It wasn't long in coming.

'All right. Let's assume that there is some sort of conspiracy of silence. Two questions arise; two that are possibly connected. The first is why are these particular prostitute murders so special and the second is who has the sort of authority to enforce this silence?'

The questions were greeted with something of a puzzled silence by Gant who just frowned into his glass. In the end Drangnet broke the silence.

'All right, let's do the simple things first. We have three prostitute murders. What connects them?'

Gant grunted and took his usual inordinate amount of time lighting his pipe.

'Well if you're looking at this wall of silence we are finding, you might as well list a couple of unexplained corpses in the river as well. We know even less about them. No-one's talking about them either.'

Drangnet thumped his glass down on the table.

'Bravo, *mon ami*. We mustn't forget about them. We have Dankovich's vanishing corpse from Saturday and the one from last night that we intercepted and managed to hang on to. I just assumed they were a couple of uninteresting corpses but not only have the politicos shown more than usual interest in them as well now in the murder of these women, there's no word on the street about them either. Are these two things somehow connected?'

'Ah.' said Gant, Now someone did open his mouth about them. I heard from one of my spies that the word in the town is that they're anarchists.'

'Anarchists?' Gants was less than impressed. It was a common accusation almost invariably with absolutely nothing to back it up.

Gant shrugged.

'That's what I was told, Boss.'

'That's complete rubbish. Who on earth goes around killing anarchists for heaven's sake?'

'Mark you,' Drangnet continued after taking another sip of wine. 'That is precisely the sort of fiction that the politicos would invent to hide some other nefarious activity or other.'

Again, a contemplative silence descended over the little table. Drangnet signalled for yet another glass. It was turning into that sort of a meeting. It was clear to Drangnet that introducing the river bodies into the conversation had actually complicated matters. Now they had to find reasons for the wall of silence to extend to them too.

'All right. Let's get back to the start. We have the murder of three prostitutes in the space of three days. Similarities?'

Gant's puffing on his pipe became even more determined as he thought hard.

'Well, sir. The similarities are that all three killings took place at night, they were all young women, of course. All three were living in the houses and they were all discovered in the morning when the girls didn't come to breakfast. No-one in the house or outside says they saw anyone unusual. All the houses were relatively easy to get into.'

Dragnet just nodded. He couldn't add much to the very short list of points.

'Differences?'

'One suffocation and two stabbings,' offered Gant before tailing off. 'Two right bank one left. Can't think of much else.'

Drangnet had to agree. This wasn't getting them very far.

'What about the locations. Anything special there?'

'One each in the second, the fourth and the sixth.'

Drangnet sighed. 'Not enough of a pattern there as far as I can see.'

This time it was Gant's turn to nod. 'All very similar types of establishment.'

Dragnet's interest perked. 'What do you mean, Roger.'

'Well, sir,' he shrugged. 'They're all nice, middle of the road *maisons*. Clean and tidy, professionally run and, as far as we know, properly managed. They abide by all the rules. The girls are all young and attractive and properly cared for and ply their trade in the house not outside on the street. The prices are reasonable, I'm told,' he added quickly. 'They're neither the luxury bordellos inhabited by the *grande dames* we all know about and can't afford nor are they the filthy hovels that you find further from the centre of town. As I said, they are just good, middle class businesses; never any trouble.'

They were both silent for a moment until a thought struck Drangnet.

'Good, middle class businesses, you say. You're quite right. And if they were a chain of jewellers or clothes shops that were being robbed, what is one of the first questions we'd ask?'

'Who owns them,' was Gant's immediate reply.

'Precisely my friend. So, who owns these brothels? Unless I miss my guess, it is the legendary Madame Fernier.'

Again, both men became silent while they changed their focus. Madame Fernier was an almost mythical figure; a woman who had inherited what amounted to an extensive criminal empire in the city from her equally mythical and famous father. Dragan Fernier had started life as a market porter at *Les Halles* more than fifty years ago and had risen to being the man who controlled most of the petty crime in Paris. It was a thriving business that he had passed on to his daughter on his death. Almost all the crime was of a very low level, petty thieving, pickpocketing, protection for local businesses, nothing very serious or ever too violent. For a perpetually understaffed *Sûreté* there was seldom much to trouble them unless the housebreaking was at the home of someone rich or famous. In any case the trail of evidence stopped always stopped a very long way short of Madame herself. The brothels were one of her many legal enterprises.

'Maybe this is some sort of war or revenge on Madame Fernier; someone trying to muscle in on her territory, as it were.'

'Perhaps.' said Drangnet.

There had been a number of attempts over the years against both father and daughter, but none had succeeded, and the perpetrators seldom survived the experience. As the dead bodies that resulted from these occasional attempted coups were mostly people who Drangnet thought Paris was well rid of, the *Sûreté* seldom got seriously involved in any investigation. He changed the subject.

'I've been thinking about these bodies in the Seine. We lost the first one and only managed to keep the second by virtue of having half the police in Paris spend the night in the *Hôpital Salpêtrière* to keep him away from the clutches of the politicos. We should have Dankovich's autopsy report by tomorrow morning, by the way. We need to have made some arrangements if, true to form, a third so-called anarchist drops in the river tonight.'

Gant listened with interest. Whatever his boss had in mind he was pretty sure that he was going to have to spend the next couple of hours arranging it. So much for a nice evening at home with his family.

'I want you again to have enough men down on the river so you can take possession of any body that might appear drifting towards the west end of the *Île St. Louis* and that means keeping it away from any other branches of our noble police forces who might want to poke their noses in. Then, if a body does actually turn up, I don't want it taken to the *Salpêtrière*. I want you to take it down to the old gendarmerie in *Vaugirard*. The commander there is an old army colleague of mine. He won't let anyone interfere with our body. You might not know that there is a small mortuary in that station. We had to use it during the Commune. If something turns up in the night, get a message to Dankovich to get down there first thing in the morning and do the autopsy there. He won't like it, of course, but it'll mean that we should get the report a good deal earlier than normal.'

'Do you want us to get a message to you as well, boss?' suggested Gant somewhat mischievously.

'Kind of you, old chap,' Drangnet replied with a straight face. 'I'll be happy to hear the news in the morning, thank you all the same.'

The evening crowds were beginning to fill the street outside the café and they both felt that their conversation had reached some sort of end, no matter how unsatisfactory.

'All right, time to go. I'm going back to the office for a while to catch up on paperwork.'

Gant nodded and they left the café and headed back to the *Quai d'Horlorge*; Drangnet to his papers and Gant to organise tonight's watch on the Seine.

Chapter 4: Monday 4th April   Scene 3: Contact with a Possible Ally

He arrived back at the office and put in an hour or so going through the usual pile of paperwork that accumulated on the side of his desk. In spite of Gant's best efforts to intercept much that needn't concern him, there was still always enough to be working on. It was coming up to seven in the evening and, having finished initialling endless pages of reports and information sheets, he fell to contemplating the little picture newly restored to its customary place by his door. It was by the modern artist Camille Pissarro. He had attended the first exhibition of the group that called itself the Anonymous Society of Painters, Sculptors and Printmakers at the former studio of the photographer Nadar a few years before and several of the artists had caught his eye. The group had recently christened itself The Impressionists. He had been slowly collecting a few of their smaller pieces ever since. Even on his modest salary, he could still afford a few of their less expensive works from time to time. This one was a small oil painting of the Seine in springtime. It glowed vividly and magically caught the spring light over the river. It was as he gazed at the picture that he remembered the two corpses that had washed up just a few metres upstream from where he was sitting. He had wondered whether he could find some sought of thread to link all this and now he thought it over more deeply as he looked though his notes. Leaving aside that the politicals had tried to take the men's bodies away, he knew that they were each found during the night following the murder of a prostitute. There was also the matter of the interest shown in all of this by these political police. Could the two sets of murders be connected in some way? Now there had been a third killing of a young girl, tonight's events would prove the connection one way or another.

Then there was Gant's very valid point about Madame Fernier. He also recalled the chance remark by Monsieur Blanco in the *Café du Marché* the other day to the effect that "madame" took care of the people associated with the market. Perhaps it was a line of enquiry that he might walk along for a while, at least. An idea formed in his mind about the same time as he realised that it was some time since he had had anything to eat and the wine he had taken recently was lying slightly heavily on his stomach. He made up his mind and thought "why not?" It was certainly worth a try. He reached into his desk drawer, took out a sheet of headed notepaper and wrote a short note. Once finished, he put it in an envelope and got to work with a candle, sealing wax and his official stamp. Soon the note was sealed with an official-looking and ornate "RF". He left the front unaddressed. If his plan worked, the lady would get the note soon enough. He looked at the elegant little clock on his office mantlepiece and saw that it was nearing eight o'clock. Just the time for something to eat. So, slipping the note into his inside jacket pocket, he took his hat, coat and stick, left the office and set a brisk course for the *Café du Marché*.

An hour or two later he sat back in his chair on the edge of the busy café, replete with a simple but delicious meal of moules followed by cassoulet. The wine was a simple red from the Rhône and yet again he sat there marvelling at how such a well-cooked meal could be provided for such a low price. The clientele was again drawn primarily from the market workers and they were people who knew both a good meal and the value of a franc. He succumbed to a piece of the house tart. This time it was apricot. As before, as the last of the delicious tart passed his lips, the proprietor again sat down opposite to him, uninvited at his table.

'This time you can pay for your own meal.' he said gruffly. 'But you can have your digestif on the house.'

With this he pushed a large measure of cognac across the table at his customer.

'You're developing a taste for our cooking, Monsieur Chief inspector.'

'Indeed,' Drangnet replied. 'You do simple things here very well as opposed to many others in Paris who complicated things badly. You, your wife and your chef are to be congratulated.'

The man hurrumphed with some pride. *'Le chef, c'est moi.'*

Drangnet was amused by the reference coming from someone who he would assume was a stanch republican.

'I'm sure that *Le Roi de Soleil* never cooked as well as you, Monsieur Blanco.'

The man positively bristled with pride. Drangnet raised his glass in tribute to his host and the gesture was received with a smile and a nod. The policeman thought this was as good a moment as any.

'Monsieur Blanco. Might it be possible to have a short word with you in private? It is an important matter but perhaps it might be better to go somewhere more private?'

Blanco looked a little startled but replied very quickly.

'I have an office in the back of the café, monsieur. If you go past the toilet it is the door at the end of the corridor. I can meet you there in five minutes if you wish.'

Sure enough five minutes later he was sitting in a tiny office next to the kitchen facing a by now somewhat suspicious restaurant owner. He immediately set about to reassure the man. He had carried his cognac in with him and took another sip before he started. It was an attempt to make the man slightly less defensive.

'Monsieur Blanco. As you know I am trying to catch the people who murdered these poor prostitutes and, I will be perfectly honest with you, I'm not making too much progress. Now I don't want any information from you but the last time I was here you made a very brief reference to someone who takes care of those who are in, shall we say, her extended family. I feel that I would like to be able to ask her advice about this terrible business. She, like you, is not under suspicion of doing anything wrong nor is she in any danger from the police. It is just that I would like to talk with her, and I don't feel as if I should demand that she visits me at the *Sûreté*. What I want would be a purely private personal conversation.'

He paused to finish his drink and then reached into his pocket, withdrew the letter, and laid it gently on the table between them.

'This is a note making this request. It is a personal note from me to Madame Fernier. Unless I'm mistaken, I think that you might be able to ensure that it gets to her. If I am mistaken, then please think no more about it and just destroy the note.'

With that he got up and started to leave the little room. Blanco just looked up at him with appraising eyes.

'They say you're an honest man; for a flic, that is.'

'I try to be, Monsieur Blanco,' replied Drangnet with a slight smile on his lips. 'I try to be.'

Blanco got up to face the policeman.

'I'll see what I can do, Chief Inspector. No promises.'

He fixed Drangnet with a very hard stare indeed and dropped his voice to a whisper.

'You should know, however, if any harm comes to Madame Fernier as a result of this. You'll be a very dead honest policeman. Make no mistake.'

Drangnet nodded and left.

It was with a slower pace and a heavier stomach than when he had arrived that he walked home from the café along the length of the *Rue de Rivoli*. It was about ten o'clock and the road was still thronged with people and horse drawn vehicles of all sorts. Some of the early theatres were emptying and there were still many cafés open waiting for the late trade. For a while he forgot the pressing business of the murders and just strolled along, taking pleasure in the town and in the joy he always felt of living there. It was almost a warm evening too and although they were all wearing their coats and scarves, here were many people standing around and taking drinks in the gardens that occupied the centre of the *Place des Vosges*. Spring seemed truly to have arrived. Once in his apartment, he poured himself a whisky and set down in an armchair to read while the remained of his excellent supper continued to digest itself.

A little later he was awakened from a light doze by a shark knock on his front door. He opened the door. There stood an absolute mountain of a man; considerably more than six feet tall and obviously more than two hundred pounds in weight. What looked like a wrestler's build was well disguised by an immaculately tailored black wool suit and waistcoat. A sober tie and stiff collared white shirt, and highly polished, expensive-looking leather shoes completed the ensemble. He held a black bowler hat in his left hand while his right was outstretched and held a letter. Only the battered and scarred face betrayed a life that would be more suited to the boxing ring that anywhere else. The man offered no smile of greeting. Drangnet assumed that the man wasn't on social terms with too many policemen. He reached out and took the letter from the man's outstretched hand and thanked him. A slight nod on the head preceded a surprisingly nimble about turn as the man mountain returned back towards the stair well.

Drangnet closed the door went quickly to the front windows in time to see the man getting into a cab which lurched perilously to one side as the man mounted and was driven off around the square. He smiled. Madame Fernier's reply had obviously arrived. He sat back down and drained the last of his whisky, turning the envelope slowly, over and over, in his hands. It was small, almost square; near ivory in colour. Heavy for its size. It was the stationary of a fine lady; the finest. Not that of a master – or should it be mistress – criminal. But it was more than that. This lady, the author of this note, was almost a legend in the City of Paris. She had never been arrested, never even questioned by police. He had never seen her, yet he held in his hand what was hopefully an invitation to meet her. He couldn't help but feel a frisson of excitement as he crossed to his disk and reached for his letter opener to slit the wax seal on of the envelope.

Dear Chief Inspector Drangnet

I would be pleased if you would take tea with me tomorrow at 3:30pm.

Angèle Fernier   *38 Quai d'Orléans, Île St. Louis*

It wasn't the longest letter he'd ever seen. But it held out more promise than almost any he had ever received.

Chapter 5: Tuesday 5th April   Scene 1: Another Fish is Caught

It was about seven in the morning and he was just on the point of leaving home for the office when there was a knock on his front door. As he went to open it, he heard his deputy.

'Chief. It's Gant.'

He opened the door and let the man in.

'I don't know how you did it. You've got the luck of the devil, I suppose, but you were right. We've got another one. It looks as if our third prostitute's killer, if that's who it is, has ended up the same way as the other ones.'

'All right. Where's the body right now?'

'At the moment it's on the mortuary cart down the police station in Vaugirard. I explained to the commander about what you wanted and he's waiting for your instructions. I've sent word to Dr. Dankovich and left men to supplement Constance's people to guard the body in case the ungodly get to hear of what has happened. I'm not sure if they're going to be needed. Constance gave the impression that he would rather relish being invaded by a few political policemen. He shares your feelings, I think. He said he was an old army buddy of yours. Likes a fight.'

'Yes. It's a tough beat down there in Vaugirard and he's the right man for the job. The man fights tough and dirty when necessary. So how many people know about this latest body?'

'For now you, me, four of our men and the mortuary cart driver and his assistant. The local men at Vaugirard of course. That's all as yet.'

'Good Roger. Well done as usual. Maybe we'll hang on to the body slightly longer this time. Strict secrecy obviously. Make sure the cart drivers keep their mouths shut. I'll come down there immediately.'

'Don't forget you've got a meeting with Dancart at ten. You really shouldn't be late for that. He's got company, I gather.' warned Gant rolling his eyes.

Drangnet just grunted and followed Gant down to the waiting cab. As they set off south, he was pleased to see that Gant hadn't used one of the *Sûreté*'s own cabs. There was less chance of tongue wagging with a civilian hire.

The more recent reorganisation and renumbering of the original twelve *arrondissements* established some eighty five years ago had increased the number to twenty and incorporated most of the country areas that had surrounded the inner city out to a distance as far as the universally unpopular Wall of the Farmers General with its tax collection stations. Thus, the fifteenth that included the commissariat of police where it ran alongside the more fashionable sixth and seventh arrondissements, consisted of substantial residential and commercial buildings while further out it became more rural where the arrondissement had been extended to include the villages of Vaugirard itself and Beaugrenelle.

The police station on the *Rue de Vaugirard* was not particularly large or important. It occupied a drab building that seemed perpetually in need of repair and housed the normal compliment of police of various ranks carrying out the usual range of tasks associated with domestic policing. Possibly because of its relative isolation from the centre of the city it was a police station that housed not only cells and stables and offices but also basic medical facilities including a morgue. It had also been at the centre of fierce fighting when the city was re-occupied by the army to end the weeks of the Commune. It had remained a tough area.

The station was commanded by an old friend of Drangnet's, Pierre Constance, a veteran of the Paris police and one of his comrades during their army days. They had fought together at Sedan. He was a man who seemed to have been on the verge of retiring for more years than Dragnet could remember. The two had known each other for a sufficiently long time for the customary and somewhat elaborate greeting between to two men to be ignored when they arrived.

'Dr. Dankovich arrived about half an hour or so ago; none too happy, I should add, about being dragged out of bed so early. However, he started his examination immediately. Come into my office so you can have a coffee while you wait.'

Drangnet accepted the invitation with pleasure. He was all too well acquainted with the good doctor's reluctance to be interrupted while performing an examination even when he hadn't been dragged out of bed at dawn. Lord only knew what sort of mood he was in now. The three of them were old friends and colleagues. While Drangnet had been in and out of the city during the conclusion of the German siege and the brief turbulent life of the Commune, the other two had worked through; all three had played prominent rolls in trying to minimise the terrible effect of the *Semaine sanglant* that ended the communard's brief attempt at power ten years before.

Constance's office was tiny and completely filled with memorabilia; photos and certificates, a table set with toy soldiers, some small portrait busts and piles of books arranged higgledy-piggledy in shelves and on the floor, a game of chess set out. A paper-strewn desk faced two almost threadbare leather chairs. Amongst many skills that his friend regularly demonstrated was his ability to make coffee. Once the two men were suitably equipped and seated, Constance addressed his old friend.

'All right, Louis, what the hell's going on?'

So, it was without hesitation, Dragnet gave him a résumé. For the moment he left out Madame Fournier. But the rest of the story was as complete as he could make it. This was an old school policeman who would understand. Constance waited in silence just watching his friend.

'So, I get the impression that you don't think this has anything to do with anarchists.' he said finally.

Drangnet sighed and shook his head slightly.

'I honestly don't think so, Pierre. You and I are a lot closer to what is actually happening on the streets that these new political characters who never seem to leave their offices. We know most of these so-called anarchists since before the days of the commune. Most of them are all talk and I don't think there are too many bomb throwers amongst them. As for strangers, there are always new people in town and obviously we don't always get to find about them immediately. But we all have good sources of information and by and large nasty foreigners are unwelcome as we tend to know. We always get to know one way or another. And in any case, I think that we are being side-tracked, perhaps on purpose. I have no evidence, of course but just call it an old policeman's nose. The point is that some prostitutes are being murdered and miraculously those responsible are themselves being polished off by persons unknown. It's all rather odd but, to be frank, I'm not ungrateful.'

Constance nodded slightly. He was very used to trusting his own "policeman's nose"

'So why did you pinch this particular corpse.'

Drangnet smiled a little.

'Probably because I could, I suppose, and I was unhappy with what had been happening when I had the first body stolen from me. In any case I wanted the doc to have a look at him. Maybe he can tell where this man came from. I'm pretty sure I can guess how he died.'

The two took to reminiscing for a while until Gant again came in to report.

'The good Doctor is taking his time. He says he won't be hurried so you might as well not wait. He also says that he actually hasn't finished the one from yesterday yet. He'll get a report on both to you by *** tomorrow morning. Not before.'

'Did he say anything at all?'

'Well he did say that this one was garrotted like the other one and with the same sort of cord.' replied Gant holding out a paper packet to Drangnet.

He looked in it and started for a moment. Suddenly a lot of things became clear including how he was going to introduce his conversation with the good Madame Fernier this afternoon.

'Don't forget your meeting with Dancart, sir.' said Gant with a sly smile on his fact. 'You know you don't want to be late.'

Drangnet gave his deputy a very dirty look and, having said goodbye to his old friend Constance, he set off back to the office and his meeting.

Chapter 5: Tuesday 5th April   Scene 2: A Meeting with the Boss

He had already been warned by Suzette who else would be at the meeting, so he wasn't much looking forward to it. This was not because they were members of the great and the powerful of the city but because he usually found it almost impossible not to say the wrong things when he met them. He had little time for these people.

The atmosphere was formal and frosty. Two other men sat one on either side of Dancart's elegant writing table. He knew both of them by sight and was pleased that he wasn't on personal terms with either of them. He had spent considerable time avoiding that sort of thing. The first, resplendent in full uniform with much gold braid and medal ribbons was the grandly moustachioed Louis Andrieux, the actual Prefect of Police for Paris. The second was a certain Monsieur Jean Antoine Ernest Constans, the current Minister of the Interior, no less. He started to feel a little sick. However, he knew that it was not the result of last night's excellent meal at the *Café du Marché*. He had dined well but modestly. No, it was, he knew, entirely because he was faced with politicians. He didn't have a political bone in his body and to have them forced on him when he could be out there chasing villains felt unpleasant in the extreme. However, he was a courteous man, if not always polite, so he just sat with a calm that seemed to annoy the others. They were clearly used to a greater degree of subservience. His boss started things off.

'Chief Inspector, I wonder if you might give us all a briefing on the recent spate of killings of prostitutes in the city?'

He was intrigued more than startled. He knew what this was all about, of course. What sort of an idiot did they take him for? But for the moment he was forced to oblige these two with an account of the crime when, in reality, they were much more interested in the potential damage that might be done to their own reputations.

'Well, in the last four days we have had the murders of three prostitutes. One strangled and two stabbed while lying on their beds in their own, shall we say, places of business.'

He couldn't resist as he added: 'Hardly an actual spate though, I would have thought.'

Hardly something either that should cause the Minister to prise himself loose from the powdered magnificence of his office in the *Place Beauvau* to attend the office of a humbler inferior. The Minister frowned at him.

'Be that as it may, have you solved these crimes?'

'Well yes and no, Sir.'

He fought hard to keep cynical smile from his lips as he continued: 'It seems that the three women were stabbed by their clients.'

'And?'

The Minister was clearly getting slightly hot under the collar. Putting his best innocent face forward, Drangnet went on. Dancart shifted uncomfortably in his seat. He recognised the signs all too well. Drangnet was all set on annoying his superiors again. It was something he was very, very good at. He sighed silently, waited for the inevitable and offered an equally silent prayer that the damage would not be too great this time.

'Oh, the three men who were most likely responsible were themselves each found dead shortly after the deaths of the prostitutes, floating in the Seine very near here. In fact, just over there.'

He gestured over the shoulders of the men in front of him in the general direction of Notre Dame and beyond. Two of the three involuntarily turned around and looked over their shoulders. They both returned to face Drangnet with faces like thunder. He paused somewhat mischievously until he felt his superior was about to make a comment and then carried on.

'Fetched up, or dumped possibly, on the little beach on the north bank where the river divides between these two islands to be precise. Just around the corner from these offices, in fact.'

Both the Prefect and the Minister looked grim. Drangnet smiled inwardly. He was beginning to enjoy himself.

'And how were they killed?' insisted the Minister, heading headlong towards Dragnet's mischievous bear trap.

'Strangled, I think, sir,' he replied innocently.

The Minister bristled.

'You think, Drangnet? You think?'

'Well sir, I can only really guess as at least one of the bodies was removed from my morgue before my pathologist had had a chance to examine it.' he replied with commendable inexactitude.

Constans was outraged while Louis kept his most innocent of faces firmly fixed in spite of a strong desire to enjoy a slight anticipatory smile.

'Removed, Drangnet, by whom may I ask?'

Drangnet smiled as he heard the unmistakable of a bear in the shape of the Minister of the Interior falling into a carefully-laid trap.

'I gather that it was on the orders of the Ministry of the Interior, Sir.'

There was a very uncomfortable silence in the room as the good minister went a similar colour to his mulberry-hued embroidered waistcoat. The man finally spoke. One could see that he was trying to control an outburst of temper. Drangnet tended to have that effect on people sometimes especially when that was his intention.

'Chief Inspector. Did you manage to find out anything about these men while they were in your care?'

Drangnet looked directly at the man with some contempt.

'You mean in the very short time they were in my morgue? Hardly in my care as you choose to put it, *Monsieur le Ministre*. I did ascertain that each had been strangled. Had they remained in my care, as you put it, longer, I might have discovered more.'

'Oh bugger,' he thought immediately to himself with surprising lack of concern, 'There goes my career - again.'

He probably didn't actually want one in any case. In fact, he was about to discover considerably more about these three dead men through the kind offices of Dr. Dankovich but he was damned if he wanted to pass that on to these idiots; yet at least. It was left to the Prefect to take the meeting forward and to attempt to pour some oil on the troubled waters created by Drangnet's report.

'Chief Inspector, it has come to our notice that these three men are of interest to our colleagues in the political division. There is some evidence to suggest that they are members of this anarchist group that is beginning to cause to much trouble. Anything that you could pass on from your investigation would be greatly appreciated.'

Drangnet became a little angry.

'Sir, I have no information from my own investigation, as you put it, let alone anyone else's, as without bodies I have nothing to investigate.'

Now he was stretching the truth more than a little but he was beginning to get fed up.

'If you think there is a political aspect to all this, then I would suggest that you and your newly formed and excellently-funded political department would be the ones to investigate it. They at least have the bodies, I presume. I have nothing to add to what I have told you already other than to offer the personal opinion that this theory about anarchists is complete rubbish.'

A now thoroughly red-faced Minister couldn't restrain himself.

'As I recall, Chief Inspector, you were offered the post of commander of this new division and you turned it down. May I enquire why?'

Drangnet faced the man squarely.

'I don't like politics, *Monsieur le Ministre*. Nor do I find it easy to work with politicians.'

The man clearly wasn't used to being addressed like this and was about to lose his temper in a substantial way. Fortunately, Dancart interrupted hastily in an effort to calm things down.

'Thank you, Chief Inspector. I think that will be all for the moment.'

Drangnet got up, nodded, and left very quickly indeed, leaving a thoroughly disconcerted meeting behind him. The door closed and it was the Minister who spoke first with considerable anger.

'I want that little man gone. I want him out of the police force immediately; today; disrespectful little swine.'

Dragnet was well above six feet tall so clearly the Minister's description was pejorative rather than literal. Dancart was about to come to his colleague's defence but to his surprise and delighted it was the *Préfet* who replied.

'Jean, that's probably neither a good idea nor might it be possible.'

The man refused to be diverted.

'And why not?' he snapped.

Andrieux sighed.

'Well there are a number of reasons actually. Firstly, might be that Drangnet is by far the best detective in the Department and that probably means in all of France. Then, he is widely liked and respected by everyone in the *Préfecture*. He solves more crime in a year than most of the rest put together. He is feared by the criminals as well. He is completely honest, unbelievably hard working, never gives up and is without fault in his work. Finally, he had friends in high places so getting rid of him will undoubtedly cause more trouble than you might imagine.'

The man scoffed.

'Oh yes. In high places?'

'Er yes.'

'Higher than mine?'

The Préfet looked at the man directly.

'Yes, Minister. Higher even than yours.'

There was a silence as the man realised what had been said. Without a further word he rose and swept angrily out of the room.

The *Préfet* turned to his Superintendent.

'Does he?'

Dancart smiled.

'Actually yes. Drangnet is a regular player of the great game of *Jeu de Paume* and one of his regular partners is Monsieur Jules Ferry, our current Head of State and President of the Council and Minister of Public Instruction and Fine Arts. I gather they are good friends and also form a highly successful doubles partnership. I gather from those who know about these things that the relations between tennis doubles partners are often very close.'

The man, being a politician, quickly had second thoughts. With little more ado the two men left. Dancart called Suzette.

'Oh, for God's sake, get Drangnet back in here.'

Soon a surprisingly calm policeman was back sitting in the room. Superintendent Dancart looked at his man with exasperation but with less of a frown than might be imagined. He was well used to the errant ways of his maverick Chief Inspector and ignoring their differing ranks, the two were good the best of friends.

'Louis, you really must stop doing this sort of thing. One of these days you'll get up the nose of someone who really matters. Fortunately, this particular iteration at the Ministry of Interior is probably on his way out soon. But it's a worrying habit. Not good for the department or your promotion prospects.'

Drangnet smiled. 'I'm a little more bothered about the former than the latter. So, what's this all about?'

'I'm not sure if you been told officially, but you've probably guessed. This investigation has been given officially to the political people.'

Drangnet sighed. He had even less time for the newly-formed political police department than he had for the more traditional politicians. Dancart went on.

'They seem to have decided that your three dead bodies are Romanian anarchists. What do they really think. Are they?'

Drangnet simply shrugged.

He tried quickly to think of a way of avoiding his nascent investigation being trampled to death by hordes of heavy-footed politicos.

'I'm sorry, Sir. Do you mean that they are Romanians who happen to be anarchists or anarchists who happen to be Romanian? It would be as well to be clear.'

That particular piece of sarcasm was rewarded with a long stare by his superior. It was also ignored.

'Don't be a smart arse with me, Dancart. I know you too well. So how far did you get before the first body vanished?'

'Not far at all, Chief.' replied the policeman, looking a little sheepish. 'But now there have indeed been three killings. All three men were found in the river. They had each washed up on the island. They were also all found less than a day after each girl was murdered and each had been strangled with a ligature. Garrotted. Although I had no idea whether they were Romanian or not, the two we saw certainly didn't look particularly French. General enquiries revealed no witnesses at all although, of course, it wasn't possible to find out where the men were killed. That's about it.'

His chief looked thoughtful for a moment before adopting a more informal tone.

'Louis, I'm as uncomfortable as you are about this new unit. They don't seem to be answerable to me and I don't receive any reports - or at least none of any substance. It looks as if yet again the government is playing with their favourite secret police game. However, whether or not there actually is a political dimension to all this, and I have my doubts, by the way, we have six murders to solve and that is still a Paris police matter, however unlamented three of those killings might be.'

Dancart shared his junior's sympathy for the prostitutes although probably for slightly different reasons.

'We just have to do the best we can with what we have.'

'Also, if there really is a political element to all this, Louis, then please find a way of keeping it off my desk and leaving it firmly in the hands of our colleagues who apparently are responsible. They have the budget for this sort of thing. This job is complicated enough without all that and we have enough crime of our own to keep us busy.'

He got up and made to end the meeting and to allow Drangnet to leave, this time with a little more dignity than before. As he left, Drangnet found himself thinking:

'If the stabbing of three prostitutes and the garrotting of their three killers in central Paris isn't anything to do with us, then I'm damned if I know what is.

Chapter 5: Tuesday 5th April   Scene 3: Tea on the *Île St. Louis*

She sat upright almost at the front edge of the high-backed wing chair, her own back not touching that of the chair. It was a pose that for most people would be stiff and unnatural. But this instance was entirely to the contrary. The slim, elegant lady in front of him sat perfectly still, head held high; her eyes looking steadily and directly into his. She didn't speak; just looked at him with an expression on her face that was neither nervous nor was it in any way aggressive; these being the two expressions that he most commonly came across when talking to people.

Being a senior policeman tended to have that effect on them. No, this lady showed neither of these. She was just relaxed and, interestingly, seemed perfectly content to remain silent until he, as the guest, was completely ready to start taking. It was he, after all, who had requested the audience.

She sat with her back to but not obscuring the long, floor-to-ceiling window behind her. It was one of six that pierced the majestic curve of the wall that ran around the building high at the west end of the *Île St. Louis* on its fourth floor. There was not quite enough of the early spring sun coming through to obscure her from view. But he admitted to himself that she could look at him with much more clarity than he could observe her. Beyond the window lay the very eastern end of the *Île de la Cité* and, of course, the great fantail of flying buttresses that was the east of end the cathedral of Notre-Dame. He wondered how the view might change if he were able to walk slowly around all six windows. However, for now, he just satisfied himself with taking in the room and its occupant. He found it indeed a gratifying process.

The room into which a simply-uniformed maid had shown him was high-ceilinged and perfectly reflected the lady opposite. It was elegant and restrained as well. Pale grey silk walls were lined with bookcases full of a mixture of volumes from expensively leather bound to cheap paperbound. Between them were pictures under picture lights; an affect softer and, for him at least, comforting. Stuccoed ceilings above ornately detailed with exuberant floral patterns and a deep golden brown parquet floor beneath covered, he noted with approval, with thick and obviously high quality oriental rugs. He was no great fan of hard wooden floors. He noted that the whole apartment had been converted to the newly available electricity that only the wealthiest inhabitants could afford to have installed. His more modest apartment was still heated and lit by gas.

He was intrigued that many of the paintings were very modern indeed. The little Paris group of so-called Impressionists were a particular favourite of his too. Madame obviously shared his taste and his initial positive impression of her deepened. It was a comfortable room indeed.

As he looked out through the window he noticed a small coloured shield of stained glass hung high at the apex of one of the windows' arches. It seemed to be a coat of arms, brightly coloured and at that distance almost indecipherable. The afternoon sum had just caught it and projected an out of focus multi-coloured image down on the little table in front of him. He immediately thought of the much greater splendour of the rose window in the west façade of the cathedral spread below him. That too would now be projecting an infinitely greater but equally colourful blaze of light into the cathedral's interior in an attempt to transform the lives of those who fell into its path. He wondered not entirely idly whether a similar fate was in store for him in this beguiling woman's apartment. He hoped not; or perhaps not yet, at least.

The lady across from him gave a similar impression of a restrained elegance. She was fashionably attired in a high-necked day dress in a deep blue material with small white lace touches at neck and cuff. The dress was tightly tucked in at the waist as was the current fashion. Little dark leather pumps protruded slightly from the low hem of the dress. She wore a pair of small pearl earrings and a single strand necklace of similarly-sized pearls around the high neck of the dress. To say that he was impressed would be an understatement but that was the least provocative way he could think to describe his feelings.

Finally, he felt that he should at least start their conversation. After all, it was he who had requested their meeting.

'Madam Fernier. Thank you for receiving me.'

It was a pretty feeble effort but at least it had the virtue of honesty. Unusually for him it was the only thing he could think of to say. Her eyes twinkled and she made as to reply but the whole introduction was interrupted by the maid coming into the room with a tray of tea that she arranged over the low table in front of him. All the usual accoutrements of afternoon tea were laid out but only one cup, he noticed. Madame obviously was obviously not taking tea with him. He noticed a small jug of milk. How did Madame know of his preference to tea in the English style?

By the time the maid had retired, and he had taken a sip of the undeniably excellent tea they had both seemed to have forgotten whose turn it was to speak. He suddenly remembered something. He too had collected a little information about his hostess and had brought a small gift that was customary on these occasions. He reached into his jacket pocket and put a small package on the table in front of her. It was a small, square, bright pink box of delicacies from the newly re-built patisserie of Monsieur Ladurée on the *Rue Royale*. The very slight but neutral smile that had hitherto graced her face broadened into one of genuine delight.

'Monsieur Drangnet how very thoughtful. Thank you.'

She stopped for a moment as a thought crossed her mind.

'Perhaps you are too well informed about me, monsieur.'

The little pink box was a famous trade mark of the *Maison Ladurée*. He couldn't resist. For a moment he thought that perhaps the ridiculously large amount of money he had spent on this little trifle might have been worth it - just. He leant forward and poured a tiny amount of milk into his tea to emphasise the point.

'As you seem to be about me, Madame.'

This time he won a genuine laugh. She tossed her head back.

'All right, Monsieur perhaps we should get to the substance of our meeting. How can I help our distinguished *Inspecteur en chef de la chambre criminelle de la gendarmerie de Paris*?'

He hadn't really planned this conversation. Now he felt that he should have. For he was the guest of someone who was more than just an elegant lady of an uncertain age. The elegant, restrained, and undeniably attractive woman who sat across from him was the lady who ran almost all the street crime in Paris. There was hardly a pickpocket, footpad, house breaker, petty criminal or prostitute in central Paris that didn't in some way connect with her. Each regularly paid a small proportion of their income to her or at least to her organisation. It was a system that had been in place since her father had founded the business from a base that was a lot less salubrious than the *Île St. Louis*. His kingdom had been based in the so-called Belly of Paris, the vast market of *Les Halles*, in the north east corner of the first arrondissement. He had started to work there as an eight-year-old porter and worked his entire life in that difficult, often violent world. In time, his ability to negotiate - or perhaps argue would be a better word - with his bosses found him developing an increasingly important life away from that of a market porter. He often gave voice to his fellow workers' concerns and, protected by their support, made a reputation of a successful negotiator with the politicians who owned and ran the market. From there it had been a natural progression into crime, minor at first, then more serious and by the time he reached middle age with a wife and a young daughter, his interests had branched out into protection; protection first for businesses, then people who wanted it or needed it, prostitutes, petty thieves. Anyone who could pay. The market supplied his workforce. There was never any shortage of strong young men willing to work extra hours for a few extra sous. He had died at the age of seventy. However, for some years he had been sharing the essentials of his somewhat unusual business with his beloved daughter to the extent that on his death she simply took over.

She proved to be a better employer than her father, increasing the business while paying more to her employees and taking less from her customers. Above all she had reduced the violence, although not entirely. She had on occasions proved to be as violent an employer as her father when it was necessary. That it seemed to be necessary less often than before was all. Almost as important as all that, she was much loved. It was as much to that as anything that she owed her success and her security.

She wasn't simply beautiful, he thought as he prepared to come to the point, at least not in any conventional way. She was, however, a very handsome woman; very handsome indeed in that particular way that often defeats younger women who labour too long and too hard to create their own beauty.

'Madame. In the last few days three young prostitutes have been murdered here in Paris. Two stabbed in the heart, one strangled. Almost simultaneously with the deaths of these unfortunate girls bodies of three men have been found fetched up on the little beach on the side of the river, hardly stone's throw from your window.'

He allowed his gaze to linger on the view outside before returning to his narrative. The beach was indeed only a few tens of yards from that very window.

'Two of the women were stabbed, one suffocated. Each of the men had been strangled: garrotted, in fact. I gather from my, er, colleagues in the political division, that the men were Romanians and, in all probability, in France under false papers. These colleagues seem to think that they were involved with these anarchists that seem increasingly to be troubling us here in Paris.'

He paused while the maid reappeared to replenish the water in the teapot in front of him and departed again.

'As I am sure you'll know I've already interviewed many of the girls in your *maisons closes* before starting to look for their killers. Whilst I'm not particularly happy that someone seemed to have decided to do our job for us. Unless it is a complete coincidence, it does seem as if those responsible for the women's deaths have been found and dealt with and at the same time saving the City of Paris a considerable amount of money in the process.'

She had hardly moved throughout his explanation. Even now she remained remarkably still and relaxed as she replied.

'So, Chief Inspector, I presume that in your opinion, and probably in those of your rather unsavoury colleagues who specialise in what they perceive of as political matters, these men were anarchists and that I am, in some way involved in their deaths; timely as that might have been or not.'

Drangnet moved a little uncomfortably in his seat.

'Well Madame, not precisely.'

She didn't have to ask the obvious question. She just waited without saying anything.

'Madame, my political friends are claiming that the men are, indeed, Romanians and are almost certainly anarchists or some sort. Perhaps even paid assassins. Who can say? I can't say one way or the other and they won't, obviously. One body were removed from my morgue and out of my jurisdiction with what might be termed indecent haste before we could give it anything more than the most cursory of inspections. I am still examining the others.'

She now looked at him quite directly.

'Monsieur, delighted as I am finally to meet you and to have the chance to have this conversation, but I'm still not quite sure why we're talking. Do you suspect me of something? Some sort of involvement in the deaths of these Romanians, perhaps? In which case, why, Chief Inspector, am I having this conversation with you in the comfort of my own apartment and not in some dark and damp cell under the *Quai de l'Horlorge* in the company of men who I imagine would make that interview much less agreeable than you do now?'

Now it was his turn to smile although this time his was a little winterly.

'Ah Madame, I said that these dead men might have been identified by others as Romanian anarchists. I didn't say that anyone had concluded that there was any connection with the killing of the three girls. They might be suspect. No more.'

She again paused to consider if she understood correctly what this intriguing policeman was saying to her.

'So why are we having this conversation, pray?'

Enjoying a small moment of theatre, he just replied.

'Madame you haven't yet opened your offering from Monsieur Ladurée.'

The little pink box had remained untouched on the low table between them since he had presented it earlier. Now she leant over and took it up into her hands. No rings on her fingers Drangnet noticed. She was about to pull one end of the bright pink ribbon bow that was tied around the box when she noticed that there was a second, narrow tie following precisely the same path as the ribbon. However, this was less beautiful; much less. It was a narrow string, predominantly white in colour but stained periodically along its length by patches of that deeper ochre that blood can turn into when left for a time. It was the length of butchers twine that Dankovich had sent up to him in the paper packet. Her gaze was now much more penetrating and somewhat less friendly.

'Chief Inspector I see that your brief inspection of the dead bodies of the Romanian anarchists was not entirely cursory. Also, now it seems that I have you to thank personally for this conversation not taking place in the cellar of the *Quai*.'

He smiled at her and nodded slightly while she delicately untied the string and let it fall slowly and gently in a rough coil on the table in a gesture that was almost tender. Perhaps they were both thinking of the dead girls. They had both recognised the cord that was commonly used by the butchers of the *Les Halles* to tie up butchered joints of meat. Then he shrugged in an innocent sort of way.

'I thought that the information would be of more use to me than to them, Madame.'

She looked at him sharply.

'And to your colleagues at the Quai?'

'At the moment, just me, Madame.'

Madame Fernier's response was to do nothing other than to ring the smallest of hand bells that Drangnet noticed for the first time lay in her lap hidden by the folds of fabric. The maid appeared instantly. It crossed his mind to wonder what sort of signal would have heralded an intervention of a much less genteel kind.

'Louise, please could you get a glass of whisky for the Chief Inspector. I will take the same.'

There was silence between them for the short interval before the return of the maid carrying two cut glasses filled with whisky and soda. The water had already been added. Madame had indeed found a lot of information about him. They both took a sip while the matter of a formal toast was dealt with by a slight mutual inclination of their heads. Their eyes met. In fact, it took a while to remember which of them should take the conversation forward. It was she who very quietly whispered:

'Thank you, Chief Inspector. Everything I have heard about you seems to be true. That is most unusual.'

He just smiled for now came the crux of the matter; the reason he was here.

'I'll be candid with you Madame. My first concern is not with catching who strangled these so-called Romanians if that is, in fact, what they were. They got what they deserved, in my opinion. I am more concerned with the murder of your girls.'

'Surely, Chief Inspector,' she shrugged, 'they are just common prostitutes. If they break the law like any other criminal they should be punished and, in any case, theirs is a risky profession.'

'If you truly have done your homework on me as you seem to have done,' he glanced at the whiskey in his hand, 'then you would know that you're mistaken. In the first instance these women are not doing anything illegal. Your *maisons closes* are run correctly and within the current laws. These girls are under my protection as much as any other citizen of Paris who has a right to expect it. I don't take it well when this sort of thing happens. Protecting the residents of this city - all of them - is my duty and one I take very seriously.'

She looked across at him.

'Yes, they said that you were a gentleman when you talked to them. It's unusual. Most of your colleagues treat them with very little kindness. Quite the opposite in fact, in spite of many of your colleagues using their services and paying very little for them.'

He shook his head slightly with more than a little regret.

'I'm genuinely sorry for that, Madame.'

'You are unique, Monsieur. My girls all like you. I'm pretty sure that you're the only man in Paris who can command a welcome into more than five hundred Parisian bedrooms without any charge at all. Perhaps you should try it sometime?'

He grinned:

'That's the first truly intimidating you've said to me since I came here, Madame.'

She tossed her head back again and joined in his laughter before settling back to the business of the day.

'Well, Chief Inspector, I'm enjoying your company of course but there must be something you want from me?'

Drangnet was reluctant because he too was enjoying himself, but they came come to the point of the meeting. He put his whisky down and squared up to his hostess.

'As I said, I may be a little uncomfortable with the new political department of the Gendarmerie. However, I understand why they are there and as long as they don't seriously get under my feet then I will put up with interference from time to time. I want to solve the murders and, more importantly, to stop it happening again. However you did it, you seem to have uncovered the identities of three men who killed the girls in a time when the police haven't got within a country mile. If there are more of them, then we need all the help we can get. You seem to be very much better at finding them than we are.'

She just sipped her whisky and said nothing as he continued.

'If it's true that these men are using your girls before then kill them, then you might well be able to help find them. We might even be able to find ways of protecting the girls a little better. Recent events have made me very sad.'

He went on, feeling that a little more explanation was required for his unusual proposal.

'Between us, I'm also little worried about the political police, Madame. Their methods tend to be less than subtle, and they seem to answer to a higher authority than mine, if indeed they answer to one at all. I don't want them to, shall we say, disrupt life in Paris as we both know it. If I can stay in the middle, as it were, I might be able to prevent some of the consequences of their misplaced exuberance.'

'Does that mean you want to protect us from the police as well as from the Romanians, Chief Inspector?' she offered teasingly with a charming smile.

'Well, not quite in those terms, Madame, but essentially that is the case.'

She didn't give up easily, this woman.

'Even me, Monsieur?'

He returned her smile.

'Especially you, Madame.'

She looked across at him almost fondly. What an extraordinary policeman this was sitting in front of her sipping his whisky. She thought of her father. How things have changed. The improbable thought of him sharing a glass with a Chief Inspector of police made her smile. There was a silence while she thought a little. Drangnet realised that the interview was coming to an end, to his regret it should be said. So, he used the quiet to finish his whisky and take one last look out of the window in front of hm.

'Thank you, Chief Inspector. I think that we may be able to do that for ourselves, but your concerns are reassuring. If you're asking for our help to identify these people, then I will have to talk to others. There are matters that need to be considered. But perhaps there may be something we can do. If these people wish to continue killing my girls, then perhaps we must. However, as I said, I'd like to take a little time to think about it.'

They both rose together, and the maid entered the room as if by magic. Madame Fernier offered her hand and he took it lightly in his and dipped his head in the customary way. He released it with a slight frisson of sorrow.

'Thank you for meeting me Madame. I have enjoyed it and I hope that it won't be the last time.'

She smiled at him.

'Oh, I think it won't be, Chief Inspector Drangnet. I think not.'

And with that he was ushered away by the maid and shown courteously down the broad curving stair to the front door of the house.

Chapter 5: Tuesday 5th April   Scene 4: Tennis with the President

It was not invariable given the jobs of the two men involved but as often as they could they played together at least twice a week, The early evening of each Tuesday was a regular date at the tennis count at the western end of the Tuileries Gardens. Other than his work, tennis was Drangnet's great passion and he was a highly skilled practitioner.

The game has been close, as it normally was, with the policeman, on this occasion, emerging with a hard-fought win against the politician. Very occasionally it was the other way around. The two were well matched. So, he took his shower feeling a warm sense of satisfaction. His opponent still showed the glow of energetic exercise even after the shower. They didn't often play singles against each other as games tended to become rather too competitive. They sat together on the wooden bench while they finished cooling off. They didn't normally repair to the club bar after the game. Even in the confidential intimacy of the club it would not be good for the Head of State to be seen drinking; nor could he risk being overheard.

'Louis you've made a bit of an enemy, I hear recently. Not for the first time, I might add. My Interior Minister is after your blood. What on earth did you say to him?'

Drangnet shrugged and took a sip of his weak whisky while his opponent did the same. Here they could chat. There was no-one else in the changing room.

'The man is an idiot and a politician. There is no worse combination, in my book.'

Ferry was amused. 'You should remember that I am a politician too.'

Drangnet nodded: 'But you, at least, are far from being an idiot and, more importantly, you are my doubles partner.'

His distinguished opponent shook his head as if he were dealing with an incorrigible child.

'Louis, Louis. What am I to do with you? You are the best policeman in France but even that can't protect you for ever. Sooner or later I'll not be able to clear up behind you. One day they will catch up with you and kick you out. What will you do then?'

Drangnet looked completely unconcerned.

'Well sir, I will retire to play this wonderful game, so I don't have to work so hard to beat you. I will look more to music and cooking to fill my life. I will read all the books for which I don't have time now. I'll wander the streets of my beloved Paris and just look at them. I might even take up crime. I seem to have a lot of friends in that particular profession here in Paris who would be delighted to advise me if I wish.'

Ferry looked completely appalled.

'Christ, God forbid. But a word to the wise, Louis. Be careful with this political thing. There are things here that even I cannot control. You need to watch your back.'

The time had come for his Head of State to return to his affairs of State. Having dressed he went to leave and join his bodyguards who were waiting outside. He turned back to address his friend whose slow pace of dressing clearly reflected the fact that her had less pressing matters to attend to.

'You know, Louis, anyone else would let me beat them from time to time. I after all Head of State of the Republic of France.'

Drangnet shook his head.

'When you occasionally win then you can be sure that you played better than I did. You wouldn't forgive me if I let you win. That is why we are friends *Monsieur le Ministre de l'Instruction publique et des Beaux Arts et Président du Conseil*.'

The great man grinned and gave his friend a very rude hand sign as left the changing room for the affairs of state and the resumption of his heavy mantel of greatness.

It was much later in the day after his return home from tennis and meeting on the *Île St. Louis* there was a knock on his door, not loud or particularly hard but firm. He was unused to receiving uninvited visitors at home and actively discouraged it when he could. He opened the door to be slightly taken aback by the sight of the same mountain of a man standing rather awkwardly in front of him as delivered Madame Fernier's invitation to tea. The man filled the small space outside his door as he was almost as wide as the door itself. Again the man was immaculately dressed and again there was no effort to shake hands. The man simply held out a small envelope for him to take. Once he had done so, the man again simply nodded and turned away.

Once back inside he sat down on his sofa, took another sip of the whisky that was more often than not his customary and only companion in the evenings. The envelope was unaddressed but felt weighty. It was stationary of the highest quality. It was also sealed. Suddenly he was happy that he had spent rather too much money at Ladurée. Rather than just inserting his finger and ripping the envelope open in his usual manner, he got up, went into his study, and sat at his desk. On it and directly in front of him was a rather ornate desk set and he took up its letter knife. For some reason he purposely took his time slitting open the very top of the envelope. Inside was a single sheet of thick paper. There was no letterhead. The note was short, handwritten, and simple.

Monsieur Drangnet

I am told that tomorrow there will be a fine, sunny afternoon. I would be delighted if you would join me to take tea in the Tuileries Gardens. Perhaps we can meet by the Grand Basin Rond at 3:30pm?

Please reply only if you cannot come.

Angèle

Chapter 6: Wednesday 6th April   Scene 1: Autopsy and Clues

Unusually for him, he felt a little stiff when he got up. Perhaps the game yesterday had been a more strenuous than usual. It often was in singles and almost always when he played Ferry. They were both competitive men on court and when they played each other they tended to get carried away. While the game of doubles required a higher level of collaboration, of course, it certainly involved a lot less running around.

A brisk walk to work relieved some of the stiffness but he still fidgeted a little during the morning meeting. There was little enough in the business of the meeting to divert him from his slight discomfort.

Office work took up the rest of the morning. It was the day when they were interviewing some new recruits to the *Sûreté* and Drangnet always insisted on sitting in. He didn't chair the panel, but he always wanted to run a ruler over the new people. Today they had four to see. Two were from the Paris gendarmerie. Some time ago he had realised that the opportunities for the ordinary street policeman to gain advancement to the *Sûreté* were almost non-existent. He had started encouraging the commandants of the various precincts to recommend suitable candidate who were willing and seemed able. Many of the men who came this way were pretty good. Most of the commandants cooperated and took pride in sending good candidates up for interview. The other two were from other parts of France. Again, Drangnet maintained good links with other *Sûreté* branches across the country and again, he was happy to hear of anyone who wanted to move to the capital from one of the regions. He never forgot that neither he nor Gant were natives of Paris.

For most of the time he just sat silently and watched while Dancart ran the interviews with two of their senior sergeants. The session took most of the morning and when they had finished, they had a discussion as to who to choose. In the end they chose all four as they had been a particularly good quartet of candidates. Drangnet agreed.

Then after a good lunch with Gant at a local café, Drangnet returned to his office and sank into a certain reverie. He still had no real idea how to get his investigation going and it was beginning to annoy him. What he needed for that confounded fellow Dankovich to come up with something useful. Lunch began to take its toll and he found himself falling into a light doze.

Just as he was on the point of slipping into a proper snooze he was awakened by a somewhat peremptory knock on his door and an entrance before his had time to ask the caller in. Dr Dankovich strode purposefully into the room and sat, unbidden, in the chair in front of the Commissars desk.

'Got anything to drink in here, Drangnet, old chap?'

The policeman refrained from glancing at the clock on the mantlepiece and he went to the large cabinet at the wall. He took out a decanter of red wine and two glasses. He had a fresh supply from a local café put each morning in the cupboard precisely for such eventualities. If the decanter still contained wine by the end of the day it was Gant's job to make sure that it went to whoever was working the night shift that day. He set a full glass on the side table beside the chair and returned to his desk with his own.

'Dr Dankovich. How nice to see you. I hope that your unannounced arrival as well as your obvious thirst mean that you have some news for me.'

The man took a good pull at his wine, paused a moment to savour it, and then replied.

'Good wine that. I suppose it's some of your infamous stuff from the Rhône Valley. Very nice. What did you say?'

Drangnet just frowned at his guest. He was fully aware that the distinguished doctor was having a joke.

'Well, the two men you brought to me, the one you brought to the hospital and the one that you hauled me halfway across Paris to examine, both died of strangulation. You know that already. A length of butcher's twine was used in both cases. It was used by someone with great strength as it actually cut most of the neck muscles and tendons as well as just asphyxiating the man. Close to a decapitation rather than just a strangulation. Not an easy thing to do with such a small piece of string. I would speculate – although you will remind me again that it is not my place to speculate – that the perpetrator was well used to handling this stuff. Someone like a butcher, perhaps. The victims were remarkable similar, they were thin but in perfectly good health, had recently both had sex and a good meal and had nothing remarkable about them. They looked to me to more of central European origin than France but these days one can never be sure. There are so many foreigners here these days. Unusually there was no alcohol or drugs in their blood. The first had a slight liver disease but nothing too serious. They seemed to a perfectly normal people of average height and weight.'

Drangnet frowned. He was hoping for more and said so. The doctor looked pleased as he had clearly come to visit for a reason. The doctor had more.

'So, Doctor. Other than a completely regulation strangling, did you find anything out of the ordinary.

'Well actually, my friend, I did turn up something that might be of interest.'

The good doctor took the opportunity of another, somewhat theatrical, pause to take another sip of wine.

'Well, I found one rather interesting thing or rather two. Both victims had small tattoos on their left shoulders, at the very top of their arms.'

Drangnet looked expectantly at his guest, as if to the increase the tension of the moment.

'Was it the same tattoo, by any chance?' Drangnet asked with mounting excitement. Perhaps here was a clue at last.

By way of reply Dankovich just pushed his now empty glass across the little table. Drangnet took the hint and was around the desk to perform a refill in an instant. He regained his seat.

'And…?'

His companion took his time sampling the wine with an excess of diligence. Drangnet was beginning to get fed up with this play acting. However, with not without inconsiderable self-control, he remained silent and waited patiently for his guest to continue.

'It was a small tattoo consisting of an inverted pair of dividers with a small pyramid beneath.'

Drangnet frowned slightly as he thought about it.

'Sound like a masonic symbol of some sort?'

Dankovich nodded.

'That's precisely what it is, I believe. It is a type of symbol I know well as I am a member of the brotherhood myself. It's certainly unusual to have masonic symbols tattooed on one's body, but I assume it's by no means unknown.'

'Is that all? Nothing else?' Drangnet asked.

'Well actually there is something else. There seems to be a small circle drawn within the pyramid. It is rather indistinct so I can't make out whether it is meant to be anything in particular. If this is, in fact, a masonic symbol then it might be an eye of some sort. All-seeing eyes do tend to appear in masonic symbolism occasionally. Oh, and at the bottom of the tattoo there was also a number.'

'And?'

Drangnet was beginning to get annoyed. This was worse that drawing teeth.

'There were numbers; two, one, three or perhaps it was one number, two hundred and thirteen.'

There was a pause while the policeman again thought.

'Is this a significant number in masonry?'

Although he knew that there were many policemen who were members of freemasons' lodges, he had never been in one himself.

'Not that I know of, Louis. I've certainly never come across it.'

There was a silence while they both thought about it. For the first time Drangnet had the sense that he might have the glimmer of something to go on.

'Well, if the dividers and the pyramid are normal masonic symbols then clearly the numbers are the significant things. And you're sure when you say that you haven't come across them at all in a masonic context.'

Dankovich shook his head.

'No. Never.'

'Well that's interesting. I'm grateful to you. You've given me something to work with at last, old friend.'

The glasses were topped up and Drangnet raised his in a symbolic gesture of thanks. The doctor seemed a little quieter as he slightly struggled with what he wanted to say next.

'Louis. You're not a mason. That's fine, of course. But I feel I should offer you a bit of friendly advice. If you want to follow this line of enquiry, I would suggest that you proceed with caution. If you start asking difficult questions then you could run into problems. Some of these masons are powerful people and don't take kindly to interference from people who aren't, as they say, one of their own. The Prefect himself is a Mason as is his deputy. There are plenty of others in your squad and in neighbouring ones who see masonry as a way to advance their careers and are members of the brotherhood. Now there is no reason why they should object to anything you ask or get in the way of your investigation but you should, at least, be aware that if you do find your wrong-doers in the world of masonry then you could come up against some opposition.'

This was a problem new to Drangnet. It added just another layer of complication. But he rather relished it.

'Doctor can you describe this tattoo to me in more detail or make a sketch of it. It would be very useful.'

Dankovich smiled triumphantly.

'Well, you old Luddite, I can do better than that.'

111

He reached into his briefcase pulled out a file. It was a standard manilla folder that always contained his reports. He handed it across Drangnet's desk and waited.

Drangnet open the file. In addition to the usual sheets of paper now prepared on Dankovich's new typewriter toy there was a photograph. It showed the tattoo in commendable clarity. He said nothing but leant across and refilled the man's glass. The decanter was almost empty.

'Thank you, old friend. I have no idea what this means but at last I have something to work with on this damned case. This is wonderful.'

Dankovich raised his glass and downed its contents in one and bid the Chief Inspector farewell. As he reached the door he turned back with a grin.

'You know, Louis, what you really need in the office is a telephone.'

Drangnet just growled at the doctor's departing back.

Chapter 6: Wednesday 6th April   Scene 2: Tea in the Tuileries Gardens

It indeed turned out to be a beautiful spring afternoon. He had arrived at the gardens early. However much he looked forward to the meeting - and perhaps he did a little too much – he couldn't forget that the elegant lady who was to be his companion for an hour or two came from a very different part of the Parisian world than he. He was supposed to be the one trying to put this lady in jail for a long time. He was not supposed to be spending time fussing over his appearance, checking his hair more times than was necessary in the mirror before leaving and making his way to the Tuileries Gardens. The same world, perhaps but different parts of it.

He had entered the Gardens at the opposite end from the round pond that was their proposed rendezvous. He called in briefly at the gracious building at the north west corner of the gardens that housed the two courts of the *Club de Jeu de Paume.* He walked the relatively short distance from his office across the *Pont Neuf* and down through the very garden through which he and Madame Fernier would walk this afternoon. After a game and a sojourn in its comfortable bar, he would usually then either walk home or take a Hansom cam, depending how long he had spent at the club chatting to the very few friends he had. It was a regular routine and was one that at least kept him fit.

He was early not just because that was what he usually did. This time he wanted to see what was going to be around them as they took their tea. He was under no illusion that Madame would be protected. That would be her habit on the occasions she ventured so far into the public eye. But he was interested to know what form the protection would take. He had purposely not told anyone of the meeting; no-one in the department. He didn't want the all-too-heavy feet of the Gendarmerie galumphing about and confusing everything. No, oddly, he felt perfectly secure under Madame's shadow. Nothing would happen to him unless she wished it and on that he would just have to trust his own judgement.

He sat, feeling the sun warm on his back, just watching the world go by in the true French manner but actually looking very closely at the people who passed by enjoying the afternoon sun. He was pleased to see that there was little out of the ordinary. Children played with their little sail boats in the pond watched nervously by their governesses or less nervously by their parents. The garden was popular, and many Parisians were taking the air. Families, courting couples, single men deep in thought looking closely at the ground; poets probably he mused; all sorts, in fact. For a moment he felt almost completely relaxed. It was a quintessentially Parisian scene.

He was still dreaming slightly when she arrived and, as a result, he was taken a little by surprise. A cab, in somewhat better fettle than most of those that filled the Paris streets, drew up beside the pond; a good deal closer than was usually allowed to ordinary people. It was a traditional back Hansom cab but glisteningly clean and drawn by a horse of much greater quality than those customarily found plying their trade around Paris. A fine beast he said to himself then smiled a little when he was struck by the thought that he could have been referring to the cab's occupant as well as the animal that pulled it. The driver jumped athletically down from his seat high up at the rear, having quickly looped the reins around the hand brake handle that would prevent the whole thing driving off if the horses got impatient. He opened the carriage door and let down the steps. Lastly, he offered his outstretched hand to assist his mistress.

For a brief second, he found himself wondering about the regal arrival of this daughter of a market porter. But such ignoble thoughts vanished as the lady in question alighted delicately from the cab. He was not, as a rule, a man easily impressed. His job had seen to that. People from all walks of life could take his attention and he found himself always less interested than he should. He learned a long time ago that what appears on the surface is usually the least important. But this time he was impressed as Madame Fernier stepped lightly down on to the gravel path around the pond.

Oddly, he hadn't really thought much about this afternoon's rendezvous, so the arrival of a woman fashionably dressed in flowing layers of flower printed chiffon, looking twenty years younger than she had on their last meeting, left him speechless. What he saw was a woman of striking beauty. He had only a few seconds before she came close to regain the power of speech. Fortunately, he succeeded - just. He took the proffered hand and raised it, as was correct, to within an inch or two of his lips. As the same time, he dipped his head towards it. Her response to this entirely correct greeting was equally formal.

They turned away together and, as they started to walk down the gardens, she slipped her left arm through his right as was traditional. Completing her outfit were a pair of delicate but practical shoes peeping from the hem that lightly brushed the ground, a broad brimmed hat set at an angle with a small but completely transparent half veil. A matching parasol was hung over her right shoulder. He noticed with some pleasure that the rather jaunty angle at which her hat was set, accommodated their proximity as he felt her against his side, moving sinuously as they walked. He was finding it difficult to concentrate. However, it was she who came straight to the point.

'Monsieur. I've thought about your proposition and talked to some of my colleagues. In principal we wish to accept. But before we get down to business, as they say, I would like to get to know a little more about you. I talked to a number of my associates from many parts of my little community and I gather that you are held in some respect. My girls think you are a gentleman and always treat them with courtesy and fairness. My men think you are tough and honest and dangerous because you don't give up. Believe me, Monsieur Drangnet, that's a rare combination to find here in Paris and even rarer for these qualities to be admired in my particular world. I know you are one of the few honest policemen I have come across and believe me my life would be less expensive but more difficult if all your colleagues were like you.'

She slightly squeezed her arm against his as they walked. This was turning out to be a more interesting walk than he hoped. She continued.

'You were born in Aix-en-Provence, I believe, the son of a respected local judge. You were well educated and ended up entering the Grandes écoles system here, finally graduating respectably from military academy of St. Cyr, no less. You had a successful career in the army and served with some distinction, I gather. and ended up as Aide-de-Camp to Marshal MacMahon, the commander of the army at Sedan. Much to everyone's astonishment and anger in some parts who thought your talents would be wasted, you decided not to continue in the army but decided to join the police force where understandably you were welcomed with open arms. You rose through the ranks very quickly, as they say, to be the youngest Chief Inspector in the history of the *Sûreté* but have consistently refused further advancement. Most people I have talked to, including various Ministers past and present are baffled by this. It seems that the great and the good of the establishment cannot wait to enfold you in their collective bosom. However, you are reluctant to cooperate.'

'I know you live in a large apartment on the *Place des Vosges* for which you pay too much. You employ a housekeeper, but she only comes once a week. You really ought to have a living-in one.' she said with a smile. 'If you wish I could supply a particularly attractive one with all the right attributes. However, I digress. You walk the mile or so to work at the *Quai* most mornings. You buy a newspaper and take a coffee at the brasserie on the *Quai de Bourbon* most mornings but you patronise other establishments as well. After work you play *Jeu de Paume* at least three times a week and I gather you are quite expert. You have no regular lady companion although you are often invited socially; invitations that you almost equally often decline, usually pleading pressure of work or some such. You are not, apparently, a homosexual, however. You attend the opera and the theatre regularly, often alone, and numerous concerts, also often unaccompanied although I am told this is by choice rather than necessity. You are much in demand, I gather. You play the piano slightly more than competently and are a senior member of the choir at the *Eglise St. Gervais et St. Protais* which means that you're very much more than competent at that. It is a very difficult choir to get into and it is almost unheard-of for the choirmaster to allow one of his members to miss as many rehearsals as you seem to. You obviously have a voice, monsieur. You are a subscriber to the *Bibliothèque Forney* in the Marais which is idiosyncratic but interesting. Finally, you occasionally buy art from Monsieur Monet and his friends although never spending very much. However, you usually get good prices because they like you. They think that you seem to understand well what they are trying to do. You dress well but modestly. One of your few extravagances is the purchase of English shoes; a preference of which I personally approve immensely. You can tell a lot about a man by his shoes and the way he keeps them. You eat mostly at local restaurants near *Les Halles* and in the *Marais* where you are known as a discerning customer with a more than usual knowledge of the wines of southern Rhône. You usually dine alone but not invariably.'

At that point she paused for a little thought.

'That just about does it, other than to say, with some admiration on my part, that you speak both English and Italian quite well and can read a little Greek and Latin.'

They continued on their gentle amble. He was conscious of seeing one or two couples more often that coincidence would suggest. He assumed that by the quick occasioned glance in their direction that they were something to do with Madame. He was pleased that he had told no-one at the Department of this meeting. It could have led to some awkward moments. She nudged him a little provocatively with her hip.

'And now, Monsieur Chief inspector?'

He laughed a little before starting, if for no other reason that he was slightly shaken by his companion's precise with highly accurate characterisation of him and his life.

'Madame, I will admit to being very pleased that your colleagues, shall we say, are reasonably well-disposed to me. That actually means more to me than you might imagine.'

Now she was making contact though their linked arms that went well beyond the purely correct. She was almost leaning on him as if she was going to lay her head on his shoulder. She didn't of course, and he found himself a little disappointed that a fantasy wasn't fulfilled.

'But why, Monsieur? Surely, we are the people who you should be trying to arrest and lock up. I am sure that many of your colleagues would like to do that although a major source of their income would dry up if they succeeded.'

The laugh that accompanied this remark was slightly hollow. He replied as they continued to stroll in the sun.

'Well, I don't expect you to understand really but perhaps you, more than many, might. I think that a good policeman understands where he lives. Paris has a life of its own. It has a population of all sorts, most of whom are not-strictly law-abiding. I can't explain but there are differences between serious crime and a general penchant for bending the rules. It's been like that before I came here, and it will remain so after I'm long gone. We are, after all, only very temporary additions to the life of this great city. You, Madame, are in control of most of the prostitution in central Paris. You derive a significant part of your income from it. But as far as I have found out you are an extremely popular boss. You never use intimidation; in fact, if I didn't know these were brothels, I would get the impression that you run a benevolent institution of sorts. Come to think of it, perhaps you do. There is never any violence towards you girls, no intimidation and no coercion. Your girls are all well cared for, have medical attention when they need it and you provide for them way beyond the rules that govern prostitution in this city. They are all given places to live and they are protected. That is why these recent deaths are particularly difficult for you. All your girls, as you describe them, actually want to work for you. The same goes for all the other businesses you control; the protection, the pickpockets, the petty house breakers. The others who form your group. Don't get the impression that I condone all this, but this is part of Paris and its life and if we choose to live here, we have to understand that. It is part of what makes Paris and these people have a right to be treated with respect and a certain amount of tolerance. I will catch people when they go beyond what is acceptable behaviour, but I draw lines. I don't expect everyone to understand, at least not publicly. That is the main reason why, as you have so cleverly pointed out, I would prefer to avoid promotion. I also try to avoid politicians and that is another reason.'

'As for you, I probably know much less about you that you do about me. I know little about your early life except that you are the only daughter of Dragan Fernier who started life as a porter at *Les Halles* and built up, often with extreme violence, the business empire that he bequeathed to his only daughter. In know where you live, of course, but other than that I know very little about you; certainly, nothing about your personal life.'

He had obviously finished. She turned slightly towards him.

'Well, you will find that my personal life, as you put it, is not that different from yours.'

It was an intriguing thought as the casual informality of their walk continued. They drew near the little cafés that were arranged in the slightly wooded area towards the end of the gardens. Tables were set out under the lightly sun-speckled shade and most of them were occupied with couples taking tea. They had passed a few and he was beginning to wonder whether they would be able to get a table. However, Madame headed purposefully toward one in particular and, miracle on miracle, there was a single table for two located almost in the middle of a terrace of about fifty souls. They approached the table and he was a little surprised that the waiter who would normally have made them wait for some time before taking their order, actually greeted them, escorted them to the table and then held Madame's chair for her. Then he remembered with whom he was taking tea.

He sat down opposite her and for a second, he was overtaken by a moment, for him, of complete madness. He looked across the little table and saw his companion as if for the first time. She sat erect as usual; hands folded loosely in her lap. He saw her elegant hat tilted a little on her head with her hair piled up on top of her head under it. Her gaze rested on him lightly through the little veil. What affected him so deeply was that she seemed decorated in the same dappled sunlight falling across the filmy dress that so often adorned the so-called impressionist painting that he loved. He caught his breath. Without thinking he looked at his companion absolutely sure that he meant it, and just said:

'Madame, you're the most beautiful woman I have ever seen.'

Even she gasped slightly and raised a hand to her mouth. It didn't take her long to recover but he detected a slight blush through the inadequate veil and a slight lowering of her head as she replied:

'Well thank you kind Sir. You really are an unusual policeman. But perhaps I knew that already.'

He wasn't sure whether she meant her beauty or his idiosyncrasy. However, the possible difficulty in the moment was relieved by the arrival of the waiter in spite of the fact that nothing had actually been ordered. His policeman's nose began to twitch a little so as the waiter filled the table with afternoon tea he looked around while also running over the past few minutes in his memory. His expression must have changed for as the waiter withdrew, she looked at him again.

'You have been thinking more, Chief Inspector. I hope you haven't changed your mind.'

He laughed out loud.

'No, Madame. Changing my mind is something I seldom do. If ever. No. I was just, yet again, thinking that I am dealing with a very special person.'

'And what, in particular at this moment, brought that to mind?'

He saw that his hostess had already poured the tea into Meissen cups not Limoges he noticed. Milk was put in first and the rest of the tea set matched the cups.

'Well, at first I was impressed at how lucky we were to find what seems to have been the single vacant table in this busy café. But I did spot the waiter removing something from the table as we arrived. I assume it was a reservation sign. Then, apart from the unusually accommodating waiter, a great rarity here in Paris, I note that while everyone here is seated on these particularly elegant but very uncomfortable iron seats, we are the only two who actually have cushions. I see also that although space is often at a premium in these cafés, there is a good deal more space between us and our neighbours that usual. Presumably, this ensures a higher than normal amount of confidentiality for our conversation. I note also that somewhat intriguingly that we are more or less surrounded by tables occupied by men who, in in spite of being well-dressed in very well fitting suits are all rather large and, shall we say, in very good condition. These men are accompanied by ladies who are all young and quite exceptionally good looking. There isn't a plain one amongst them. We are taking tea in Meissen crockery while everyone else is using plainer stuff. Finally I notice that the man who is obviously the café's proprietor is working very hard behind the counter but this is being made more difficult by the fact that he keeps on looking over here like a puppy who is off the lead but nevertheless wants to know where his master – on in this case mistress - is.'

Her smile was broad as she asked: 'And what, Chief Inspector, do you infer from all this?'

He returned her smile.

'I infer, Madame, that you own this café.'

She gave a bell-like guffaw.

'Monsieur Drangnet, your reputation as the best detective in Paris seems well-founded. You are completely right in all respects. However, I have an admission to make.'

He lifted his hands in mock horror.

'I hope I won't be forced to arrest you, Madame.'

He glanced around with some amusement before continuing.

'Although I have a feeling that I won't have much chance of getting you back to the cells at the Quai if I do.'

She her broad smile showed how entertained she was at the prospect of his trying.

'No Monsieur. My admission was of a more personal nature. We obviously have to talk in some detail about how any collaboration between us might work. While, like you, I can see a number of virtues, I can also see some difficulties. These are better discussed in private; I think. I would prefer my people think that this is a purely social meeting for they will naturally assume that I have found a way of taking advantage of the only incorruptible policeman in Paris. You have no idea how much good that will do to my reputation. The same might go for any of your colleagues who might be skulking in the undergrowth.'

'There are none, Madame.'

'None?' she asked with some incredulity.

'None at all.'

'Well, I never. You are a trusting soul.'

He shrugged.

'I am accustomed to trusting my own judgement, Madame.'

The rest of tea was taken up with inconsequential small talk as if any conversation with this woman could be regarded as small. But all to soon he felt it was time to return his companion to her own world. Like her, he wasn't particularly inclined to mix pleasure with business. After a while they rose and made their way back slowly to the little pond to her waiting Hansom cab. He had no idea whether it had left and returned somehow magically at the correct time or whether it had remained there all the time. Normally cabs like these were moved on pretty quickly by the gendarmerie. But perhaps not in her case.

However, he reminded himself that there were very few cabs in Paris like this one. As they neared, the driver dismounted and held the door open. She turned to him.

'Monsieur, may I offer you a ride home, unless, that is you are going on elsewhere?'

For a moment he hesitated. Was there any danger in being seen to accept a ride from this notorious lady? After a very quick thought he decided that there wasn't. In any case ever if there was, he scarcely cared at this point.

'Thank you, Madame. I will be going home, I think. I have little to do this evening other that cook myself something to eat. I have to look over one of the pieces that we are practicing for Holy Week at

St. Gervais. I must do my homework, I fear. It is a price that our Master of Choristers extracts from me in exchange for my all-too-frequent absences from choir practice that you rightly pointed out. I have to come prepared to sing correctly. That means I sometimes must work on piece at home in the evenings sometimes.'

'Very well.' she replied.

They both mounted the cab and settled themselves comfortably if intimately in the limited confines of the cab. The driver set off without any seeming instruction from either of them, he noticed.

'So, what is it?'

He was momentarily flummoxed, diverted as he was by the feeling of a warm thigh pressed quite firmly against his.

'Er, what, Madame?'

'The piece of course.'

'Oh, it is a group of motets by Couperin; a collection called his Little Motets.'

'These are motets for soloists, Monsieur, not pieces for a full choir. What part so you sing?'

'*Basse-taille*, Madame.'

She smiled radiantly while looking at him with admiration.

'Now, Monsieur, I am really impressed. To be a soloist with the choir of *St. Gervais* is an achievement and an honour.'

He shook his head self-consciously.

'At the moment it feels a little more like a burden rather than an honour. But now you see why I must practice.'

'Yes indeed. You had better practice well or the old man's ghost will come to haunt you.'

Yet again, he was surprised by this extraordinary woman. Francois Couperin, like many of his family, had been a famous

123

organist at the church and his works were particularly prized by the choir. He was beginning to like this woman a lot. He replied smilingly.

'We will do our best to honour the great man's memory, Madame.'

The journey back wasn't far and he found himself outside his front door with a slight feeling of disappointment. He got out and turned to say goodbye, but she got there first.

'You cook, therefore?'

Unsure of what was coming he was as non-committal as he could be given his earlier admission.

'Er yes. I do a little.'

'Well? Do you cook well?'

He nodded in a diffident sort of a way.

'As well as you sing?' she persisted.

'As well as a policeman can.'

She looked quite thoughtful at this admission.

'Well in the case of this particular policeman, that might mean something. Perhaps you might like to cook here for me, and we can discuss the more practical details of our arrangement in private. Unless, of course, you think that is might be unwise for you to be seen entertaining me at your home?'

He noticed the twinkle in her eye as he replied. She had, after all, invited herself most elegantly.

'Madame, I have never been one to take the wisest course. I would be delighted.'

He stood on the payment and took the usual proffered hand in his and raised its back towards his mouth, stopping the customary inch or two before actual contact. He was flabbergasted to feel that she pressed it gently up until he was forced to lay the intended kiss directly on the back of her hand.

'How does the day after tomorrow sound? Next Friday, Chief Inspector. Is that enough time for you to prepare? At eight, perhaps?'

And with that the cab sped off leaving him a surprised man on the edge of the pavement of the *Place des Vosges*; a man surprised and delighted in equal measure.

Chapter 7: Thursday 7th April   Scene 1: Preparing the Feast

As Drangnet woke, it would be wrong to say that the culinary adventure set for the next day obsessed him. He had a job of work to do after all. But if truth be said, the matters of tomorrow evening and more particularly his cooking was not far from his mind.

It was clear that in spite of the tattoo clue, he would make no real progress in his main investigation until he had talked with Madame so he would fill the day with finishing off a good deal of paperwork on a number of smaller cases that had been sitting on his desk awaiting attention. Unlike many he didn't mind paperwork. He knew it was necessary and therefore inevitable. Why decide to hate something from which there was no escape? Actually, the tying-off of all the various threads of even the most mundane investigation was, for him at least, a satisfaction; a sign that a job had been done well and matters concluded. There as a finality about it and he liked that. If he had to sit for a few hours at his desk to achieve it then so much the better. It was, after all, what he was paid to do.

But first he decided to take his time getting in to work and make sure that everything was organised for tomorrow night. Therefore as he sat taking his early morning breakfast and his mind was not on murder. It was on what to cook. Now that was a question. He was not at all an un-talented cook; for an amateur, that is. He knew the basics well enough not to be nervous about the whole thing. However, he knew that his guest was someone who could eat at the very best places in Paris when she so wished; and that meant to him, at the best places on earth. He could not out-cook the world's best. No, he would settle on something that was simple to make, which also meant relatively risk free, but something that might surprise her for being unusual, unusual for her, that is. Perhaps a menu from his youth; something simple, almost peasant food but cooked well. He had always retained a taste for the cooking of his native South of France which despite recent fashion in some of the newly opened restaurants in the capital was at its best when it was it is least complicated. It would also be a chance to indulge his own preferences.

A main dish of *alouettes sans tête*, veal rather than beef, with its traditional rich and slightly lumpy, rough tomato sauce full of the herbs of Provence that would distinguish the dish from its northern, Belgian equivalent. *Paupiettes* as they were called here in the north. *Pommes gratinés* and perhaps a *ratatouille* to accompany it. All could be prepared in advance. He didn't want to spend too much time getting flustered in his kitchen while his guest remained a tranquil observer in another room. He would have a word with his butcher and ask him to put more than the usual herbs in the stuffing. In his view they were rather too cowardly about that here in Paris. Pudding could be a simple lemon cream. He was good at those and, again, they could be prepared in advance. He had his own storage space in the basement of the apartment house and there it was cool enough to keep the pudding relatively firm. That only left the first course and the wine.

He disliked the new fashion of offering a tiny starting event that, in his opinion, might as well not be there at all. He liked a proper first course. A personal passion was for *tellines*, the tiny clam that he grew up with as a boy as they were found in plenty along the Camargue coast. They were small and sweet and definitely unfashionable. That made them more interesting to him, rather than less. However, there was only one problem. They were usually impossible to find in Paris. They were too small and too odd to make the effort of getting them here from the coast worthwhile on a regular basis for any merchant. Again, his local fish seller would have to help.

It was one of those inevitable coincidences that as he walked from his office or the tennis club to or from the *Place des Voges* his route would often take him near the market of *Les Halles*. He had always preferred to shop there. It had both retail and wholesale sections in most of the halls. He had been doing it for years and they seemed to put up with him. Being known as a senior policeman had its advantages. It was always a vibrant, noisy place and he loved it.

He finished his breakfast and headed off to the market, now popularly known as the Belly of Paris after the famous novel by Emil Zola published as few years before. Perhaps it was his imagination but as he walked through the huge space that he felt less than the usual indifference as he passed. A few people who knew him would normally raise a hand or even call out 'Bonjour Chief Inspector' as much as a warning to others as a friendly greeting to him. But this time more faces seemed looked at him or catch his eye, and many did so without suspicion or hostility.

Santier, the butcher, was easy. He also came from the south anyway and relished the chance to make some proper *alouettes*. "Proper" meant with a thicker layer of veal, more pork fat around the outside than usual to give moisture and a filling fuller of dried herbs from Provence, salt and pepper than was usual for the normal, more refined, Parisian taste.

'Chief Inspector,' said a delighted butcher. 'I would be happy to make them for you. It is many years since someone asked for them to be made properly. Don't worry about the filling. You will be able to taste the herbs in the meat not just in the stuffing, I promise. In fact, I will offer you them as a gift. I'll make enough for you and for my family too. I promise you that Madame will enjoy them. Just make sure you don't use tomatoes that are too ripe. You need to taste the acid of a slightly unripe fruit. Oh, and don't cut the tomatoes too finely.'

Drangnet held up his hand. This was the classic advice on making a good Provençale tomato sauce. He noted that the identity of his dinner guest was known even here. As usual in life some advice might be welcome depending where it came from. Too much, never. Alexei Dassin, the fish merchant, took more convincing. He came from the north and, like many fish merchants was habitually bad-tempered. Drangnet has always assumed it was something to do with cold wet fish and the ice necessary to preserve them.

'Monsieur Drangnet. What on earth do you want these little things for? No one in Paris bothers with them. They are too small and uninteresting. Let me get you something much better.'

Drangnet was adamant and shook his head.

'No, Monsieur Dassin, I want *Tellines*. Nothing you can offer me can match the taste if they are cooked properly. I'm sure your people in Brittany can let you have some, though. They deliver other things to you every day. I want three or four kilos and I want them alive. Can you do it by tomorrow?'

The old fish merchant shook his head slowly as if dealing with an errant child bent on doing something wrong, something of which he should know better.

'Of course, Chief Inspector, of course. For you anything. But they won't arrive until the afternoon. I'll get someone to deliver them to you at the *Place*.'

So that was the main part of the menu settled. There remained only the wine and that, he knew, was going to be simpler.

'Hum, Drangnet, as usual you set me a challenge but, also as usual, I am equal to it.'

He had been buying his wine from the house of Gravalet for years. He had started with the father and now the son had taken over. Both had been trusted but unadventurous wine merchants. He remembered that own his father once said to him that the two most important people in his life, probably the only really important people, were his bank manager and his wine merchant. That was the reason his wine merchant addressed him by surname only; a familiarity that he would not have put up with from anyone else - other than his bank manager, of course.

'Right, my friend. I suggest we offer all your wines from the south, just like your menu. A Crémant de Bourgogne as an aperitif, a Chateauneuf du Pape for the main course and a perhaps a Meursault with your beloved *tellines*.'

Drangnet frowned slightly. 'I wonder if a Meursault might not be a little heavy for the *tellines*. Something lighter, perhaps and with a little less perfume. A touch sharper, perhaps?'

'Well I can get a dry white from the same region as the Chateauneuf. It is quite light and fruity. It is no great wine and a bit thin in my view, but it might suit you?'

Drangnet nodded. 'That sounds fine.

The man asked further.

'Anything for the pudding or cheese?'

Unusually for a modern Frenchman, Drangnet disliked both a cheese course and a salad that seems to have entered into French table etiquette to be taken towards the end of a meal. To be frank he couldn't see the point of it. He was no great devotee of cheese in the first place. The South of France has few great cheeses. Something to do with the lack of cows, he always felt. Goats and sheep were a poor substitute. He hadn't really bothered about them since he came to the capital. As for salad he was no rabbit.

'No, thanks. Just give me another bottle of the Crémant to cover the pudding, please.'

Gravalet shook his head in exasperation.

'Chief Inspector. You must the only man in Paris who has no time for cheese. What on earth would we be without our great French cheeses?'

'Slimmer?' Drangnet volunteered as he grinned at the man.

The food would be delivered to his apartment the following morning. He reminded himself to tell his housekeeper. His next stop was at his local greengrocer with an order for the rest of the makings of the dinner. Obviously, he could have ordered the vegetables from *Les Halles* as well, but he had a particular soft spot for the local man and his small shop located in the *Rue de Birague*. The produce came from the market but he had been going to Monsieur He ordered the makings of his ratatouille, as well as the tomato sauce.

'Please make sure that the tomatoes aren't too ripe. I need them quite hard.'

The man was quite used to the idiosyncrasies of his near neighbour and just acknowledged with a wave of the hand as he scanned down the list on the note from Drangnet that has been hastily pressed into his hand. The Chief Inspector had clearly decided that he was now late for work.

He sat back at his desk happy that it was settled. A small token of flowers for his guest and that was all and that could be done tomorrow. He was sure that she would get her revenge with something unusual from Ladurée. He had asked his housekeeper to come tomorrow morning as opposed to Saturday to make sure that place was in good order and he knew he had clean shirts. That was about as far as he could go. It did not, however, stop him both fretting about the arrangements slightly and becoming annoyed at himself for doing so.

He didn't spend every minute of the rest of the day thinking about cooking the following evening. That would be an exaggeration. He had his job to do and, after a few hurried conversations with his Chief, it had been made plain that this murder of the three prostitutes should be his priority. Actually, this made him unhappy. He had always chosen his own priorities and had set the speed with which he pursued each of them. He didn't like being told what to do. He had known this for many years and it was one of the main reasons that he hadn't followed the glittering career in the military that had others had mapped out for him. He was not about to get tangled in a career that would have forced him to take orders no matter how far he progressed. He guessed, correctly as it turned out, that he could get himself quickly into a position in the police force where his successes would insulate him from the day to day vagaries of superiors. He knew that while he was delivering the right number of arrests and subsequent prosecutions, he would be left alone to enjoy the privileges of a rank that was neither too high nor to low. It was a recipe for contentment which was why he objected to the pressure that he was beginning to feel now from above. So out of bloody-mindedness he spent the day perusing trivia on a number of current cases well away from the death of these three ladies and all that followed.

But even as he worked through the old cases, adding something here, editing something there, occasionally noting something that still needed to be done by others, much to own annoyance, he kept on coming back to the matter of tomorrow's supper.

Chapter 7: Thursday 7ᵗʰ April   Scene 2: Tennis Practice

The full day passed and little news came in from the streets. No-one still seemed to know anything. To be honest, the bodies in the Seine were crimes for which he could raise any great enthusiasm. He was pretty sure that these were the men who killed the girls and if he was honest, he found it difficult to produce any great indignation at their demise. He was more interested in why they decided to murder a series of prostitutes and on that he hadn't much progress. Other things were also fighting for space in his mind.

There was, of course, Friday's meal to anticipate. There was also some tennis to play. The final stages of the club's annual doubles tournament were on him. It was easily the most hotly contested competition of the club year and one for which he and his illustrious partner were the current title holders. The tournament had been going on for some time over the previous weeks. Tennis clubs tended to have only one court. But the Tuileries Court was a fortunate exception in having two and therefore the competition that took place with a lot of contestants and a larger number of rounds could be spaced over a period of weeks. Club members who were not entered in the tournament also wanted access to their beloved court and that also meant that doubles competitions took longer. They had arrived at the quarter final stage. Both Drangnet and his partner felt that they could benefit of a practice session and given that his partner was trying to run the country when he was not playing tennis, time for that practice was limited. The great man had stolen a couple of hours that afternoon and a session between them and the club's current professional and his assistant had been scheduled. The club's *maître paumier*, the idiosyncratic Charles Delahaye, know universally as "Biboche", may have been in his late sixties but was still one of the most skilful players in France. It would be a hard couple of hours, but he was looking forward to it. He knew the president would refuse the handicap that was usually offered between players of very different standards, even an idiosyncratic one for which the old master was famous. Biboche, after all, had once played a match in full dress uniform of the National Guard: suited and booted with belts, webbing, knapsack and carrying a musket with fixed bayonetin his left hand to even the odds with a less talented player. This time, more prosaically, they would ha ve to rely on the *maître paumier* and his young assistant to make the game just challenging enough to extend them and make them work hard. A victory, of course, was out of the question. Actually, he was looking forward to it. Biboche was one of the very few men who could shout and swear at the Head of State and get away with it.

The day wouldn't end after the gaem as he had a choir practice at 6pm and he had been told in no uncertain terms that he was to be there. So, it meant no lingering whisky after his game or at least time only for one. That would have to wait until after the choirmaster had done with him.

As for the murders themselves, the men were dead. He was interested in preventing it happening again irrespective of whether these were anarchists or not. He needed to work out some sort of strategy to help Madame Fernier and to protect her ladies.

The only thing on his desk was the list from Madame Bondine. Each of the seven girls in the house that day had six visitors, some identified by name and some by pseudonym. A total of forty-two clients. Drangnet did a quick calculation that at fifty francs a time the house was earning about two thousand francs a day. Multiply that by the number of such establishments Madame ran, and he soon realised how much even this small part of her empire earned. He presumed that somewhere there was a list of names that provided the key to the code of pseudonyms that were used on the list and if even some Madame Bondine clients included any sort of selection of public figures then it could be a powerful weapon had she a mind to use it.

Given the exertions of the afternoon to come he had a very light lunch of a lamb cutlet with some vegetables and a single glass of wine taken at a little cafe on the *Quai Malaquais* on the left bank. It was not a regular haunt, but their cooking was passable and it was on the way to the tennis club.

Three hours later he and his illustrious partner were sitting in exhausted silence in the panelled changing rooms at the tennis club. Neither man had the strength for much conversation. They just sat side-by-side on the wooden bench after their showers clad only in towels knotted at the waist each staring silently at the floor. It had been an energetic hour on court. The unscheduled entry of the young *sous-maître* who seemed completely unmoved by his recent exertions, brought a couple of glasses of whisky. He put them down on the bench between the two men.

'Yes Sir, I know that you instructed that there were to be no refreshments but Maître Biboche thought they might be required for medicinal purposes.'

The two seated figures just nodded thankfully. The young man turned back slightly as he reached the door.

'Messieurs, perhaps it is not my place to mention this but the Maître is himself taking things rather slowly at the moment.'

Ferry raise a smile at that.

'Good.' was about as much as he could manage.

After a further pause filled mainly with slow but regular consumption of their drinks, Ferry turn to his companion.

'How are you getting on with this anarchist business, Louis. I heard that there was another murder last night.'

Not for the first time Drangnet wondered about the man's sources of information.

'Well there was indeed another murder, sir. Another prostitute was killed in the *Rue des Tournelles* and there was another corpse in the Seine, but we have no evidence that it was another of your supposed anarchists.'

Ferry raised an eyebrow at the word supposed but decided to say nothing but continued:

'I'm getting a lot of pressure to get this matter cleared up. I'm relying on you.'

Remembering his speculation about the actual content of Madame Bondine's list, Drangnet could well imagine where at least some of the pressure might be coming from. But he kept silent on the subject. The less the great man got involved in his investigation, the better. He looked across at his playing partner. Jules Ferry had endured a difficult time during the days of the Commune nine years before. He was a republican from the Voges and a political moderate by nature. Solidly anti-monarchist, he had been Prefect of the Seine during the siege of Paris by the Germans and was regarded as the reason that so many citizens went short of food during the city's difficulties and ended the brief but unsuccessful uprising of the communards. He had been forced to resign from office and had spent two years away from the spotlight as Minister for Greece. He returned to form part of the republican opposition and once the left regained power it had not been long before he had been appointed President of the Council. Ferry, Drangnet thought, was precisely the sort of moderate, intelligent politician that Paris and the rest of France needed to continue the healing after the German invasion. The great man paused as he was putting on his cravat.

'You must remember, Louis, that I had experience of these Proudhonists nine years ago. They're dangerous.'

Drangnet nodded.

'But are these our present-day anarchists, Jules? I thought that was more to do with these violent new disciples Bakunin and Kropotkin these days than our dear old Pierre-Joseph?'

Ferry shook his head, slowly.

'Unfortunately, old friend, the ideas these men hold are often more dangerous than the bombs they throw.'

Always respectful, Drangnet still pursued his point.

'That may well be the case, but I do find it a little difficult to see the of murdering prostitutes as an act anarchism. In my view, your new political police are making something out of nothing, possibly to justify your generous funding.'

'You never pull your punches do you, Louis?' Ferry laughed. 'Even when addressing your Prime Minister.'

'If you mean the man who needs to improve his volleying at the net before the quarter finals in a few days' time, then I will agree that I don't, Monsieur.'

'Pah!' replied the man.

They both finished dressing and as they left the club to go their separate ways, the Prime minister having been met by an escorted carriage and Drangnet heading on foot back through the Tuileries Gardens, the policeman entertained the thought that if things ran true to form the problem of catching the murderer would be taken out of their hands before too long. It had happened before when some politician or other interfered for his own reasons.

Chapter 8: Friday 8th April   Scene 1: The Feast

The knock on his door came precisely at eight. He had heard the front door bell but there was little point in hurrying down to try to beat his concierge to the. In all the years he had been living there he had never managed to do so, nor had he managed to come or go himself without being observed irrespective of what time of the day or night he might try. So, he opened his own door and waited. She was wearing a floor-length black velvet cape, its hood up against the evening chill. He stood back to allow her in and took and kissed the gloved hand. He noticed that her driver was still standing on the landing outside holding quite a large parcel.

'May I ask my driver to bring the parcel in Monsieur.'

Slightly surprised he gestured his permission.

'Of course, Madame.'

She motioned him in. The man entered carrying a parcel that he put down against the wall while his mistress looked on. Having done so he bowed slightly to them both and departed, pulling the door silently shut behind him. Drangnet noticed that there were flowers in the usually empty vase on the hall table. Presumably, his housekeeper had decided to make some of her own arrangements for the events proposed for the evening in the full knowledge that her master would have probably forgotten.

Madame Fernier then turned her back to him and loosed the cords that held the cape closed and waited him to take the weight. She then simply walked out of it, leaving him to lay it carefully across one of the hall chairs. Having thrown back her hood, she put down her head and extracting a couple of pearl hat pins she took off a very elegant little bonnet and handed it to him, together with her gloves. These he put on the little table under the hall mirror. Again, she continued for a few steps before turning. The effect, in order to give him a good view for his inevitable inspection, was both memorable and completely successful.

The dress stopped short of a ball gown, of course, but not by much. It followed the fashion of the day being full length, slightly flared at the hem and pulled tightly into a very narrow waste in an open waistcoat. The material was a heavy silk floral design in an ivory colour with the floral designed in pink and olive green. A heavily decorated panel sprang from her waist and formed the tight bodice that was cut square across her breasts, low enough to leave an attractive décolletage in view. She twirled around for him to inspect the back. The material had been gathered into five long pleats that were drawn up tightly to emphasise her tiny waist. She returned to face him with a mischievous smile on her face.

'I don't get the chance to dress up very often, Chief Inspector. Most men are reluctant to be seen out in polite company with me. So, I thought I would show off little. I hope you approve.'

For a moment he didn't know what to say.

'Madame. You look completely ravishing. Beautiful. I would be honoured to be seen anywhere with you.'

She laughed.

'Perhaps you're one of the few men brave enough to do so. But I'm not sure what that would do to your promotion prospects, Monsieur.'

'I'm not sure if I have too many of those any more. Nor do I think I want any. I sometimes think that I have more enemies in the National Legislature than I have on the streets of Paris. But even if I didn't that wouldn't make the slightest difference. You look wonderful, Madame.'

He wasn't sure but he thought he detected a slight blush on her cheeks.

'Well thank you, kind sir. That is gallantly said.'

She sank to a theatrical, low, slow courtesy; a manoeuvre that had the most exciting effect on her already considerable décolletage. Judging by the smile on her face as she rose this was precisely what that she wanted to achieve. This time it was he who felt that he might be colouring a little. He finally led her from the hall into the sitting room although she was reluctant to sit.

'Monsieur. Please forgive me if I seem rude but I have an insatiable curiosity. I love looking around other people's homes. Would you allow me to see yours?'

He remembered that his housekeeper had worked hard during the day so the prospect of an inspection worried him less than it might have on other occasions.

'Madame, I would be honoured. Would you prefer to be escorted or to look around on your own?

She was astonished.

'You mean that you would let me, me of all people, look through your apartment unsupervised?'

He was genuinely surprised. Any difficulty hadn't occurred to him.

'Why ever not? You are perfectly at liberty to go where you wish. In any case I have to check some things in the kitchen. Just don't be too long as I want to bring some wine up from the cellar and I don't want it to get warm.'

'You really an extraordinary man, Monsieur. I won't take long.'

He left her to it while descending to the cellar and fetching the wine. Everything seemed in order in the kitchen when he came back. He caught the odd glimpse of her flitting from one room to the next but by the time he had opened the wine and poured it she was standing once again in his sitting room. He was about to offer her a seat but again she interrupted his plans.

'I am happy to have a toast standing up monsieur before getting comfortable because I want to give you your present. Actually, I'm a little excited about it myself for I think you will like it.'

So, they touched glasses, standing very close together, and she savoured the wine. Then she was off again. This was a long way from the rather dignified and reserved lady he had first met only a few days ago. She was almost girlish.

'Now go and get the parcel please and bring it is and put it on the table.'

He had known that something was up when he saw her driver bring in the large rectangular parcel, wrapped in that particular brown paper which is used to wrap meat by the butchers in the Les Halles market. Rather like his gift to her of a few days ago it was also tied with butcher's twine. This time, however, it wasn't bloodstained. It was white and hitherto unused. It certainly wasn't one of Monsieur Ladurée's little pink packages. She came over to him as he examined over the parcel; disconcertingly close as she bent over with him.

'Now you may open it. I hope you appreciate the wrapping paper and cord,' she mocked him very slightly.

It took him a little time to undo the knots as they were butchers' knots and unfamiliar to him. She took up the conversation without actually moving from her bent position at his elbow.

'I am very pleased that you undo knots. Most men would take a knife and cut them.'

'Ah,' he replied. 'My grandmother in Aix-en-Provence wouldn't hear of such a thing. Cord was valuable and was to be saved.'

Quite right,' she nodded. 'Also, for us butchers cord has a special significance, too.'

Remembering recent events he couldn't resist trying to look her straight in the eye to see the look on her face when she said this. But she hadn't moved from her close observation of the parcel and he succeeded only in looking more closely at her breasts. That was informative too but in a somewhat different way. She giggled. Finally, he got the parcel open and the sight that he beheld simply took his breath away. What lay before him was a richly bound manuscript book. The book was a deep burgundy leather-bound folio volume with gold decoration at the edges and on the spine. In the middle of the front cover, also embossed in gold, was the title "*Maître Francois Couperin, Le Grand. Les petits Motets*". He opened it and saw on the inside of the front cover the ornate bookplate of the *Comte de Toulouse*. It was dated 1705. Inside were hand-written voice parts of a full set of the motets including some that that he was currently trying to learn.

'I thought it might amuse you to practice from the parts written down for the good Count while the great composer was still organist at St. Gervaise.'

Dragnet was quite stunned and it was some time before the power of speech returned.

'I don't know what to say. I can't possibly accept this. This ought to be in the *Bibliothèque Nationale*. I knew about these copied manuscripts, of course, but I thought that they had been sold to an English collector forty years ago when the *Comte de Toulouse's* estate was broken up.'

'Not all of them, Monsieur, although I suspect the Englishman would be displeased to know that. There are still a few copies in France and I managed to, er, acquire this copy.'

This time he stood and looked rather sternly at his companion. She knew exactly what he was thinking.

'No, Monsieur. I didn't steal it nor did I commit any crime to obtain it. I promise. I just happened to know the person who had possession of it, and I negotiated a price with him. It was just sitting on a shelf unused and I thought it would be nice if it were put to use. Especially by someone singing in Couperin's own church. All above board. Really'

Drangnet's face must have shown a certain level of disbelief as she continued with a mischievous look on her face:

'However, it might be a good idea to keep it here rather than anywhere else. My negotiation was, shall we say, a little robust.'

He held up his hand. He didn't want to hear any more. She rightly took this as a signal that there was to be no more interrogation.

'Right,' she said briskly. 'I'll go and put this on the music stand of your beautiful Boisselot piano and you can pour me another glass of this excellent Crémant.'

With that she whisked the book away leaving him slightly at a loss for words. He did as she asked and before long, they were back seated opposite each other at either end of his sofa. She obviously thought that her part in the opening events of the evening was at an end so she waited for him. It took him a not inconsiderable effort of will.

'Madame. We have a little business to discuss and I would like to enjoy your company a little more. I suspect that our business won't take too long as all we have to do it to agree on whether or not we collaborate and perhaps how we might start. The rest can wait for another time depending on whether we agree anything. The food can wait long enough for that. After we can sit at dinner and I can indulge one my very favourite activities if you agree.'

She looked rather archly at him.

'And what might that be Monsieur?'

'Sitting at dinner and talking with a beautiful, intelligent woman about anything that comes into our heads. '

She tossed her head back and laughed.

'I agree. I too wouldn't wish to spoil our food and our conversation by talking business and eating at the same time. Let's do that now.'

As if to emphasise the point she leant forward holding her how empty glass out for a refill. He found it surprisingly difficult to concentrate on not spilling the wine conscious that her smiling eyes never moved from his. Finally, she settled back in her seat and became very business-like very quickly.

'Chief Inspector. I have talked with my colleagues and we have decided to offer you help. We have discussed exactly how we can help and why we should do it. There are conditions, of course, and we would require you to agree with them.'

'And what surety do you have that I'll keep my word Madame?'

'It's only necessary that you give us that word. It's not only my girls who have a high opinion of you. We only require you to assure us that everything we say will go no further than you personally. There will times when we will give you information or help but this must be for you alone. We do not hold your colleagues in the same high regard as we do you, Chief Inspector. There will also be times when we don't want to tell you things and you must respect that. At all times you must not make any reference to our help with your colleagues and information from us must make no appearance on police files. We are risking much by agreeing to collaborate with you.'

'As I am with you Madame. Especially as you are requiring me to keep secrets from my colleagues and superiors. But I give you my word nevertheless.'

She nodded gracefully in acceptance. But before she continued he felt he had a point to make.

'Madame, you must also understand something. Not only am I investigating the deaths of your girls, I am also investigating the deaths of a group of so-called Rumanians that have been found murdered and dumped in the Seine. You know and I know that these are connected and irrespective of how I feel about you, Madame, I will continue to my job correctly. Part of that job is indeed to see if there is such a connection and, if so, what I should do about it.'

Her smile returned lightly as again she nodded her understanding. He continued.

'So I suggest that you're very careful about what you tell me. I'll start from the premise that you and your colleagues are telling me the truth and that I won't spend too much time proving that one way or another. But if I find that any of your people are guilty of a crime worthy of prosecution, I will arrest them.'

The ambiguity of what he said wasn't lost on her. However, before the conversation progressed, she wiggled her glass at him slightly. The charming smile was enough to rob the gesture of any discourtesy. He returned to his seat and continued.

"Perhaps, Madame, I can offer some suggestions as to where I think that you can help us and then you can decide whether you can offer that help.'

She just nodded, looking at him very levelly over the top of her glass. He noticed that she had yet to sample the refill. She did, however, note that he had slipped seamlessly into being a policeman. She knew how dangerous was the game they were playing together.

'As far as I can guess, Madame Fernier, to date three of your girls have been murdered by unknown people who may or may not be their clients. There seems no obvious reason for this. Subsequently three male bodies have found washed up on the edge of the *Île St. Louis* very near the Police headquarters. All three were garrotted using butcher's cord. Attempts were made to appropriate these bodies by the new political police but fortunately they succeeded in only getting the first of them. I'm having the unpleasant experience of being pressured by them for any information.

I'm very reluctant to tell them anything as I regard this as a *Sûreté* investigation and none of their business. But they have their supporters. I know that they have visited the houses and have been asking questions and they tend to be much more direct about these things that we are. I think that it might be an idea for the three concierges to stay away for a few days and have advised the ladies to that effect. But that is your business not mine. The political police seem to think that three men are Romanian anarchists. They care more about this than they do about the murders of your girls and, on the face of it, I can't see why they should be taking the interest they have. I can only assume that these six killings are all interconnected in some way and that, in particular, makes me very interested indeed.'

Madame remained motionless and silent.

'I'll continue to investigate these deaths. But...' as he looked directly into her face, 'I also believe that your people are responsible for the deaths of the three men in the river. And that means you. You will probably be responsible for the death of a fourth when we find him like the three others if this lamentable trend continues. I'll be quite honest with you, Madame, my main concern is not with these

Romanians; if that is what they are. It is with the safety of your girls. We must put a stop to his as soon as we can. That is my priority. My other major concern is that while we and the political police have found no connection with these foreigners, you seem to have found them and executed them within hours.'

He paused to see if she wanted to reply but still there was nothing from her; just a steady gaze that now he returned.

'I am concerned for you too, personally. You are in danger from the political police because you know more than they do. They will assume that you are connected with these anarchist groups. That could bring much trouble down on you and your people. I believe that you are also in danger from others. Normally I would locate and interview all the clients who were in the houses on the days of the murders. I have seen some lists. That too will be dangerous for you. There are some powerful people on those lists.'

Now he would wait for her reply and it was not long coming.

'As usual I need to talk my people and then we must have a proper meeting. In secret and completely confidential. Soon I think.'

She reached across the small space between them and took his hand.

'Thank you, Chief Inspector. I thank you for your honesty and loyalty to the people of Paris. Particularly I thank you for wanting to protect me. That is the sentiment of a gentleman.'

He smiled at her.

'Also, perhaps the wish of an ordinary man, Madame.'

'So now,' she smiled. 'It is time to see if you are as good a cook as you are a policeman. Can I do anything to help?'

He too was pleased to get to more domestic grounds.

'Well, I have to do a little work in the kitchen for the first course which means leaving you on your own for a little while.'

'Is a woman not allowed in your kitchen, Monsieur?'

He was somewhat set back until he remembered actually who he was talking to. He laughed.

'It is just that the few women who come into this apartment are usually not interested in the kitchen. However, Madame, you would be an honoured guest in my kitchen.'

As soon as she entered the kitchen, she saw the bowl of tiny clams glistening under a layer of water.

'Ah, so this the surprise that Monsieur Dassin told me about.'

And before he could speak, she went on:

'No, he didn't give away your secret other than to say they are called *tellines*.'

So, he talked as he cooked. The whole point was that it was done quickly so most of the time was spent waiting for the water the water to boil for the pasta.

'*Tellines* are, as of course you know, small clams. Contrary to Provence local lore they are not unique to the stretch of beach between Arles and Montpellier. They're found in a number of places around the Atlantic coast in Brittany and around the Mediterranean, notably on the Italian coast, in the province of Lazio. But they are well-known in the cuisine of the Camargue. As with all shellfish the secret is to try not to overcook them or they will become tough and rubbery.'

Within a few minutes he was finished. He escorted her to the table placed two bowls of pasta in front of them and had poured them both a glass of the white wine. They ate in virtual silence both seeming to understand that eating was far too important to be relegated to a background activity. The *tellines* had been very simply cooked, quickly in the same white wine, a touch of olive oil, salt, pepper and a suggestion of lemon. Nothing else. The remains of the liquid were mopped with pieces of rough bread. A broad smile set itself on her face.

'Delicious, Chief Inspector. Fresh, natural. You can taste the fish and the sea. In future I will have Dassin deliver them regularly to the *île*.'

It was an admission that gave him much pleasure. He laughed at the thought.

'I'm not sure that your Monsieur Dassin would be happy with that. He was reluctant to supply even these few.'

'Ha!' she exclaimed, tossing her head back as Drangnet saw the streak of steel returning in a flash. 'My Monsieur Dassin will do what he's told.'

It was clearly a moment of some significance. Drangnet sought to regain their increasing familiarity.

'Madame. In the future there will be many times in public when we must observe the social niceties of our time or of our relative positions. However, I would be honoured if, at times when we are alone, we could use our Christian names. Mine is Louis.'

'Mine, Louis, is Angèle.' She smiled with a genuine pleasure.

'It is a beautiful name, Madame.'

She frowned a little. Yes, it is. Certainly, better than my second name of Heike.'

It was a surprise to say the very least. Heike was a German name, a sort of female equivalent of Heinrich. He had heard of its use in Germany and Scandinavia and even the Low Countries but never in France.

He must have looked surprised. She nodded.

'Yes, it is a little odd I admit but it was my mother's choice. She came from the Alsace and some of her ancestors and relations were German or Friesian or something.'

He smiled and said virtually without thinking. 'It is a charming name and completely suitable for a beautiful lady.'

She seemed genuinely complimented and ducked her head slightly with a girlish grin.

'Time for the next course, I think.'

He rose and immediately she did too. They both carried out their respective plates to the kitchen. Before long the next course's dishes had been taken out of their warming compartments of the policeman's cooker and two plates filled with the *alouettes, pommes gratinés* and *ratatouille*. The tomato sauce had thickened up nicely and the ratatouille had managed to retain its structure while still remaining tender. They served themselves in the kitchen and carried their plates back and Drangnet poured two glasses of Chateauneuf. He noticed that Gravlet's wine was not only from a great vineyard but also a great year. He would never have got such a wine by himself. There were clearly even more advantages to entertaining this lady.

This time they chatted; informally and candidly. He asked about her youth and her father and her taking over and development of the business. She asked him about his early career and his early life in the army before the police force. She was obviously well enough informed about his profession. All to quickly the main course and a second glass of Chateauneuf for each were finished.

They had wandered over a wide area together and learned a lot about each other. Without taking a special notice of it they were becoming friends and good ones at that. He realised that he was talking to her without the slightest reservation and it seemed her with him. They passed easily to the lemon creams which met with enthusiastic consumption and it seemed only a few minutes before they were sitting together again at the sitting room sofa close but not entirely inappropriately. Each had a final glass of crémant in hand.

It was well past midnight and much to both their regrets the evening had to draw to an end. The fact that matters had inevitably to revert to reality helped a little.

'I'm concerned. Angèle, that we have a problem that we haven't really talked about'

She just looked at him and waited.

'When I talked with Madame Bondine I obtained a list of your girls' guests during the night poor Mademoiselle Flandrette was killed.'

She just nodded. She knew.

'There are some significant names on that list and if I find myself having to ask too many questions there maybe consequences.'

Again, it was as if she had slipped effortlessly back into her official personality.

'Louis. My clients are their own responsibility. I don't ask them to visit my girls and if they have to answer your questions that's their problem. I am sure you will ask them in whatever way you require to. It is a matter of no consequence to me. In fact, if it helps your investigation, I would actively encourage it.'

Dragnet found himself wondering if the possibility of discovery would make her clients slightly less comfortable than she imagined. However, time would tell.

It felt too soon but at last it was time for her to go. He fetched her cloak and hat, laid the former gently over her shoulders and watched admiringly as she adjusted her hat in front of the mirror that hung to one side of his front door. She turned to face him and took both his hands in hers.

'Louis, thank you for a wonderful evening. I have not enjoyed myself as much for a long time. You are my favourite sort of company. You have also demonstrated that this policeman, at least, can certainly cook very well indeed. Don't be surprised if you are treated with even more respect when you next visit the market. They like people who respect their produce and can cook it properly. For the rest I will help you all I can. It's not just in my own interest nor is it just my duty. I want to help you as a friend because I want to become a close one. I trust you and I'm sure you will make the right decisions along what may be a very difficult road. Finally, and above all, I hope we can see each other again before too long. Apart from everything else, I enjoy your company.'

'Thank you for coming, Angèle.' he replied. 'I too hope we will meet again very soon, even if we don't have business to discuss. I would enjoy seeing you again.'

She smiled again in that direct was in his face and inclined her head slightly to one side. He placed the anticipated kiss on er cheek, enjoying lingering slightly longer over the process that was usual under the circumstances. He opened the door and escorted her down the stairs to the front door where inevitably her carriage was waiting.

He passed her up into the cab and felt a final squeeze of his hand as she settled back into it.

'Bonsoir, Louis,' she said quietly.

'Bonsoir, Angèle,' he replied equally gently.

He stepped back and nodded the coachman and he drove off down the side of the *Place des Vosges*. He stood following in the cab until it passed through the entrance at the south side of the Place and down the *Rue Royal*e and out of sight.

He felt not at all like going to bed so he cleared the dishes into the kitchen for his house keeper to deal with the morning. He poured himself a whisky and sat down at his piano and opened the handsome manuscript. It was a careful and ornate copy almost without damage. He found that all the motets he was learning were there of course and he started to follow his lines, silently, hearing the music from inside his head.

Chapter 9: Saturday 9th April   Scene 1: Episode with and Angry Policeman

Gant stuck his head around the door to the office.

'Someone to see you, boss.'

Drangnet waited expectantly for something more. His deputy was hardly garrulous at the best of times, but this was an unusually uninformative start to a conversation even for him. Gant had obviously said all he was going to.

'Roger,' he asked with a sigh. 'Do I get any more information than that or do I have to guess the rest?'

'Well sir, I don't think you want to see him very much.'

Drangnet just raised a hand slightly and made a sort of tired, flapping gesture.

'In that case, Roger, I suggest you send whoever it is away and leave me in peace.'

'Er. I can't sir.'

'And why not exactly?'

'Well I don't outrank him me.'

Now Dragnet became interested.

'Outrank? You mean he's military?'

'No, boss. He's policeman like us, sort of.'

'Sort of? What on earth do you mean?'

'Well,' replied Gant looking more and more uncomfortable. 'He's one of those politicos. He is an Inspector and I am too so I can't tell him what to do.'

'His name, Roger?'

'Inspector Tergia, Sir.'

'And you can't get rid of him, I suppose.'

Gant shook his head.

'He's most insistent, boss. Wants to see you personally and at once, or so he says.'

Before either could say another word, the man himself flung back the door and strode into the room.

'Inspector Drangnet. I want to talk to you about the dead man who you seem to be hiding from us. The anarchist who you have hidden in the mortuary at Vaugirard'

He just stood there bristling with outrage waiting for Dragnet's reply. He was a squat man in a badly fitting suit.

Drangnet just stared to the man, then shouted:

'Clement!'

It took the man less that a second to come into the office. He must have been standing outside.

'Sergeant Clement. Do I gather that you have just authorised this man to come to visit me?'

Clement was obviously upset at what had been a recent encounter downstairs.

'With respect, sir. I did no such thing. This man just arrived unannounced, pulled rank on me and barged straight past me. He didn't even bother to identify himself.'

Drangnet looked calmly at the man still standing indignantly across the desk from him while continuing to talk to his sergeant.

'Sergeant kindly get four constables up here immediately and arrest this man who has broken into my office without authority. Lock him up in the cells and then send someone to Chief Inspector Cordiez of the Political Police and to inform them that we have a man claiming to one of their inspectors in detention. If they want him, they had better come to collect him.'

The man in front of him was outraged and was about to remonstrate violently when Drangnet ordered him to be quiet.

'Inspector Tergia. You are not addressing an Inspector of Police, someone of equal rank to yourself, but the senior Chief Inspector of the Criminal Police of the City of Paris and you will be taught some manners. I will not have you barging in here and abusing me or my officers of whatever rank. If you or one of your colleagues wants to talk to me, I expect that request to come in writing from a member of your department of commensurate rank to myself. Once I receive such a request, I will consider it and reply in like manner. Your arrogant and boorish attitude does no credit either to your department or to the force we both serve. I will issue a formal complaint to your superiors as to your conduct and I will make it my business to ensure that they enact a suitable punishment. In the meantime, you will remain a guest in our cells until once of your colleagues sees fit come and get you.'

The man made to speak but again was cut short by a gesture.

'Another thing you might get into your arrogant brain is that the investigation of crimes of murder in the city are the responsibility of this department and ours alone. If I happen to think there is a political element to one, I will inform your department in the usual way. At the moment there is no evidence that the dead man presently residing in the morgue at Vaugirard is a victim of any form of politically motivated crime and, as such, it is none of your business. If any of your people tried to get near him until I have finished with him, I will arrest them as well for impeding my investigation.'

The man remained shaking with rage as four very large constables handcuffed him and dragged him away. As the door closed behind him, Gant sat down in one of Drangnet's chairs, a large grin on his face.

'I don't think you're making many friends at in the political department, sir.'

Drangnet just shrugged.

'Personally, I don't give a damn. How dare the arrogant bastard come charging in here and throw his weight around. You just make sure that no one releases him until I say so. That goes for Dancart all the way up to the prefect. Make sure the cell staff know that too. He is to be released only on a direct order from me.'

Chapter 9: Saturday 9th April   Scene 2: Another Meeting with Dancart

He decided to take himself off to do a bit of his favourite sort of detecting; in a library. He had been a reader's ticket holder of the *Bibliothèque nationale* since the new building on the Rue de Richelieu was opened just before the beginning of the war with Germany. He was also a personal friend of the current director Léopold Delisle. He often found a good reason for using the place. Mostly he just had questions to be answered, questions that he either thought that no one he knew could answer or that no one would give him an honest answer to. Sometimes, like now, he had a question that he didn't want anyone to know he was asking. In that case he simply had to find the answer himself and the *Bibliothèque* was the best place in France to do that. The other great advantage of the place was that no-one could disturb him. You needed a pass to get in and that was available only on application. Having left word with Gant that he would be out at least until mid-afternoon if not the rest of the day he set off to walk to the library. With him he took a notebook and pencils and the all-important photograph that Dankovich had given him.

It took him more than an hour to find what he wanted. The library catalogue was hand-written on small index cards that were stuck in one of more than a hundred large volumes, more or less in alphabetical order. This was necessary as new books were added to the collection every day. There were more general subject indices but these were often vague and invariably misleading. In fact, his friend Delisle had set himself the task of publishing an up to date complete printed catalogue which was an enormous venture as the library contained many hundreds of thousands of books and manuscripts. He found a number of reference books on iconography and, in particular, on masonic symbolism, and settled down comfortably under Henri Labrouste's wonderful vaulted roof. He felt yet again the pleasure of sitting in that immense, book-lined oval room as he set to work to try to interpret the symbolism of the tattoo.

Four hours later he realised that he had better be getting back to the office. Dancart would be very unsettled by now although not to the point of releasing their guest in the cells. He would certainly want to talk to his subordinate. Drangnet had spent the four hours enjoyably but completely unproductively. He had found a large amount of information about masons and seen an equally large number of illustrations of masonic symbols containing triangles, pyramids, circles, eyes in bewildering variety but nothing that matched his image exactly. A few numbers even appeared from time to time but nothing like the ones he was searching for. He closed his notebook and got up from his seat. Reluctantly he returned his pile of books to the issue desk and stepped out of the building and into the late afternoon sun.

Whether it was luck or not, he doubted but Gant was in the *Sûreté* reception when he got back.

'Well that's it boss. Something of an eventful day, I think.'

Dragnet smiled at his old friend.

'You might say that, Roger. You might well say that. How is our guest, by the way? Is he adjusting to life in the cells?'

Gant laughed.

'I'm not sure I can accurately describe his mood, sir. Actually, I've been avoiding going near. But I think we can both make a pretty accurate guess.'

'Yes, I suspect we could, my friend. Who's in charge down there tonight?'

'Lodec and Leclerc.' replied Gant with a grin on his face.

Dragnet laughed with his deputy.

'Excellent. I don't think there is a harder, bad tempered, more disrespectful pair of policemen in this whole nick. Our friend should feel at home.'

'I'm a little surprised that he's still here. I would have thought they would be in a hurry to get him back.'

'Oh, these things take time, you know. The head of the political department would have to register a complaint with the prefect who would then pass on a bollocking to Dancart who wouldn't, of course, know what the hell is going on. By the way, is he in?'

'Er, actually he is. I passed him in the corridor about an hour ago. He asked me where you were and I said, of course, I didn't know but perhaps you were out investigating something. He said that you shouldn't go home without seeing him first. I then said that perhaps you might be going home directly and not coming back to the office. So, he said something along the lines that I could bloody well send someone around to your place to sit outside your door to make sure you got the message.'

'Which, of course, you didn't do.'

'No sir.'

'And why not?'

'Well, I knew where you would be.'

'Ah. I see. And what sort of mood was he in do you think?'

'Pretty fierce, boss. Pretty fierce.'

'And this was about an hour ago, you say?' replied Dragnet,

'Yes, sir.'

'Well perhaps I'll let him cool down a little more which I catch up on some paperwork.'

'I would advise exactly that, Sir.'

In the event, he let almost an hour go by before folding his newspaper and descending the ornate spiral staircase down one floor to his boss's office. Dancart' secretary had long since gone home and doors leading from the landing, through the commissioner's waiting room, his secretary's office and to his own office were all wide open. Dragnet set his shoulders and marched resolutely through this ornate corridor towards the inevitable dressing down that awaited him with all the foreboding of the trip to Madame Guillotine to whose tender caress he had been responsible for sending a large number of criminals during his rise to Chief Inspector of *Sûreté*.

Much to his surprise he found not an irate Superintendent but one with a wide smile sitting in one of the two less uncomfortable chairs ranged on either side of his magnificent fireplace.

'Do sit, Louis,' he said gesturing to the chair opposite. Alongside each chair was a low table bearing a open bottle of red wine and a glass.

'Help yourself, dear chap.'

Drangnet wasn't completely surprised. He and Dancart had followed parallel careers with the old man one rank above him almost ever since he joined the force. They got on very well and the senior man knew all the idiosyncrasies of his talented but occasionally headstrong and wilful junior. He also knew how to handle him and was a skilful proponent of the carrot and stock method of management. Tonight, obviously, was the carrot. Once they had settled, filled their glasses and silently toasted each other's heath, Dancart began.

'All right, Louis, what are you up to this time?'

'What on earth do you mean, sir?' replied Drangnet innocently.

Dancart looked over the rim of his wine glass.

'Well I was just wondering why we are playing host to one of our esteemed colleagues from the political police, somewhat, I gather, to his displeasure. I was told he was under arrest but while everyone on this building I have talked to seems to think its a thoroughly good idea; indeed a highly amusing one, that opinion is not shared by the Prefect of Police of the City of Paris who has received an official complaint about it; A complaint that he had passed on to me. Indeed, I was summoned to the Prefect's office this very afternoon.'

'Ah, I see. I'm sorry about that.' replied Drangnet. 'And what did you say to him, if I may ask?'

'I was able to delay proceedings a little, firstly by pleading ignorance, of course, and secondly, because I gathered that Chief Inspector Cordiez, the boss of the politicals, had been in such a hurry to complain that he presented his official complaint about your conduct to the Prefect in person and verbally. His harangue was not to the Prefect's taste at all and he rejected the complaint on the excellent grounds that all official complaints to the Prefect have to be presented in writing. So, the man was turned around and told to get his pen out. However, I was also summoned, and the essence of the complaint was passed on to me by a Prefect who managed to be both angry and amused at the same time. It will be tomorrow before Cordiez has finished his essay and handed it in and therefore also tomorrow before the complaint is handed on to me, equally, of course, in writing. I will then have to summon you to explain yourself before I make a formal reply to the complaint probably later tomorrow afternoon or even the day after.

'Also in writing, sir?' was Drangnet's only reply.

'Yes, Louis, in writing. However, that is the point at which your luck will run out completely and explanations will be necessary.'

'In the meantime, sir, Inspector Tergia remains our guest?'

Dancart grinned. 'Of course. Unless the arresting officer releases him himself, and I am pretty sure you won't. He can only be released by the order of an examining magistrate and, as you know, that can actually take a day or two as they eat, sleep and make love in writing.'

But now a much more solemn look came over the superintendent's face.

'So, in theory you have until tomorrow afternoon or the day after to explain yourself. In practice, however, you have until I finish this bottle of wine. So, as I said at the beginning of this conversation; what on earth are you up to?'

'Well sir. As regards this idiot Tergia, it's fairly simple. He barges into our offices, refuses to identify himself correctly to the desk sergeant and is verbally abusive to all and sundry. He then forces his way, without authorization, past my inspector and comes to rest in my office and abuses me too. His insists on having the body of a dead man we are investigating released to him at once without a shred of authority or paperwork. I attempted to explain that dead bodies in Paris are our bailiwick not his and should keep a civil tongue in his head when addressing a superior officer. He continued to make an exhibition of himself and I concluded that he was impeding our investigation so I arrested him and put him in the cells. I have a fond hope that the experience might teach him some manners, but will admit to having my doubts.'

Dancart nodded.

'I had a feeling it was something like that. I won't even begin to scold you because you've done this sort of thing before and, to be frank, I agree with you. But we need to have a reply to the Prefect ready. Perhaps you'll draft one?'

'Yes of course. I'll have one to you by tomorrow morning.'

'Good. Now tell me what's going on with this investigation for yours. Are you actually making any progress?'

Drangnet gave his boss a resumé of the case.

'So let me get this right.' said Dancart after Drangnet had finished. 'We have the murder of three dead prostitutes, each of which has been followed by three dead men, the body of the first of whom has been snaffled up by the political police before we could examine it while the second and third are in our possession, which is as it should be. These bodies are being autopsied by our own Dr. Dankovich. Right?'

Drangnet nodded.

'Is there any actual connection between all these deaths?'

'The women's deaths or the men's?' he asked innocently.

Dancart just frowned.

'Not really. Well, it's hard to tell. The politico's think something is up. They are the ones sniffing around the prostitutes so we have to assume they think there is a connection. Apparently, they think that the men are all anarchists.

"And what do you think to that particular theory, Louis?"

'To be honest, sir, Not much. I think we have to bear in mind where these new police came from. Tergia and Cordiez were both military back in the days of the Commune and they played an active part in arresting and executing a goodly number of communards during *la semaine sanglante*. They are definitely not nice people. They enjoyed their work too much for that. That experience may well have contributed to their getting their present jobs explaining as well why they tend to act like bullies with no manners. It also explains that they are regarded with complete loathing by most ordinary people here in Paris. If they rely on intelligence from the streets to do their jobs, they are going to have a difficult time. But they do have a lot of money so they can buy their information, I suppose. My belief is that their fixation with anarchists dates from the days of Louise Michel and Eugène Varlin and the Reclus brothers and they are now happy to blame unnamed anarchists for anything untoward they come across. Proudhon and Bakunin are behind us. They would be too intellectual for this lot anyhow. In any case the current major figures in the anarchist movement are currently not in France at all. Kropotkin, for instance, is in Switzerland. The rest are mostly in London.'

'Surely, Louis, anarchists are still a danger.'

'Obviously, sir, but there are precious few here at the moment. The trials after the Commune killed off many of the leaders and the remained scattered abroad. Many went to London and some went much further afield than that. There is little evidence that they have returned in any great numbers. You have to remember that most ordinary people here don't want a bunch of bomb-throwing anarchists on the streets of Paris any more than we do. I'm pretty sure I would have heard about it if there were any about - at least in any sort of organised way.'

'Louise Michel is still among us, proclaiming as loudly as ever.'

Drangnet smiled.

'Yes, when she's not in prison or touring abroad. But however well she speaks and no matter how many stop to listen to her speeches or watch her plays, she is a lone voice, or at least, one of very few and one that increasingly drifts away from advocating violent action and comes closer to political theorising. I rather enjoy listening to her myself. She's an intelligent person and a good speaker. In any case, I can't see her being involved in anything to do with killing prostitutes. Killing the prostitute killers, I could believe, however. But that wouldn't be an anarchist thing in my view. That would come from her feminist views.'

'So, you're saying that the anarchist threat is over here in France.'

'No, Sir. I'm by no means saying that. In fact, I think it will be an increasing threat over the coming years and it's one that before long will be one that we will have to face in the streets of Paris. But I think it will be a threat posed by individuals not organisations. There is already a new philosophy being talked about, the so-called "propaganda of the deed" which means that anarchism should embrace violent acts performed by individuals not groups. You recall that man Clément Duval two years ago? He burgles a house on the *Rue de Monceau*, steals fifteen thousand francs, sets the house on fire, is caught, stabbed poor Brigadier Rossignol who was trying to arrest him and when he is sentenced to death, he starts shouting "long live anarchy."'

Dancart nodded.

'I remember the case well. He should have been executed. Instead some soft judge gave him life on Devil's Island. What did he write? "The policeman arrested me in the name of the Law, I struck him in the name of Liberty". Bullshit, the man was a common thief. Rossignol lost an eye.'

'Well he's now something of a folk hero to these anarchists; this Duval. I think what we have to fear from the anarchists is more individual acts of violence not some organised conspiracy. The same goes for Charles Gallo and that attempt to throw acid on the members of the stock exchange. He also went on about it being an act of anarchy. That's why I don't think this particular case has anything to do with the anarchists. Remember we have two crimes that seem to be rolled up into one. Firstly, we have the murder of three prostitutes.

Secondly, we have the murder of three men. The only connection between these two groups currently is that each man seems to have been killed very soon after one of the prostitutes and that the political police have made some sort of connection for us. There is no evidence that any of the three men was seen anywhere near any of the brothels. We also have the fact that each man was dumped in the Seine and washes up at the same place on the western end of the *Île St. Louis*. The prostitutes came from different houses and don't seem to be linked in any way other than that most prostitutes are connected in some way or another in this city. I haven't been able to establish any link between the men as I have only had the chance briefly to examine them.'

'So, Louis. You want to have the first body back?'

'Yes, I do. And if these politicos have had any autopsy done, I want a copy of the report too.'

'All right, Louis,' Dancart sighed. 'I'll see what I can do. Just you make sure that I have your report on our friend in the cells by tomorrow morning. I don't need to tell you we need some progress on the case pretty soon. Our lords and masters are getting jumpy as the newspapers give it more and more attention. And for heaven's sake keep clear of the politicos. I've got quite enough trouble on my desk without you waging a political war that you won't win.'

Drangnet saw no reason at all why he couldn't win that particular confrontation but wisely decided to keep that opinion to himself

Chapter 9: Saturday 9th April   Scene 3: Rehearsal at St Gervais and a visit to the Theatre

Finally, at about 8 o'clock, *le maître* was happy with them and the group was dismissed. Slowly the choir gathered up it's belongings, chatted amongst each other for a while and started to make their way down the nave of St Gervais to the doors at the west end. Drangnet was one of the first. Almost alone, it seemed, he always had something to do or somewhere to be after the practice. The rest usually headed for a bar or a café to continue chatting. The last thing he expected was to be greeted on his way out by anyone let alone by a beautiful woman. Actually, being greeted was something of an overstatement. The lady in question sat, fully clothed against the cool that even now had invaded the great arcaded nave of St Gervais, in the back row of pews that was placed fully under the overhead of canopy above which towered the great Clicquot organ that had so graced the church since the days when the Couperin family were in charge. She just lifted her head and looked at him. It was enough to divert him from his exit and to make him slide into the row and sit beside her. He took her hand, freshly taken from its glove, and dipped his head to follow the conventional greeting that required him to stop short of contact between his lip and the back of her proffered hand. Good intentions, they might have been, but at the last minute she raised her hand to press it none too gently against his mouth and left it there slightly longer that he expected.

'Madame Fernier, what a delightful surprise. What on earth are you doing here?'

She finally allowed him to lower his hand onto the seat between them where, continuing to hold it, she swept her skirt across it to shield it from any curious glanced from the rest on the choir whose exit from the church was now noticeably enlivened by one of their member being so interestingly intercepted .

'I came to listen to you, Monsieur. Why else?'

Leaving aside an obvious suggestion as to why it would be normal to visit a church in the first place, he followed with another question.

'So why, Madame Fournier, are you here at the back rather than nearer the front? That would surely offer a better view?'

'A better view, perhaps but not a better sound, I think.'

Drangnet was immediately interested.

'How come, Madame. What do you mean?'

She turned to smile at him, still, he noted, holding his hand hidden under the folds of her long skirt.

'Normally I listen to my music here when the full choir is singing and the Couperin's great organ in thundering away. It takes a certain amount of time for the organ sound to travel up to the choir and I find if I sit too close to the choir up there in the chancel, I hear things a little out of time. If I sit here by the time the organ has travelled from there above me here, up to the far end on the church it seems to have caught up with the sound from the choir that has only travelled half the distance. So, it all seems to have caught up with itself, so to speak. At least that is what we think; my friends and I. It's probably not very scientific but there it is.'

'On the contrary, Madame, I think it's all too scientific. Worryingly so.'

She frowned very slightly.

'Why would you be worried, Monsieur? Is it perhaps that you don't think women are capable of such scientific considerations?'

Her tone was a slightly mocking one although he noticed that she was still holding his hand.

'Not at all Madame. Quite the contrary. And in your particular case very definitely not.'

'Good. For tonight I have something in mind that might test your credentials, as they say. That is, of course, unless you have something of importance that will take you away from me tonight.'

Drangnet lost track of the *entendres*. He also immediately decided that there was nothing that he could think of that was more important than spending some more time in the company of this enchanting woman.

'Madame,' he replied as gallantly as he could. 'I would be delighted to attempt whatever you have in mind. I'd be grateful if it could include food of some sort, though. I seem to have forgotten to have eaten much today.'

She looked a little pensive while she obviously was rearranging her plans a little. They were interrupted by the young man who had been in charge of their rehearsal as he too left for the exit.

'Monsieur Drangnet, I must congratulate you. Not only were you in excellent voice this evening but you were singing extremely accurately. You must have been examining the score carefully since we last sang together.'

'Oh, I have, *maître*, I have.' he replied smiling to accept the compliment as he remembered that grand volume currently sitting on the music rest of his Boisselot.

'Well. All I can say is that you should keep up the good work. I wish all the members of the group were so diligent. So, I will wish you both a good evening.'

And with that he went to tip his hat before remembering that, being in a church, he was carrying rather than wearing it and departed with slightly less dignity that he hoped. The two in the pew both laughed before Madame asked:

'And who exactly is this rather pretty boy who seems to be *maître* of the choir. I haven't seen him before.'

'Ah,' he replied. 'That's the new man who is taking over year and he is doing two concerts in advance to introduce himself, so to speak. The first is a performance for the large motets with full orchestra, organ and choir and the second is our little effort. He is twenty-six years old and has some rather interesting ideas about Gregorian chants amongst other things that will shake up our little choir, I think.'

Before she could reply, the verger came towards them having extinguished most of the church lights. The message was clear. His companion finally loosed her hold on his and they made their way out of the church to stand under the great elm tree that traditionally had obscured the baroque façade of the church. Even under the dim glow of the streetlights they could see that the tree was coming into spring leaf. Her carriage appeared as if by magic and the coachman jumped down from his seat at the back and attended to their ascent. It was again the same elegant version of the now ubiquitous Hansom cab that was used for everything from smart conveyances like this to the everyday taxicab. The coachman spread a light rug across their knees and before long they were travelling off from the church eastwards in the direction of the *Place de la Bastille*. She didn't volunteer their destination to him, but he decided not to give her the satisfaction of asking. Two could play at that game. She did however re-find his hand under the cover of the blanket. Madame was obviously in both a flirtatious and a serious mood. He found that oddly seductive. As they passed his home on the *Place des Voges* and continued eastwards she finally decided to give him a clue.

'I am taking you somewhere both to see something interesting and to meet someone who might help us. These two are related. However, you will I think, find it illuminating and possibly useful as we should not completely lose sight of why we became acquainted in the first place.' She paused before continuing. 'Much as I might wish to.'

As much to his own surprise as hers he gave her hand an involuntary squeeze and was rewarded with a brief kiss on the cheek. He glanced upward quickly to check that the little trap door in the roof of the cab that normally allowed the occupant to converse with her coachman, was closed. It was. She noticed and leant across and kissed his cheek again, this time lingering little longer. He was taken aback somewhat. Madame was certainly in the flirtatious mood,

Their route passed east across the *Place de la Bastille* and headed on towards the *Place de la Nation*. Some few years before the circle had been called *Place du Trône-Renversé* and had been the site of one of the most active guillotines during the revolution of the seventeen nineties and after. It had played a prominent role in the horrors of *le semaine sanglant*. Dragnet started to feel a little uncomfortable. This was getting further and further from the part of Paris where he felt most comfortable. As if she sensed this, she again squeezed his hand before leaning towards his ear.

'Please don't worry, Chief Inspector. You're with me now. I'll protect you.'

Just before they arrived at the grand circle the cab turned off into a side street and pulled up outside a café. It was brightly lit by gas lamps, the new electricity, so championed by the government, had yet to reach this far out from the centre of the city. They entered and madame led the way confidently though the café to the back of the main room and they entered what seemed to the auditorium of a small theatre. They slid into a couple of seats at the very back. The performance was is progress and it didn't take him long to realise that he was present a production of a play he had actually seen before. Nadine had been first produced in Paris some years before and had been written by the legendary Louise Michel, one of the great working-class heroes on the Commune and a woman that Dragnet had also come across before.

As usual the play was a rowdy affair portraying a highly political if highly inaccurate account of the 1833 worker's revolt in Krakow interspersed with interruptions from the audience and numerous sound effects most of which seemed to consist of only half-controlled explosions. The place was little short of a riot but that, Dragnet assumed, was half the point. He had attended this sort of performance before. What he couldn't figure out was why Angèle had brought him here. There was obviously some reason behind her madness, so he just settled deeper into his uncomfortable chair and decided to wait it out, ignoring the pain of an empty stomach that was increasingly preoccupying him. At least, the thought, they had come in relatively near the end. To that extent, madame seemed to have been merciful. He just sat there not taking much notice of the action on stage. It was as usual a completely amateur production; a constraint made a requirement by both an absence of budget and by good proletarian principals. The standard of acting was inevitably dreadful.

Before the departing audience could fill the exits, Madame had taken him firmly by the elbow and marched him back into the café and sat him with little ceremony at a table in the corner. An un-labelled bottle of red wine and three glasses adorned a linen tablecloth. Drangnet also counted three sets of cutlery. So he said very little, sat quietly, returning his host's smile, and, other than pouring them both a much-needed glass of the wine, waited for events to unfold. It wasn't long coming for the thick throng of departing theatregoers parted and suddenly the whole point of the evening stood in front of them. Dragnet rose, of course, and greeted a woman he had met on a number of occasions in the past in circumstances that were not always felicitous.

'Madame Michel, how nice to see you again.'

The great lady smiled in a way that indicated how little she believed him.

'Chief Inspector, how nice to see you again too. I do hope you enjoyed our production this evening – at least for the short time you were there.'

'I apologise, Madame. I am afraid that *Maître Couperin* proved to be a difficult task master as usual. With a simpler composer the rehearsal might have been shorter. As it was, Madame Fournier hastened us here as quickly as she could.'

They broke off as a waiter appeared to their table with three plates of food. He shot a surprised glance across to Madame Fournier who just smiled and inclined her head slightly in answer to the unspoken thanks. It was, as far as he could tell, mutton stew with carrots and potatoes. It was not Drangnet's favourite by any means, but it was at least food. He tucked in and found, to his delight, that it was excellent. Having felt a certain frisson in the opening exchanges between her two guests, Madame Fournier was first to get the conversation going by confronting the issue.

'Well, I arranged this little visit as I thought that you two hadn't met before. However, I see I was mistaken.'

Madame Michel seemed to be reluctant to admit it. It was left to Drangnet to reply.

'Madame Michel and I have certainly met before on numerous occasions, not always under pleasant circumstances.'

The lady in question remain engrossed in her stew. Dragnet got fed up quite quickly and addressed his companion.

'Madame Fournier. Whatever reason you had for arranging this meeting tonight your friend seems to greet the idea with her usual lack of courtesy, especially when dealing with members of the police force. In spite of what happened in the past, a past incidentally in which Madame Michel might have had reason to be grateful for policemen like me rather than being so contemptuous of us, today is now and the world has changed somewhat since 1871. Perhaps not as much or in a way that she might like but nevertheless changed it has. So, I see very little reason for continuing this conversation in spite of the stew being acceptable. Perhaps you would ask your coachman to drive me home where I would prefer to renew my study of Couperin's motets than suffer the opprobrium of this bitter and impolite old *petroleuse*. Whatever she might think of us, her stay in New Caledonia, however difficult was preferable that her original destination on *l'Île du Diable*. She has us to thank for that although I recall she never got around to it.'

Much to her concern, Angèle Fournier saw her policeman put down his fork and make to rise. He clearly intended simply to walk out and make his own way towards his home on foot in the hope of hailing a passing cab to help his journey. Actually, it was a bluff although if the bluff were called, he was content to take his chances.

Angèle started to reply, perhaps to try to pacify her obviously upset companion, when the taciturn woman across the table stopped her with a wide smile.

'You always were a touch impatient, Chief Inspector, even in the old days when we were both somewhat younger. But I will admit that you were always fair, unlike many of your colleagues. And yes, I remember that you are one of the people that I have to thank for seeing to it that my head still remains attached to my shoulders.'

'Amongst others, madame. Amongst others. More than you might imagine.'

She nodded as they both fell silent as the memories of those violent weeks returned. Mercifully, he had been absent during the main events that had led to the brief flowering of the revolutionary uprising that led to the Commune. He had been attached to Marshal MacMahon's staff and sent to Lyon to supervise the investigation of the outbreak of violence that had taken place under the auspices of Michael Bakunin in September of 1870. It was a relatively straightforward business, but the antagonism of the local police hadn't helped. They resented his intrusion in spite of their own inability to control things. By the time matters were wrapped up and the various people who had been arrested were readied for trial, the violence between the Government forces and the Communards was well under way in Paris and he was prevented from getting back into the city for a while. He had to wait until almost the end of the fighting until he got back in and by that time the main fighting was all over. The great revolutionary adventure had lasted little more than two months. The government took its revenge and what came to be known as *la semane sanglante* took place. Thousands of communards were arrested, submitted to summery trial and executed, often on the same day. Drangnet and what was left of the official police force was often powerless to bring any discipline to proceedings. The soldiers had been finally let loose on the communards and they were making the most of it. Drangnet could little other than to wait and hope that at least some on the communards would be arrested and brought to him safely. Possibly because of her fame, Louis Michel appeared without notice in his office for her interrogation.

Louise Michel was a legendary figure in the city. Denied active service in the commune forces because she was a woman, she had been tireless during the defence of the city against the French army. She had helped to build barricades, carried ammunition to the commune's soldiers, tended the wounded, distributed food, carried intelligence, encouraged the soldiers, comforted women and children. She had finally been arrested once the republican army entered the city and taken control. Drangnet had been one of the policemen who had been charged with interrogating her before her very public trial. Fortunately Madame Michel had become too important just to be taken out of her prison cell and shot in some dark alley.

Dragnet bought himself back from his memories. 'I am pleased that you survived the attack in Le Havre earlier this year, Madame. I thought you were not only very lucky but rather generous in trying to excuse your attacker.'

Michel just shrugged.

'I felt that the man was unbalanced and therefore didn't deserve to be put on trial.'

Drangnet nodded slowly.

'I am nevertheless pleased that the bullet that, I've been told, is still lodged in your head hasn't caused permanent damage.'

She smiled in rather a wry way.

'I rather think that you would have hoped it would've knocked some sense into me but as you see, it hasn't. No, Chief Inspector, more or less I'm still the same person that you interviewed before my trial almost ten years ago.

'So, it seems, Madame. So, it seems.'

She turned to Angèle.

'I will admit that, almost uniquely Angèle, this man treated us with some respect. He was still a policeman doing a job, but he nevertheless interrogated us with a measure of courtesy. I suspect he got a lot more out of us that those other thugs who regularly resorted to violence when they didn't get the answers they wanted. We all remember that, Monsieur, even now. That is the reason you have your stew in your plate rather than in your face tonight.'

It was Drangnet's turn to smile slightly as he inclined his head in acknowledgement of her compliment. He well remembered those chaotic days as the Paris police tried in vain to re-establish some sort of law and order while the chaos had surrounded them.

'Yes, I remember all too well those days and nights we talked. I always found our conversations very interesting although even now after all those years I still don't entirely understand how you and your colleagues held so strongly to what was so obviously a lost cause.'

'Faith and belief, Chief Inspector. Faith and belief. Not unlike your beloved Maître Couperin, I feel.'

'Perhaps, Madame. But even he didn't need the courage that you showed. I remember that most of all as we sat together in amongst the ruins of our *préfecture* in the *Palais du Cour d'Appel* that had so recently been burned to the ground by you and your colleagues.'

This time she tossed her head back and laughed loudly.

'Yes, I remember that very well. It must have been the first time that an examining policeman asked his prisoner whether they minded being interrogated in their own cell rather than in his office.'

He too smiled at the memory.

'I recall that your cell was in much better condition than my office, Madame.'

Again they fell silent for a moment. The memory of what had been going on around them at the time and the extra-judicial assassinations of hundreds the communards soon removed the smiles from their faces. Her subsequent imprisonment at Satory Prison and the exile to New Caledonia for next seven years seemed silence him more quickly that it did her.

'I do hear about you from time to time, Madame, although you now seem to be the business of another department rather than mine.
'

Immediately her friendly countenance dropped.

'Yes,' she almost spat. 'We now attract the attentions of these disgusting political police and their secret agents all the time. I wouldn't be surprised to find that there were some in our audience tonight. They're usually are waiting for some pretext to arrest us again for incitement or something else. I'd much preferred it were you lot were still chasing us. At least you were honest about it.'

'I hope you're right, Madame. I'm afraid that I made it perfectly plain when the political department was set up that I wanted nothing to do with it. I don't think they are necessary and I certainly don't like the fact that they seem to operate outside the law. There is plenty enough crime in Paris to keep us busy.'

'But monsieur, surely our plays and meeting are seditious enough to regarded as criminal. Are we not all anarchists, revolutionaries and criminals?'

Her tone was highly sarcastic. It was as if she couldn't resist provoking him.

'Madame we now live in the Third Republic and since the Constitutional Laws of a few years ago, there was intended to be a limited guarantee of a certain freedom of speech and action. Whatever these political police may think or do, I for one do not regard making speeches or putting on political plays as criminal acts.'

'Even if they incite others to violence or to break the law, Monsieur, for that is what we are being accused of all the time?'

'If indeed you are breaking the law, then I believe it's our job to catch the law breakers and bring them to court. It is not our job to prosecute people for what we might guess is in their heads. The burden of proof is too important a basic criterion of justice for it to be the product of guesswork.'

Madame Fournier had remained silent throughout this interchange as she looked from one of her companions to the other with a look on her face not too distant from admiration. However, she was taken a little by surprise for Drangnet to change of tack and to address her directly.

'Now, Madame Fournier. I have enjoyed your company, as always, and I have enjoyed meeting Madame Michel again and, indeed, the stew. They were both were sharply spiced and a little tough. The play was less to my taste. However, I must now ask you why I am here?'

She almost looked annoyed to be forced into the limelight.

'Chief Inspector. Firstly, I would say that, in the matter of my murdered girls, Madame Michel is my confidante. She is also my friend and I trust her. So, if you wish to go forward with our collaboration then you should know that I trust her completely and you must too. The police seem to think that the men who have been murdering my girls are anarchists of some sort or from somewhere and I feel that Madame Michel knows more about this topic that I do. Certainly, she knows more than your colleagues in the blundering and unpleasant political police about these anarchists.'

'Yes,' Drangnet agreed. 'That's probably because she is one. A certain hands-on experience is always useful in these matters, I believe.'

Louise Michel's face became very hard for a moment. It was well known that since the Commune all but a few of her more extreme colleagues had either been shot or had fled abroad, She, almost alone, had returned to France soil and preached an increasingly anti-government line. His comment had been a little light-hearted but like all the best jokes it had more than a grain of truth to it and she didn't enjoy that.

'That may be so, Chief Inspector,' Angele continued, 'but on this occasion, it is Madame's view on the rights of women – my girls in particular – that is helping me. These are views that I think are somewhat similar to yours, I think.'

Drangnet felt it was time to lay down some ground rules, not only for Madame Michel, but also for his new lady friend, even if it risked everything he had built to date. Now Drangnet was finally becoming interested in this hitherto rather pointless evening.

'I'm not at all sure what you mean by rights, Madame. But if you're saying that I should be investigating the recent murder of three prostitutes in central Paris then I agree that I am doing exactly that. But that is nothing to do with their rights, as you put it, that you claim they possess just by virtue of being women. It is because the laws of France say that the taking of life is unlawful and within the boundaries of Paris it is my responsibility to enforce the law and try to find out who did it, to arrest them, make a case for the courts for their prosecution and to present that case to the best of my ability with a view to obtaining a prosecution under the law. The law, Mesdames, is my mistress and she takes precedence over all other ladies. She is a constant and exacting mistress. She is a woman who demands much, I have found, in a world that is inconstant and often untrustworthy but ultimately, she gives everything too. Without her, I feel that we are lost. We will lose all hold of civilised behaviour and with that we will lose hold on life itself. So, Madame Michel, may I ask as a policeman with every right to ask what views you may have on this little matter of murder?'

She was slightly taken aback, he could see, but the old antagonism was still there. So, she came back fighting.

'Well, Chief Inspector. I should first ask you whether you are more interested in who killed the girls or who killed their murderers.'

He was also direct.

'Apart from noting your evasion of my question, Madame, I would suggest that is none of your business. I am a policeman and, as I warned you, I am asking you this question officially. If you refuse to answer I will have you arrested and you will be taken to the *concièrge* on the *Île de la Cité* for further interrogation. Given your track record, I doubt that you would emerge to some considerable time. I could keep you there for weeks and, given how I'm feeling now, I'm minded to do just that.'

Angèle gasped and even Madame Michel looked surprised and uncomfortable. This was a very different policeman to the one who had faced them a few moment before. Drangnet had suddenly got fed up with being pissed about by these women and even the presence of the delightful Madame Fernier couldn't prevent his getting angry. He had other and better things that he could be doing tonight and, above all, he was getting bored with this little charade. He wasn't even concerned about the black looks he was beginning to get from some of their fellow diners. He no longer cared. This was just a great waste of time and all he wanted to do was go home. He offered only a cursory answer to her question.

'Both, of course. They are all murders in Paris and thus each is my responsibility. To me there is no difference. Each will be investigated correctly without favour to the best of my ability and that of my colleagues. And, in passing, I would be interested in why you've immediately jumped to the conclusion that the three men we have recently found floating dead in the Seine have anything at all to do with the murder of three prostitutes. It isn't a connection that I've made as yet. Perhaps you know something that I don't. As present I am more inclined to regard it as a coincidence.'

They both hesitated. He didn't.

'Be under no illusion, both of you. If I find that either of you, or even both, are actually responsible for any murder, these or any others, I shall endeavour find the evidence, arrest you, and see that you are convicted. I will make sure the prosecutor demands the death penalty and I will attend your execution. This is the demand that my mistress, the law, puts upon me and I am no cuckold. You would do well the understand that before this conversation goes any further at all.'

Madame Michel looked rather aggressive.

'And what, Chief Inspector, if your mistress, the law, is wrong.'

Drangnet became angrier.

'And who, exactly, do you think you are to be the sole judge of whether a law is wrong or right. If there is a general feeling that a law should be changed, you sanctimonious old bitch, we change it until it is right. You're not always right about everything yourself and your infallible self-belief may be seductive to your so-called followers but it cuts very little ice with me. If the law has to be changed because it's not up to the job, then we, the people, will decide that; openly and in public We don't go around killing and bombing people or hiding like rats in dirty corners conspiring and having endless meetings or putting on meaningless plays that tell more lies than offer truths about the history of the workers you are so proud to think you represent. We are all both the servants and the masters of the law at the same time. It is a position that you and your friends all around us here in the café completely fail to understand. If the law is wrong, as you put it, and needs to be changed then that must be done but by us ourselves and we do that by debate and reason, in public and subject to public scrutiny, by consent and voting not by guns and bombs. It was an Englishman who wrote recently that the pen is mightier than the sword. He was right and we would all be well minded to remember that.'

'It is unusual,' opined Michel, very shaken by Drangnet's unexpected passion, 'to find an Englishman with such wisdom.'

Dragnet nodded.

'Perhaps, old woman, you might be surprised to find wisdom in the mouths of others, In any case the words come from a play about our own Cardinal Richelieu.'

'And what happens,' returned Michel, 'if no one listens, especially if you are poor or old or a woman? What then? How do you then take part in this great debate for change?'

'Then you speak louder and perhaps longer or as long as you have to. But still just with words not guns, Madame so that people will finally hear you and listen to you. The one thing you can be sure of is if you stop talking and just throw bombs only thing that will happen is that people will stop listening. Then you are completely lost and you will have achieved nothing.'

'Perhaps you are right. Monsieur. Perhaps. But the time is coming soon when the world here, in Paris at least, will be controlled by men and women who don't agree with you. Then holding on to your principles then will be difficult.'

'That is when holding to them is even more important than before.' he replied with conviction. 'When life is settled and easy, you don't need such convictions. But if, as you say, some time in the future, Paris will be controlled by people who don't agree with me, unless they are democratically elected, I will oppose them with everything I have. I don't risk my own life and that of the men under my command every day to let anarchy reign here.'

Again, there was silence as both took stock of where they were. They were both thinking of how much they could trust each other and how far to go before confidences would go too far. It was also time to bring the conversation back to where they started, with the dead women. Somewhat to Drangnet's surprise, Louise Michel was quite relaxed as she spoke.

'Chief Inspector, I can't tell you who killed the women or who killed the three men. But I can tell you that the men were no anarchists. Certainly not in any sense that you understand it. I think that you and I both know how the men were killed if not actually by whom. As far as I can, I'll help you in your investigation. I do this for two reasons. The first is that Angèle is my friend and I, like you, I think, value friendship. The second is that I have always spoken out on the subject of women and their rights. While I certainly don't approve of a society where women are submitted to the carnal desires of men in exchange for money, I accept that prostitution has been with us throughout history and probably will be in the future. Therefore, if there is anything I can do to protect these women, then I will help in any way I can.'

'Thank you, Madame. Any help would be appreciated. Our jobs are made much easier with cooperation from the residents of Paris.' he replied somewhat sarcastically. 'But you've avoided answering my original question. You seem to associate the deaths of the three men with those of the three prostitutes. I admit there is a considerable coincidence, but I would be interested to know why you think there is a connection and if so, of what sort.'

She just shrugged unhelpfully.

'Just precisely it is exactly that? The coincidence is too great to be just by chance.'

Drangnet was getting very fed up now. Whatever had been intended by this somewhat unorthodox meeting, it was clearly getting nowhere. The woman was reluctant to give clear answers, being more intent on scoring debating points. Perhaps that was the world she lived in now.

'Well, thank you again for your valuable insight, Madame Michel.' he replied somewhat sarcastically.' I think I might have been able to work that particular insight out for myself.'

He turned to his companion.

'Madame Fournier, I think perhaps I should be getting back now. Are you going to offer me a lift back to the centre of town or do I have to make my own arrangements?'

Angèle was a little startled. The evening seemed not to have gone at all the way she had hoped.

'Er, of course, Louis, I'll take you back. I don't think that you will find too many cabs in the streets around here at this time of night.'

He looked at her rather pointedly.

'I wouldn't worry too much about that, Madame. As has been pointed out, there were certainly one or two representatives of the political police here tonight and I am pretty sure that one or two have remained behind. They'll give me a lift back. They're good at that sort of thing. I won't be without assistance.'

'No, Monsieur, I brought you here and I will take you back.'

'Then, Madame,' he said making to rise to his feet, 'I'll settle up with the waiter for the meal and then perhaps we might leave? I still have much to do, this evening.'

Turning to Madame Michel, he nodded his farewell to her.

'Goodbye, Madame, it was interesting meeting you again. No doubt we will again before too long. It is the way of things these days, I fear.'

And without further ado he rose before she could say anything and went over to the bar reaching for his wallet. The bar man gave him a very dirty look. He obviously knew Drangnet was a policeman.

'Sixteen francs.'

'For all three of us, Monsieur?'

The man just grunted and nodded.

Drangnet placed eighteen francs on the counter, none too gently and walked towards the café entrance. He arrived at the door at the same time as his host. Madame Fournier's cab was waiting outside and before long the driver had installed them and was driving back up the Rue du Faubourg St. Antoine towards the *Place de la Bastille.* This time there was no handholding under the blanket. But she seemed intent to patch repair whatever damage seemed to have happened to her plans.

'Chief Inspector.....'

Then she stopped and again found his hand.

'.....Louis. I had hoped that it might be a helpful meeting. Louise is a friend of mine and I know she is concerned about the deaths of my girls. I also know that she knows a lot about the anarchist community here in Paris. I just thought that it might help if you two talked. But obviously I was mistaken. I should apologise. I hope that nothing has happened to make things difficult between us; just as things seem to be going on so well.'

Drangnet's mood had softened a little now they were alone. It seemed he was incapable of remaining angry with this woman for long. He squeezed her hand in what he hoped was a reassuring way – whatever that was.

'Don't worry. Madame Michel has had a long and not altogether felicitous relationship with the police whatever she might say and they with her. Actually, I hold her in high regard. She is a woman of principal. She is a dedicated and fearless political animal but she has for years encouraged many people to follow paths that have led them into difficulty if not actual criminality. We have laws in this country against inciting people to these sorts of things and when they follow her advice or perhaps what they take her advice and break the law as a consequence, then my job and that of my fellow policeman, is to catch them and to try to ensure that are put in jail. I respect her courage and, unlike many of my colleagues, I respect her opinions. In my view she has a right to them. I even agree with some of them. But when they lead to other things, it all gets a little complicated. Like many people who hold their own ideas above all those of others, she has become a bigot. But no, in answer to your question, we are still what we were before tonight - whatever that is or was.'

She laid her head on his shoulder.

'I know she has many connections in the world of anarchism; in London too where there is more fertile soil for that sort of thing. I have read many of the works of Proudhon and of Bakunin, of Marx and even Kropotkin. As far as I can remember, none of these writers said anything about the importance of killing Paris prostitutes. As for Madame Michel, like many great people, she can be a bit of a pain in the arse.'

Angèle giggled.

'You said you still have much to do this evening. Does that mean you are not going to offer me a nightcap?'

Dragnet didn't hesitate for long.

'Madame, I'd be delighted to offer you some refreshment. That sheep stew was very good, but it was a little fatty. I need something to clear me out a little. I had a mysterious delivery a day or so ago that might fit the bill.'

It was, as he anticipated, no great mystery to Madame and that was proved by the fact she said nothing. The case of wine in question had been delivered a day or so before, much to the amusement of the concièrge who had to take delivery for him .

Before long they were sitting together on the sofa in his apartment each holding a glass of vintage Juglar Champagne, twelve bottles of which had been the anonymous and unprompted gift delivered to his door. The bottle stood on the low table in front of them.

'Madame. This bottle still a Juglar label on it which means that it was bottled at the latest before 1829. So, it's older than either of us.'

She smiled.

'So should all good wine be, Monsieur. My father always said that throughout your life you should never drink wine that is younger than you are.'

'He was a wise man, Madame. But what would he think of our dinking the favourite wine of His Imperial and Royal Majesty Napoleon the First?'

She frowned slightly as if to take seriously what had been a light-hearted question.

'I think that, like many Frenchmen, he admired Napoleon for much of his career but came to hate him when the emperor emerged from the soldier.'

That was, if course, true, certainly amongst that part of the populations that was suspicious of anything that smelt of monarchy.

She changed the subject.

'So Chief Inspector, how are your investigations getting along? Any news of progress?'

They both took another sip of Napoleon's champagne as if to make a transition to a more serious business.

'Not well, Madame. Not well at all. Not for the killers of your girls, nor for the bodies that seem to wash up against the *Île St. Louis* with such coincidental regularity.'

He couldn't swear to it, but he imagined he detected a fleeting smile cross his guest's face. Yet again he decided to trust his own judgment and be candid with her. Sooner or later it was an investment that he felt would pay dividends.

'As I said before, I don't subscribe to the opinion held by some of my colleagues, that this is some sort of anarchist plot to kill Paris prostitutes. I can see no reason for such a plot to exist and I'm pretty sure that this view is being promulgated by the political police as another way of feathering their own already well-lined nests. Unless you are unbalanced, most murders have some dividend; money, love revenge; something like that. I can't see any such dividends in these murders. No, I think there is a completely different explanation both for the killing of your girls and, actually, for the corpses in the Seine.'

She leant across him, momentarily allowing her torso lie across his legs as she reached for the bottle to top up their glasses.

'So, what do you think, my dear Chief Inspector?'

This was the moment that he had been waiting for some time; ever since he saw the crumpled list that Madame Bondine had handed to him a day or two ago.

'To answer that, Madame, I have to ask you a few questions. May I do that, or should I wait until we meet in slightly less social circumstances. I am beginning to value our friendship and I don't want to blur the lines between that and our more professional association.'

She smiled broadly at him. He had clearly said something that pleased her immensely.

'Monsieur, we are adults. When we first met, I told you that I would tell you what I could. That is still the case. Do ask your questions. Please.'

Taking a deep breath, he started, full in the knowledge that could be a crucial point in a relationship that he really didn't want to end in spite of the very real possibility that he was being taken for a fool.

'The other morning, Madame Bondine gave me a list of names; people who had visited her house on the day that Mademoiselle Flandrette was killed.'

Angèle nodded. The giving of the list had obviously been sanctioned by her.

'Do all your houses keep these records?'

'Yes, they do they do – now.'

'It that your normal practice. Madame?'

'Well it wasn't really but a little time ago we had a disagreement with the tax people about the number of clients we had.

I found that I couldn't prove how many there were. So, I started the policy more as evidence of our business than anything else. Obviously, I hoped it might be useful to you.

'Do your clients know about this list?'

'No, they don't. Ever since we have had this problem with the murder of the girls, we now ask them to sign into a visitor's book of sorts and they almost invariably use a false name. It is a bit silly really as most of them a well-known or regulars and we know them and the ones that aren't, we find out about pretty quickly.'

'How do you do that?'

'We just have someone follow them home.'

He could immediately see some problems with this rather simple explanation. However, he let it pass for the moment. However he saw that the question about how the murderers were identified was very easily answered. He also realised that here, somewhere, was an admission of guilt.

'What happens if they refuse to sign in?'

'Then we now no longer admit them. They are turned away.'

'Don't you run the risk of losing customers?'

'Clients, Louis. We prefer to call them clients.'

Drangnet thought that this was a distinction perhaps but no difference and said nothing.

'It doesn't seem to have much difference. But we've always been a little choosy, even before this business. There are many other places where men can go, places that have lower standards.'

'But interestingly, Madame, those other places, as you put it, don't seem to have had any trouble. This business seems to be targeted on you.'

Again, she just nodded.

'Do your visitors sign out as well?'

'No, but the concierge usually makes a note of the time they leave in her house records, if she sees them.'

'And where are these records kept?'

'At each house, Monsieur. The concierges keep them up to date and in safe keeping. We never know when a tax inspector might come calling. She collects the payments, of course, so she notes the details of the visitor, their time or arrival and departure and the amount paid for each girl. she is also responsible for paying the girls and keeping all the house accounts. The full record is made up at the end of each week and sent to me. My accountant then compiles a full record stores it.'

'I'd be grateful for copies of these records from the three days when the murders took place, Madame.'

Yet again, she just nodded.

'I'll have them for you by tomorrow evening, or rather by this evening,' she replied as the clock on Drangnet's mantlepiece chimed a musical one o'clock. He noticed that the bottle was empty and made to offer to fetch another. But she held up her hand.

'I think it's quite late enough, Louis. I know I have a busy day in front of me and I would have thought you have too. I'll send a man with the copies of the house records to you by the morning.'

'Thank you.'

Just as she made to get up, he took her hand.

'Angèle, I should thank you for being so candid with me and for trusting me. It means a lot to me. Rather looking amongst the anarchist community of Paris, I think that we'll find our killer in the pages of your record books, although I have a feeling that their identities will come as less of a surprise to you than they will to me. However, in the interest of stopping this gruesome little campaign for violence against your girls, I will persevere.'

'And those responsible for the bodies in the Seine, Chief Inspector?'

He smiled a little tiredly at that.

'All in good time, Madame Fournier. All in good time.'

And with that he escorted her down to his front door where, to no surprise at all, her carriage was waiting.

Chapter 10: Sunday 10th April   Scene 1: Complaints and Rebuffs

Next morning at eight o'clock sharp all twenty six members of the *Sûreté* sat around the polished conference table as, one by one, the officer who was in charge of each of their current cases got to his feet and gave a weekly progress report. Strictly speaking it wasn't completely necessary as Drangnet was kept informed of all the important developments by Gant, but it was a necessary part of his management style. Very often the squad had to prioritise and deal with many different matters from murder to petty street crime, with the squad divided up into smaller groups as the difficulty of the cases demanded, each led by a more senior officer. It was all too easy for these groups to get isolated from the squad as a whole and for those involved in slightly less important cases to resent some of their fellow officers who had more interesting or prestigious work. The weekly meeting was a good opportunity for the cohesiveness of the squad to be maintained. It also allowed Drangnet to make sure that individuals were not side-lined and that even the more senior of them occasionally were put to work on the less exciting crimes. It was Drangnet's way of reminding them that they served the whole community not just some of it.

Nothing he heard came as much of a surprise. Gant's ready access to his boss had seen to that. So, the meeting lasted no more than its usual hour or so. He was able to offer a few words of advice or encouragement where appropriate, approve a few changes within each group where progress was too slow or where too many men were looking at a simple case. All had been agreed with Gant beforehand. This time, however, he did say a few words about the prostitute murders as he was leading that enquiry and many of the other groups would come across the case while out and about the Paris streets. There was obviously little that he could say in public about his progress. It had been very little and his somewhat unorthodox method that he had adopted to try to solve it was not really a matter he wanted to discuss. But it provided the opportunity of remind them all that they were all part of the same squad.

The meeting over, he retired with not without a certain anticipation and shut himself in this office having told Gant that he wasn't to be disturbed. Gant, in any case, had his hands full as he had received his boss's instruction to write the response to Cordiez's official complaint that had finally landed on Dancart's desk in its written form. Drangnet had been wakened by Angèle's large messenger at seven who presented a number of leather-bound ledgers. They were weighty enough to make him take a cab to work. He had sent out for a notebook to a stationary shop close to his office and now he set to about transcribing the ledgers. It did cross his mind to try to copy all of them but that would have been an immense task. He knew he could always refer to them again if he wanted to. For now he contented himself with three or four weeks before the murders in the three brothels.

It didn't take long for him to realise the value of the information that Angèle had entrusted with him and that, in the wrong hands, was capable of doing substantial damage. The fact was, of course, that prostitution was not illegal in Paris. It hadn't been since the days of Napoleon. But it was regulated. Women were not allowed to solicit from the street and they should work in a registered house under licence. The house had to be supervised by a woman, financial records kept, and the fees and taxes set by the city paid. The health of the women was regularly monitored Some of these *maisons de tolerance* became famous for their design and for the welcome they gave their clients. Some even boasted celebrity clients like the then Edward, Prince of Wales, the heir to the British throne who was a regular visitor to the famous Madame Kelly and her establishment, *le Chabanais*. *La Fleur Blanche* in the *Rue des Moulins* was also well known for its aristocratic and famous clientele. Madame Fernier's houses might not have been quite so famous, but she owned more than thirty of them in the city generating a tidy income.

Of course, the problem was that while prostitution was legal and socially acceptable in general terms when it came down to individuals attitudes were very different, especially amongst men's own families and colleagues. A man of position and reputation in the community would not be thought well of if it were known that he frequented *maisons de tolerances*. Wives and mothers-in-law would have something to say about that. If the identities of many of the names he was copying out of madame's ledger were to be made public there would be some interesting domestic consequences.

Gant had a broad smile on the face that he put round the door almost as Drangnet started his perusal of the ledgers. He held out a piece of paper.

'I think you won that particular round, sir,'

The paper was an official letter from Chief Inspector Cordiez requesting an appointment with Drangnet.

'Well,' said the Chief Inspector. 'I have to say that I'm surprised. I wonder what he wants?'

Gant shrugged.

'He probably just wants to know what we found out from the autopsies and whether he can have the bodies.'

'Tough.' said Drangnet. 'They're definitely not his.'

Certainly his visitor would be on a fishing trip. Presumably he wanted the case to revert to a chase after some sexually crazed anarchists and, as such, he would get it back onto his own desk. However, the note was friendly enough without being informal.

'Write a nice polite reply, would you Roger? Have it hand delivered immediately. Take it round now, Tell the good Chief Inspector that he is welcome to call after lunch today. Say about 2 o'clock?'

Gant left and Drangnet returned to Madame's records. They made very interesting reading. A surprisingly large number of entries were familiar to him; some highly surprising. He tried to stop himself just reading through out of some vicarious pleasure. The most significant records, of course were those for the three dead girls on the nights in question. There seems to be a convention that none of the girls took a new client after eleven o'clock and of the three girls only the second had this last client of the day. The other two had had clients who were listed as departing well in advance of midnight. Drangnet recognised one of those in any case. Mme. Flandrette had had a late client too, but he was also recorded and identified as leaving around midnight.

His secretary brought in some coffee and he sat back in his chair. However interesting this was, entertaining even, it wasn't really getting him anywhere. It looked highly unlikely that any of the women were killed by their clients or, at least not their last one of the day which would have been logical. Either that or Madame Fernier's system of record keeping was not as fool proof as she thought. That just left the possibility of either another client sneaking back in unobserved to kill or a total stranger doing the same thing. Yet again Drangnet felt that he had made absolutely no progress at all. These were the options that he started out with.

So, it was at precisely 2 o'clock, that Sergeant Clement knocked in Drangnet's door. His voice just betrayed enough of an amused tone for Dragnet to realise that his invitation to his colleagues from the political department was common knowledge throughout the station.

'I have a Chief Inspector Cordiez downstairs, to see you, sir.'

'Thank you, sergeant. Please have him shown up immediately.'

Being a branch of the French army, the Paris gendarmerie generally wore military style uniforms commensurate with and very similar to the general army uniforms. The conventions for the criminal investigation divisions were slightly different and it was generally accepted that for every day work, civilian clothes were worn. For official and ceremonial occasions, however, they reverted to full military uniform. On this occasion, however, Cordiez was smartly attired in a dark suit, dark sac coat, white shirt and the new style of necktie. Drangnet was slightly less formal as he paired his dark trousers with a dark tweed cut away coat.

Drangnet rose from behind his desk and came forward to greet his guest with an outstretched hand and broad smile of welcome.

'Chief Inspector. Welcome to the *Quai d'Horlorge*.'

He gestured away from the formal pair of chairs that were placed directly in front on his desk to a pair of slightly more comfortable looking chairs arranged to either side of the small stone fireplace to one side.

'Do sit down. I've taken the liberty of organising some coffee for us. I hope that's suitable?'

Cordiez responded to this initial show of courtesy with and equally broad smile.

'Thank you, Chief Inspector. That would be very welcome.'

The coffee was brought and the two settled. Dragnet waited for his guest to start. It was, after all, he who had requested their meeting.

'Chief Inspector. I feel that we've got off on the wrong foot, so to speak. Perhaps we should have arranged to meet before now. But perhaps the first thing I should do is to offer you my sincere apologies for the behaviour of my Inspector recently. I gather he forgot himself and was extremely rude to you, his superior officer and a number of your colleagues. I apologise to you personally and I am quite prepared to do so on his behalf in public to your colleagues. It should never have happened, and the man will be severely disciplined.'

Drangnet was impressed. It was a handsome apology.

'Thank you, Chief Inspector. Of course, I accept your apology and let's think no more of it. It certainly isn't necessary for you to talk to my men, although I thank you for the offer. I wouldn't want them to get used to that sort of thing. Perhaps Inspector Tergia can do that for himself when he is returned to you.'

A slight grin crossed Cordiez's face.

'Yes, I am sure that being your guest here for a couple of nights will have given him more than enough of an opportunity to think on his behaviour. Your cells here have a certain reputation in the city and a long history of changing characters rather quickly, I believe. I am perfectly happy for you to release him as and when you think appropriate. I'll catch up with him later, no doubt.'

'Thank you. As it happens, I have arranged for him to be returned to you as we speak. I assume in spite of his, shall we say, overexuberance, his is an able officer and if you are as busy as we, then you have need of all your people. I hope he has learned a lesson. Time will tell.'

'I'll make sure that he has, Chief Inspector. You're right. He is an able officer but, as you found out, he can be somewhat hot headed at times. This is not the first time that his, er, impetuosity has led him into difficulties. He is, however, loyal, hardworking and very persistent. But he does lack subtlety, I will admit.'

Drangnet couldn't resist the chance.

'That must be a difficulty sometimes in matters political. Such dealing as I have from time to time with our political masters shows that a light touch is often necessary - essential, even.'

'Yes. Inspector Tergia tends to take a sledgehammer to crack a walnut occasionally but with political matters, as you put it, we do occasionally come upon some exceedingly hard nuts.'

Dragnet just nodded. All this was not the only reason that the man had come to see him and sure enough the main topic was broached next.

'So, may I ask what conclusion you have drawn from your examination of the last two bodies that were found near the *Île St. Louis*? It seems that we might have a common interest there.'

This was a part of the conversation that Drangnet had prepared carefully.

'I've asked for a full report to prepared for you, including Dr. Dankovich's autopsy reports and it should be ready to hand over by the time we finish our meeting today. But essentially the two men we saw were both strangled to death. We don't know when and we're not sure where they were dropped in the Seine, other than it would be somewhere upstream from the western end of the *Île*. We don't know the time of death except that they didn't seem to have been in the water very long. We estimate no more than a couple of hours each. They were strangled by a length of thin cord and seemed to have no other injuries. We don't know who they were as they were both completely naked and had no personal possessions on them. They were both white men in their early thirties, of European appearance, in good health. One had had his appendix removed and the other showed signs of a mended break in his right arm. They were unremarkable in every way. It's all a bit of a mystery.'

'And the connection with these prostitute murders you are dealing with?'

Drangnet sighed as he continued to observe his guest closely.

'I am aware that these deaths might seem to coincide with the deaths of three prostitutes in the town. But at the moment we can find no evidence that it is any more than just that - a coincidence.'

Cordiez shifted very slightly in his seat, a movement that Drangnet noticed with interest.

'Were there any distinguishing features on the bodies; scars, physical deformities of any sort?'

This was obviously a crucial question and Drangnet had thought long and hard about how he would answer it. If the symbol they found was a masonic one then admitting to finding it might open the possibility of Cordiez claiming some sort of interest, especially if Cordiez was a freemason and could claim some specialist knowledge. He had yet to hear the answers to his questions on the subject from Ferry. Drangnet put on his best poker face while he shook his head.

'No. In fact, you could say that the most unusual thing about the two bodies we examined was their lack of unusual features. They were young men in excellent health. Nothing that stands out. Nothing to identify them at all.'

For a moment there was a slight shadow that crossed briefly across Cordiez's face. It was fleeting but it was enough for Drangnet to notice. He carried on, refusing to give up on the topic.

'And did you find anything at all during your examination of the first body, Chief Inspector Cordiez?'

'No. Like you we found nothing. Although I must admit that perhaps our examination was less than thorough. We are a relatively new department as you know, and we don't yet have all the facilities in place that perhaps we should.'

'Ah,' replied Drangnet softly without making further comment. There was a slightly uncomfortable silence before he spoke again.

'Chief Inspector. I wouldn't dream of telling you how to do your job, of course. I am very happy indeed to stay as far away from the world of politics and political crime as I can. I have no feel for it and, to be frank, no interest in it. I have quite enough on my plate as it is. But I have been a policeman here in Paris for a long time and have bumped into politicians from time to time. These have not always been felicitous meetings. But I have a little experience of the consequences of the events of the Commune and the political manoeuvring that both proceeded and followed it. I have also come across the growing phenomenon of anarchism in our society, at least on the street where I can actually see it and I'll be frank with you. I can't see any connection between the deaths of these three young men and the anarchist movement just as I cannot see any evidence to link them with the deaths of my three prostitutes. It may well be that you have information that I lack, of course, but that is, at present, my opinion.'

'Yet,' persisted Cordiez, 'you have to admit that there could be a connection between the deaths of the prostitutes and these three men. The coincidence is very strong.'

'On the face of it, perhaps. But only in the timing of the crimes. We have no evidence that these men were anywhere near these brothels on the nights in question. We have no witness statements from local residents or from people in the street. In addition, there are simply too many unanswered questions. You have to ask yourself why three anarchists would even want to kill prostitutes. I have a certain familiarity of what these people believe in and I can't see any justification for killing prostitutes in the writings of men like Proudhon or the speeches of Kropotkin. It simply doesn't make sense. Then there is the difficulty of connecting the murders. How were these three killers identified by their own prospective killers in the first place. The women were murdered in three separate *maisons de tolerance*. Who actually killed the men? The method of strangulation was indeed the same in each case, so it is possible to assume a connection there but what it that connection? Are we to assume that because the method was the same, the men were killed by the same individual? In any case are easier ways of killing people than by garrotting them. Garrotting is a highly specialised art especially if the intended victims are fit young men in their prime as seems to be the case here. Is it symbolic in some way and, if so, what is the symbolism and to whom is any message intended? There is also the question of whether the three prostitute murders are themselves connected at all. We have to consider the possibility at least that they are not. There could be an element of copycat in all this. There is also the more general point that there are four or five suspicious deaths in Paris every week and coincidences do happen.'

Again, there was a pause as both men got lost in their own very different thoughts. They also both realised that there was little more to talk about. The situation was rescued by Gant knocking at the door and bringing in the copy of the report to give to Cordiez. This having been passed on, both men rose.

Cordiez was polite as he made to leave.

'Thank you for seeing me, Chief Inspector. I was pleased to meet you and to clear the air a bit. I wish you luck with this investigation, of course. If there is anything we can do to help, please do not hesitate to ask.'

Drangnet was equally polite.

'Thank you for coming, Chief Inspector. I will certainly keep you informed of developments should they take a political turn. I trust that by now, your inspector has made his way back your office and is a slightly wiser man for his experience.'

Gant escorted their guest to the door where he was passed to a constable to be escorted the rest of the way out of the building. Gent returned with an envelope which he passed to Drangnet without a word. It contained two photographs.

He was not unacquainted with Paris' new passion for photography and, indeed, he had been one of the first to press for its wider adoption by the police as a way of documenting crime scenes and as an aid for the rapidly developing science of police forensic science. They had been recording pictures of suspects and arrested prisoners for some time. Photographs had yet to appear in newspapers and broadsheets, of course. Illustrations there were still often highly fanciful representation of current events by artists who took considerable liberties with the reality of what they were trying to portray. Here, however, were two more photos of the tattoos found on the two bodies. They were of higher quality than the previous one. They had been considerably enlarged and showed a remarkable amount of detail. He bent over the pictures intently for a long time before sitting back slowly and looking across his desk at his deputy.

Gant drew his chair up to the desk until he was directly opposite his boss. He slid one of the photographs towards himself and turned it around as it moved. Like Drangnet he bent low over it to examine it closely.

'These two aren't precisely the same. But given that no two tattoos are identical anyway, it certainly looks like some form of identity badge. This bloody case gets weirder and weirder.' he muttered after a pause.

'Hum,' replied Drangnet contemplatively. 'On the face of it it does seem to be rather odd. No doubt it'll make sense once we've cracked it. In the meantime, what did you think of our visitor?'

Gant leant back slightly from the desk.

'He was fishing, boss.'

Drangnet nodded.

'Certainly, but what was he fishing for? Other than the rubbish about his inspector, he didn't seem to contribute to proceedings much.'

'He was interested in what we found on the bodies. He didn't seem to be very happy that you said you had found no marks or distinguishing features.'

'He was indeed. It was almost as if he was expecting a different answer. Odd that.'

There was long pause while they both stared at the photographs. Drangnet was conscious of the picture almost going in and out of focus as his attention passed from what he was seeing to what it all might mean. Finally, he pulled himself together.

'OK. For the moment, let's forget what this damn thing means and concentrate on our visitor. He came to find out whether we found any markings on the body. Either he found some on bodies on the first body or he didn't. If he found nothing that might have been because there wasn't anything or there were and his forensic people were incompetent. If he found nothing, then he shouldn't have been surprised when we said we didn't either on the next two. If he did find something, then he knew that I might be lying, and he has to come up with a possible reason for that. Or I was telling the truth and there really wasn't anything. If there was a tattoo on the first body that he is not telling us about, the other question to be asked before we go further into this is why he was so interested in the matter in the first place. If he found nothing there would have been nothing to be interested in and the question wouldn't have arisen in the first place. As I denied finding anything then he had to figure out why I might have lied, if that is what I was doing. Is it just to keep him out of the investigation or do I have an ulterior motive? Does he know about the tattoo and perhaps he thinks I know what it means? Does he?'

Gant frowned before replying and not for the first time did Drangnet realise that his rather portly and urbane deputy contained hidden intellectual depths.

'Another set of circumstances arises if Cordiez not only knows about the tattoos but also knows what they mean.'

It was, of course, an obvious conclusion as Dragnet readily acknowledged.

'That, my dear friend, would mean that our friend Cordiez is part of whatever is going on.'

'Now that would indeed be interesting. But actually boss, come to think of it, however strange that seems, it would certainly explain why he came up with this ridiculous idea of the anarchists being responsible for killing prostitutes. Maybe it really is a cover up of some sort. Whatever is going on it's not anarchists. But if the three deaths are connected it can't be personal. So, it must be some weird sort of conspiracy. Maybe it's somebody who just doesn't like women.'

'This is all a bit of a guess, Roger. We still have to find some evidence. Let's stick to the facts we have. We have three dead women and three dead men. We are assuming that the men died at the hands of persons currently unknown the connection is that it is some sort of retribution. A message is being sent out. That, my friend, is the sum total of the facts we have, and it is precisely the same small list of facts that we started with. All we really seem to have achieved is a slightly bigger list of guesses. These are that it is about killing women and there is some sort of a group, a secret society, possible masons, that might be doing it – note I said might – and they may have this tattoo as their badge of membership. We can also guess that the men who were killed were the bottom of the chain of command. There are others above, one of whom might be Cordiez judging by his interest today. This group might have masonic connections, but that assumption is based only on the badge which only might be a masonic symbol. But we don't really know any of this. It could all be garbage.'

Gant had listened in silence.

'Cordiez.' he said. 'That's where we must start. One of us should investigate him and the other should concentrate on this damn symbol.

Chapter 10: Sunday 10th April   Scene 3: The Quarter Finals

They were having a successful run. This evening's match was the quarterfinal and they were not being troubled by their opponents. Although the club was one of the few that boasted two courts instead of the usual one it still took a certain amount of time to play a full tournament. But the annual Club doubles was the most prestigious competition and there was always a large entry for it. The time required to play all the matches was also affected by the fact that only one court could be used in order to keep the playing members who weren't in the doubles competition happy as they too required to be able to play their games. Playing time for the early rounds also tended to be limited to the evenings or, at least, late afternoons as the players were amateurs and had their livings to earn during the day.

The match was duly won without a great deal of trouble. Their opponents were perfectly competent. Indeed, taken as individual players they were at least as good as Drangnet and Ferry. But they were a pair that had formed especially for the tournament. *Jeu de Paume* is a game of tactics and the doubles game especially so. In addition those employed in doubles play are very different to those for singles and they take a long time to develop properly. Drangnet and Ferry had been playing together since well before the German war and by now they knew everything they needed to beat most opponents. That is why they were firm favourites to retain the title. Tonight they had a straightforward three set win without any great effort and alarms.

The traditional sporting handshakes were exchanged across the net and both teams saluted the *sous-maître* who had been marking the game and after acknowledging the generous applause of the watching crowd, the players retired for their showers. As they walked to the changing room, Drangnet leaned close to his partner's ear.

'Jules. I wouldn't mind have a word in private with you fairly soon if you have a moment.'

Other than their tennis, their social and professional lives kept them apart these days, much more that they would have liked. Unlike Drangnet, Ferry was married, and he and his wife had a full range of official responsibilities. It was difficult to get together, especially as Ferry's current eminence tended to prevent him having professional contacts with the policeman. However, he also knew that Dragnet wouldn't have mentioned it had it not been important. In any case, the club changing room was not the place for a confidential chat today as it was somewhat overcrowded with all the comings and goings of an active doubles tournament. So just before they went into the little room, Ferry laid a hand on Dragnet's arm.

'Why don't you come for supper tonight, Louis? I had planned a rare quiet evening at home given the fact that we were playing this match. There will be Eugénie there of course and her sister who is staying for a few days. But no one else. I'm sure that my dear wife would be delighted to see you. She was only saying the other day that it has been too long since we last saw you. In any case as you know she's been trying to get you and her sister together for years.'

Dragnet smiled. It was true that this particular piece of attempted matchmaking had been going on for some time. He actually enjoyed the woman's company and had escorted her to a number of operas and theatre performances. That was, however, as far as either of the wanted to go, much to Ferry's wife's frustration.

'Why thank you, Jules. I'd be delighted.'

'About eight?'

It had been a quiet and relaxed meal. Rather than Ferry's official residence, they were at his elegant but secluded private house in the Rue Bayard and, as his host had promised, there were only four around the table. Ferry's wife, Eugénie and her twin sister Fabienne were both attractive, intelligent women with well-expressed views of their own. Drangnet knew that Eugénie had been trying to get her sister and him together for a long time but although they got on perfectly well there was little attraction beyond that. The conversation was resolutely unpolitical. They covered the recent game and their prospects for the semi-finals and possible finals that were to be held over the coming days; the final being on the following Sunday. After that, the talk was generally about the cultural life of Paris. Ferry's duties included attendance at many plays and concerts, so they were well-versed in the newest events. Fabienne worked with the newly established publishing house of Ernest Flammarion so the conversation also centred around the young writers like Émile Zola and Guy de Maupassant who the new publisher had taken on. It was, however, not late when the ladies excused themselves and left to go to an early bed. Ferry also got up.

'Let's go into my study, Louis. It'll be more comfortable to talk there than with just the two of us on either side of an empty dining table.'

The study as a small, intimate place, book-lined with a few pictures on the walls. The curtains were drawn, and a fire burned cheerfully in the grate against the still cool spring evening. Drangnet settled into one of the leather armchairs that stood on either side while his host poured two generous glasses of cognac.

'Now old friend. What's this mystery that you want to talk about?'

For a moment, Drangnet who hadn't done much preparation for this meeting, hesitated.

'Well. I'm not sure if it is something you really want to talk about, Jules.'

Ferry laughed.

'It's not like you to be so reluctant, Louis. Perhaps you better just dive in and leave it to me to tell you if you're crossing any boundaries.'

'I want to talk about the Freemasons, Jules.'

Immediately the man stiffened slightly. The whole topic of masonic lodges in France could be a difficult one. They were mistrusted by those who weren't members and held in secret by those who were.

'Well,' said the great man. You know that I'm a mason. I have been for some time. That's public knowledge. I've never tried to hide it or deny it.'

Dragnet agreed.

'Yes, I know that. You're a member of *La Clémante amiliée* lodge here in Paris. No, I was wondering if I could ask you some questions about masonry in general? Not being one, I know very little about it.'

'You have an enquiry where this has come up, have you?'

'Yes. Well, yes, I think so. I can't be sure but there seems to be some sort of connection.'

'Is this to do with the prostitute murders, Louis? I wanted to ask how all that was going.'

'Yes, it is.'

'Then ask your questions. I'll answer them as best I can. But you have to understand that there may be some that I can't answer.'

Dragnet paused for a moment to collect his thoughts. He was a very long way from linking these murders directly with masonry. All he had to go on were two dead men who has the same tattoo on their bodies. It wasn't even certain that the symbol had anything to do with the masons. So he started off with some basic information.

'About how many masons are there is France at the present time?'

Ferry shrugged.

'About twenty thousand, I believe. Somewhere around there, anyhow.'

'And in Paris?'

'Six or seven, probably. But that's a guess.'

'Divided between how many lodges?'

'Between thirty and thirty-five, I think. Come on Louis. What's this all about? It's not like you to beat about the bush. Tell me what you're really after.'

In a way he was right. Dragnet could spend a long-time asking background questions and with a different audience he might have done just that. But this was one of the important men in the land and, irrespective of any personal friendship, he had limited time. So Drangnet reached into his inside pocket and extracted a photograph of the tattoo. Without saying anything he passed it across to his host and sat back, looking very intently to see if there was the remotest sign of recognition. Whether it was a pretence, he couldn't tell. Ferry was a relatively unemotional man who kept his emotions firmly under control. But all he could see was an expression of mild interest change quickly to a slight frown.

'Ah. I understand you questions about freemasons now. Well, taking this little picture bit by bit, it is true that the pair of dividers is a common masonic symbol – probably the best known if not actually the most common. But it is also used in plenty of other places as well, not least in school textbooks on geometry. As far as I can remember dividers are also used in art to symbolise God, as architect of the Universe, Uranis who is, as you know, the Muse of Astronomy, and of Astronomy and Geometry personified, Astronomy in the Quadrivium of the Seven Liberal Arts, as well as two of the Cardinal Virtues, Justice and Prudence, I think. Also, one of the Four Temperaments, Melancholy as well as one of the Four Ages of Man; Maturity. I think there are uses for it in eastern art as well.'

Drangnet was impressed. He knew all this but only after considerable research. Ferry seemed very well versed in this sort of symbolism. So he pressed on.

'And the Pyramid?'

Ferry looked slightly more little perplexed at this.

'Well, it certainly true that a pyramid does appear on some masonic documents and bit of regalia, but it actually has no specific relevance to any ritual. It may refer to the building of Solomon's temple. Sometimes an eye is shown as well, the all-seeing eye of God which is meant to be a reminder that humanity's thoughts and deeds are always observed by God who sometimes is referred to in Masonry as the Great Architect of the Universe. This eye is sometimes surrounded by a triangle but not necessarily by a pyramid.'

He got up and fetched a magnifying glass from his reading desk.

'Actually, this doesn't look like an eye at all. It looks more like an empty circle with something sticking out of the top.'

Dragnet moved on.

'And the number?'

Ferry frowned.

'Ah there you have me stumped. For, while I knew something about dividers and pyramids in a masonic context, two hundred and thirteen isn't a number that I can recall as having any significance at all. It's certainly not a number that occurs in masonic ritual or regulation. As far as I know there is no lodge numbered 213 either.'

Now it was Drangnet's turn to frown.

'Don't you masons have some sort of membership number?'

There was a pause while his host thought about his answer.

'Not really, no. Well it's true that each lodge has a number and one can look this up. Each lodge also keeps a register of its members and these do have a number associated with them. It is a sort of accession number and is simply represents the order in which members were admitted to the lodge. But before you get excited you should know that each lodge keeps its own register which is independent of all the others. So as long as a lodge has been around for long enough to have two hundred and thirteen members then they will have obviously a number 213. This number would never be never used in ceremonies or on formal occasions nor are they ever really referred to. I doubt whether most masons know what their register number is. It's probably just written down in a ledger of some sort. I can't see it being particularly important.'

'It was certainly important enough for these two men to have it tattooed on their arms.'

'I'm not sure that you've actually established that all this has anything to do with freemasonry in the first place, Louis.'

Drangnet had to admit that this was perfectly right.

'What about the first victim?' asked Ferry.

Dragnet looked sharply across at his companion.

'I'm not sure in the description of these men as victims is entirely appropriate give that they were probably murderers before they became victims, as you put it,' he growled.

'Again, Louis, you're making assumptions here for which you have no evidence as far as I can see. Unless you know more that you are admitting to me.'

Drangnet was reminded that he was talking with

Ferry just lifted his hand slightly and let it fall in mild apology as the policeman went on.

'I have no idea whether the first man had a tattoo. The body seems either to have vanished or we have reached the extent of the accommodation to the Interior Minister's instructions. Your precious political police are not particularly co-operative, as usual.'

Ferry smiled weakly. He wasn't about to get into this debate for the umpteenth time.

'All right, Louis. I can see what you're getting at and, to be honest, I can find no way to disagree with you. The symbol certainly looks like some sort of masonic one and obviously we have to find if there is a significance to this number that I don't know about. I'll do some checking for you, of course. Whatever the traditions of secrecy that exist within the brotherhood, they certainly don't amount to covering up murder, you can rely on that. I'll find out what I can.'

Dragnet smiled at his friend.

'Thank you, Jules. You can certainly ask in places that I can't. *Jeu de Paume* is the only brotherhood to which I aspire.'

Ferry also smiled broadly.

'Yes, indeed. I tend to think you're right. I certainly thought we played rather well today. Your defence of the galleries was exemplary and your interception volleys to the base of the tambour completely flummoxed them.'

'Well, your defence of the back of the court was also very effective. They were unable to set decent chase the whole game. I noticed that Biboche gave us a surreptitious clap of his old hands as we came off court. I think he enjoyed a win for the oldies over the others of tomorrow. I have hopes that we might go all the way again this time.'

Ferry looked pensively at the magnificent old silver trophy standing in pride of place in the centre of the ornate pate grey marble mantel piece above the fire.

'Yes, my old friend. That beautiful old silver trophy would look well up there for another year, I think.'

He put a few more logs on the fire and refilled their glasses before sitting down.

'Louis. There is one thing I should say to you. I have no idea whether this business has anything at all to do with masons, but you ought to take a little care.'

'Oh why?' he said with an effort to look innocent.

'Because, you idiot, there are a lot of powerful people around who won't take kindly to having you poke around in their masonic lives. Many people take these things much more seriously than I do.'

'And, Sir, who might these worthy and completely innocent people be, may I ask?'

Ferry frowned as if at a recalcitrant student.

'You know perfectly well. Apart from me, your current Prefect of Police, Louis Andrieux is one as is our current President, Jules Grévy. They are all freemasons. That you probably know. What you might not know is the more than 30 percent of the senior members of your own department are members and probably the head of the Political Police Cordiez is as well.'

Dragnet just nodded as his friend continued.

'These are all people who could make life difficult for you. Some of them regard the masonic oaths as sacrosanct, including the stupid ones about giving preference in life to fellow masons instead of non-masons. For these men, freemasonry is an indication of superiority and solidarity. Many have joined the brotherhood because they think that it is a way for personal advancement as masons have to swear that they will always favour their colleagues. Many regard it as an exclusive and privileged men's club. In many cases they are right. You will find a much higher proportion of freemasons in, for instance, the higher ranks of ministers and senior civil servants that would be suggested by the law of averages. So if you have to ask questions of these people, I advise that you do so with care and restraint.'

Dragnet was silent for a while as he digested what had been said. After a while, he stirred:

'Dancart and my man Gant?'

Ferry shook his head.

'Not as far as I know but I'll find out.'

'Can you do that? Without arousing suspicion or something.'

'Oh yes.'

'How?'

'Because I am a Deputy Grand Master I can find anything I want to about my fellow masons.'

Again, there was a long silence before Dragnet utter a single word.

'Christ.'

'Quite,' said his host with a broad smile on his face. 'There is one thing you should know, however, Louis. Most people assume that

Freemasonry is a single entity, certainly within each country. It isn't. There are a number of different groupings that have quite different traditions and rules. The biggest group is called the Grand Orient of France. but over the years there have been many schisms and splinter groups formed. Indeed, the most recent was caused only four years ago when we decided that we should abolish the requirement for members to believe in the existence of God and the immortality of the soul. Relations between the various groups vary and some of the smaller and more conservative ones are highly secretive and resistant to outside interference even from other masons. I'm telling you this because for all my seniority in the Brotherhood, even I might not be able to find out what you want.'

It was getting late, but Ferry sensed that his friend's questions weren't completely over. So again, it was a while before the policeman collected his thoughts; a gap filled by Ferry again refilling their glasses. Dragnet gave his host that characteristic little gesture of slightly raising his glass against the neck of the inclined bottle to signify that he just wanted a short measure this time.

'Jules. More than anything I want to know what these numbers mean. At least two of the three dead men had them tattooed and maybe the third did and it is obvious therefore that they mean something to them at least. It links them together and, assuming that these three are actually the murderers of the prostitutes, it seems to me to be the key to solving this mystery. Maybe this is no masonic thing at all but if it is, then I want to know about it.'

'Of course, my friend. I'll try to help. But what about the person or persons who killed these three. What about them? Have you any idea who did that?'

Dragnet gave his doubles partner a very long hard look before finally replying. Theirs was long and deep friendship. It was a friendship that has survived wars and the Commune and the ups and downs of life after that as they both had worked hard on rebuilding the Paris that they both loved so much. The years after *le semain sanglant* had left deep scars and it was only now, some ten years on, that, their efforts were beginning to bear fruit. The new Paris was a fragile beast and made up of a cacophony of different things, many of which made for difficult and sometimes inappropriate bedfellows. These two men were partners on a tennis court and friends over life and they thought the same about the city over which they had charge. However, Drangnet knew that even the deepest and most trusted friendships sometimes have their limits.

'Yes, I know who did that, Jules. It's not an investigation that I intend to pursue much further although I would never tell that to anyone else. As far as I am concerned whoever killed these men has done us a service. That is my choice and my decision.'

Ferry just nodded slowly. He understood even if he didn't know the facts. That was his skill as a politician. More importantly, it was also his skill as a friend.

Chapter 11 Monday 11th April   Scene 1 Others walk in Luxembourg Gardens

Émile Sandrat was not a man to lose his temper very often. Nor did he usually let problems or difficulties, however great, affect him. He prided himself on his self-control and his refusal to get exercised over much, at least visibly. His was almost invariably the voice of calm, if not actually reason, in most of the regular weekly meetings of the senior members of the governing body of the *Paris Préfecture*. His superior, the Prefect, was a political appointment; all too susceptible to the political whims of his masters. There had been an average of one such appointment each year for the last ten years with, apparently, yet another coming up imminently. He, however, had been in place throughout that time because, as Deputy Prefect, he was a long-serving bureaucrat; a civil servant, whose job it was to translate the variety of whims and fantasies of the next incoming Prefect into actual policies and instructions that the actual police under his command could carry out. The new political police group had been his idea. He had to pick his Prefect carefully as some of them were not completely in favour. But he found one whose political ambitions outweighed his wish to improve the everyday policing of the city and had been given virtually carte blanche to set it all up.

He sat in the morning sunshine in the *Jardin de Luxembourg* waiting for his colleague to arrive for their meeting. He looked around him with some satisfaction. The garden had been created some two hundred years before by Marie de Medici and had twice been reduced in size by the avarice of property developers, firstly a hundred years ago and secondly just twenty years before but the place was still a magnificent example of French garden design. It was his favourite place to walk in Paris as he contemplated his achievements to date and planned the future.

Now, some three years after his appointment as Deputy Prefect, he had created what he wanted all along; a small, secret private force that answered to him alone. He had taken personal control of who was appointed to the squad and what sort of people they were. Most importantly he had managed to create a group that had almost no connection with other police departments and therefore operated in almost complete secrecy. He had created strong connections with the politicians that controlled his budget too. He had access to almost unlimited funds.

The department he created wasn't particularly big; not more than fifty or so strong but they comprised a wide range of skills. He had brought in a group from the old military intelligence service that they had used during the days of the Commune. These were men who knew the secrets of the city's underworld and where to find information. Most importantly, the citizens knew them too, and they were feared. He had a small group of officers and planners, with Cordiez at their head. And he also had a force of soldiers who operated out of uniform and very much beyond the law when they had to be.

All this was secret. It was a police force within the police force. Free from supervision and fully at the behest of its political masters. Loyalty was assured by money. They were paid very well; much more than usual. Sandrat had the budget for that. Objectives were set, plans made, operations carried out seemingly without any independent oversight or control, which is exactly as Sandrat wanted it. He had strong support high in the political establishment and while he retained that he was his own man.

In a sense, France had always had its secret police, dating back to the revolution and then to the notorious Joseph Fouche and his highly competent network of spies, informers and enforcers that served Napoleon so well. His nephew Louis-Napoleon had used his political police to great affect during his Coup d'état in 1851. The tradition had continued throughout the Second Empire, through the Commune and after as France rebuilt itself. In a sense the whole of the Paris operated like a secret police force, having to rely to a very large extent on agents, spies, and informers to gain enough intelligence to operate effectively at all. But the embryonic Third Republic that followed Commune had started the long business of organising the police into a much more structured service, administered and directed in an orderly and correct manner. Men like Drangnet and his immediate boss Dancart had seen what had gone before and even been part of it. They knew enough to avoid the pitfalls.

But even as the force had taken shape and had started to gain a modicum of public respect, the need of a secret police had grown again, and the political section had been born. Most people just thought it was a necessary. This was Sandrat's kingdom and he had set about taking on the investigation of all matters that affected the state itself rather than the people of France. French society was still shaken from time to time by the actions of subversive elements; anarchists, revolutionaries, foreign spies, obscure and occultist groups and the political police established a strong and unassailable place in the administration of justice. The general population was well used to being spied on and never had the police in the first place. The new force had gained ground without opposition except, perhaps, only from people like Drangnet from time to time who sought something new and fairer; something to suit the new republic. But beyond the political police itself, or rather, perhaps, inside it, there was another layer; and that was very small and very secret indeed.

Sandrat had two great passions in life: the exercise of power and the Brotherhood of Freemasons. All his life he had been a devoted member of that most conservative of lodges, *L'Ordre Fidelité*. There he found his friends; people with whom he had most in common; people who shared his passion for secrecy and personal, male, friendship. The lodge had long set itself against the reforms that were beginning to sweep through French society since the monarchy had been abolished; reforms that were beginning to infect the Brotherhood. Everything that he believed in; loyalty to God and the Church, to the Monarchy; all the traditional values to which he believed France owned its greatness, were being questioned by this new obsession with republicanism and a secular society. He believed passionately in the right of a few to govern the many. The elite who had passed through the French system of *Grandes Écoles* and had demonstrated their abilities to take decisions and to shape the institutions that were essential to govern France. These men alone mattered. The rest were nothing. Worker bees only fit to labour in the hive of life. Destined to serve and to be ignored. Above all he hated these women who now wanted powers and responsibilities that they were so clearly unsuited to. Women had their role, of course; to produce and raise children, to keep their husbands' homes well managed and provide their husbands with entertainment. But they had no place at all with the elite. Now, God forbid, the Grand Lodges were suggesting that they should be allowed to become freemasons. It made his feel physically sick to think about it.

He'd made sure that the lodge of which he had been a senior member for fifteen years admitted only those who thought like him and would never entertain these modernist thoughts. There, at their monthly meetings, he felt safe surrounded by like-minded men of principal and courage who would never bow to these new ideas. There he was surrounded also by fellow masons who knew how to keep secrets. They knew, like him, the correct role of women in society. They were there to serve men and only that. A woman had been the originator of the Original Sin. She had brought Adam into depravity. Without her, man could have continued to live in Paradise for ever. Woman's role was to continue to be punished for this for all eternity; to serve and never to rule. To be useful and once that had ceased for any reason, to be discarded like the evil rubbish they were. It was from within his own small community of *L'Ordre Fidelité* that he had quietly created his own conspiracy. He knew full well that he had limited power but within that which he had he could at least do something.

He had picked his co-conspirators carefully. His three senior colleagues were members of the Senate. They were like-minded men and fellow masons, but they were members of different lodges. His own *L'Ordre Fidelité* was too small to escape attention if these important men had joined it. They had other, more prestigious lodges of their own. But these men were his supporters and the basis of his power and security. The man Cordiez whom he had chosen to lead the political police was equally suitable as his opinion about women very much coincided with his own. He was not one of them, of course. He was very much below true officer class, but he was highly ambitious and not above getting his hands dirty. He had had some difficulty in the beginning with other police departments over the autonomy give to his creation but now there was a general, if grudging, acceptance that the political department's remit was one that few of the already overworked sections really coveted. In any case, political areas such as the observation of foreign spies, anarchists and other political agitators and troublemakers was very close to every politician's heart and that in itself gave him the power he needed. He had certainly been able to keep most of their activities and all of their budget well away from interfering scrutiny especially that of the other departments and the *Préfecture*.

Today he had been called by one of these colleagues to discuss the progress of their campaign. He had always expected some difficulties, of course, but he hadn't expected what had happened. He had assumed that by putting it about that these were killings by foreign anarchists that Cordiez could have kept the investigation to himself and thus scrutiny to a minimum. But this had proved not to be the case and now his partners wanted to see whether Cordiez had got things under control. He was about to be asked some awkward questions by his colleagues. He looked up to see one of them approaching.

All through the great Jardin de Luxembourg there were signs of spring. Trees were greening up and the carefully tended flowerbeds were beginning to show their colours. As with many of the gardens and open spaces throughout the city, the parc was alive with people, women pushing children in perambulators, couples wandering arm in arm. A small army of gardeners went about their business. The two well-dressed men walking together deep in conversation would not have looked even slightly out of place. The *Palais de Luxembourg* was the seat of the Senate of the French Government and the gardens often saw a fair smattering of senators and their acolytes taking their ease; discussing matters of state or just enjoying the sun. They were mostly wearing business suits, hats and walking canes and ambled slowly appearing to be oblivious to whatever was going on around them. Only a close observer of these two would have noted that the conversation was animated at times with the younger of the two gesticulating regularly to make some point or another.

'Well? What's going on? How come this man Drangnet is interfering in this whole thing?' Comte André de St Germande was insistent.

Sandrat shrugged slightly in reply. His companion was highly agitated; so much so that he looked quickly around him as they were walking along the path in the garden. The last thing he wanted was anyone to become too interested in them or, God forbid, overhear them. Neither of them was exactly unknown to the public. The man continued.

'Come on. Are you or are you not in charge of this enquiry?'

Sandrat sighed. More than once he had explained that it wasn't as straightforward as all that. In a way it was the Prefect's fault. He had reacted to the public pressure to curb the petty street crime that had been on the increase since the end of the Commune and given the police more independence from the overall control of the public prosecutor and his tame police. Now it was not unusual for the *Sûreté* to do most of the investigation themselves and only hand the case over to the prosecutor's office when it was virtually complete. His plan to portray the killings as anarchist crimes and thus to win jurisdiction over it had failed. How he had to take a back-seat while Drangnet ran the case. But he sought at least to reassure his young colleague.

'As far as I can see, my friend, Drangnet isn't actually getting very far. He doesn't seem to know who killed the women and equally his investigation into the murder of our people seems to be going nowhere. But I'm not too directly involved, as I said.'

'Well bloody well get involved and soon. I want to know what's going on.'

Sandrat just thought to himself that getting more involved now might raise some unwelcome questions. He was conscious that his actions could be scrutinised closely. He had to be careful.

Their course through the garden had taken them away from the Palais through the formal garden to the south. There were more and more people taking advantage of the spring day and they found themselves increasingly interrupting their own conversation for fear that it might be overheard. Sandrat steered them off to the west along a narrower path where they found a bench. It was easier to keep track of who was around them. He turned to his companion sounding rather defensive.

'Look, if anything significant happens, I'll certainly be informed but I can't now simply barge into the investigation and take over. Apart from the fact that both Drangnet and Dancart would get very unhappy and therefore suspicious, it simply wouldn't do any good. Yes, I know, I have the power to interview witnesses; to do what I want, but I'm also trying to avoid making too much of a fuss about Drangnet's business when I haven't on many previous occasions. You'll just have to be patient.'

His colleague just grunted angrily. The pressure was getting to him. Sandrat laid a hand on his arm.

'My brother, remember our purpose. It is a divine and moral one. These policemen and their investigation are minor against the task we have set ourselves. We must succeed and set an example. Then other men will follow in time. If that means that life is less safe for us personally then so be it. We all knew the risks that we would run.'

The man was obviously less than convinced.

'Madame Guillotine awaits if we make a mistake, my friend,' came the mumbled reply.

'In which case, my brother, we will each die a martyr's death and there is no nobler way than that.'

They walked on in silence. It was true and they both shared the conviction. They were all doing what had to be done. It was God's work. Sandrat felt that perhaps that man had been reassured a little by the lack of success with the investigation, a progress that might have reassured him that it was headed in the right direction – away from them. He was however, troubled by the fact that their three messengers had been so quickly eliminated. It was something that no-one had foreseen.

'I think perhaps we should change our plan a little. For some reason, the whorehouses we targeted seem to have some system for tracing the people who use them. I have no idea how they do this but all three of our people have ended up in the Seine in very short order. I think we should now change and target the unregistered *maisons* for a while. We feel that there will be less pressure on our members who do our work for us. I feel that our colleagues might have been identified because some of the men who visit these registered *maisons* are often well-known and therefore are important. What we must remember that while it would be good to think that our brothers who are carrying out our instructions are as dedicated to the cause as we are, they also might not be. We agreed that they should receive payments and already there are some who are demanding more for future assignments as the job is clearly not as straightforward as we thought. If we change to the less reputable *maisons*, we will still be carrying on our mission, but the subsequent investigation will certainly be less. No-one cares about these women.'

His companion remained silent for a while. He didn't agree with this at all. Whatever the dangers, a part of their mission had been justified by the fact that it was all in the public eye. People would know what they were doing, and, in time, they would come to know why and understand. Somehow to head for the less fashionable or less salubrious parts of Paris was less noble, less principled. He felt the opposite. He felt they should transfer their attention in the other direction, to the granddames of the profession. The women at the very top of their so-called profession. He'd argued before that these were the right targets. They were the ones who lauded their sexuality over men. They had the big houses on the fashionable boulevards in the city centre. They were supported by rich men, many of whom had families; wives and children whose lives were belittled by their masters' obsession with these evil women. They had turned their faces away from their duty as men and fallen all too easily into the depravity that these women offered.

'I don't like it, Émile although I can see why you're suggesting it. However, this is something that all the founding brothers should discuss not just you and I. It is more that a small adjustment. It affects our very *raison d'être*. My lodge meets tomorrow tonight. Perhaps you would like to be my guest? We could meet after without raising much attention. I've already invited Phélypeaux and de la Trémoille. We are initiating some new people so there is a good reason for us to entertain guests.'

Sandrat was delighted. His companion belonged to one of the oldest and most prestigious ledges in Paris and one of the richest too. They were well known for their hospitality.

The two men parted and went their separate ways back into the centre of the city. Sandrat knew it was time to move on. Perhaps the change of target would throw Drangnet off the scent. He had less influence around the periphery of the city.

Chapter 11: Monday 11th April   Scene 2: Lunch in Montmartre

The morning meeting with his men was over and Drangnet made his way back to his office. There was the usual small pile of correspondence sitting on his desk. It had taken him a long time to persuade Gant to fillet the day's post. In the beginning, the man had been very reluctant to make any decisions about it at all. He merely saw his role as just opening each envelope, extracting the contents and adding them to the pile of work to be transferred to Drangnet's desk. The envelope was also preserved and took it place in a separate pile of its own. He had become braver over time as he realised that Drangnet had no real interest in most of it. His boss hardly gave the pile any attention at all and had gradually became more and more censorious as he became more confident and the pile to be kept on his own desk grew as that destined for Drangnet's diminished. Today, however, one letter had given him pause for thought. It was small, blue, sealed with wax and unfranked. It bore only the Chief Inspector's name and rank in a rather flowing, cultured hand and a note at the bottom bearing the word 'Personal'. This, he felt, was for the boss only and so it was that when Drangnet arrived at his office on the Monday morning, his first action, having quickly glanced across the daily incident report was to reach for his letter opener and to slit his way carefully into the missive.

Dear Chief Inspector,

Perhaps I was a little impolite to you when we met yesterday and I wish to apologise. I know now that you are trying to help Madame Fernier and you deserved my assistance rather than my approbation. My only excuse is that I am unused to meeting men, especially policemen, who treat me with any real degree of courtesy and perhaps I have become too accustomed to that.

You are obviously helping Angèle and she trusts you. I respect that. She also obviously likes you. I find that somewhat more worrying! But perhaps I should also see what I can do to help you too.

I would be pleased if you would take lunch with me today at the Café du Quartier at 40, Boulevard Ornano in the 18th. I am sorry to ask you to come to Montmartre, but I have been in less than the best of health since my return from exile and this café is very near my apartment. One eats moderately well.

With kind regards

Louise Michel.

He was certainly surprised, and his first impulse was to ignore it. He obviously could decline the invitation, but the note did not seem allow for the possibility. However his progress through this melancholy case was slow and help of any kind would be welcome. He also had to consider the effect of a refusal on Angèle. He shouted through the open doors between his office and that of his deputy.

'Roger!'

There was a brief pause as Gant got up and came in. They had been on excellent terms of years now, but that informality did not extend to the junior man shouting back.

'Yes, sir,' he said as he arrived at Drangnet's door.

Drangnet waved the blue letter in the air.

'Did anyone see this arrive this morning? It must have been delivered by hand as there isn't a stamp.'

'Ah yes. I was sure you'd want to know, so I checked. It arrived at about six in the hands of a scruffy little urchin with his arse hanging out of his trousers. He chucked it at Sergeant Clement across his desk in reception and scarpered as fast as his legs could carry him.'

Drangnet just nodded. It reminded him of something that he had always known but too often forgot. In this city there were groups, networks, associations that operated in ways and at levels that he seldom really experienced. It was all too easy to see the world from his side of his desk without remembering that it was only he who saw it that way. Madame Michel could clearly call upon the services of boy to deliver an important note for her early in the morning right across most of Paris in the absolute certainty that it would find its destination. He wasn't entirely sure that he could do the same thing. The boy had obviously not wanted to hang about in a police station or, perhaps, even be seen in one, but he had done his job. It said much about many things not least of the reverence in which this famous woman was held and equally the power that she still wielded even now after she had returned from a miserable six year exile in New Caledonia; an exile to which he had been instrumental in sending her. Perhaps, he thought, that he shouldn't have been surprised at her attitude at their previous meeting. Perhaps, too, this next one might be more informative.

'I'll be out for lunch, Roger. Please organise a police cab at about 12:30am to get me up to Montmartre and to stay until I want to come back.'

Seeing that his deputy was more than curious he offered only the briefest of explanations.

'Another fishing expedition, Roger. Little more, I suspect.'

Gant just nodded and went back to his desk.

Drangnet stepped out of his cab at the stoke of one o'clock. He noted that the horse was breathing rather heavily. He made a mental note to have a word with the stableman and remind him that his horses had to be fitter than that. The short rise up to Montmartre had caused the animal to blow and that did not auger well if they were ever required to give chase to fleeing criminals. He turned into the *Café du Quartier* to find himself in a restaurant interior of the sort that Paris had in profusion. He could quite believe Madame Michel's remark that one would indeed eat moderately well. He was greeted at the door by the maître who shook his hand with an overenthusiasm that indicated a distinct nervousness. He was expected and the customers who already almost filled the small café shot suspicious glances at him as he was led to the back to a table near the kitchens were Madame Michel waited. They obviously knew who he was.

To his surprise two ladies awaited him as he saw that Angèle had been invited as well. Once everyone was again seated after the customarily elaborate exchanges of kisses was over, his host opened the conversation.

'Chief Inspector, I'm very pleased that you could accept my invitation, especially as it was made at such short notice.'

'Madame, I was delighted to receive it.' He replied. 'It is an added delight to see Madame Fernier here as well.'

He didn't add that it was nice to see the woman smiling and in somewhat better spirits that at their last meeting. As if reading his mind, she continued:

'I feel that out last conversation didn't go too well, and I have been reminded by my young friend here that that was largely my fault. It is never good to be scolded by one's younger friends. So again, I offer my apologies.'

Drangnet just raised his hand slightly off the table.

'Please, Madame. Think no more of it. It is past and, most importantly, we are talking again and here of all places.'

'Oh. Why doe this place strike you as significant, Monsieur?'

'Well, you have come back from exile and have returned to the Montmartre where you lived before the Commune; here in the shadow of the great *Butte de Montmartre* and the canons under the *Tour Solferino* where it all started ten years ago. You were there then. Perhaps one could claim that without you it might not have started at all. In many more ways than one you have come home.'

He saw a tear in her eye and knew what she was feeling.

'Many good people died because of our actions on that day, Monsieur. I have always wondered if anything has really changed.'

He looked directly into those rheumy eyes and replied quietly but forcefully.

'Oh yes, Madame. Never doubt that for a moment. France has changed. Perhaps not exactly in the way you wanted or as quickly as you wished, but changed it has. You did great things that March day and in the days that followed. You achieved much at great cost. France

230

will never again be ruled by a king or an emperor. We owe you and your fellow revolutionaries a great deal.'

She nodded slowly as if revisiting those events in her mind.

'But what now, Monsieur? We are still governed by men in fancy waistcoats.'

Drangnet smiled at the image. She was right, of course.

'You may not like the politicians, Madame, but at least they are elected.'

She frowned and he knew what was coming so he continued before she had a chance to speak.

'Not by universal suffrage, I know, but that too will come one day.'

'You were involved too, Chief Inspector, I seem to remember. Not exactly fighting at our side on the barricades but you were there.'

'Yes, I suppose, I was.' His reply was almost a whisper.

'Perhaps you had a more difficult job that we did. For us it was simple. There was only one side. You were one of the few who tried the impossible. You tried to maintain a civilised middle path between the extremes. It can't have been easy. I have been making some enquiries about you. You may not have been on our side of the barricades, but you seem not have been on the other side either. Many people around here remember you with surprising affection. Insofar as there is such a thing, you were a fair policeman and you seem to have retained that reputation. I'm not sure how you manage it. In any case, I you an apology for my recent behaviour.'

'Perhaps,' piped up Angele who, up until now had been an interested spectator. 'A certain independence of mind be one possible explanation?'

Madame Michel harrumphed.

'That's just another word for pig headedness.'

Dragnet was still interested in the older woman who had invited him to lunch, and he wanted to get to know a little more. It had been some time since he had come across her and he was interested in where she stood now. So, as the food and wine were set out in front of them, he continue their conversation a little. Louse Michel was still very much held in both reverence by the local population and with suspicion by the establishment. Although she had come back for exile in the south Pacific French colony of New Caledonia as a result of the general amnesty at the end of the previous year and was thus released under licence, she had lost little of her the zeal of ten years before and her very public espousal of both the cause of women's rights and the wider matter of anarchism had served to keep her in the public eye. She was still a person who often made politicians and police very uncomfortable and he smiled slightly that, in all probability, this lunch was being observed by at least two representatives of the political police. As he started on his delicious plate of a lamb ragout that was significantly better that on their previous meeting together with dumplings he returned to his host and her resumed life on the Montmartre.

'I think I can guess what you think of the new addition to your beloved butte, Madame. I'm personally sorry that this monster of a church is going to be built. It seems to be an insult to the lives of many good Parisians who fought with you. To live under its growing shadow must be difficult.'

The new church, to be known as the Church of the Sacred Heart, had finally been authorised and construction was beginning. A huge turreted basilica, utterly inappropriate in both the old Paris and the new one constructed under Haussmann, was an unashamedly political project, promoted by both Church and State. It was, according to its instigators, not just a church perched high above the rest of Paris on top of the *Butte* but also double monument, both political and cultural. It was to represent both a national penance for the defeat of France in the 1870 war with Germany ten years before and, according to the Archbishop of Paris, also to expiate the crimes of the Commune.

'I carry my disgust silently, Chief Inspector,' she replied. 'I spit at it every time I pass. But I thought you were a man of the Church. You sing at St Gervais, I hear.'

'I do indeed but that's more a matter of music than it is of faith.'

For a moment they fell silent as the continued to eat. The plates were taken away and replaced with three portions of *crème brulée* and some plates of fruit and cheese. The now empty bottle of wine was replaced.

Michel continued what was essentially seemed to be an interrogation. He began to get the impression that she was asking some questions for which Angèle wanted answers and as it was his intention to enlist more of her help he decided to continue to play along. Michel let a charming smile spread across her face. Drangnet was reminded of a fox.

'All in all, Chief Inspector, you are a bit of a mystery; a conundrum as they say. You are a tennis playing, church singing, policeman. As I can't imagine too many old members of the commune gracing the courts at the *Jeu de Paume* in the Tuileries Gardens, all three of these activities are thoroughly institutional and conservative. You mix with these conservatives and seem to be admired by them. Some of your friends occupy or have occupied the highest positions in the government and in the hated military. You play tennis with our current Head of State, for heaven's sake. You also show few republican tendencies, publicly at least, but when I mention you to any of my friends, I find a significantly degree of approval, even from people that I know came across your door ten years ago and even, most extraordinarily, by men you have arrested and imprisoned since then. Most of Angèle's girls seem to adore you. This is a disease to which I am beginning to suspect that Angèle herself is not completely immune. The word enigma hardly seems to fit.'

'So, Chief Inspector Drangnet,' she continued. 'What sort of man are you? To whose tune to you dance in the grand masked ball that is life in modern France. What or who are your particular mistresses?'

Drangnet took his time. It sounded a little like a challenge. But he was all too well aware that this woman was well connected with parts of Paris life that he was not or at least, not as well. He reached for the bottle and topped up the three glasses. He then took a long draw and savoured it for a while, holding it in his mouth and drawing a little air in over the top of his tongue before swallowing.

'I don't think I actually dance to anyone's tune, Madame Michel. At least I hope I don't. In any case, I've never found that to be a particularly satisfactory way to proceed. I like to think that I make my own mind up about things.' He thought for a moment about what she had just said. 'But, to use your metaphor, perhaps I do have a mistress; or more precisely, just two of them. And my allegiance to these is unyielding. My first is to the Law that, as a policeman, I have sworn to uphold. The second is the population of Paris that I have sworn to protect. The Law, however imperfect, is what it is. However it has been constructed and by whom, it still provides the only sensible way to conduct one's life, I believe. I see it failing a hundred time a day, but I know that without it there is no hope for us. If it needs to be changed, then I can confident that changes will happen, but it'll never be a council of perfection. But if we have to live by something, then the Law of the Republic of France is indeed my first mistress.'

'Using this law, I address the demands my second mistress, as you might put it, every day of my working life. The people in this town are under my care – or that is what I believe - and I work to make their lives as good as I can; as free of pain and difficulty from crime, as far as I can influence matters. I try to treat everyone the same, I hope, from the grandest rich to the totally destitute.'

'So, Madame, those two might well be my mistresses and if you insist that I must be dancing to some tune or another then it is to theirs perhaps. All I can do is to serve these two mistresses as well as I can.'

Madame Michel looked thoughtfully at her guest while Angèle just looked at him with something approaching adoration. There was a slightly uncomfortable silence as they all felt slightly that the conversation had strayed into areas what were slightly too personal.

In the end it was Angèle who was able to get things onto more practical subjects.

'Now, Louis. How goes your investigation? Have you made any further progress?'

'I'm afraid we've not really made much progress at all.' he replied feeling slightly relieved. 'We still don't know who murdered your girls and there is almost no information reaching us from any of our usual sources.'

Drangnet didn't want to say much more. His suspicions about Cordiez and his colleagues were not for public consumption. Equally, his suspicions about a connection with freemasonry had remained very much concealed so far. In any case while he had already decided that as and when the time came, he might confide in Angèle, he was much less certain about Louise Michel. She was a woman with a strong and unyielding reputation of holding views with the passion of a fanatic. The question of the significance of the tattoo was equally not something he wanted to raise at this point, and these were the only significant clues that he had stumbled across. Then a thought struck him. Perhaps Angèle or this schoolteacher turned anarchist revolutionary might recognise this mysterious number 213.

'There might be one thing that you might like to have a guess at. During our investigation of one or two of the few avenues of enquiries that we seem to have in this business, we've come across the mention of the number 213 a couple of time. We have no idea what it could mean. Does it seem familiar to you in any context?'

He had expected a period of silence while the ladies at the table tried to bring something to mind. But Madame Michel burst into laughter almost at once.

'At a risk of stating the extremely obvious, Chief Inspector, you are clearly not a modern woman. Or if you can't figure out this particular puzzle, perhaps you should think of employing some women in your completely male police force.'

Drangnet looked at her with considerable surprise. He hadn't actually expected any reaction at all.

'This is ironic.' she said, 'Considering the remarks you have just made about the rule of law, Monsieur, but you have possibly have just answered your own question.'

A somewhat bemused Drangnet could do no more than wait.

'I have no idea if this is of any great significance to your enquiry, Monsieur,' she went on. 'But this is an infamous number in the lives of every woman in France. I am sure that Napoleon's Civil Code figures greatly in your life, as it does in ours but if you ever read it through completely, ultimately you would arrive at book one, section five, the section that deals with marriage. This part of the code effectively takes away all independent rights from women; all right to be heard, to own property of any significant sort; to have an independent life of their own. In chapter six of this section appears an infamous paragraph. It is a paragraph that specifically demands unquestioning obedience of all wives to their husbands. That, Chief Inspector Drangnet, is paragraph number two hundred and thirteen. So yes, you could say that this is indeed, a significant number; to women, at least.'

He hoped that his face remained calm, but in that instant he saw what this whole business was about. Ever since seeing the tattoo he had known that this must have been some sort of masonic group, however obscure, but he couldn't work out their motive. Now is was simple; even obvious. This was group of woman-hating masonic lunatics who were obsessed with killing women who weren't content to be subservient and quiescent wives.

'Does that help?' she enquired.

He looked across the table as calmly as he could, anxious not to arouse too much interest.

'It's certainly interesting, Madame. I'll have to go back to my files and see if I can work out how significant in might be. At the very least you have come up with one explanation of these numbers and that's more than anyone else has. For that I thank you.'

Louis Michel nodded her head in acknowledgement.

'Now, my children, I will leave you two in peace. It's time for an older woman to take her rest. I'm not as strong as I was before I went for my holiday in the South Pacific and I find that I tire all too easily. I remind you that you are both my guests today.'

Drangnet, who didn't for a moment believe that she was remotely tired, and Angèle both rose with her as she stood to leave. She offered her hand to Drangnet and looked at him directly.

'Chief Inspector, I find myself being slightly seduced by you as well. I feel instinctively that I should trust you. That isn't the same thing as actually trusting you, of course. It may well be that there will be new barricades to man in the future and I can't always guarantee that we will be standing on the same side, you and I. But if that happens and we find ourselves with opposing forces, I feel that you and I, at least, will talk with each other before we shoot.'

'I think I can promise that, Madame,' he offered with a smile.

'Then, at least, I have achieved something this morning,' she replied and with a wave to Angèle she swept out of the café.

They sat together for a moment while they both digested the conversation. Louis was excited as he finally saw a possible way forward. Angèle sensed that something had changed. Typically, it was she that brought the conversation back to the table.

'So, what can I do, Louis.? What do you need from me?'

The moment had clearly arrived, so he took a deep breath.

'I think I know what's going on, Angele. It sounds ridiculous even to me and I certainly have no proof but if I'm right, part of my own police force is involved.'

She was astonished.

'Surely not, Louis. What on earth do you mean? My girls are being killed by policemen? I can hardly believe that. We know most of them and we know the ones that visit us. If this was the case one way or another, we'd know about it, I'm sure.'

'No. I don't think it's a simple as that,' he said, shaking his head. 'But I'm pretty sure that some police, probably not my department, are involved in some way.'

'Who?'

'Well my theory is that the political police, or some of them at least, are involved somehow and if I'm right then I need to get some information on some of my colleagues. I need to have them watched. I need to know where they go and who they meet. Obviously, it's impossible to ask members of my own staff find out. I can't ask them to spy on their colleagues even though I could certainly find enough of them who dislike the politicos to do the job. But even if they did there's no real chance of keeping it a secret. The prefecture leaks like the proverbial sieve. Most of my policemen look like exactly what they are and that would make following anyone in secret rather difficult. It occurs to me that you might have some people who might do some following a lot less obtrusively that us and see where some of these men go and what they are up to.'

She hardly hesitated.

'Of course we can do this, Louis.'

Well, I know how many people you have. Many more than I have in my *Sûreté*. I need you to follow some people for me. I want to know the movements of these people. I need them tracked day and night and I want to have regular reports of where they go and who they meet. I have nowhere near enough men to do this properly. You'll need at least four people permanently following each man all day and all night and I need reports, preferably twice a day. Can you do this for me?'

She reached across the table with an intimate gesture and touched his hand lightly.

'Obviously, we've plenty of people who can do this. Who do you want us to follow?'

He was slightly taken aback at how quickly she agreed and how simple she obviously thought it would be. So equally briefly, he listed three names.

'Louis Andrieux, Prefect of Police, Henri Sandrat, his deputy and Serge Cordiez, Head of the Political Police.'

Even she looked a little shocked as he went on.

'I want to know, where they go and when, who they meet and, if at all possible, what they talk about. I don't know where they are at the moment, but you can probably pick them up on the Quai.'

She fell silent as she thought about what he was asking. To give her credit, it took her very little time to organise her thoughts.

'Yes, I think we can manage something. It shouldn't be too difficult. We have numerous market traders, delivery drivers, unemployed youths of all sorts who can stay close without arising suspicion, especially if these men themselves don't expect to be observed. These three they are well known to my girls as well as you will see from the lists I gave you. I think we can offer a report, say each morning first thing, if that would be satisfactory?'

'You can do that?'

'Why not?' she shrugged. 'All these three will presumably go to bed sometime just after midnight, and that would give me enough time to get a report drawn up and put under your door by the time you get up. How does that sound?'

Drangnet couldn't hide his surprise.

'That would be wonderful, Angèle. I have no idea what we'll learn. It might all come to nothing. In one way I hope that we find nothing untoward. That at least would indicate that the police service is not involved in this business. But anything will help at this stage. Do you want any help finding these people?'

He was instantly shamed by a thoroughly patronising look from his hostess. She didn't even bother replying. Instead she just smiled a little patronisingly.

'One thing occurs to me, Madame. There may be occasions when we wish to be in contact in an emergency, as it were. I am sure that you can get a message to me at the Quai easily enough but I'm

239

not sure what happens if I want to contact you as I certainly don't know where you are and, in any case, I may not want anyone from my office to know about it.'

She thought only for a moment.

'If I want to see you, I'll either send you a message with the report each night or in an emergency I'll risk a message to your office. Your Sergeant Clement can be trusted. His brother works in the market. If you want to see me you can leave a message for my man bringing your report or Monsieur Blanco can also be trusted.'

It all sounded to simple and normal. He was flabbergasted to know that his long-serving desk sergeant was also connected to the world of *les Halles*. She went on in a thoroughly business-like manner.

'Right, I have a lot to organise in a short time Louis, so I wonder if I could let you go now? I had a feeling that something like this might happen when you sent me your message, so I have arranged from some of my people to come here for a meeting after lunch. I don't think that they would be particularly happy to sit here making arrangement to carry out your spying for you with you sitting at the table. Leave it all to us and I'll have the first report to you tonight.'

Thoroughly taken aback by the speed of events, he found himself back out on the street without much ceremony. Madame was obviously someone who didn't allow grass to grow under her feet.

Chapter 11: Monday 11th April   Scene 3: A Conspirators' Lunch

It was lunch time and, as usual, the restaurant was busy. The clientele was mainly made up of businesspeople and professionals. There was also a fair smattering of academics too. Since the foundation of the *École Libre des Sciences Politiques* in the nearby *Rue Saint-Guillaume*, the restaurant *A La Petite Chaise* had become a favourite of the better-heeled teachers at the school, many of whom were also, by tradition, visiting senior civil servants and politicians. There were two levels with the bar and a smaller number of tables on the ground floor and a larger suite of three room on the first floor. Both were crowded at lunch time and after seven in the evening. The décor was not particularly luxurious. Unlike some of the other popular restaurants in the town like *Le Tour d'Argent* or *Bofinger* who had developed highly decorated and ornate styles, *La Chaise*, as it was familiarly known to its regulars, had remained sober but comfortable; as had its cooking. It was always a safe place to eat.

The noise level was high as well as everyone tried to make their conversations heard in the crowded rooms and there was a constant clatter of plates and serving dishes as the staff struggled to keep up with the lunchtime rush. It was ironic, therefore, that in the middle of the cacophony the three men ran little chance of their conversation being overheard. They too fitted perfectly into the scrum of Paris bourgeoisie. Each was dressed in the sober respectability of middle-class businessmen and were tucking into their meals with gusto. It was a clever place to meet. There were many more secret places in Paris to talk but they knew that the more clandestine the location, the more they ran the risk of being observed. They could have talked at their gentlemen's clubs or in their offices but again there were always others, secretaries or colleagues who might have noticed the three or even remembered that it was not the first time these three had met to talk. Their beloved temple was obviously not possible. In spite of freemasonry being at the very core of their beliefs, their fellow masons wouldn't necessarily have shared their particular ideology. A few did, but the process of recruiting them to their cause was long and painstaking and they simply couldn't make any mistakes.

The three each had luxurious houses or apartments where they could meet but again these were in places full of curious neighbours or vigilant concierges. Given their shared mission and the penalties that would attend their being discovered, they had to take the utmost precautions. They had decided that meetings held in the opposite of secret were the best. No one seeing them sharing a regular convivial lunch regularly would regard it as particularly memorable in a place like *La Chaise*. It was, after all, what everybody was doing there. Even had they been recognised, they were all politicians who dined there regularly so returning to that same restaurant would be regarded as unremarkable if it was noted at all. The general mood amongst their fellow diners was boisterous and good humoured but it would have taken a very close observation to see that there were few smiles being passed between the three. The oldest of them started the important conversation.

'I wonder if we might better change our methods, my friends. We have lost three brothers in the last week.'

The other two nodded. It had been a worrying start to their self-appointed journey.

'Do we know what happened?' said another.

'No. They did their job. Each of them. The women were killed as we instructed, and our brothers escaped. But we don't know what happened then. The next thing we knew was that our brother in the police found out that one by one, some few hours only after they had done their duty, each was found floating dead in the Seine just below the downstream end of the *Île St. Louis*. No-one knows how they got there, and no one know who did it. Each of the three was apparently garrotted.'

There was a respectful silence for a moment. These men had died doing their bidding and they felt that deeply.

'How is the police investigation going?' asked one.

'Ah. That is where we might have something of a problem too, I think. We managed to get to the first body ahead of the criminal police and disposed of him safely but after that we lost custody of the second and never got close to the third. It seems that this man Dragnet in the *Sûreté* is being entirely too active. We had anticipated that our brother in the political police would be in charge after we decided to spread the story that this was an anarchist conspiracy, but Dragnet seems to have friends in high places.'

'Can we do something about him?'

'I really can't see how. He is very well respected and has the highest reputation as a detective. It would very dangerous indeed to move against him. In any case that is definitely not what we should be doing. But here is one slightly odd thing. In theory he should be investigating the murder of our brethren too, but for the moment he seems more intent on finding out why the women were killed. Perhaps that means he hasn't yet made a connection between the two cases.'

Again, the conversation paused slightly while they thought the matter through. One of them voiced what they were each thinking.

'We didn't anticipate that we wouldn't have control of the bodies. In fact, we didn't anticipate that there would be any to have control of. The only investigation that should have been happening is into the dead women. We seem to have presented this man Dragnet with an important clue. Our own people.'

One of the three silently slipped his hand beneath his jacket and onto his shoulder. It was a gesture that their leader noticed. He needed to take control.

'Brothers,' he said is a slightly lowered voice, 'we mustn't lose sight of our mission; the mission that we all agreed and believe in. We all bear the sign of our belief and that is the most important thing to remember. It is the symbol of the fellowship that binds us together. It's even more important than our own lives and we swore on the Holy Bible. Remember what we are sworn to do is holy work and that still matters more than anything. This is perhaps to test our faith. We must not be found wanting.'

Again, there was a slight pause in the conversation.

'From a practical point of view we have two problems, brothers. The first, and most important, is that we continue our holy mission. The second is that, perhaps, we might have to do something about this policeman if he gets too close.'

Both his companions look decidedly uncomfortable at this. They had never imagined that they would be discussing killing a policemen as part of their great plan.

'There has to be some reason why our brothers were identified or followed and killed. I don't know how that was done. Nor do I think we can find out easily. So, I propose we change or policy a little. We decided on the *maisons* controlled by the people at *Les Halles*. They are officially recognised and licenced and thus they represent the approval of the secular state in France. They still represent the beginnings of the so-called emancipation of women in our lives and that is what we and the good book forbids. We are the protectors of the Word. Don't forget that and that is why we embarked on this great and dangerous journey. That is what we were founded to combat. Obviously, these people have some arrangement that we didn't anticipate to protect their women. It would be too dangerous to try there again. We should go to some of the unregistered houses and start our campaign again.'

Surrounded as they were by the hubbub of their fellow diners, there was still a palpable silence around the little table. This was not the way they had envisaged their task. From the start they had planned to strike at the very centre of the bourgeois world; the places where the great and the good of Paris took their leisure and where they fell most surely under the influence of the women. Their brotherhood would bring back the old values or at least show men the way to achieving them. The new masonic flight from their own history, traditions and their biblical origins was progressively leading the whole brotherhood of freemasons away from the purity of mind and body that had been at its foundation. The first bringer of evil into the world after the Creation was a woman and women had been the custodians of the Devil ever since. The evil had finally arrived at the doors of their masonic temples and the Grand Lodge of France was proposing to admit women into their brotherhood. They had decided that it was time to fight back. They had formed their little group to take the fight onwards.

'The project must continue, my brothers. We will still be taking evil from the world. Nothing really changes. We must be more careful about who we use to carry our mission. Perhaps it would be better not to use brothers who hold the sign. It would also be wrong to allow this policeman to connect the future with the past. Sandrat thinks we should switch our targets to the less well-known brothels further into the outskirts of the city. Some sort a security has obviously been organised at Madame Fernier's places. We could try to avoid them, perhaps.'

Neither of the others agreed.

'I don't think we're serving our great mission by making it less visible. If anything, it should be the opposite. You will remember that originally I wanted to attack the biggest and most famous of these places. Heading off into the outer suburbs is simply not what we had in mind. In fact, it would be the opposite. No, André. I really don't think that is a good idea.'

'I suggested to Sandrat earlier that you all come to my lodge meeting tomorrow evening. We are doing some initiations and there will be plenty of other guests. We can meet with Sandrat afterwards in privacy and decide if we should change our tactics at all. Whatever we decide, we do need to keep him part of us. He is the line of control to Cordiez and his men. We must make sure that we send a clear signal. Remember are lives are at risk here including out own.

The other two nodded slowly. It seemed a logical precaution and they certainly needed to plan their next moves.

The second of their number raised the next issue.

'We need to know what this man Drangnet is up to. Why he seems to be looking for our brothers rather than looking for the people who killed them.'

'Or both,' the third added.

'Again, we can bring our concerns to Sandrat tomorrow.

With that the conversation went on to other things for the rest of lunch but each man gave it very little attention. This was the first

245

real sign of difficulty with their project and they would each be happier after tomorrow evening's meeting and they could see a less confused way ahead.

Chapter 12: Tuesday 12th April   Scene 1: Surveillance and Precautions

He had thought that he might stay up and see what time the first report would arrive but as he had no idea when that might be, he went to bed. The morning would bring its own news. He slept well as usual, waking just after six. Sure enough, a large envelope was waiting on the mat have been slid under the front door. He forced himself to leave it alone, unopened on the kitchen table while he conducted his usual ritual of getting himself ready for a day's work. Whatever the envelope contained, this was a regular working day and some rituals were necessary. As he finally finished dressing, he also realised a slight flaw in their surveillance planning. In the event that the report carried something that needed some immediate action, he hadn't organised a way of getting in touch with madame to inform her or to assess any direct consequences given that he was probably going to have to rely on her for that as well. In any case he thought that it would be a good idea to meet and discuss the first night's surveillance. He quickly adjusted his route to work to go via the *Café du Marché*. It wasn't much out of his way.

He was ready by seven o'clock and the sun had risen in the sky sufficiently to start bathing the *Place des Vosges* in a bright, optimistic light. He felt the need to get into the fresh air and take this coffee and the diversion via the market would do well. He could also read the report then. It would make an interesting addition to his usual morning newspaper. So, a little later, he had settled into his seat on the sunlit terrace of the *Café du Marché*. He waited for the waiter to bring him a customary grand café noir and quarter of a buttered ficelle and apricot jam. Finally, he got to slip his penknife blade through the wax seal that closed the large envelope.

He was astonished. He was accustomed to receiving many and various reports in his department. Paperwork flourished and most of it took a considerable amount of deciphering. Very few of his colleagues possessed legible handwriting or the ability to spell and the same could be said of most of the secretarial staff at his disposal. Punctuation was completely beyond them. What he had in his hand was a sheaf of beautifully written and laid out pages written in almost perfect copperplate handwriting. Headings, columns, and times were exactly arranged and aligned as was the main body of the text. Each of the three men under surveillance had been followed from mid-afternoon the day before and through the night until each had retired for the night. Their movements were documented, and precise times given. Most interesting were surprisingly detailed lists of the people they had met and talked to. These came mostly from cafés and restaurants, but it was clear that some of the watchers had got near enough to overhear conversations.

Louis Andrieux, Prefect of Police, was the least interesting. The prefect was also an Assembly Deputy for the Rhône Area and he had been in an official sitting of the Chamber of Deputies that had gone on until ten in the evening after which he had gone straight home and presumably stayed there. Sandrat had been in his office in the *Préfecture* until early evening when he had taken dinner with a group of friends at a restaurant. As the group included wives, it was assumed, probably wisely that nothing conspiratorial was discussed. Cordiez had also been at the *Préfecture* until about eight when he went to a *maison de tolerance* - not one of Madame Fernier's it was pointed out but a much more expensive one. He went from there to a café where he too sat with some friends eating and drinking until midnight. The report informed Drangnet that a variety of topic were discussed but main topic had been the prospects for the upcoming first race meeting of the year at Longchamp. The conversation centred almost exclusively on horses and jockeys, owners and trainers. It was noted in the report that the men around the table were clearly betting men and there was no effort to prevent anyone overhearing them.

The whole report was complete, concise, and factual. That it bore little of great significance was of little consequence at this stage. These were early days and it was clear that the system, at least, worked. He was intrigued at how quickly she had set it all up. There was obviously an extensive intelligence street-level intelligence network already in existence that was nothing to do with the police. He still had some misgivings about the overall security, but these could be discussed when he next met Madam. But was did astonish him was that two extra sheets of paper were appended to the main report. These were detailed biographies for both Sandrat and Cordiez.

He assumed that Andrieux wasn't included as he was a public figure and much of his information was on the public record. But the lives of the other two men were outlined in great detail and he felt his pulse quicken slightly as he read them. Perhaps Madame was trying to make a point, but the two lives were listed in a way that emphasised how similar were these two. They came from very similar backgrounds, had similar military careers – nether had risen too much up the officer ranks. Sandrat seemed to make more progress after the Commune when he had been sent to New Caledonia with a promotion to set up the military police and to supervise security. Drangnet wondered whether he and Madame Michel had come into contact much during her imprisonment there. There seemed no lack of detail as to Sandrat's activities. He had returned to Paris at about the same time as she had and had immediately got himself a plum job in the *Préfecture*. He had established the political department and it was he who had appointed Cordiez to run it. Cordiez's entry was less detailed. He seems to have spent the years since the commune in the Paris gendarmerie serving mainly in outer quartiers. Drangnet's interest was further drawn to a concluding section on the accounts of each man. Both these pages concluded with a note in a slightly different hand to say that both men were apparently members of a Freemason's lodge called *L'Ordre Fidelité*.

Before continuing his walk to work he wanted to sit and digest what he had just read. So he asked for a second coffee. On balance Drangnet was satisfied. The report had given him little that was world-shaking, but it illustrated how very well organised were Madam Fernier and her associates. It also showed him that they kept as many dossiers on him and his colleagues and they did on hers. Possibly more. However there remained some details of their arrangement that troubled him a little. He also needed to get a message to Ferry before their tennis game this evening. He needed to find out about the *L'Ordre Fidelité*. He finished his coffee and motioned for his bill. Unsurprisingly it was Monsieur Blanco who presented it.

'Please can you tell Madame Fernier that I would appreciate a few moments of her time?'

The man just took his money and turned away. He had received the message he was expecting and that was that. Drangnet completed his journey to work and held yet another inconclusive departmental meeting. He was pleased to see that the day-to-day business was being capably dealt with by Gant without anything having to trouble him directly. A few more reports had come in from the police precincts nearest the murders with a few eye witness statements claiming to see suspicious looking people leaving the houses at around the estimated times of death but these contained very little useful information and certainly no descriptions of actual people. These sorts of statements often appeared some time after the original crime was discovered as people found out there may be some money to be had. Drangnet generally ignored them. He had a regularly meeting scheduled with his boss Dancart for late morning. It was just a sort of catch up and wouldn't take long. Before that there was the usual pile of other office paperwork that theoretically needed his attention but, having passed under Gant's eagle eye, all he really needed to do was sign it. As very few of these endless bits of paper actually had any material effect on his life or on that of his department, the was perfectly happy to trust his deputy's judgement. He got to the bottom of the pile and had just written a note to Ferry when there was a tap on his door.

'Got a letter for you, boss.' said Clement from the front desk.

He put the envelope down on the desk.

'Came a couple of minutes ago. Delivered to the front desk by some urchin off the street. Ran out before he could be asked who it was from or what his name was. Raggedy little lad, arse hanging out of his shorts and socks round his ankles.'

Drangnet glanced down at the envelope. It bore his name written in the same copperplate script that he had recently been reading with his morning coffee.

'Thank you, sergeant,' said Drangnet. 'I don't think there'll be a reply.'

'But,' he said, handing his own note across the desk, 'Please send this by a reliable courier to Minister Ferry at the Palais the Luxembourg as quickly as possible.'

The man nodded and left, closing the door behind him. The note on his desk just said: '12 noon at the *Café Normande, Rue St Victor* behind the *Halle des Vins.*'

Dancart listened to Drangnet's briefing with a slight frown on his face.

'Louis, it seems that you're still not making much progress. Have you really no idea what is going on or are you're doing your usual and keeping it all to yourself?'

Drangnet grimaced.

'Well to be honest, Émile, I think I do know what is happening, but I haven't a shred of evidence. Just a collection of guesses and bits and pieces. Rather like an unmade jigsaw with none of the pieces actually fitting properly together. I know it's all part of a single picture and one day it will fit but now…'

'Can I help?'

'Well, I'd be interested in hearing your impression of this man Cordiez who seems to run the political department.'

Dancart settled down a fraction in his chair and gave the matter some thought before replying.

'Well, Louis. It's pretty obvious that personally I don't like him or the crew he runs with. They don't seem to be real policemen at all. No-one seems to know what they're doing or who controls them. They certainly take no notice of me. Whenever we come across them on the street, they ignore rank and just do what they want. They have the reputation of being pretty violent, too. They certainly don't bother about liaising with other departments. As for Cordiez himself he just seems like the rest; pushy, arrogant; bit of a law unto himself.'

251

'Yes, you're right. That's my impression too but he must be a law unto somebody, as they say. Someone must control him. Who's his boss?

'No idea.' returned Dancart. 'Presumably, someone further up the tree at the *Préfecture*. I don't think that they can operate completely outside the prefecture.'

'Well, that basically just means the Prefect and his deputy. The rest of them in that office are just pen pushers.'

'Do you mind if I ask you if you're a freemason?' said Drangnet changing the subject abruptly.

Dancart looked extremely startled.

'Good Lord, Louis. Whatever made you ask that? As it happens, I'm not. Never really had the time for all that mumbo jumbo. Why? Are you?'

Drangnet held up as apologetic hand.

'Don't get me wrong, Émile. I'm not accusing you of anything, but one of the leads I've got – one of the few, in fact – is a masonic connection of some sort. I don't know how it fits, if, indeed it does, but I want to find out whether our lords and masters are masons. I have a feeling that a lot of the are. I'm not, by the way.'

'Well I don't know about our superiors, but I do know that a surprising number of the lower ranks have joined. I think a lot of them think that it helps their promotion prospects. We could probably get a list of some sort together just by asking around. However, what about the problem of whoever is bumping the supposed killers off in such short order. Any thoughts on that?'

Drangnet had been working with Dancart for long enough to regard him as a friend so had no hesitation in being honest.

'To be frank, sir, I'm not spending too much time on that. As far as I'm concerned, someone is doing us a public service. I have a pretty good idea what is happening but the investigation of all that is somewhat down my list of priorities at the moment. Stopping more prostitute murders is more important.'

'I understand, Louis and, to be honest, I rather agree with you. But yesterday I was in a meeting with the Prefect and I was asked about it. I made the usual 'we're following various lines of enquiry reply and hope to make good progress before too long' sort of reply, of course.'

Drangnet was immediately interested.

'You mean that Andrieux himself was interested in this?'

'Well actually, no. I think it was more his deputy, Henri Sandrat.'

'Sandrat. Now there's a name you don't hear very often. What do you now about him?'

Dancart shrugged.

'Well, not much really. He seems to be just one of those time-serving bureaucrats that we breed in such profusion in this country. He's been in the deputy prefect's job for some time, I think. About as long as we've been in the service ourselves. A bit of the furniture.'

'But what does he actually do, Boss.'

'To be frank, I've no real idea. I report to the Prefect regularly and his office staff usually give me what I want when I ask for it. It's a system that works well and I don't really question it. They don't seem to want to be involved in the day to day stuff here and that suits me fine. I've no idea where Sandrat fits in. I'm not really sure what he actually does. I can't say I'm particularly interested.'

As he sat there, Drangnet's plans for his lunchtime conversation got a little clearer. At last a strategy was beginning to form in his mind. He made to go.

'So, if that's all, boss I'd better go and see what my people are up to.'

'All right, my friend. Just keep me in touch with things as they progress. I don't particularly like being asked questions by the top brass that I can't answer.'

As he left, Drangnet thought, somewhat uncharitably, what were heads of department supposed to expect? It was one of the main reasons he had avoided becoming one of their number. It came as no surprise that he returned to his office to find absolutely nothing new of any consequence lay on is desk. Gant was out doing something and the whole place felt empty. So, he passed some time with the morning's paper until it was time to leave for his luncheon appointment.

His destination was south on the river almost as far as the Salpetrière Hospital so he crossed over to the left bank across to the *boulevard St. Michel* before turning eastwards along the *Rue des Écoles*. It was a route he enjoyed travelling as it reminded him that all of Paris was not just somewhere for crime to occur. Here were closely grouped buildings of the Sorbonne Academy, *L'École Polytechnique*, numerous *Lycées*, libraries and other academic institutions. These were places of education and learning, vibrant and alive as much with students as with ideas. Indeed, many of the inhabitants could still converse in Latin, an ability that gave the quarter its nickname three hundred years before. The *Rue St. Victor* ran south from the *Halle aux Vins*, the main distribution depot for imported vine from across France with its four main thoroughfares: the *Rues Languedoc, Bordeaux, Champagne* and *Borgogne*.

The *Café Normande* proved to be another thriving place full equally with workers from the *Halle aux Vins* and students taking advantage of the prices. He was obviously expected as no sooner than he had got in though the door than a white aproned waiter greeted him and escorted him though the throng of people scrumming for a place at one of the few tables left to the back of the café and into a small room with three more formally dressed tables. Two rather well-dressed couples occupied two of them while Angèle sat at the third. Drangnet took her hand and made the customary bowing towards it.

'Madame, I'm delighted to see you again. I hope you are well.'

'Thank you, Monsieur. I am indeed well and delighted also to see you. I'm also pleased to see that our little arrangement for swift communication works so well.'

Drangnet glanced slightly nervously at their dining companions before replying.

'As am I, Madame. I am sorry that the message must have come so late.'

She waved her hand dismissively.

'Oh, don't worry about that. And please don't worry about being overheard. These are good acquaintances of mine and will keep a good confidence in the unlikely event that they hear something.'

Bodyguards, he thought to himself, as she continued.

'I have taken the liberty of ordering for you. The veal is always very fresh here and the cook here does a particularly good Armagnac sauce. Their pear tarte is also one of my very favourites. It was my father's too, and he often came here for it. If fact I'm proud to say that it bears his name, *Tarte père Fernier* or *Tarte aux poires Fernier* if you are brave enough. He was very fond of pears, you see,'

She stopped abruptly, colouring very slightly, as she realised, she was running on a little with her enthusiasm.

'Perhaps you might like to choose the wine?' she finished slightly lamely.

He smiled gently with genuine affection.

'I'm happy to trust the owner's recommendation, Madame. If you can't get good wine here of all places, less that fifty yards from probably the greatest selection of French wine in the world, then there's no hope for us.'

'Now Chief Inspector, how are you getting on?'

They paused as a cold glass of white wine was put in front of each of them as an aperitif together with what looks like some small pieces of *fougasse*, the olive strewn bread from the South of France. He picked up and savoured the strong taste of the black olives and olive oil. His pleasure must have shown as she seemed genuinely pleased.

'I thought you might like a taste of home, Louis.'

'Ah that is all a long time in the past, Angèle. A very long time.'

'Perhaps, but our childhood and are parents are never far from our memories.'

'True. I look forward to meeting you late father a little later in the meal.'

She smiled radiantly at him.

'I think he would have liked to have met you too, Louis. Now tell me what this is all about.'

Two plates of thinly sliced veal with a creamy sauce, scented slightly of Armagnac and some little green beans and plain boiled potatoes were delivered to the table together with a carafe of red wine and two more glasses. She shook her head when he offered her the new wine and just poured himself a glass. He was actually quite happy as the white had clearly been from Burgundy – a Meursault or some such. He was rather hoping that her interest in his background would have extended to the red wine from the south of which he was so very fond. So it proved as the unmistakable taste grenache grape of the southern Rhone valley wine came to him.

'Firstly, I should thank you for the report, Madame. It was a great surprise to see how complete and detailed it was. I'm grateful and impressed.'

'I did hope it was what you wanted, Louis. Unfortunately, it didn't seem to offer anything very exciting.'

'Well we can't expect to be lucky first time around,' Dragnet laughed. 'That would be too much to hope for.

Angèle pouted attractively. She was obviously someone who wanted fast results.

'Perhaps it would help if you told me what this is about. Why are we following policemen rather than anyone else? If we knew what we were looking for it might help.'

This was the moments he had been reluctant to confront. While his ideas remained in his head no one could see them and see how very farfetched they seems to sound. Now he had to expose them to scrutiny. He took a deep breath.

'I think I've guessed what's going on with the killing of your girls, but it is a story that almost beggars belief. It's pure speculation on my part and I have absolutely no proof of what I think and at the moment I am incapable of getting any, certainly enough to make a case that will satisfy the Courts of Justice of the Republic of Paris.'

'Tell me what you think, Louis. Obviously as I have always said, if there is anything I can do to help, I'll do it.'

'Well. You already know that I suspect that some members of the police are involved. But that is only part of a bigger picture, Put at its simplest, I think that these girls were murdered by men, working for a small group of highly conservative and fanatical freemasons who hate women and want to prevent the emancipation of women into French life and society. I think they see it as a sort of divine cause, and they form a very small secret brotherhood within the masonic orders. I also think that these men are mostly from one particular freemason's lodge here in Paris. Your notes identified this link without my influence, and I think that is highly significant. I believe that some of the senior members of this conspiracy are members of the Paris police force at a very high level and might even be using the police itself actually to carry out the crimes. I think they started with your houses because they knew them as clients. They probably felt that yours had the right status and reputation. If they started with the most famous and expensive, they run then the risk of some very important people getting very upset. The whorehouses at the opposite end of the scale were simply not important enough to generate publicity for their cause.'

With that he took another mouthful of the delicious veal and waited for her reaction. They finished their main course in silence. She was clearly thinking it through. At least she hadn't dismissed the idea outright or laughed. Strangely he found himself a little nervous waiting for her reaction. He had been mulling over his theory in his head for so long that, in a way, he had got used to the idea. It was only when he spelled it out loud that he realised how ridiculous it sounded. He was astonished to hear her say:

'Yes, I think you're right – or pretty near.'

'What? You really think so?'

'Yes, I do. In fact, I've come up with a theory that's not a long way from yours. I did talk to Louise and she reckons that's exactly what's happening.'

'I hardly think that Madame Michel is the most objective opinion about women's rights and all that.'

'Perhaps, but she's one of the cleverest woman I know, and I value her judgement. She likes you, by the way. She thinks you are honest and trustworthy.'

Drangnet was at once pleased and appalled.

'I'm not sure that illustrates her good judgement, especially given what I want to talk about.'

'Then I suggest we wait until we've had pudding.'

The famous tart arrived, and it was indeed something special. There was nothing extraordinary about it and the way it was cooked. A simple pastry base, with sections of pear fanning out in concentric circles, covered with a glaze that was neither too sweet nor too bland with just the slightest whiff of some pear brandy. The generous slice was served without any accompaniment, slightly warm but alone on the plate. The pastry did indeed, as they say, seem to melt in the mouth and the pears were precisely "al dente".

'That, my dear Angèle, was easily the best tart I have ever tasted. My complements to both the cook and your late father. Both obviously know what they're doing I particularly like that the peel was left on the fruit.'

She smiled delightedly.

'Yes, my father always said that that was really here the real taste of the fruit was hidden.'

'Ha! Madame. That's exactly why I dislike so many of the so-called great chefs in Paris these days. Most of them would have spent hours peeling the pears so it looks more elegant on the plate.'

'I think of all the many, many things that my father did in his long life, both good and bad, making pear tarts here in this café was one of his favourites – and perhaps one of the most successful. I often came here as a child to watch him and it was here that I began to learn about his life and about Paris. He taught me to cook by his side and talked to me. He treated me like an adult. He got me slicing pears with a very sharp knife at the age of four and I learned much from doing that.'

'I'm surprised you've still got the right numbers of fingers, Madame.'

She tossed her head back and laughed.

'I'll admit it was close sometimes, but I never forgot the lesson behind it; that trust is probably the most precious gift of everything both to the giver and to the person who accepts it.'

Drangnet thought for a moment. It was true, of course,

'And I,' she continued. 'trust you. So, tell me what you want. Why did you send me the message that you wanted to meet?'

He paused while an cognac un-requested was placed at his elbow.

'Well it did occur to me that what I asked you to do is not without danger. I wouldn't presume to judge your people or their competence. You obviously know them much better than I but I know that the police use civilian spies and informants all the time and I have no idea whether any of them are your people as well. Additionally, I don't know if any of them is a freemason. There must be a good chance that some are. I use informants myself and not only don't I know where their loyalties lie exactly – other than to money, of course - but I don't necessarily believe that they have any great loyalty to me. I also know that there are plenty of informants amongst police ranks. Information about our operations often finds its way into the hands of journalists or other criminals. I'm not questioning their reliability but if information that you were doing this surveillance got back to someone like Cordiez and his men, there could be unpleasant consequences for you.'

To do her credit she neither dismissed his concerns, nor did she object to them. She seemed to consider carefully before replying.

'There's obviously no way to prevent this. All we can do is entrust the matter into the hands of the people we know, our own people, and we must rely on them. They all know the consequences of betraying our trust. We decided that we should use only as few as we could and only ones that we know well and will keep their mouths shut. I am pretty sure that none of them is a freemason, but you never know, I suppose. Plenty of our people are. That's a risk we'll have to take. As for me, I am personally well looked after. The people nearest to me are as loyal to me as they were to my father. They have proved that many times over the years when other came along and tried to take my business from me. I'm not concerned, and you shouldn't be for me either.'

Drangnet could do little more than accept what she said. In any case it was not really officially his business. Except, of course, that it was.

'Well, Madame. Then all I can do is thank you again for doing this. I do think it's important and perhaps we'll just have to be patient. I am please that my message got through to you and it has resulted in a fine lunch and, as always, it's a pleasure to spend some time with you.'

She smiled.

'We both want to get this matter cleared up, Louis, and all of us appreciate how seriously you are taking it. I have told my people that we have a responsibility to help, not matter how reluctant some of them might feel. We and the police do not normally make easy bedfellows. So, we just have to try to help where we can, and this is something concrete we can do.

Chapter 12: Tuesday 12th April   Scene 2: Tennis Semi-Finals and After

The match had gone well for them. In spite of the game being changed to the Tuesday from the traditional Wednesday, there was a substantial turnout of spectators wanting to see if the reigning champions could keep in this year's competition. The *maître's* betting book was a full one. It was the most prestigious of the club's numerous competitions, even more so than the singles title. The first game to be played on the occasion of the official opening of the new court in 1862 was by the Emperor Napoleon III. Their old court had been demolished to make way for the Garnier's new *Opera* and Biboche had applied for a licence to build a new court on a piece of land at the western end of the Tuileries Gardens. After considerable local opposition he had obtained it and the Emperor had agreed to join in the opening festivities. The great man was, however, only an enthusiastic amateur player rather than a skilful one, so the game became a doubles match and it was arranged for him to be partnered by Biboche himself. Needless to say, the Emperor won.

Their opponents tonight had been good ones. In a game where experience counts for much, both pairs were well matched, and they had played each other numerous times before. It was a small club after all. But in doubles play experience of playing together in a pair was the most valuable of all and Drangnet and Ferry had been doubles partners for more than ten years. The game had never really been in doubt in spite of the set scores being close. There are, of course, different ways that gentlemen should win. Then after the customary round of drinks and subsequent small talk they both took Ferry's cab and went back to his house for a quick supper. The second semi-finals had not been re-arranged so they were denied the opportunity to stay and see their prospective opponents for the final in action.

Madame Ferry was out on one of her innumerable charitable committee meetings and supper was a selection of cold meats and some cheese with bread and salad. Neither man was particularly hungry after the exertions of their game. It was only mid-evening when the two sat together with that warm, slightly tired feeling after a good meal and slightly more good wine to drink that perhaps they should. There was a comradely silence while each nursed a digestive glass. For Ferry it was a cognac; Drangnet a whisky. It was Ferry who started after a long and satisfied pause.

'I think that was as good as we've played together, my friend. They never had a hope really.'

Drangnet nodded gently in agreement.

'Yes. If we keep it up, we'll win again on Sunday.'

'I agree,' said Ferry with a smile breaking out on his face. 'I rather think we will. That'll disappoint the younger members.'

Drangnet just shrugged. The last thing he wanted to do was to appease the younger generation.

'There's more than one way of teaching respect, Jules. It's one of the great things about our noble game. It teaches that experience and calm can be more effective that strength and power. I'm sure that if we play on Sunday like we did today, we'll win. Whoever wins the other semi-final tomorrow, they'll be as good a pair these two tonight, no doubt. Unlike many of the people who play this competition they understand some of the subtleties of the doubles game. I've watched them. They both have good all-round games as single players. Even as a doubles pairing they understand about defending the galleries and they know that the pursuit of chases in different in doubles than singles. But, being young, they sometimes can't resist going for the glory of hitting winners when they should be going for position or for the more psychological subtilties for the doubles game. They don't understand the pleasure of keeping the ball in play simply because you can or playing shots just to demonstrate one's ability to get your opponent out of place or just where you want to put him. They'll get a bit ragged under pressure especially when a rest goes on for a long time. The longer it goes on the more they are likely to end it with an attempted force and make a mistake when they shouldn't or needn't. I think all we need to do is to keep things going and let them beat themselves.'

There was a silence while they both adjusted to the conversation that they both needed to have. Drangnet was direct.

'Jules. I need you to talk about Freemasonry. Other than some basic stuff, I know nothing about it really and I have a feeling that somewhere it is the key to solving the prostitute murder business.'

'All right. I'll do my best. But it is a vast subject. Rather than just giving you a long and rather tedious lecture, perhaps it would be better if you asked me specific questions.'

'All right. Let's start with some basic ones. How many masons are there in France in general and in Paris in particular?'

Ferry frowned for a moment and the replied.

'Somewhere between twenty and twenty-five thousand in France; slightly less than half that number in Paris, I would guess.'

'You don't know exactly, Jules? I would have thought that a secret society like yours would keep a pretty close account of membership numbers.'

Ferry frowned in an exasperated sort of way.

'Louis. Like many people, you seem to hold all sorts of misconceptions about freemasonry. Maybe this little chat will put some of them right. It is not a single, homogenous group. Nor is it a group of completely like-minded people. It has over-arching rules and conventions, to be sure, but only in the most general of ways. There are a surprising number of divergent opinions and beliefs amongst masons.'

'So, there's no single governing body, as it were. Some committee or something that makes the rules?'

'Well. It is not quite of clear as that. You must remember that masonry has been in existence in Europe for a long time in many different countries, not just France. Links and connections exist between countries but essentially masonry in each country goes its own way. There are different governing bodies in most countries. Here in France we have two main entities that tend to be responsible for making the rules, as you put it. They tend to take the lead and all the individual lodges are affiliated to them or, at least, most of them are.'

'And these two are called?'

'The Grand Orient of France and the Supreme Council of France.'

'And all masons belong the one of these?'

'No, Jules.' said Ferry with a slight look of annoyance. 'Individual masons belong to individual lodges. The lodges are affiliated with one of these two bodies to whom they look for guidance and authority. But lodges themselves have considerable autonomy.'

Drangnet paused while he digested this.

'So, if there are these two main authorities and hundreds of lodges more or less in bed with one or other of them, can I assume that there is a fair degree of agreement between all parties? No particular "sides" as one might say?'

'Well no, not really. There have been a number of significant disagreements since the time of the Emperor and they're still going on.'

'Are these disagreements between all the members or just a few?'

Ferry got up and refilled their two glasses before embarking on a very abbreviated history of what was, in reality, a long and complex story.

'Freemasonry started, we're told, with a trade union of master stone cutters who, it is said, possessed the secret of the building of Solomon's temple. The brotherhood was formed to keep that secret. From the very beginning, therefore, there was a connection between that group and God – Christianity basically. Members throughout history have sworn allegiance to that God and this is what is currently our biggest difficulty. As time has gone on that link was perpetuated and Freemasonry and the Church became connected and then with the leaders of the Church which in many cases in Europe was Royalty. So, if you want to paint the general picture in the very roughest of terms, freemasonry and the Church and the State all become interlinked if not actually connected.'

'Then as you know, about a century or so ago, all our ideas about the world began to change and people started taking about man not God being at the centre of things or the origin of everything and that revolutionary politics, democracy and so on started to take hold culminating here in France at least with actual social revolution. Freemasonry had always been an intellectual pursuit and it followed suit and gradually the old masonic philosophy also changed into the more revolutionary version that wanted to incorporate more modern ideas. By the time we got rid of the Emperor and survived the Commune, masonry was set to drop its old relationship with God and adopt a more secular agenda. Then the Third Republic was born, and many masons were and remain its chief architects.'

'Including you, Jules,' Dragnet remarked.

'Yes,' his host nodded back. 'Including me.'

A thought struck Drangnet.

'Is everyone happy about this? There must be some who prefer the old, less progressive ways. I assume masonry still has places for them'

Ferry seemed to become uncomfortable with the thought. It seemed to Drangnet that the man was having difficulties reconciling his own beliefs with those of some of his masonic brothers. It was with a certain reluctance that he went on.

'Yes, I'll admit there are still groups that wish to remain back in the days where links with the monarchy and the church were strong, but they are few and getting fewer. Obviously, we don't have a monarch anymore and there seems very little chance of our having one again, thank God.'

'Soon if there remains an old guard, as we might say, it will increasingly be made up of fanatics who are isolated from the mainstream?' said Drangnet, not wishing to ask how Paris-centric was this new progressive direction of Ferry's. It wouldn't be the first time that Paris would regard itself as the centre of everything.

Ferry just shrugged and Drangnet continued.

'These reactionaries. Do you know them? Are they identifiable? Do they belong to any particular lodges?'

Ferry suddenly realised that Drangnet was taking the conversation is a particular direction.

'Louis. What's this all about? Why do I get the idea that you're on to something?'

Drangnet just raised a hand slightly.

'Just be patient with me for a few more moments. I'm beginning to see a bit of light in the mystery of ours. Let's just change the topic a little. Before coming back to the issue of people, how about the question of women and their membership of the brotherhood of freemasons. How does that sit at the moment?'

Ferry blinked at the abrupt change of subject.

'Well, as it happens, we are getting close to admitting our first women into the brotherhood.'

Drangnet smiled slightly.

'So not very well, in other words. I thought that the Empress Josephine had got into that club seventy years ago.'

'Only in Strasbourg and only into a lodge of adoption,' grumbled Ferry, sense of humour wearing a little thin at this gentle teasing.

'Ah, I'm not sure what sort of difference that makes. But what you're saying is that in spite of efforts of enlightened people like you, women are still effectively excluded.'

Ferry rose to the challenge.

'Not, I really don't think that's fair. There are many initiatives to admit women on an equal basis to men and given the speed with which changes like this usually progress, I think we are doing rather well.'

'But here are still people opposed to it?'

'Oh yes.'

'Many?'

'Yes.'

'Violently?'

Ferry now began to look concerned.

'What are you driving at, Louis? I think you'd better tell me where all this is going?'

'Before I do that, Jules, can you tell about this Lodge, *L'Ordre Fidelité*?'

Ferry answered in a somewhat exasperated voice. He wasn't someone who liked being kept in the dark.

'Ah, the lodge you asked me about. Well, there is very little to tell. As far as I know it is a small lodge, founded during the reign of Louis XVI in 1776. So, it can claim to be one of the oldest lodges in France. From the start it comprised military officers who were loyal to the king. It originally had charitable ambitions, as do many lodges, giving support to families of army officers members who died in action. They refused to accept the attempts of the Pope to forbid Catholics from becoming freemasons and actively encouraged practicing Catholics in the army to join. They still exist albeit in a much reduced form. As far as I can find out their active membership is little more than twenty of thirty. As with most lodges, they probably meet once a month and I'm told that their meeting place is above the *Café Dragon* on the *Rue des Capuchines*. That's about all I know.'

Drangnet was disappointed.

'Surely you have more information than that? Aren't you some sort of senior freemason? You can find out what you want.'

'Ah, Louis,' Ferry replied shaking his head. 'You really don't understand. Freemasonry is a very loose knit community. There is no sort of fixed hierarchy and no one is really in charge. Masonic lodges are held together by allegiances of discipline, shared values and beliefs. Individual lodges have a surprisingly large amount of autonomy in what they believe and in the way they operate and organise themselves. Many lodges hold surprisingly opposing views. Insofar as there are generally accepted rules, these are very much open to individual interpretation. Although there is theoretically one governing body, the Grand Orient of France, there are other groups, as I said. In the case of *L'Ordre Fidelité* lodge this is complicated even further by the fact that they are a Clandestine Lodge.'

Drangnet just waited for an explanation, just raising an eyebrow.

'Sometime a lodge decides to follow policies that diverge significantly, even fundamentally, from what are the generally accepted norms and they step outside the family and then they are classified as Clandestine lodges.'

'And what has *L'Ordre Fidelité* done to deserve this?'

Ferry sighed as if he was being called on the explain something to wilfully ignorant schoolchild.

'Well, in essence, we've already covered this. Freemasonry is modernising. Many of its old attitudes are changing and, in France, in particular, it's following the more general movement towards to republicanism, popular democracy and a more liberal and enlightened attitude towards the world. As a consequence, it is also distancing itself from the official state church and allowing allegiance to a supreme being or supreme architect to the universe rather than just to God. They are also looking at ways to include women in their number. A number of lodges, especially the more traditionally minded ones find some of this hard to accept. I suspect the *L'Ordre Fidelité* is one of those.'

With that he felt silent leaving Drangnet more than a little dissatisfied.

'That's it? That's all you can tell me?'

Ferry was obviously not happy about being put on the spot.

'Louis. To be honest before your sent me your note this morning, I hadn't even heard of them. But I really can't see what more you expect me to say. What do you want?'

'Well a list of members would be nice to start with.'

Ferry shook his head.

'I'm sorry but I can't give you that. Lodges keep their own membership records. There's no central list and in any case, it would be confidential.'

'Secret, you mean,' retorted Drangnet somewhat waspishly.

'No, Louis,' Ferry sighed. 'Membership lists, where they exist, are not secret but individual lodges have the right to keep them confidential if their members wish it. For instance, I don't mind in the least if people know that I am a member of the *Clémente Amitié* lodge. In fact, all people who are standing for elective office in France are now encouraged to make their masonic membership public.'

'Encouraged but not required,' Drangnet replied.

'No,' sighed Ferry. 'It doesn't work like that. In any case, don't you think that you owe me a bit of an explanation? Why are you so interested in all this?'

'Ah well,' he replied with a slight smile passing over his face, 'The conduct and progress of my investigation is a confidential matter, I'm afraid.'

'Confidential?' said Ferry with an expression that seemed to show that he was undecided, whether to be amused or outraged.

'Yes, confidential.'

'Not secret?'

'Oh no, Sir. Merely confidential.'

'And who holds this confidence, may I ask?'

'My superior in the prefecture, of course Monsieur. Who else?'

'Not the *Ministre de l'Instruction publique et des Beaux Arts et Président du Conseil*?'

'I am sure that Chief Superintendent Dancart would be happy to take the responsibility of sharing the confidence, sir.'

'Jules,' Sighed Ferry trying a more conciliatory approach. 'You're really being difficult. I really know no more about this damned little lodge and it would look a little odd if I decided to instruct others to find out more.'

'I understand, of course. I'm grateful for what you told me. I'll simply have to find out more for myself.'

'You always were a stubborn bugger, Louis.'

Drangnet just nodded. He was already thinking that Madame Fernier might be a more useful source.

'Jules, believe me, I'll tell you when I have really got something to go on other that a wild speculation, mostly my own.'

Chapter 13: Wednesday 13th April   Scene 1: The Morning Report

This morning it was raining and cold. The wind had turned northerly and was blowing at a brisk pace that drove the unwelcome rain through the long, open streets of Haussmann's new Paris with nothing to stop it. There were fewer people about as a result and those that were just scurried from one bit of shelter to another. Many of the cafes had their usual collection of early customers seeking breakfast before continuing on to their jobs. It was that, as much as anything that made Drangnet decide to forgo yesterday's pleasure at opening the new morning's report over a relaxed cup of coffee and a *ficelle*. This morning, he would feel uncomfortable in a crowd. That and the fact that he had woken up later than usual and people would be waiting for him at the *Sûreté*. He joined the others, head down, hat pulled firmly down over his face, coat tied closely around his waist and hurried down towards the river and the *Quai de l'Horloge*. As usual when it rained there wasn't a cab to be seen.

He arrived somewhat breathless and very damp. But fortunately, some years ago, he had spent far too much money in a good quality overcoat, and it was an occasion like this that made him remember what a good investment it had been. He requested coffee from his secretary, conducted the morning meeting with some brevity and then had retired to his office to spend a few moments with the morning newspaper. Having found little of any great interest there he turned to the large envelope had again appeared under his door during the night when Gant came in in something of a rush. He was in a state of considerable excitement.

'Sandrat's been killed!'

'What?'

'Killed, boss.'

'When? How?'

'An accident apparently, sir. He was hit by a delivery cart slap in the middle of the *Boulevard St Germain*. He seems to have been crossing the road and fallen over in front of it. It ran right over him. One of the horses seems to have kicked him in the head too.'

What do you mean one of the horses?'

'They were a pair, sir. It was a fully loaded dray wagon delivering to the wine market.'

'What time was this?'

'About eight o'clock this morning. Sandrat apparently lives somewhere around the Luxembourg Gardens and was presumably walking to work. After the accident someone put him in a cab and taken straight to the Salpetrière Hospital but he seemed pretty dead.'

Drangnet just looked thoughtful. Maybe it really was an accident. Such things weren't uncommon especially in the busy early morning traffic. But this was all something of a coincidence.

'Right,' he said decisively. 'Does that new-fangled telephone gadget of yours still connect you with Doctor Dankovich at Salpetrière?'

'Yes, sir,' he replied looking a touch put out. 'Of course, it does.'

'Then talk to the good doctor and check that the man is indeed dead and whether he thinks there might be anything odd about it. Do we have any witnesses?'

'Yes, plenty. I already have some preliminary statements from people who said they were passing by. The local gendarmerie got there pretty quickly too, and they commandeered the cab. By the way, I think that we'll probably be getting a bill for that sooner or later. From what I can find out he tried to run across the road in front of the wagon and slipped.'

'Have we got anything from the driver, his details and some sort of a statement?

'Yes, He's one of the regular drivers; drives the route every day, so we know where he lives. He says that he tried to stop but he was fully loaded so there wasn't much chance of his doing so. He did say that he was going a good pace as he was late with his delivery, but he denied anything excessive. Some of the pedestrians confirm it. He certainly wasn't going at a gallop or anything like that. It's also true that the wagon was very well loaded, and a good load of wine is very heavy as we know. All seems quite straightforward. Simple accident. But I'll speak to Dankovich.'

Drangnet looked long and hard at the door as it closed behind his deputy. He was no great believer in coincidence but maybe this was just one of those unlucky things. As long as the good doctor didn't discover something untoward or some eyewitness didn't come forward to say that they say the man being shoved into the horses' path, he could close the book on it pretty quickly. Perhaps it wouldn't do to delve too deeply. It certainly solved a problem for him. The Prefect himself was departing from office soon in one of those many and seemingly continuous changes of senior appointments and ministers that seemed characterise the new Third Republic and its perpetually unstable politics. So, if he could try to persuade his tennis partner to take more than a passing interest in his replacement as deputy prefect, it might go some way to breaking up this dreadful conspiracy while making the whole department somewhat more to his taste. It was an opportunity.

He took up the envelope that still lay in his desk and took his paper knife in hand. But again, before he had time to use it, the door opened again. Not for the first time he noticed that Gant seemed to knock, turn the door handle, and come in all in one movement.

'Look like an accident,' he said. 'Nothing to make the good doctor think otherwise, apparently. Cause of death was having his head stood on by a full-grown dray horse. Numerous broken bones and internal injuries. The cart's wheels got him too. Pretty comprehensive job.'

'All right, Roger. Wait for Dankovich to send his report in, then write it all up and put it in file. Unless we get anything new in from the streets in the meantime, I want it closed off and looking like a death that we don't have to concern ourselves with.'

'No chance of anarchist horses then by any chance, boss?' Gant suggested mischievously but had to the presence of mind to leave before Drangnet could reply.

Once the door was closed Drangnet was finally able to get to the envelope. The report was again beautifully laid out and clear. Cordiez has spent the day in the prefecture as had Sandrat. Both had lunched at different local cafés. The observer clearly couldn't get close enough to overhear the conversation and little was reported about either event or the rest of the day. The two did, however, come together in the evening when they had attended a meeting of the *Lodge Sagesse des Parfaits Maçons*. There followed a particularly detailed account of what went on with the initiation of five new members described in some detail and Drangnet realised that the report had been written by someone who was actually there as well. Other than that there was just what the writer described as the usual masonic business affairs. The writer also noted that, apart from Cordiez and Sandrat who both attended as guests, there were two other guests that evening, Armande Louis Phélypeaux and Claude de La Trémoille, both Senators from the Upper House. It was, apparently, not unusual for guests from other lodges to be invited to these ceremonies. But all four had been invited by the same man, the Master of the Lodge, Comte André de St Germonde, also a senior Senator and, apparently, the man who Sandrat had met the day before in the Jardine de Luxembourg.

Drangnet got up from his desk, went to a bookshelf and took down the current political directory. It was published after each election and listed all the elected members of both houses as well as all the elected and appointed officers of the state. All three men were indeed Senators and permanent ones at that.

He was fully aware that there might be good reasons for these five to meet and talk. Something masonic was the obvious first choice. The fact that four of them were guests of the fifth might again not be particularly suspicious. Three were also senior members of the National Assembly. Cordiez was not, on the face of it, likely to be an everyday colleague. Sandrat seemed to be neither one thing nor the other and maybe, Drangnet mused, that was precisely his position. Three bigwigs at the top, Sandrat passing orders to Cordiez who had direct access to men on his staff who would actually getting their hands dirty. Enough everyday social and professional contacts and private masonic meetings to keep things confidential and enough distance from the sharp end for deniability.

The whole thing, thought Drangnet, smacked of a hastily arranged meeting of conspirator masons under cover of the regular monthly get together of the Lodge. The reporter went on to say that while all the rest, including, it seemed, himself, left at the end of the meeting at about nine thirty, the Master and his four guests stayed for almost another two hours before making their various ways home.

So, he thought, we seem to be getting somewhere at last. We have a meeting between five men under the pretext of a Masonic lodge meeting where only one of whom, the Master of the lodge, had any real right to be there. The others were outsiders. So, he could at least tie these five together. Now, a few hours later, one of the five was dead. He didn't believe the accident story for one moment. He was all too well aware that the author of the surveillance report worked for Madame Fernier and she would have been the first to know about the meeting. It may be a considerable step to go from that to planning this morning's accident on the *Boulevard St. German* but it was by no means an impossible one. The remaining four conspirators would now have to think about what to do next especially, if he was right in his guess, an important middleman had been taken out of the picture. He was sure that the noble senators wouldn't be comfortable getting close to the dirty, executive end of their conspiracy. He smiled quietly to himself. He felt that the tension was rising. This, he felt, was the sort of moment when criminals started making mistakes and he settled back into his chair with a slight feeling of anticipation without realising that he was rubbing his hands together gently.

Drangnet smiled. He always thought of himself as a logical and disciplined sort of man. He disliked doing anything in a hurry. He prided himself on a cool head and a calm mind. Now things seemed to be moving fast and he needed to catch up and start planning. There was movement in the case at last.

Chapter 14: Thursday 14th April   Scene 1: A Message Arrives

Yet again his thoughts were interrupted by Gant's knock and enter performance.

'Yes?' Drangnet exclaimed somewhat forcibly in a sharp tone of voice that showed his annoyance slightly.

'Er, sorry to disturb you, sir,' said Gant realising that the Chief Inspector wasn't too pleased at having his morning interrupted yet again. 'Just got this.'

He came fully into the office and put another envelope on the desk.

'Same sort of delivery,' he said briskly. 'Another kid off the street. Ran off again almost before he had arrived.'

The door closed again. He slit open the envelope and took out a small note. Carrying it unread, he walked across to one of the armchairs he had arranged so that he could look out of the window and see out onto the river and the right bank beyond. He took the decanter of his beloved red wine from the Rhône valley, poured himself a glass and sat down, staring out for a moment at the river traffic without a conscious thought in his head; as if to clear it. Some random thoughts came and went, each following the last rather like a dream. A fragment of Couperin, a glance at the game on Sunday. Madame, yes, she flitted in and out as well. A corpse of a murdered young girl and a blood bespattered body of a deputy prefect of police. Who was grinning at that, he wondered? None of the thoughts was, of course, as random as he thought. They were all bits and pieces of the case and this was the seemingly random way he tended to order his thoughts about a case and to plan what to do next. Many times, in the past he had found that this seemingly disjointed cascade of jigsaw puzzle pieces would fall into some sort of order if he let them. His mind would do the work if he didn't insist on driving it in any particular direction. Usually it would work the better for that.

He sat looking vacantly across the water, seeing the view without taking it in, letting some bit of his mind that he didn't control do the work for him. The new note remained loosely in his hand unread as he sipped gently at the wine. There would be time to add the new after the old had been sorted and organised.

Oddly, this was the only place where he could do this. He'd tried it at home or while walking around the Paris streets, but it never seemed to work. Here in his office, just looking out over the river, it did. Perhaps it was matter of context. He was in the middle of the Paris judiciary system here on the *Île*, surrounded by policemen of all sorts and their offices, soldier's barracks, courts of justice, lawyers and court staff, prison cells. The place positively reeked of it all, while sitting just a few metres to the west along the *Île* was the great cathedral church of Notre Dame, standing imperiously looking down over their attempts to administer justice to low and high alike. Disapprovingly too, perhaps, these days, he felt, given the new republican ambition to remove the Mother Church from her centuries old influence on affairs of state and society. This was the place where Church and State truly intersected; not in the tasselled chambers of the *Palais de Luxembourg* and the *Palais Bourbon* where the two chambers of the National Assembly played their games. It was here on this little island where the two laws, those of men and of God, intersected. He smiled with contentment. This was where he was at his happiest. This was his home.

The picture was almost clear in his mind. He knew he was on the right track. He had it right. He also had not an iota of evidence. He also had an uncomfortable feeling that the beautiful Madame Fernier was toying with him; or at least she was as interested in using him as he was in her. Again, the smile came to his lips. It was a situation that he slightly relished. The game was coming to a conclusion and it was all the more intriguing for the fact that he wasn't completely sure what side she was on.

At some stage he opened the note. This time the handwriting was less elegant but still it was readable and in an educated hand. Not Madame, he thought, but perhaps one of her men. The message was a short one. They had found out – God knows how, Drangnet thought – that the group of conspirators was meeting again tomorrow. The venue was a café in the *Rue de Caille* in the 14th *arrondissment*.

His attention again drifted to the window and view beyond. He just sat and tried to add this latest snippet to the picture already in his head. Given what he now thought, it made sense for the conspirators to meet again. Sandrat's death had forced that on them. There was always the possibility that it had been no accident – a conclusion that Drangnet had already come to – and if so, they would be forced to decide what it meant and what to do, especially if they thought they were under threat themselves. Presumably some plan was already in play, perhaps another murder, and instructions would have to be given. The chain of command had been broken and it had to be restored. A meeting therefore had to be arranged and tonight, apparently, it would happen.

The next question he had to ask himself was what, if anything, he was going to do about it. If he was right there was an opportunity of catching all the major conspirators in the same place or at least the ones he knew about. With Madame Fernier's good offices he might get a report of what was being said if one of her people could get in secretly to observe. But it would be hearsay testimony at the very best and irrespective of whether it would be any use when he tried to take all these people to court, it would raise some very difficult questions about him and Madame. A testimony from him, Chief Inspector of the *Sûreté*, would carry much more weight. He could also explain his present there. The much used standby "acting on information received" would more than suffice. Yes, he had to go himself somehow. Any other way would also compromise his relationship with Angèle.

Chapter 14 Thursday 14th April   Scene 2 Plan, Action and Betrayal

Drangnet sat alone in his office lost in thought. There were a number of ways he felt he could approach this opportunity. The most official was a large operation, fully resourced and planned. But there was nowhere near enough time to organise something of that magnitude. It would have to be a big operation involving a lot of people and costing enough to flag it to the attention of a number of people he would have preferred not to get involved. He was all too aware how thin was the amount of actual hard evidence he had that could be used to justify such an investment. Dancart would back him of course, but others further up to hierarchy would hear about it and some of those could be connected with the conspiracy. He could mount a more limited operation with just a few colleagues from the *Sûreté*. That would certainly be easier but again the questions of evidence loomed. He couldn't go on a fishing expedition especially when another police department was involved. He could also just take Gant and a few men.

The problem really was that he had no evidence that anything untoward was actually planned for the evening and getting official sanction for an operation would be especially difficult at this late stage. There was no legal reason why this group shouldn't meet and discuss anything they liked. There was also the little matter of having absolutely no evidence at all against any of them. He was pretty sure that would be Gant's reaction. They might indeed overhear something but in the absence of time to arrange the surveillance, there was very little chance, it seemed to him. He needed to be there if only to confirm his suspicions rather than anything else. The chances of picking up any actual evidence were small. If it was truly just Drangnet satisfying his own curiosity then he certainly didn't feel that he had the right to get others involved.

All these thoughts were passing through his head and he was slightly depressed that he really couldn't decide what to do. There was also the possibility of ignoring this meeting completely as there was very little chance of his getting anything particularly significant from it in any case. But he didn't want to ignore anything coming from

Angèle given that it was her people who were being put at risk in helping him to get the information in the first place.

Gradually he found himself coming to the conclusion that he was going to have to do the job himself, more or less. He and perhaps a couple of others would go and take a look. Not Gant. His faithful deputy still had a career in front of him and had a wife and three children to support. He had too much to lose by getting involved in something that was going to have to be unofficial.

There was a knock on his door; one that he didn't immediately recognise. Over the years, most of the people who had regular access to his in his office had recognisable knocks. They tended to do it in the same way each time they came in. This one was less familiar. Before he had a chance to guess, his boss came in bearing a harassed expression. Drangnet got up to greet him. It wasn't unknown for the Superintendent to visit his Chief Inspector, but it was rare. He sat in the chair opposite.

'I'm getting a lot of pressure from the powers above about this prostitute killing business, Louis and now with Sandrat's accident it's getting worse. I'd like to think that you are making some progress even though you seem content to keep me in the dark, as usual.'

Drangnet decided not to remind his superior that it was less than a day since their last meeting. Dancart was as up to date as Drangnet wanted to keep him. The pressure must have been considerable for his boss to make the trip to see him.

'You know how it is, boss. In our business we often get situations where we know what it is happening pretty well but have no real evidence; at least not enough that will be enough to arrest someone and make a case for the Judge.'

Dancart just made a harrumphing noise before going on.

'What all this about there being a list of these girls' clients? What's that all about?'

Immediately it was obvious why Dancart was sitting in his office. Someone or some people weren't concerned about the murders at all. They were worried about their wives finding out what they got up to in their spare time. Drangnet was immediately less sympathetic.

'Well, Sir. It's true that we have located a list of people who frequented these brothels and we're hope that it might provide a list of possible suspects.'

'Some people are getting a bit rattled by that list. Some are even lobbying for me to forbid you to use it.'

'I admit it's a long shot, sir, but I can't afford to ignore the possibility that these women were killed by one of their clients. If I have to ruffle a few feathers by asking some people questions, then I would just say that is rather tough luck on them. I'll try to do it as quietly as I can, but I have a difficult investigation on my hands, and I don't have the time to bother too much about these people. If they're so worried about their reputations perhaps, they should go home to their wives more often. If some people actually want to confiscate the list, I would be very interested to know some names. It strikes me as a good place to start asking my questions.'

Dancart sighed.

'Louis this is exactly the reason why it'll be difficult to get you appointed to my job when I retire. You have to learn to keep on the right side of these people.'

'I wasn't aware,' replied Drangnet, 'that I ever said I wanted your job, sir.'

'All right. As you wish. Are you making any progress at all? We've enough trouble with this dreadful accident with Sandrat. We have to find a new Deputy Prefect as well as everything else.'

'That, my old friend,' said Drangnet with a smile, 'why you are paid so much more than I am and have a nice big office. I am getting somewhere, as it happened, with the murder of these prostitutes but it'll be a little time yet.'

'You better hurry up. The newspapers are also beginning to take much more than a passing interest too. It could all get a bit ugly if they get wind of your infamous list.'

'Well if they do, sir, it certainly won't be from me.'

Ah, he thought to himself. Newspapers. A new and unwelcome pressure on police work. So far he'd manage to avoid journalists to a great extent but even he saw that there were an increasing number of them around the places where crimes took place; talking to witnesses with fistfuls of money in their hands and getting stories before the police. Making them up too when there wasn't enough information to make a good story. There was always a ready market for sensational stories of murder or violence.

'I'll do my best, sir.' he replied, pleased that, for the moment at least, he didn't have to deal with these people.

In the end he just decided to do it himself. In truth it was a matter of having no alternative. There was now little time to organise anything else. He decided on two people to help him, men he had known for a long time dating back to the difficult days of the commune when no-one knew who was a friend or who an enemy; who was denouncing who. Both men now served in the uniformed gendarmerie in the outer arrondissements, one in the 14th itself.

The *Rue de la Caille* was a short street that linked the *Boulevard d' Enfer* with the streets bearing the same name just at south east corner of the *Cimetière Mont Parnasse*. It was a narrow lane scarcely wide enough for a carriage and the café was almost halfway along it. It was a generally scruffy part of southern Paris near the newly built railway station that serviced the Paris to Sceaux line. The comings and goings of travellers would mean that the café would have regular strangers dropping in for refreshment in addition to any regular customers it might have. It was some chance for Drangnet and his two men to sit unobserved or so he hoped.

It had taken Drangnet most of the afternoon to find his two men. Both were, of course, on duty on the streets. One he found in the *Parc de Montsouris* right at the southern end of the 14th. The second had been on duty at the *Château de la Muette* on the western edge of the city. They were old friends of his from his army days and were very happy to earn some overtime. He arranged to meet them at ten o'clock at the entrance to the forage market next to the cemetery. His information was that the conspirators would assemble at 11pm so that gave them time to walk to the place and settle into the café and try to get themselves in a position to overhear what was going on when the meeting began.

Drangnet returned to the office and worked late. He often did so there was nothing unusual for the dwindling number of staff to remember. There were always plenty of bits of paper to be attended to and by the time nine thirty came around, the building was virtually deserted. He took a key from the locked centre drawer of his desk, got up and went over to the safe in the corner of his office. Inside was his Chamelot-Delvigne MAS 1873 revolver. He had been given it as a replacement for his old service gun when the new model became standard issue seven years ago. Although he practiced with it fairly regularly, cleaning and oiling it, making sure it was in good working order, he had actually never carried it in anger. He usually felt that if he needed a gun to help him enforce the law, then perhaps he wasn't doing his job properly. This time felt different. He put it in the pocket of his overcoat, walked out of the building past the night sergeant on duty at the front desk and started as if to walk home. He wanted to get away from the *Île* before hailing a cab. He also wanted to avoid catching one of the many cabs that regularly patrolled near the *Préfecture* in the hope of regular trade. Most of those drivers would recognise him too. He wanted to find one who didn't know him if at all possible. He struck off north to the *Rue de Rivoli* and got almost as far at *Les Halles* before hailing a passing cab. He asked the driver to go towards the *École Militaire*. There he intended to change cabs before finally arriving at the rendezvous.

The two policemen were waiting when he got to the fodder market and before long they were walking down the street that had recently been renamed as the *Rue Denfert-Rochereau* after the commander in charge of the defence of Belfort during the recent German War towards the entrance of the *Rue de la Caille*. The night was cloudy and there was very little light.

Drangnet entered the little street first with his companions close behind and made his way down towards the café keeping close to the wall, his two companions just behind him. The street was barely illuminated by two gas lamps, one at either end. Out here, away from the great boulevards and buildings of the centre of the city, the provision of street lighting was less much generous. There was barely enough light to see across the road let alone illuminate the buildings opposite and although the street was barely more than fifty metres long it was almost completely dark for the most part. Suddenly Drangnet felt unsure. There should have been at least some light coming from the café and as far as he could see there was none. He drew the revolver from his pocket and held it in front of him as they neared the café entrance. The whole café was dark. He found himself reverting to his military training. The MAS 1873 was a double action revolver which meant that the hammer was cocked before firing by the first part of the action of pulling the trigger. This partial first pull enabled the shot to be fired just by further pulling the trigger, making the actual firing of the gun smoother and thus more accurate. It was also hazardous to keep the gun at this "half cocked" position as an accidental discharge was much more likely.

His suspicions deepened while looking at the dark doorway of an obviously empty café and it was as he raised his gun towards his eye level that he was hit a huge blow to the back of the head. The gun fell from his hand and he crumpled, lifeless in an unconscious heap on the cobbled street.

Chapter 14: Thursday 14th April   Scene 3: Interrogation and Survival

The black fog that filled his head hardly cleared as he came back to consciousness. The pain was intense. He could feel that he was seated, fixed to a chair by ropes around his chest, arms and legs. His head was spinning, and his eyes wouldn't focus. He just sat there moving in and out of consciousness. Suddenly he was drenched with a shock of cold water. Someone had got tired of waiting and had hurled a bucket-full in his face. Now he began to see around him.

He was in a low room lit by a couple of single gas flames on burners coming out from the bare brick walls. Above him was a low, vaulted brick roof. He was obviously in a cellar and judging by the rubbish piled along the sides of the room and in the corner he could see, it could well be the cellar under the café he had been aiming for. They had obviously been waiting for him. There was an empty chair directly in front of him. He regained enough of his thoughts to realise that he was alive and therefore someone wanted to talk to him. Sure enough someone came from behind him and sat down. It was Cordiez. Drangnet's revolver held loosely in his lap.

'I'm disappointed Chief Inspector. I had thought we would have much more of a problem getting you here. Some of the others thought that your ego would get you to come but I had my doubts. I thought you would see the note as a trap. But then I realised that you were getting so used to trading little notes with Madame Fernier so you probably wouldn't pick the bad one in the apple box.'

Drangnet knew that they weren't going to let him go. His capture and Cordiez facing him directly without a mask or disguise of any sort showed him that unless he could think of a way out, he wasn't going to leave this place alive. So as Cordiez crowed he tried to explore his situation a little. Apart from the man in front he could sense at least one other behind him. The ropes around him were tight and there was no way he could even thing of getting loose with at least two armed men looking at him. Cordiez went on. He didn't seem to need a partner in his conversation.

'You've found out, of course. You have figured it out while all those stupid policemen that you surround yourself with at the *Sûreté* flounder about. But you have no proof. No evidence indeed. You're stuck. So, you decided to come here tonight to get some sort of eyewitness evidence. Better than nothing, I suppose.'

Perhaps, thought Drangnet, there was some sort of chance to talk to this man. He was the one who was vulnerable. He wasn't nobility or a politician of high rank. Nor was he a thug off the street. He was the link between these two sorts and now that Sandrat had gone he had an even wider gap to bridge.

'They won't save you, you know, Cordiez. As soon as this comes close to them, they'll drop you in the shit and run fast in the other direction.'

There was a silence while Cordiez decided whether to admit his prisoner into what had hitherto been a monologue.

'They won't you know. They need me. They wouldn't know how to kill a prostitute and get away with it.'

Drangnet smiled at the man's naiveté.

'Oh, they would, my friend. Believe me. People like that have been doing that sort of thing for centuries and getting away with it, consuming thousands of little people like you in the process. We've had five revolutions in France in the last hundred years and our Senate is still full of people like St Germonde and Phélypeaux and Trémoille.'

This time Cordiez paused before replying. Perhaps he was actually thinking about what Drangnet was saying or maybe he was just digesting the fact that Drangnet knew who were the men at the top.

'Yes, Cordiez, I do know about these people and so does my department. Their time will come soon. They'll no longer be your passport to the top. I guess that's what all this is about for you, at least. You're no man of principal, are you?'

He was rewarded with a scowl of recognition.

288

'You don't know what you're talking about, Drangnet,' he snarled taking a firm grip on the revolver for the first time in the conversation.

Drangnet realised that he was playing a very dangerous game. But he had nothing to lose.

'I'm afraid I do, Cordiez. I've met people like these many times before. Like you too. I've had to deal with them time and time again. They may affect the manners of gentlemen, but they're sharks. Dangerous men. Killers too in their own way. Dangerous to small men like you who might put their trust in them and presume to be one of them. Whatever these men have promised you, whether it's promotion, power, influence, wealth, you won't live to get it, believe me. The second you're no longer useful to them or you're perceived as becoming a liability, they'll destroy you. You'll be the next one floating down the Seine at midnight. If you come to the *Sûreté* now and offer your testimony against these people, I'll protect you. I can get you immunity from prosecution. With Sandrat gone, there's no one else to protect you now.'

Cordiez was silenced at last. It was the only card that Drangnet had to play and he had done his best. He watched the man as a whole range of emotions played out across his face. He had, at least, given the man something to think about. But before long the face became very hard.

'Nice try, old chap. But I'll take my chances with the big guys. But I can't see any way to let you go now. You've worked it out and I know you. You won't give up. I'm afraid for you it ends here and now.'

'There are plenty of others who know, and they will come after you as well.'

Cordiez shook his head with a wry smile coming to his face.

'Maybe they'll have better luck, Chief Inspector. But you're the best and I've beaten you. The rest will be easy.'

That was the point at which Drangnet realised that he was going to die. There was nothing he could do now. So, he just sat back.

He began to think of other things rather at random. Oddly, he felt very little. The MAS 1873 revolver was a heavy weapon and at that range the 11mm bullet would kill him instantly. Cordiez lifted the gun and pointed it directly at the centre of Drangnet's forehead. Even then he felt absolutely nothing as he looked directly at it. He even saw the man's finger whiten as he started to press the trigger to cock the mechanism and fire the gun. He watched the cylinder start to rotate as it moved the bullet into line with the barrel.

There was a huge explosion in the confined space and his world went completely black and empty even before he pitched violently sideways on the chair onto the brick floor.

What followed was something of a blur. He was lying, still tied on the ground. He seemed almost completely insensible except that his head was filled to bursting with an enormous buzzing noise. A huge explosion very close to his right ear had seen to that. He dimly felt being cut free from the capsized chair and hauled to his feet by two non-too gentle men. He looked through a significant amount of gun smoke across the room to where he had last seen Cordiez pointing a gun at him. This time the man was sprawled on the floor in front of him and seemed to be missing half his head. He the felt a sharp pain in his left arm and, looking down, he saw that the arm was covered in blood. Then just as he was attempting to get his balance, Angèle appeared from behind and turned to face him. He noticed a large revolver in her hand with wisps of smoke still coming from its barrel.

She smiled down at him.

'Ah my dear Louis. we were just in time, I think.'

He tried to collect his thoughts enough to make some sort of reply, but his head was spinning and he was none too steady on his feet. His two supporters were still having to hang on to him.

'All right, you two get him into the cab and back to the *Place des Vosges*. Find Dr. Raspail and get him there as well. He'll know what to do. I'll follow as soon as I've tidied up here.'

And with that he was lifted off his feet and carried bodily from the room. He was conscious of being hauled without much ceremony and less than gently up a narrow flight of stairs and out of the building and being bundled directly bundled into a waiting cab. Both men got in as well, wedged in either side of him and as the cab moved off at pace, he felt one of the men taking a knife and cutting the left sleeve off his jacket. Immediately a tourniquet of sorts was put tightly around his upper arm. It reminded him of battlefield medical treatment which, in a sense, he supposed it was. Some form of shock then seemed to set in and without any particularly accurate sense of time he found himself somewhat to his relief in his own apartment and being undressed by his two companions. No-one had said a word to him since that moment of great cacophony in the cellar. Yet there he lay, naked on his own bed, in considerable pain from a wound in his left arm and in equally considerable surprise at actually being alive. The last coherent thought that he could muster was a terrifying vision of the inside of Cordiez's pistol barrel pointing precisely between his eyes.

He had no idea how long he lay there. He drifted in and out of consciousness or at least he thought he did. In all probability it wasn't very long before too long a fat, bustling man in a tightly fitting suit came into the bedroom carrying the archetypal medical case in his hand. His two companions started to leave the bedside. His impression that they were guards and well as guardians was reinforced by one them leaning over his just before he left the bedside.

'Just keep your mouth shut, Monsieur, or your wound could suddenly become fatal in spite of the good doctor here. You are lucky that Madam can shoot straight. You owe a debt now. Remember that.'

With that the men retreated leaving the doctor alone at the bedside. He started to try to speak but was immediately interrupted by the doctor.

'Don't say anything, Monsieur. Those were Madame's instructions.'

It had been said in perfect unaccented French, Drangnet got the point and just closed his eyes. The next thing he felt was a none too gentle stab in the arm and within a second or two, or two or so it seemed, he fell asleep.

He woke sometime later to two very different impressions. The first was an agonising pain in his left arm. It was surrounded by a tight bandage and lay inert but throbbing at his side. The second was the concerned face of a woman leaning over him. The fact was serious but still to his eyes beautiful. It was also streaked with dirt and soot. He slowly reached up with his right hand and cradled her face in it.

'Thank you, my dear. I owe you my life, I think.'

She inclined her head slightly and placed a long gentle kiss into the palm of his hand.

'Perhaps, my dear,' she whispered. 'Only perhaps.'

'What happened? Why were you there? What about the two men who came with me?'

She lowered his hand and held it gently in hers.

'Just lie still, my dear Louis. I'll tell you as far as I can. Firstly, I managed to shoot Cordiez just as he was going to kill you. He missed his aim and just creased your left arm. In fact, the wound is very slight, and the good doctor has sewn you up very easily. In fact he was slightly contemptuous. He likes a greater challenge.'

'So why were you there in the first place?' he asked. still not quite understanding what happened.

'Well, my dear, I do feel somewhat responsible for putting you in danger,' she sighed. 'It was my complacency, I suppose. Firstly, the message you received this morning didn't come from us, but I only heard about it earlier this evening from one of our, er friends, who works in your offices. I knew I hadn't sent you a message and it took a little time to find the boy who brought it. Fortunately, the boy had looked at the note so he could tell us what it said. By the time we got to the *Rue de la Caille* you had already fallen into the trap and been captured with the help, incidentally of one of the two men you chose to take with you on your impromptu spying mission. The man was unreliable but I am please to say that he is now a very dead unreliable man. We know his well. However, we managed to arrive in time. Any later and you would equally have been a very dead Chief Inspector of the *Sûreté*.'

Drangnet had too many questions rattling around in his head but one or two needed to be asked.

'Cordiez?'

'Very dead as well, I'm pleased to say. No head.'

'You must get rid of him out of the city, Angèle. If he is just dumped in the Seine or somewhere in the city, it will immediately turn into a huge manhunt. Killing of a policeman will get entirely too much attention. Better if he just simply vanishes. Take him out on one of your produce lorries that comes in from the countryside and bury him somewhere, perhaps people will be too busy to take much notice, especially after Sandrat's accident. But you never know. The other man as well, I think.'

She just nodded and turned away to give the relevant instructions to Georges who was standing in the background.

'What about the men I had with me?' he asked. 'One worked for Cordiez, you say?'

'Well one was certainly working under Cordiez's orders. He killed his colleague almost as soon you were captured. He and two others of Cordiez's people will join their boss on the proposed trip to the countryside. And, in case you are sufficiently recovered to start thinking like a policeman again, there were no witnesses, at least ones that might tell an embarrassing story. That's been taken care of.'

Suddenly things seemed to catch up with him and he felt very tired. The room was dark and there was little light coming in through the curtain. Angèle saw him fading slightly and motioned to the doctor who had been standing well back from the bedside out of hearing range. He approached his patient and gently slid another needle into this arm.

Angèle had kept hold of his hand and lent down close to his cheek.

'You go to sleep now, my dear. We've changed the sheets on your bed. The original ones were rather too bloody to stay. You need to sleep and rest now. You've just been shot after all. I'll be here when you wake up.'

'Angèle, dearest. I'll need to talk with Gant.'

'All right, we'll send a message to him to get him here in the morning.'

He was about to say something else, but the injection won, and he relaxed back into his pillow and drifted quickly off to sleep. She let his hand fall gently back onto the bed and turned to the doctor.

'No question of any difficulties or complications I presume?'

It was as much an instruction as an enquiry.

'None, Madame Fernier. He isn't badly injured at all. The bullet passed across the side of his left and the wound is really no more than a deep cut. He'll be fine after a little sleep.'

'He'll probably complain a lot,' she relied smiling gently and looking down at the slumbering figure. 'Men are such babies.'

The good doctor smiled back.

'Perhaps Madame. But from what I hear about this man he may not react quite in the way you might expect. He's experienced bullet wounds before, I think, judging by some of the old scars.'

She just nodded.

'He was lucky.'

'If you mean that he was lucky to have you there, Madame, then I think you're right. Very lucky.'

'Well. Thank you for your help, doctor. I think I can handle it from here. Pease send Georges in to see me and my maid as well. I think they're outside.'

'Very well, Madame. I'll be back in the morning to re-dress the wound. It was a pretty simple sewing job. I've seen much worse.'

The man left a small pile of bandages and medicaments by the side of the bed and shook her hand and left. The next to arrive was madame's maid.

'Louise, please can you go and get my night things and a change of clothing for tomorrow? I shall be staying here tonight.'

The girl turned away, not without letting the smallest of smiles cross her lips; a smile that Angèle decided to ignore. Next was the man who had been with her during this evening's adventure.

'Georges. I want you to get a message to Inspector Gant telling him that his boss wants to see him here tomorrow morning at ten. Not before.'

The man just nodded.

'Is everything organised from tonight. The bodies are taken care of?'

'Yes, Madame. They'll be on their way out of the city within the hour in the direction of Créteil. Eugene Tranchard has a big farm there just beyond the village and he brings a lot of produce into the *Halles* every day. He has a pass thought the city toll gate so he's never searched. The police are quite used to seeing him and his waggons coming and going at all hours. He'll get the job done all right.'

'Good,' she replied. 'And what about the bodies when they get there?'

Georges just smiled.

'Eugene keeps pigs, Madame.'

'Ah,' she replied with a grim smile. 'Again, good.'

The man left and she sat alone beside the bed. She sat looking at the sleeping figure. She was more than a little surprised at her feelings for this man. She had received many suitors over the years without finding anyone who impressed her too much. She was, in her own way, eminently suitable for courtship. She was rich, attractive, intelligent and influential. A woman to be reckoned with. And perhaps that explained it. An eligible woman in Paris had to be all those things but not to the extent that she was. The family business would always keep its secrets from the most ardent of lovers. There was also the question of her own family. She was hardly correctly born for a polite society match. There her eligibility flagged a little. But for whatever reason no one had come along who took her fancy and she had remained a bachelor and firmly unattached. Until now, that is. Until this odd, equally single, policeman had come along. He seemed to know all about her and what she was. Yet it didn't seem to matter. It was true that their relationship was based on expediency. They could both do something for each other. But she had quickly got used to having him around, to his discussing things with her. He talked with her as an equal. She had shot Cordiez tonight not out of any wish to save a business relationship but because she wanted to defend him. She had rushed to the meeting when she heard of the deception irrespective of the possible danger not just because he was helping her defend her people. She felt suddenly irrational; almost as if he was her lover. Perhaps that is what she had grown so quickly to need. She certainly felt things for him that she had never felt for anyone before.

If that wasn't complicated enough, she had now saved his life and in doing do committed murder in front of him, the senior policeman of the *Sûreté* of Paris. Hers was not the only situation that had suddenly become difficult. It had for him too.

She reassured herself that her patient was sleeping soundly and got up. She had to decide on her own sleeping arrangements before her maid returned. She had already visited the apartment and looked around but hadn't explored it. She had at least to find a bedroom to sleep in. So she set off and before long she realised that it was a substantial establishment. Apart from the usual principal rooms of a salon that contained Drangnet's beloved piano, dining room and a small drawing room, there was also a small book-lined study. Three principal bedrooms with a dressing room for Drangnet as well as rather a grand bathroom. The main corridor led to the kitchen and a scullery and, to her delight, a very small but perfectly adequate maid's apartment of bedroom, sitting room and even a small bathroom. She wandered around in wonder. This was very much more that a bachelor's apartment. She knew the history of the square well. It had ceased being the most fashionable place to live in all Paris a century ago when much of the nobility decided to adopt the *Faubourg Saint-German* on the left bank as the fashionable place to live. Cardinal Richelieu had spent almost fifteen years in residence on the Place as had Bishop Bossuet. Victor Hugo as well. Now the square contained a more arty set with a fair selection of writers like Alfonse Daudet and Théophile Gautier. The actual apartments had been designed and constructed by a variety of different architects behind Louis Métezeau's elegant facades and existed in a variety of sizes and configurations. Drangnet's was at first floor level at the eastern end of the north side, ironically the closest point to the site of the Bastille prison, just a few tens of metres to the east.

By current standards it was almost palatial; much, much bigger that most around it. It must cost a great to rent. She reminded himself to find out more. It was not quite on a par with her house on the *Île St. Louis* of course. There she had the entire building from cellar to attic. One or two on either side as well, although she kept that secret. But if she had to live north of the river, this was as good as anywhere. She wandered slowly though the rooms. She would bunk down in the maid's bedroom.

She came to the end of the Salon and sat at his piano. It was a fine example from the famous manufacturer from Marseille, golden mid-brown in colour, highly polished with much lighter inlays decorating the edges and lid. It had the customary brass inscription along the front above the keyboard denoting the proud award to the company of a gold medal at the Tenth Industrial Exhibition in Paris in 1844. In addition to the main music rest that now held the Couperin manuscript, the instrument was fully equipped with its two smaller side stands on either side to accommodate the scores for two singers. Angèle found herself wondering how often these were used and who used them. The manuscript she had given him was open and as she looked more closely, she noticed that he had pencilled small annotations all over it. This was clearly one of the motets that he was singing, and he was making a singer's notes. For him it was a working score, something to be used and venerated only insofar as it was of use. Rare, perhaps and potentially priceless as he knew full well, but a working score nevertheless. He was using it as the composer would have wished and that gave her great pleasure. She was momentarily filled with pleasure and a feeling of passion that was unlike anything she had experienced before.

Her reverie was interrupted by a knock on the door. Her maid, Anne-Marie, came in with a number of pieces of baggage, more than Angele had anticipated. The girl takes some of the decisions herself.

'Well, Madame, you didn't expect me to let you stay here alone, did you? You may wish to look after Monsieur, but someone has to look after you. So please show me where you want to sleep and where I will, and I'll make up the beds. I've also brought your linen. I believe this is a bachelor household and they don't know anything at all about linen; amongst other things,' she added as an afterthought.

That, Angèle mused, would account for some of the baggage as the girl continued.

'I've also brought you a late supper, Madame. I thought you might be hungry after your adventures tonight. I've brought a selection of things for you to wear tomorrow as well. You should, at least, have something to choose from, irrespective of what else is going on.'

It was clear that for her whatever it was that that was 'going on' as she put it, it was not approved of.

Angèle sighed. There were some things she had little control of and her maid was one on them. So she contented herself with giving the girl a tour of the apartment and then left her to it. She went back to Drangnet's bedside. He was still sleeping gently. There was nothing she could do, of course. She went back to thinking about the apartment. She assumed that he rented it but perhaps he owned it. She hardly thought so but the normal rent for a place like this would have been beyond the reach of the normal policeman, even a senior one. She had seen that he didn't have a living-in maid. He had a housekeeper who usually came every Saturday morning. She just sat there looking at him. What, she asked of herself, was she going to do with him? Leave him be or fall in love completely? She smiled. She was asking herself a question to which she already know the answer. She was already in love with him. There was no other explanation for the fact that she was sitting by the damn man's bedside. Fortunately, Anne-Marie bustled in to interrupt.

'Madame. I have made up your bed in the better of the guest bedrooms and set your toilet in the bathroom. Your clothes are hanging up. I laid a supper in the dining room. Like most bachelors who lives off cafés, Monsieur kept was very little in the pantry.'

Angèle remember with some fondness the recent supper he had cooked for her. He had clearly gone to considerable trouble for her that evening. Anne-Marie continued in most bustling and efficient manner.

'Now before you ask, I have made sure that your housekeeper at home knows what to do on the *île* in your absence. And Ludo will make sure that the place is all locked up and I have told him to stay there overnight. I have put him in the caretaker's bedroom in the attic. So, you don't need to worry about everything there. Your secretary from *Les Halles* will get in touch with you tomorrow to talk about business if he thinks it's necessary. I've told him not to bother you unless it's really important. Now, Madame, as it's late I suggest, you have something to eat and then get to bed. You'll be needed in the morning I'm sure. I'll stay up and sit with Monsieur for a while.'

Angèle suddenly did feel tired. It had been a busy night to say nothing of the strain of being in a gun fight and killing someone. She had no idea what the time was. Well after midnight she guessed. She accepted her maid suggestion, picked a little at the selection of cold meat, cheese and bread that had been set out on the dining room table and then changed into the nightdress that was draped over the bed in the best guest room. She smiled to see that it was the most sedate of many in her collection. Marie came in to brush her hair and to tuck her in as usual.

'Don't worry, Madame. I'll watch over him and wake you if anything happens.

Chapter 15: Friday 15th April   Scene 1: The Morning After

The next morning saw another bright spring day. The city woke early and business started in the streets with the noise filtering up from the square as the clatter of cabs and carriages gradually increased. Angèle woke early as well, dressed and re-assumed her place at the bedside. Drangnet continued to sleep on peacefully for a while but by 7:30 even he was roused by the general hubbub of a new Paris morning that was invading his apartment. He found that his headache had almost gone, and his arm was surprisingly free of pain.

She leant across and kissed him lightly on the cheek.

'Good morning, my dear Louis. How do you feel this morning?'

He kept hold of her hand.

'I feel surprisingly well considering what happened last night and, in particular, lucky to be alive, thanks to you.'

'Good,' she smiled down at his. 'I suggest that you stay there for a while and let Anne-Marie prepare a little light breakfast for us both. She had been out early so we have fresh bread. You can have breakfast in bed as befits a wounded soldier. I have asked Dr. Raspail come around at about nine to check on his handwork of last night.'

'Thank you, Angèle. Er. Who is Anne-Marie?'

'My maid. She sat with you for a lot of last night.'

'As usual, my dear, you seem to have thought of everything. But there is one thing you can do for me. Can you get a message to my deputy Inspector Gant and ask him to come here immediately after this morning's departmental meeting at the *Sûreté*? I think I should bring him up to date about last night. I've a feeling that he is not going to be very happy with me.'

'You asked me last night. He's already got the message. He said he will be here at ten.

Drangnet just settled back to let the events of the early morning wash over him. To be honest, now he was awake, he wasn't feeling quite as weak as he imagined when he first woke. Although his arms seemed stiff and a little painful, it was his headache that was now coming back with a vengeance. He took a little breakfast but was relieved to see the doctor who pronounced himself satisfied with his patient's condition but was able to administer some medicine to relieve the discomfort.

If Roger Gant was surprised to have the door opened by Angèle's maid who of course he didn't know, the shock had quickly been replaced by a bigger one by the time he reached Drangnet's bedside. It had been greatly supplanted by the sight of his boss sitting up in bed wearing a white nightshirt with a beautiful woman sitting at his bedside. He had worked with Drangnet for years in a wide variety of places and situations, but he had never actually talked to him in bed. He really didn't know what to say. Fortunately, Drangnet wanted to forestall any possible witticism but taking the chair, as it were, for their unusual morning meeting.

'Roger. First, I should introduce you to Madame Fernier. Angèle this is my deputy, Inspector Roger Gant.'

Roger crossed over to her and delivered a completely formal and correct bow from the waist, while taking her proffered hand and dipping his lips to within a inch or so of its back.

'*Enchanté*, Madame.'

'Monsieur.' she replied, equally formally.

The correct exchange of pleasantries having been negotiated, Drangnet continued without acknowledging the amused twinkle in both his guest's eyes.

'Roger, I feel that I should bring you up to date a little with recent events and, as I am forbidden to leave this bed for the moment, I felt that I should take the unusual step of inviting you to my bedroom.'

Gant looked around him admiringly.

'And a jolly nice one it is too sir, if I might venture.'

Angèle tittered

'Oh dear, Angèle,' Drangnet sighed. 'It's a mistake to laugh at too many of the Inspector's witticisms. It gives him wrong ideas.'

'But Louis,' she replied, 'I've only laughed at one and then only a little.'

'And that, Madame, is more than enough,' he warned. 'But there is a fair amount of explanation to be done and Roger you already know that Madame Fernier has been helping with information from her, er, colleagues around the city and in one very significant way is responsible for my being confined here to bed, I felt that she should be here to help fill in, as it were, any of the details that might have, er, slipped my mind. It did all get a little hectic last night from time to time.'

Gant didn't reply but settled more deeply, if that were possible, into the uncomfortable upright bedroom chair that was clearly made for someone considerably smaller and considerably lighter than he and waited.

Drangnet outlined the events of yesterday from when the morning report had been slipped under his door to the present. He left nothing out and Madame was able to fill in any of the details with which he either wasn't familiar or had forgotten. Gant just sat silently and listened. He looked startled when the story reached the moment when both Drangnet and Cordiez were shot but, other than that, he kept his council. It was not too long before the story was told, and the two protagonists fell silent and waited to see his reaction.

Now there was a very great deal more than met the eye about Roger Gant. Most people thought he was simply a good number two; someone who picked up and tidied away all the little bits and pieces that his more illustrious boss left behind. A man whose loyalty to both Drangnet and the *Sûreté* was unquestionable. But his pipe smoking and plain, almost agricultural predilection for tweed clothing tended to mislead people. He was no dimwit. He had a sharp mind, not just for analysing cases and the discovery of the facts that were the stock in trade of his profession. But he also how to pick quickly the salient facts out of a story and to filter out the dross. His analyses were often produced much faster that Drangnet's and much more clearly focussed. So, it might have surprised Angèle more than it did his superior when he summed the whole thing up.

'During the course of yesterday you confirmed your masonic conspiracy theory, identified three of the big cheeses at the top, all of whom are State senators, and, in passing, you confirmed Sandrat and Cordiez lower down in the hierarchy. You fell for a trap because you believed information sent by Cordiez had come from Madame Fernier here and tried to spy on a clandestine meeting of conspirators, called to discuss amongst other things the very suspicious accident of Deputy Sandrat on his way to work, that wasn't a meeting at all, escorted by one of our policemen who wasn't on our side either. Madame finds out about the trap and sets off to rescue you but only arrives in time to see you captured. Cordiez tries to shoot you but only wings you, while Madame Fernier shoots Cordiez stone dead. You leave some of her colleagues to clear up in this cellar, you are brought home, your slightly grazed arm treated and here you lie, looking, if I may say so, much too well to merit a day in bed, while, the conspiracy seems to be reduced to all leaders but no soldiers. All this leaves us with a major murder conspiracy fully solved at least the murder of the prostitutes is concerned, three major officers of the State in the frame for murder and not one scrap of admissible evidence against anyone them even on the furthest horizon. Have I missed anything, sir?'

Both of his audience had the grace to look a little chagrined.

'Er, yes, Roger,' Drangnet managed. 'I think you have covered most of the salient points.'

'In which case, Chief Inspector, There seems very little that I can do at the moment so I'll just get back to the office, make up some totally spurious reason for your absence just in case anyone notices you aren't there and wait with considerable interest to read your written report which I assume you will wish me to prepare for Superintendent Dancart.'

He rose from the chair and unwound slowly to his full height with obvious relief.

'In the meantime, I would like to express my pleasure in the fact that you have dodged the bullet, not for the first time if I remember correctly. It seems clear, Madame, that you saved the Chief Inspector's life and I would like to thank you for that just in case he forgets to. You have done both the City of Paris and me a very great service. Finally, I would remind the Chief Inspector that his arm must recover completely in time for his appointment on the tennis court next Sunday. If he does not perform or, God forbid, actually has to withdraw, the wrath of our current Head of State would know no bounds and there would be nothing that even you Madame, could do to protect him from that. He wants that cup to stay on his mantel piece.'

With that he bowed correctly in the general direction of both of them and turned to leave but was called back by Drangnet.

'Roger. Please go and have a word with Superintendent Dancart. Give him a verbal resumé of the case to date. You can also tell him that I will put it all in writing as soon as I can, but it might be a day or two before he received the full report. You can tell him everything, of course. He will have to know a little about the role of Madame Fernier as there is no other explanation for my survival but try to make it sound as business like as you can, will you?'

Gant smiled.

'Very well, Boss. I'll keep Madame out of it completely, I think. Easier that way. I'll tell him to expect you back in the office on Monday. Oh, and I should say that I am extremely unhappy about you gallivanting off on this adventure without me? But we will get back to all that when you're back in the office and I have you to myself.'

And with that, he finally left. There was a silence for a while before Drangnet smiled weakly at this companion.

'Well, that went better than I imagined. But he's not happy with me.'

'I noticed.'

There seemed very little else she could say. So, she turned her mind to the future.

'Tell me about Sunday, my dear.'

'Ah. The final of the tennis club doubles. An important date. Actually, I want to win of course but for my partner it is a sacred mission. I really do believe that he thinks his political future depends on winning, to say nothing of the approval of many of his friends who wager very considerable amounts of money on us each year. He does indeed require that Napoleon's famous silver trophy sits on the rather grand marble mantel piece at home for another year. He would not be happy at all if I let him down at the last minute.'

She then seemed to remember that the man in the bed was actually wounded.

'And how does the arm feel this morning, my dear.'

He shifted slightly in bed and gingerly flexed his left arm back and forth.

'Actually, it's not too bad. I can move it and my fingers. It's rather stiff and painful but that's probably just the stiches. Seems to work all right though. Given that I'm right-handed there shouldn't be a problem with the tennis.'

He looked thoughtful for a moment.

'I wonder if your loyal doctor could let me have a pain killing injection that I could use just before I go on court on Sunday if it seems necessary.'

'I'm sure he can fix you up with something, Louis. I'll have a word with him.'

There was a silence before she started up again.

'Well I can see that it's unlikely that I'll be able to keep you in that bed all day, but I really don't think you should go into work. You need to let Inspector Gant do his work for you and not interfere. Perhaps we should just do something together and relax. Maybe as it's such a nice day we could go out to the *Bois de Boulogne* and go for a stroll in the sun and take a long lunch at the *Café de la Cascade*.'

Certainly the prospect of lying in bed all day had very little appeal and the prospect of a fine spring day spent in the company of Madame offered an excellent prospect. But here was one thing he wanted to say before anything else. He reached down to pick up her hand that she had carefully loosed from his during his deputy's visit.

'Roger is right. I owe you my life. Cordiez would certainly have killed me and I had no way to escape. Without you and your bravery I would have been the end for me. I am unable to than you enough. Nothing I could say or offer you can express my gratitude. I am obviously totally in your debt.'

She squeezed his hand and managed to look highly embarrassed and very pleased at the same time. Louis found that it was an attractive combination. Her expression then changed a little and a sly look entered her eyes.

'Well there is something you might be able to do for me.'

'Do tell me. Anything, of course.'

'Well.' she said rather dubiously shaking her head, 'I'm not sure even you can do this.'

'Tell me, please.'

'Well you tell me that your doubles partner in no less that Jules Ferry, the current Minister of Public Instruction, of Fine Arts and the Current President of the Council of Ministers and thus effectively the Head of Government.'

'Er yes, he is.'

'And he is also a good friend of yours?'

'I have the honour to think I can regard him as that. I've known him for a long time.'

'Good. Then perhaps he is sufficiently important to help you get what I would like in repayment for saving your life.'

'And what is that, Madame?' his interest piqued at the prospect, although not without a touch of concern.

'I'd like two tickets to the opera for you and me.'

Drangent was astonished. Apart from the fact that he hadn't really considered whether or not she was a great lover of opera, he hardly thought that the simple matter of buying a pair of opera tickets need the intervention of the current Head of State. He intimated as such.

'Ah you don't quite understand, my dearest. The opera in question is the upcoming production of the opera Aida by Giuseppe Verdi.'

'Wasn't that premiered in Paris some years ago, my dear?'

'Yes but this is its first production in the new opera house by Monsieur Garnier.'

'Even so, I'm sure that I can get some tickets without needing the Ferry's help.'

'Well, I rather wanted to go the premier, my dear.'

'Ah,' he said, beginning to realise that there might indeed be a possible difficulty.

'And when is this premier, my dear?'

'Tomorrow night.'

Drangnet saw the difficulty. He was pretty sure that the place had been completely booked for months.

'I'm not sure if even Ferry will be able to grant that particular wish, but..' he said raising his hand to discourage her protest. 'I'd better write him a note and we can drop it into the *Palais de Luxembourg* on our way to the *Bois*. Even he may not succeed but I will plead our case with utmost vigour.'

'Very well, Louis. Perhaps you might like to get up as soon as you feel able. Do you think that you want any assistance with that? I'm sure that Anne-Marie can help you if you wish.'

Drangnet frowned at the mischievous look in her eyes.

'That is very kind, my dear.' he replied with exaggerated courtesy. 'I think I might manage if I don't have to hurry. If I have any problems, perhaps I can call her?'

It was about thirty minute later when he emerged fully dressed and clothed for a day in the elegant surroundings of the *Bois de Boulogne*. He had found that his arm was now no longer particularly painful, and it seemed to work more or less as it should. He walked into his sitting room to find Angèle attired in the most elegant of pale blue day dresses, parasol and bonnet to the fore, sitting reading quietly on a sofa in the salon. There was no sign of the maid.

'You look extremely elegant, my dear,' she said, 'and, if I might say, not at all like a man who was shot less than twelve hours ago. You must have wonderful powers of recovery or, at least, resilience.'

Drangnet just grunted and made his way into his study to write the all-important letter to Ferry. It had very little chance of success, he thought but he obviously had to make the effort. So, having written the note he took a light coat, his hat and a walking cane and escorted Madame downstairs to the carriage that was, as usual, waiting directly outside the door to his house. However, in keeping with Madam's thoughts about the day ahead, what awaited was not just a cab but a full four-wheeled barouche drawn by two splendidly matched hackney horses and two fully uniformed coachmen up on the high box seat in front. Madame had obviously given instructions for a stylish day out. Drangnet did wonder why two men were necessary but perhaps after last night she felt the need of some additional protection.

Soon they were winging their way down to the river and across up to the *Palais de Luxembourg*, causing many admiring glances from the pavements as they went. Even the occasional hat was raised as they passed. It seemed to be that sort of day. They arrived at the Palais gate and one of the coachmen was sent in with the all-important note.

'Make sure,' Madame instructed, 'that you tell whoever takes this note that it is to be delivered directly to Monsieur Ferry without any delay as it contains the most important information for his personal attention from the Chief of the Paris *Sûreté*. It is to be delivered at once as it contains a matter of national importance.'

The man left on his errand. Angèle shrugged with a sweet smile on her face.

'Only a slight exaggeration, my dear.'

Drangnet returned the smile weakly and said nothing. He was going to get into trouble about this. Not for the first time he was surprised by the numbers of people who seemed to be able to drop everything every time the sun came out to go strolling in in places like the Tuilerie Gardens or the *Bois de Boulogne*. To see crowds at the weekends was not unexpected but today was a working day and the great park was still thronged with people. The open space had been given to the city by Napoleon III as a public park some thirty years before and had become a favourite place for many Parisians almost as soon as it was opened. Today it was again full of different groups taking the warm spring air. The barouche stopped at the eastern entrance to the park at the *Carrefour des Cascades* and they descended. Angèle slipped her arm through his and the two set a gentle pace into the middle of the park. They strolled along the *Allée de l'Hippodrome* towards the *Carrefour de Longchamps* and the great restaurant that was their destination for lunch. All around them there were similar couples, nurses with babies in perambulators, even some family groups. People were just wandering around, taking the sun, nodding occasionally as they passed an acquaintance. A feeling of calm and an unhurried pace to life pervaded the place.

'This, my dear Angèle, is Paris at its best. There is no city that I know of that can match Paris in the early spring. Thank you suggesting we come here. I can feel the dark events of last night washing away from my mind.'

She just squeezed his arm and laid her head against his shoulder as they walked. He looked back for a moment and saw the reason for the second coachman. He was following twenty or so yards behind.

They were greeted at the door of the restaurant by the *maître d'hôtel* with an effusive enthusiasm that clearly suggested that Angèle was not unknown there and they were escorted to a prime table looking out over the park. Two cold glasses of champagne were placed in front of them and they were left to settle in.

'I hope you don't mind, Louis, but I told them what I thought we would eat beforehand. My experience here has been that chef does some things very well indeed but many others not so well. I hope you don't think I am being too forward?'

'No, my dear. Not at all. Quite the contrary.' he replied, wondering how on earth she had managed to do it. 'You seem to be taking many decisions about my life at the moment and I have to admit that I find it a rather agreeable experience.'

Lunch passed with an agreeable slowness. The food was indeed excellent and Drangnet felt himself recovering quickly. Madame made most of the conversation, regaling him with stories of her youth and of growing up in Paris. He replied happily with some of his memories of Provence. Inevitably the conversation centred around food and wine. It was as they were finishing their pudding that the waiter approached with some deference, holding a small silver plate on which lay a letter.

'For the Chief Inspector, Madame.'

It was when he took the letter that he saw the reason for the waiter's attitude. The letter was closed with a large red wax seal embossed with a large ornate "RF". He opened it with his fruit knife and read the message before handing it without comment across the table to his companion who was clearly both extremely curious and slightly annoyed possibly because the note was not for her. Her face was instantly transformed into the broadest of smiles as she read the note.

You have no idea how much arm twisting I had to do to achieve this, but you are fortunate that the German Ambassador is having a diplomatic headache. There was a queue that reached over the horizon. It's a better box than mine.

In case you are tempted, as usual, to ignore protocol, I expect my officers to wear uniform and decorations – all of them. JF

'Oh Louis,' she exclaimed. 'You really do have friends in high places. This is wonderful. What does he mean by this comment about decorations?'

Drangnet tried his best to look unconcerned.

'I really can't say, Angèle.' he replied attempting to divert her question by waving to attract the attention of the waiter who brought the note.

'Can you tell me how this note was delivered? Who brought it?'

'I'll have to find out, Monsieur,' the man said before turning quickly away to do precisely that. Almost immediately the *maître d'hôtel* himself returned and spoke with a slight bow.

'It was delivered by one of the guards from the *Palais de Luxembourg*, Monsieur. On a horse and in full ceremonial uniform. It was rather a splendid sight. Our other customers were much entertained.'

'Ah, thank you,' Drangnet replied with a sigh. He could imagine Ferry's grin as he plotted the most ostentatious method of replying to Drangnet's request knowing how much he would hate the fuss. Turning back to his companion he said rather quietly:

'I wonder how he found out where we were having lunch?' he said looking directly at her.

She had the grace to look a little sheepish with the sort of innocent expression on her face of someone who knows the answer to a question and is about to lie about it.

'Perhaps my coachman might have let something slip when he delivered the note? I really can't guess. Perhaps he thought that a reply might be necessary. Who knows?'

Drangnet didn't need to remark yet again that Madame seemed to be leaving nothing to chance at the moment. However, she was also energised by the news and became much more business-like.

'I'll have to leave you on your own tonight, I think, Louis. I have things to prepare now. Will you be all right do you think?'

'Oh, I think I'll manage, thanks.' he said seriously. 'I'll probably stay at home and get a start on my report for Superintendent Dancart. He'll want it on Monday.'

'Yes, that sounds like a good idea. I'll ask Doctor Raspail to call on you this evening to check on your arm and give you the pain killer that you wanted. Would you like Anne-Marie to come and make you an evening snack or something? Do you want me to ask one or two of my people to keep an eye out in the square?'

Drangnet smile at the suggestions almost tumbling over each other. Madame Fernier was obviously excited at the prospect of the opera. In fact, he had a few questions of his own. He had no idea in what state his dress uniform was. It was some time since he wore it.

'I accept the visit from the good doctor, but I'll decline the kind offer of Anne-Marie or some guards, if I may. I am quite used to fending for myself at home and I am pretty sure that Gant will have organised some additional patrols of unformed police to pass the house regularly. In any case my own housekeeper usually comes in on Saturday morning and I don't want to risk annoying her. Thank you all the same.'

The journey home was conducted with somewhat more haste than before. They bid their farewells to the *maître d'hôtel* and were honoured with a rare appearance of Chef from his usual seclusion in the kitchen. Drangnet was amused that yet again there was no question of a bill to be settled. He assumed that it would be sent on afterwards or maybe the restaurant got a deal on their fresh produce from the Halles market. The barouche held a good pace back into the centre of the city with Madame a good deal less talkative that before. Drangnet assume that she was making mental lists. Before long they were back at the *Place des Vosges*. Angèle offered him her cheek to kiss but made no attempt get down from the carriage.

'Thank you, my dear Angèle. Not only for a wonderful lunch but, of course, for everything over the last day or so. Even after the opera I will remain in your debt.'

'Don't be silly, Louis. It was all just something that had to be done. Good luck with your report. You still have to plan what to do about the three senators but with our Monsieur Ferry on your side, I suspect that something will be done. I'll be rather busy tomorrow so perhaps it'll be better if we met at the opera? I think the performance starts at eight so perhaps we can meet in the foyer an hour before.'

And with that she signalled the coachmen to drive off and he was left alone in the shade of the colonnade that ringed the ground floor of the square. A relaxed day had come to a rather abrupt halt. He climbed the stair to his door and entered to see that both his bed and those occupied by Angèle and Anne-Marie had been made up and a small cold snack had been laid on the dining room table. Two messages had been put under his door. The first was from Gant just saying that there was no important business at the office that needed his attention and that he had given Dancart a verbal report and had put him off anything more invasive until Monday. The second was from Doctor Raspail saying that he would call at seven. Drangnet looked at the clock on the mantel piece. That gave him three hours to take a bath, take a good look through the music for the Sunday morning service at St Gervais and start to make some notes on his report. Secretly he was pleased to have the time including most of Saturday to himself. With luck he could finish the report and do some bits and pieces of his own.

Promptly at seven there was a knock on his door.

'Good evening, Chief Inspector. It's nice to see you up and about. How is the arm feeling?'

'Actually, quite good, doctor. It's a bit sore and stiff but I'm certainly not in any great pain. Also, the bandage looks quite clean.'

'Right. Let's have a look.'

With that he undid the bandage and examined the stitches. He nodded approvingly.

'Yes. I'm very happy with that. The stitches all neat and tidy. You haven't puled any of them. There's no seepage from the wound. Just some bruising that is beginning to form. But nothing serious. I'll just clean it again and re-bandage it and then we can talk about this tennis match of yours.'

He set to work, and it was not long before the arm was re-dressed. He received another pain killing injection. Drangnet then offered the man a glass of whisky that was gratefully accepted. They sat and came to the subject of Sunday.

'Judging by what I've seen, I don't see why you can't play tennis on Sunday. I assume that you play right-handed and don't use you left arm for anything other than holding the balls and general balance. And I also assume that you don't fall over a lot and crash into other people or walls very often.'

Drangnet just smiled and shook his head.

'I agree that it might be a good idea to have something the kill the pain. But I also think that the wound should be dressed again rather more tightly just before your play. I really don't think that you should do this yourself. I assume that there will be a fair number of spectators in the club to watch the match?'

'Oh yes. There'll certainly be a full turnout.'

'Right, I suggest that I come some time before the match when you are about to get changed and I'm sure we can find somewhere private to do what is necessary. It shouldn't take too long. In fact, I'd rather like to stay and watch the match if possible. I hear from Madame Fernier that you and Monsieur Ferry are rather skilled. I am a very modest player of the game myself at the court on the *Île St. Louis*.'

'Doctor, that would be an excellent arrangement. Thank you. I'll make sure that the steward reserves a seat with Madame Ferner and Madame Ferry in the dedans. Also please let me have your account for all your kind service whenever you like.'

'Chief Inspector,' he laughed. 'You have no idea how unhappy Madame Fernier would be if I even considered such a thing. No. I gather that you and your partner are good for a small wager so I will hope to earn my fee that way. Now I'll leave you. I advise that you try to do as little as possible for the rest of this evening and tomorrow. I'll leave you a sleeping draft to use tonight if you think you need it and I'll come back tomorrow morning about ten o'clock to change the dressing and see how you are. You should try to give the wound as much of a chance to settle down as possible. Try to wear a loose shirt in the meantime so you don't rub it too much with a jacket.'

'I will, doctor, and again thank you for your help,' he said wondering how much weight he had put on since he last wore his dress uniform.

Once the man had gone, Drangnet settled down at his piano. The morning service at St Gervais was not a major one. Again the choir was observing its debt to the Couperin family, but this time there was just to be the usual musical settings to the morning mass this time composed by the last of the great dynasty that had graced the church over almost two centuries, Gervais-François Couperin. No solo parts this time for Drangnet, but there were a number of responses that the choir would be expected to lead. Given that he had not been entirely diligent in attending practice recently, he thought he had better do him homework. So, he spent the next couple of hours seated happily at his Biosselot doing just that. Once satisfied, it was still only nine o'clock, so he went into his study to start making some notes for his report to Dancart. Having started he found it remarkable easy as it was all very fresh in his mind and, in any case, this sort of report writing, no matter how boring he found doing it, never troubled him particularly. He loaded a plateful of the cold cuts, meats and cheeses from the dining room table and nibbled at it as he worked.

The clock was just striking eleven when he reached the end of the exercise and, in spite of feeling quite fresh, he decided to put off starting to write to main report until the next morning. He poured himself a glass of whisky and retired to his comfortable armchair before going to bed.

Chapter 16: Saturday 16th April Scene 1: Saturday Morning

He had slept fitfully. Every time he moved in bed, something hurt and then he woke up. It happened so often that sometimes he really couldn't really remember whether he was asleep or awake. Doctor Raspail had left him a sleeping draft which he had put off drinking until at about two or three in the morning when he had to give in and then managed to get off to sleep for a while. He woke to hear his housekeeper moving around in the kitchen. She had been his housekeeper for a number of years and was quite used to his occasionally irregular bachelor habits. She was considerably younger than he but managed to treat him like her son. She was quite used to letting herself into the apartment even while he was still sleeping. He got out of bed rather gingerly but was delighted to feel that much of the soreness had left his body and even his arm was just aching a little. He put on his dressing gown gingerly and went out in search of coffee.

'Good morning, Annabel. How are you this morning?'

'Thank you, Monsieur. I'm fine. Is it just the usual today?'

His domestic routine seldom varied, and she had long since stopped really needing instructions from him.

'Well actually, Annabel, please could you get my full dress uniform out of the wardrobe and give it a good clean up. I think it's rather a long time since I wore it. I've got to go to the Opera tonight.'

'Yes, of course, Chief Inspector. I always liked you in that. You look so dashing.'

Drangnet just coloured slightly and headed off to his bathroom to the accompaniment of a delighted giggle from Annabel. Knowing that he going to spend the day alone and that he was going to have to shave again this evening he didn't take too much trouble on his toilet. Before long he had dressed casually without feeling much discomfort and went out to a local café for breakfast, coffee and a glance over the morning's papers. He was relieved to see that the events of yesterday had so far gone unreported in the press. In fact, he sat there in the morning sun having breakfast as usual hardly able to credit that he had been kidnapped and almost killed, rescued by a beautiful woman, taken home, nursed with his injury and then almost as suddenly left completely alone. He looked around the café. Paris just continued as normal. He felt this put things a little in perspective but wasn't quite sure exactly how.

He finished his quick reading of the morning's newspapers, had a second coffee and returned to his apartment. It was time to write the report. While Annabel was still going about her business he sat at his desk and glanced through the notes he had made last night. Much of the report was easy. There was so little actual evidence and so few witness statements it was almost like writing a novel. He thought he should leave Madame Fernier's list of names out altogether. But he surprised himself about how quickly he got it finished. The only really difficult part was the events of Thursday night. He obviously had to include it as Cordiez had ended up dying. He toyed with the idea of keeping Angele's name out of it altogether but that really wasn't possible. He had always been completely honest with Dancart and that trust was important to him. He would just write it all up and rely on Dancart to give a verbal report to the Prefect. The written version could then be archived and hopefully forgotten.

He was interrupted by Doctor Raspail who was fortunately in something of a hurry. Annabel had just gone off to do some shopping for him, so he was able to receive the good Doctor who again declared himself happy with the sewing and with his patient's recovery. He decided that there was no longer any need to meet again before the tennis tomorrow afternoon and left, sparing Drangnet the difficulty of explaining the visit to Annabel when she returned.

The report was finished by lunch time. He read it through and decided it would have to do. Dancart would obviously ask some questions but they obviously had no case to be sent to the Judges for further actions. There wasn't anyone they could take to court. Then a thought struck him. Tomorrow it was highly unlikely that he could keep the fact of his bandaged shoulder from Ferry. It was certainly possible to get it dressed and changed into his tennis kit before Ferry. But the secret would be out after the game when they got showered together to go home. In any case, if he was going to get to the main characters in this story, he was going to need the help of someone of

Ferry's stature. He set about to make a second, slightly abbreviated, copy of the report. He'd give it to Ferry at his house when they were all preparing for the evening party.

Annabel just put her head around the study door.

'There I've just about finished, Sir. I prepared you uniform. It's really come up quite well. Not surprising really as you don't seem to wear it very often. And I put out some lunch on the dining room table. I assume you won't have a chance to eat before the opera.'

He handed over an envelope with her wages for the week.

'Thank you, Annabel,' he smiled. 'See you next week.'

He finished the second copy of the report, had something to eat and with only a few hours to go before he had to change for the opera, he just sat in an armchair to read. He wondered how Madame was spending her afternoon. He had no idea whether she was the sort of woman that took a long time and made a lot of fuss about this sort of thing or whether she just took it all in her stride and really didn't pay much attention. In fact, he realised that he actually didn't know much about her at all. All he did know that he had developed feelings about her that he couldn't remember having before. She was someone with whom he felt very comfortable. He enjoyed her company and was fascinated by her. He always looked forward to seeing her even though he knew that she was anything but a suitable companion for him. He was looking forward immensely to being seen with her at the opera knowing full well that many, if not most, would disapprove. In the end he let his book fall onto his lap and just contented himself with dreaming until it was time to get ready.

Chapter 16: Saturday 16th April   Scene 2: An Evening at the Opera

Tonight was a very special night at the *Palais Garnier* because Giuseppe Verdi himself was conducting his own opera, Aida. Drangnet whose musical roots were founded in the rich soil of the seventeenth and eighteenth century seldom let his musical tastes wander much beyond the premature death of Schubert. Yet he held a creeping respect for the work of the younger Verdi. There was a political core to many of the Italian's earlier operas and he respected that. This evening was the first performance of Aida in the new opera house. It had been premiered before in Paris some six years earlier in April 1876 in the *Salle Ventadour* of the *Théâtre-Lyrique Italien* on the *Rue Neuve-Ventadou*. This famous old house had been the site for many French premiers of Italian operas including fifteen by Verdi himself usually with the maestro himself conducting. Tonight's performance was Aida's second premier to celebrate to completion of the new house at the *Palais Garnier*. It was also the night of the official inauguration of the recently installed electric lighting in the famous main chandelier in the auditorium.

He had been warned by Ferry that decorations should be worn, and he knew well enough by now to realise that his usual inclination to dress down out of a combination of modesty and bloody-mindedness would not be acceptable. Angèle had also reminded him, having read Ferry's note. He felt thoroughly outnumbered and knew when to accept defeat.

'I will be dressing up my dear,' she had said. 'And I expect you too as well. If I make my entrance to find you dressed like one of my market porters, I will seek out your friend Ferry and steal him away from his wife for the evening. Be warned.'

He looked at his full-dress uniform. He hated the thing, encrusted, as it was with the gold braid, tassels and epaulettes that French military uniforms were customarily festooned. His was additionally embellished with a full gold *aiguillette* as befits a soldier who served as Aide de Camp to a Marshal of France. He had once tried to tone the whole effect down slightly by dispensing with the thing but The Duke of Magenta has seen him and ordered him to put it back. As there was a high probability that the now retired State President would be there tonight, he sighed and just left it where it was. He had no intention of causing Angèle embarrassment in the event he met his old boss. The reason he disliked the uniform so was not any particular hatred of uniforms as such but because it reminded him that his beloved police service was actually a military one. He was actually still in the army. He had always felt that the French police service should cut itself loose from the army and align itself with the domestic authorities. However, it didn't look as if he was going to get his wish anytime soon.

After checking that the uniform was all intact and in good order he went to his desk and pulled open the deep central drawer. Tucked away right at the back was a slim mahogany box, brass bound and locked. He took it out and placed it gingerly one the desk in front of him, one hand resting gently on the polished top. For while he just stared at it. "Decorations will be worn" Ferry had instructed, and Angèle had reminded him. Yes, he had some of those. Rather a lot, in reality. Apart from the moment of their presentation they all normally stayed locked in this box and equally securely hidden away in his memory. On the odd ceremonial occasion that he was forced to wear his full-dress uniform, they had usually stayed there too. He was a modest man by nature and while he was immensely proud of these little baubles, or at least of what they represented, he almost never wore them. Yet she had instructed him, and he owed her too much to ignore her.

He pulled the watch chain from his waistcoat pocket and found the little brass key hanging from it. He opened the box slowly and laid the hinged lid flat back over on the desk. Inside, resting on a piece of dark maroon velvet was a row of medals with their coloured ribbons and, at one side another rather ornate little box tucked up into the corner. The medals were military awards for gallantry including the *Medaille Militaire* and campaign medals from occasional adventure on the Mexican and Italian campaigns. There were some police awards for gallantry too. Even though he tried to ensure that they overlapped each other on the ribbon as much as possible, it was still a goodly length. These he took out of the box and laid the neat row down on the desk. Madame would have her decorations no matter how much he disliked the things. The problem, however, was not these. They were not uncommon amongst his fellow policemen in the Paris force. Most of his senior colleagues had military backgrounds. His problem was with the separate little box and what lay within it. He withdrew that too and laid it still closed in front of him while he tapped his fingers gently on it. It was another medal case, of course; quite small and coloured a dark blue. A narrow gilt decoration ran embossed around its edges while in the middle of the top there were just two ornate letters, again embossed in a now faded gold leaf: "RF".

He undid the clip, opened the little silk-lined box, and looked down at the famous white enamelled Maltese cross; the insignia of the *Légion d'honneur*, the highest award in the French Republic. For some reason this was the decoration that he was most reluctant to display but in truth he had no real idea why. Any display couldn't be done with subtlety. The award was instantly recognisable with its bright red ribbon. If worn with other medals it took precedence and was worn in front of the rest and couldn't be hidden amongst its lesser cousins. But even this subterfuge was denied him. The Legion had a hierarchy of five levels. His was at the rank of *Commandeur* of the Legion, the third level. Protocol demanded that the medal of a Commander was not worn on the chest with others but separately, tightly around the neck, suspended on a red ribbon necklet.

He touched the medal. He knew full well that although his would probably not be the only *Légion d'honneur* on show tonight, there would be few of that rank and above. The legion only permitted one thousand two hundred and fifty commanders out of a total of almost ten times that number of all ranks. He knew that a number of his superiors in the police and amongst his political masters were also members of the Legion but very few outranked him. The current Prefect of Police, Andrieux, was a member, of course, but at the rank of *Officier*, one below his.

Angèle had been wrong when she had said that he hadn't followed much of a military career. He had graduated almost top of his year in 1859 and had quickly been recruited into the general staff. He left St Cyr with the usual rank of Lieutenant and immediately posted to General MacMahon's staff for the newly launched war with Austria. MacMahon was then commander of the so-called Italian Army and very soon Drangnet received regular and rapid promotions. It was during the next war against the Germany that Drangnet, now a Lieutenant Colonel, was appointed Aide-de-Camp to MacMahon, now a Marshal of France and Commander of the Army. His original appointment of the *Légion* came as a result of his service when the Marshall was wounded at the Battle of Sedan and during his subsequent service to the captured MacMahon during his internment in Wiesbaden after the French defeat. His promotion from the initial rank of *Chevalier* to *Officier* had come later first during McMahon's subsequent command of the Versailles Army that put down the Commune and then his six-year term as President of France. Drangnet had remained one of the great man's favourites and continued to enjoy his patronage. The promotion to *Commandeur* chad come when, as a newly appointed Chief Inspector in the Sûreté, he completed a particularly difficult and potentially embarrassing investigation that had threatened to engulf his mentor MacMahon who by that time was President of France .

Annabel had hung out his uniform, freshly steamed and pressed together with a freshly ironed shirt and stiff collar and a set of clean underwear. She had even given his shoes a polish. He bathed carefully so as not to disturb the dressings on his arm, shaved again and brushed his hair. He caught an embarrassed glimpse of himself in the bathroom mirror and frowned at the reflection. He felt like a schoolboy going on his first unaccompanied rendezvous with a first girlfriend. He glanced at the clock. It was time to leave. He wrapped his dress cloak around him and wound the white silk scarf around his neck to hide the bright red ribbon. Top hat and silver-topped walking cane completed the ensemble and before long he was heading in a cab towards the *Palais Garnier*.

He arrived in good time and went to the office to collect his tickets and was a little baffled to be told that there weren't any. He was informed with more deference that he was expecting that his was a box in the centre part of the Grand Circle. The tickets, had he been called on to buy them, would have been beyond price; well beyond the reach of a mere Chief Inspector the *Sûreté.*

His surprise obviously showed itself to the clerk in the office.

'It is normally the permanent box of His Excellency the Ambassador of Imperial Germany. But he has decided not to attend tonight's performance. *Loge* number five, sir.'

He smiled in that sort of supercilious manner that men like him tend to adopt when feeling superior which tends to be often. He did, however, become somewhat more supine when he noticed the flash of red at Drangnet's neck.

'I hope you enjoy the performance, Monsieur. You don't need a ticket. The steward will be expecting you.'

Drangnet departed also with a slight smile. He had heard that it was not uncommon these days even ten years after the end of the German War that the ambassador and his guests were regularly heckled by members of the French audience when an opportunity arose. To be honest he wasn't particularly happy with the public attention that would attend their occupation of Box Five. But this was her wish. In any case, without her he wouldn't have solved the case nor would he have been alive to attend any opera or anything else for that matter. In one brave and selfless act she had saved both his life and his reputation whilst risking everything herself. He had to do something and if it meant cocking a snook at the great and the good who regarded themselves his masters then so be it.

The ornate clock above the main doorway showed that it was half past six and he stood at the edge of the vestibule to one side of the ever-thickening crowd and looked out towards the entrance. It was manned by two uniform attendants whose sole job, it seemed to him, was to act as human door stops as the great and the good of Paris society came in. A good few nodded in recognition as they came in and passed him on their way to the great double curve of the Grand Escalier stair that led up to the gilded magnificence of the grand foyer that stretched for more than fifty metres across the entire width of the first floor. More than a few both recognized him and showed a surprise at the flash of scarlet at his neck.

He just waited patiently. Then perhaps it was his imagination but it seemed to him that there was a brief lull in the procession or so it seemed to him before the door opened and in walked a solitary diminutive figure clad entirely in a floor-length black velvet opera cloak, her pale face just showing from a raised black hood, surrounded by black fur. A step behind her and slightly to one side followed Georges looking every inch of his more than six feet height wearing an immaculate plain black suit seemed to tower over her. The hiatus was such that many people stopped and turned to look. She walked steadily up to him and halted within a yard or two and, recognizing her escort with a slight smile, pushed the hood back and felt for the tasselled draw-strings at her neck. Georges stepped forward with well-choreographed timing as the cape fell away from her shoulders and caught it effortlessly, then stepped back, leaving his mistress alone to mount the final few steps up further into the foyer towards her host. The ballet was immaculate.

Madame Fernier had found a dress for the occasion. Yes. A dress. And what a dress. Heavy black silk with a narrow but deep Vee neck. It was very tight down to a miniscule waist and over her hips from where it fell heavily to the ground more fully. It was a black dress that sparkled with black light. Virtually every square inch was covered with tiny faceted black beads embroidered into complex and detailed patterns. The whole thing shimmered as she moved as if it was alive.

Her hair was piled tightly onto the top on her head. Black jet drop earrings and a similarly embroidered choker was worn tight around her neck. The only other jewellery was a small diamond inlaid silver cross on an almost invisible silver chain around her neck. She looked completely devastating and knew it.

He took her hand in his and bowed towards it to affect the whisper of a kiss an inch or so above it. As he did, she again raised her hand gently and, as a result, the kiss was planted directly on the back of her hand. When he lifted his head, he heard her gasp as her eyes fixed on the red silk around his neck, wide with astonishment. He caught her glance and offered a little apologetically with a small shrug.

'You instructed me to wear decorations, Madame. I am only doing what I was told.'

Her eyes sparkled as she took his arm and they turned to complete their grand entrance.

'One thing I can tell you, my dearest Louis, is that you will be making jealous enemies of many men here tonight.'

'And you of their wives and mistresses I think, my dear Angèle.'

Her grip tightened on his arm.

'One day, you must tell me the story. But for now, I shall be interested to watch the reaction tonight.'

He looked across at her 'My dear, you look quite wonderful. Completely devastating.'

She let go his arm monetarily and did a slow pirouette on his hand. The dress glittered and the long heavy skirt fanned out as she turned. The effect was extraordinary.

Yes,' he said quietly, 'Quite wonderful.'

Evidently satisfied with the affect, she retook his arm and they walked slowly on into the great building and up the great staircase to the first floor and towards the crown that was already thronging the ornate foyer. She turned to him.

'Louis. Would you mind if we went to our seats rather than join the crowd?' adding by way of explanation, 'to be honest, I feel a little intimidated. It will take a little time for me, a little market girl, to get used to all this.'

This was nonsense, of course, but Drangnet knew that it was not his place to disagree or, indeed, to have this conversation in public. So he tightened his arm against hers and walked her towards to curving line of doors that gave into the loges on the first level. Theirs was number five and number one at the centre was always reserved for the President of the Republic and his party. Drangnet remained uncomfortable with being a centre of attention that the occupation of this loge would bring him. But there was no point in looking too deeply. He was at the opera with a woman who he loved, for he knew that now, who looked absolutely beautiful and who provided him with company that no power on earth could persuade him to give up. She had also shot and killed a man to save his life less than twenty-four hours before. They stepped into the red velvet intimacy and another surprise awaited.

These loges could accommodate up to ten or, at a pinch, twelve, arrange with various degrees of discomfort on slim gold chairs or if one were luckier on narrow banquettes. On this occasion their loge was bare save for a rather extravagant flower arrangement at one corner, a table with a iced bucket containing champagne in the other and, in the middle, an extremely comfortable red velvet and gold sofa; seating only for two. Ferry's visiting card was propped up against the champagne bucket.

Saying nothing he led his companion to her seat and filled two glasses before returning to sit beside her. She took a sip and sat looking out over the auditorium that was very gradually filling up with wonder in her eyes. It was always a slow and glittering process. Even those in the cheap seats would have been dressed up to the nines except for the fact that there weren't any cheap seats. Performances regularly started late, caused in the main by people taking advantage of the many formal rooms and corridors that Charles Garnier had designed into his building precisely to encourage people to chat and to mingle with each other.

He just sat quietly beside her, holding her hand lightly, content to look at her and drink the sight of her beauty. After a while she seemed to sense that his attention was solely on her and turned to face him.

'Thank you, dear Louis. I needed a little time to get used to all this before diving into the throng. I'm sure we will have to be more social when the interval comes but for now, I just wanted some time alone with you.'

'My dear. Given a choice I would far, far rather hide here with you and ignore the others but you're right. We must circulate, as they say, during the interval. There are too many people here who know me or who know I am here tonight.'

'How is your arm, Louis. I hope it's not too painful?'

'Thanks to you and the good Doctor, it feels much better than I have any right to expect.'

Gradually the hall filled as people finished their conversations and took their places. The orchestra assembled and Maestro Verdi himself strode into the orchestra pit to rapturous and prolonged applause. The memory of the opera's first premier a few years before was still fresh and Verdi himself enjoyed huge popularity. The opera began with its surprisingly gentle orchestral prelude and the audience, used to more robust overtures with famous tune extracts for the main score, was instantly hushed as the tension rose.

To be honest, Drangnet only had a small part of his attention on the opera itself. It was not a story that really interested him, and the music was a long way from his taste. However, his companion was completely entranced and stared fixedly at the action on stage, taking in every nuance and turn of the drama. He was content to listen slightly distractedly to the music while just watching her. To him she looked utterly beautiful, her profile towards the stage, mouth slightly open as she gasped from time to time at the lavish production and applauded enthusiastically with the rest. The black dress sparkled and glinted as the hundreds of black glass beads on the tight bodice shifted with her breathing. The same with the full skirt that fell heavily to the ground as she fidgeted slightly as the drama in front of them unfolded. She was quite breathtakingly beautiful. He couldn't take his eyes off her. Only once did her concentration break, as the end of the first act when Radames has claimed his victory over the Ethiopians. She leant across and whispered in his ear:

'You know, my dear, that you should be looking at the stage and not just at me.'

He just grunted and continued to look at her, remembering the events of the recent past that had been much more dramatic that anything the painted hoards below could offer by way of entertainment. He was forced from his reverie some thirty minutes later by the famous triumphal march that brought the first half to an end. The house lights went up and everyone started to get to their feet to start what was, for most of them, the most important part of the evening, the promenade and the socialising.

As they rose, she came very close to him and said in a low voice.

'Louis, my dear. I am a little afraid of this next part. There are too many out there who know about me and who know who I am. I'm afraid I will be thought of as an unsuitable companion to a senior police official and a holder of the rank of *Commandeur* in the *Légion d'honneur.*'

He felt a moment of immense tenderness towards her. He put his hands very gently on either side of her face and lifted it slightly. He bet and placed the very lightest of kisses directly on the lips.

'Angèle. There isn't a single man in this house tonight who would not be proud to be seen with you and not a woman here who is not at least a little jealous. Of course, they don't know what happened two days ago, but you are more than the equal of any of them. I'm proud to be with you and to be seen with you and those in this crowd who know me well will respect that. The rest don't matter and never will. You are a woman of the greatest courage and beauty.'

She seemed to blush very slightly, took a deep breath and clung onto his right arm very tightly.

'All right Chief Inspector. Lead on.'

They left the *loge* and immediately bumped into the occupants of a neighbouring one, the current President of the Republic, and his immediate predecessor with the respective wives. Drangnet had met Jules Grévy on only a few formal occasions since his appointment a year or so before and there was an uncertain flash of recognition between the two. There was, however, no such uncertainty from Patrice de MacMahon, 6th Marquis of MacMahon, 1st Duke of Magenta, Marshal of France and President of the Republic of France until two years ago who greeted the policemen with delight and enthusiasm with both a hearty handshake and a hug in the manner of an old and dear friend. Introductions were made.

MacMahon's eye fixed on Drangnet's medal with a smile. Having both appointed him to the Legion and been responsible for his promotion within it, he knew full-well the affect it would have on many of their fellow opera goers.

'Ah ha, my old and dear friend. Someone told me you might be here, but they didn't tell me you would be with such a beautiful lady. You are a fortunate man indeed.'

He turned to Angèle while convention required Drangnet to address MacMahon's long time wife Elisabeth; a task that was made somewhat more difficult by the grand lady keeping more than an eye on her husband who had a well-deserved reputation as a lady's man. After a while she drew her husband away and they went in search of more prestigious conversation. Elisabeth had always been the power behind the man throughout his political career. It was with some relief that Drangnet and Angèle started to try to steer towards less intimidating parts of the crowd. However, they seemed to be unable to escape. That was, after all, what these opera intervals were intended for. Next to hail them was another welcoming pairing of Jules Ferry and his wife, Eugénie.

'Louis, my friend,' as his eyes also lighted on the red ribbon. 'I trust your accommodation is satisfactory?'

'Yes, thank you, Jules. More than adequate.'

'I'm delighted to see that you're correctly dressed for once,' he continued, 'You're usually are entirely too modest about it. I assume, Madame,' as he turned towards Angèle, 'that you are responsible of this welcome change in this stubborn man.'

He took her hand and bent his head towards it. Clearly formal introductions were not necessary.

'Madame Fernier. I am delighted to meet you at last. May I present my wife, Eugénie?'

Drangnet was amused to see that Ferry as the current Prime Minister merited a broad smile and the smallest of bobbed curtsies from his companion as opposed to either MacMahon or Grévy who had been greeted with a somewhat icy calm. Ferry's republican credentials were much more solid than those of the either of the current or past Presidents. Eugénie immediately linked arms with Angèle and whisked her away for a private word.

'Angèle, my dear. I've heard a lot about you. I just want you to know how pleased Jules and I are to see that Louis has found you. He is one of our oldest and dearest friends and I can see that just by looking at him he seems to have lost his heart to you. I was beginning to think that that would never happen. I want you to know that that if there is anything you need or need help in dealing with this difficult man, I am your friend. Come to me if you ever need anything.'

'Thank you, Madame. I appreciate that, of course. But perhaps I should warn you that I'm not really regarded with favour in many of the circles in which you move. I think I may have something of a mixed reputation.'

'Pah! Only a fool judges someone by their reputation. Jules and I certainly don't. All I know is that I have not seen our beloved Louis look this happy as this for many a long year and it's almost certainly you who is responsible. Now, we will have a chance to have a good chat tomorrow afternoon while our men are otherwise occupied.'

Momentarily baffled, Angèle asked: 'Tomorrow, madame?'

'The final of the tennis, my dear. The tennis. I presume Louis has invited you to watch?'

'Actually Madame, I think, perhaps it has slipped his memory.'

'Firstly, my name is Eugénie not madame and secondly I invite you. It is probably the most important afternoon in both our men's year. Men like to be watched although, of course, they would never admit it. You will sit next to me in the *dedans* and we will have the opportunity to chat quietly together while the men are occupied with their triumph on court.'

'And will they triumph? Surely there is a chance that they might be beaten?'

She was conscious that Louis was not necessarily in peak condition.

'I suppose in theory there might be a chance.' Madame Ferry replied with a pretence of thinking about it a little. 'It is after all a match. But in Louis and my husband you have two of the most determined and competitive men you will ever meet. I have seen them win on court in situations where they were both out-matched or out-manoeuvred or even out-numbered but nevertheless they won simply because they refuse to lose and for no other reason that one can see. They tend to be the same in life too.'

Angèle nodded slowly. It was a description that she was beginning to recognize. Eugénie went on.

'As he has forgotten to tell you about the match you probably also won't know that there is a club dinner on court after the match. It is formal so we have to dress up a little but not as much as for tonight. There'll be a gap between the end of the match which is usually enough for us to go home and change. If you wish you can come home with me so we can leave the men to their own devices which is probably what they would prefer in any case.'

They returned to their escorts who had been deep in conversation about tomorrow's match.

'Jules, my dear, we much circulate. Louis, I have told Angèle about the arrangements for tomorrow afternoon as you have clearly forgotten to do so. She will be my guest so neither of you has to be bothered about us. You just concentrate on winning that beautiful cup again.'

They finally made their escape from the great and the good and wandered off through the great concourse on the first floor. Drangnet recognised many but wanted to talk to few of them. Angèle too won her fair share of attention and a lot of admiring glances but in the main they were just content to wander along arm in arm enjoying each other's company more than that of others. But after a while in the distance he saw Comte André de St Germonde and tried to avoid him. But it was too late.

'Ah, Drangnet,' the man exclaimed, his eyes dropping with astonishment to Drangnet's collar. 'How are you getting on with that investigation of yours.'

Angèle gasped and her grip on his arm tightened fiercely.

'You'll know soon enough, St Germonde. Believe me.' replied Drangnet as he moved his companion quickly past the man and beyond without a further word.

'My God,' she whispered. 'The arrogance of the man.'

He stopped briefly and looked her in the face.

'Don't let a boor like that upset you or spoil this wonderful evening, my dearest. He'll get his comeuppance very soon now, have no fear.'

He set course back to the privacy of their box. There was still a couple of glasses of wine left in the bottle and he poured them both.

'To us, my love. This is one of the most wonderful evenings of my whole life. Nothing will be allowed to spoil that.'

'Oh, Louis. You're right. It is a wonderful evening. I am a lucky woman.'

He held her very close and they stayed close together as they sat and watched the house gradually fill for the second half. Just as the audience was settling in for the entrance of Maestro Verdi, she reached across and placed the gentlest of kisses on his ear. It was as faint as the touch of a butterfly as she whispered 'You called me your love. I hope with all my heart that that is true.'

Any reply was drowned by a great cheer as the great man took his place again on the rostrum. This time they stayed close together as the drama unfolded to its dramatic and tragic finale They stayed tightly together in each others as Aida and Radamés died on stage in theirs. They stood, of course, for the huge applause that followed the performance as curtain call after curtain call was won by the cast. Verdi himself was easily persuaded up onto the stage to receive the adulation of an adoring France audience.

It was nearly midnight before they got back to the *Place des Vosges*. Georges and their cab had been waiting directly outside much to the obvious annoyance of many others who regarded their own precedent. He was completely unmoved, of course, but he did offer Louis the briefest of winks as he say them safely installed. After a short drive and they were soon home and comfortably ensconced on his sofa, each with sparking glass of Juglar in hand. She sat close to him, her head bent slightly and resting on his shoulder. She tasted the wine and smiled.

'Is it really only a week or so days since we first sat here drinking this same wine when you invited me to dinner?'

'Yes.' he nodded. He refrained from reminding her that it was she who had invited herself.

'Yes, it is. A great deal seems to have happened in a very short time since then.'

They sat in a companionly silence. Both their thoughts were on the performance, although, it should be admitted, probably from slightly different points of view. His were from a combination of her intoxicating company and more generally a curiosity of how both his presence and his decoration had been viewed by people who had seen them. Whatever the reaction, he didn't feel particularly bothered with the prospects. She turned her face towards him and reached up to place another of her feather-light kisses on his cheek.

'Thank you, dear Louis, for a memorable evening. The opera was wonderful, and I don't think I have met so many important people before in my life.'

'Yes, the music was wonderful, and as for the people, well, I suspect that they were much more interested in you than in me.'

'So, my dear. What is happening tomorrow, apart from the tennis match, of course.'

'Well I have to sing at St Gervais for the ten o'clock mass. It is just a simple mass with a short anthem and the usual responses. No soloists. The after that nothing. Lunch if you like but I think as I have to play tennis in the afternoon, I'd prefer not to eat very much. But I would be very happy to watch you.'

'Fine. Let's see how I feel. I would love to come to the church, and we can decide what to do. What time do you want to get to the tennis club? Don't you have a date with Doctor Raspail?'

'The match starts at three. Usually I meet Jules for a bit of a warmup at two. I have arranged to meet the good doctor at half past one.'

She just nodded and let go his hand.

'Louis, my dear. I would like to visit your bathroom and freshen up a little. Outside the front door you should find a portmanteau that my driver has brought up. I asked him to leave it there so we wouldn't be disturbed. Can you bring it inside for me, please?'

With that she got up and walked slowly towards the door and out of the room to the corridor and the bathroom at the end, leaving a thoroughly startled Drangnet seated on the sofa holding both their glasses in his hands. He heard the bathroom door close and got to his feet and, sure enough, a large lady's portmanteau was indeed on the floor just outside his door. He picked it up and brought it inside then stopped, completely at a loss as to what to do with it. Fortunately, Angèle could be heard calling.

'Just put it outside the bathroom door, please; there's a good chap.'

He did just that, then still feeling slightly confused about what was going on returned to the drawing room and in the absence of anything else, poured himself the last of the champagne. He was not especially surprised at the visit to the bathroom. He was all too aware that his knowledge in the needs and requirements of ladies and their toilet as somewhat lacking but given that he assumed that her carriage was waiting somewhere on the square outside, he was more than a little baffled by the suitcase. He also had no idea how long this sort of thing usually lasted – whatever this sort of thing actually was. So as she had not reappeared quickly he got up and went over to the piano, sat, and started to thumb through the magnificent manuscript that had been standing on his music stand also since that day a week ago.

As he started to read the score, he slightly lost concentration for anything other than that so he couldn't tell how much time passed. He was only conscious that he suddenly felt that she had returned and was standing silently behind him although he had heard nothing. He turned and caught his breath. He had heard nothing because she was barefoot. She stood there smiling a little nervously. The great black dress was gone as was the jewellery, and she stood just in a plain white cotton night dress. Her hair was unpinned and fell luxuriantly cascading down over her shoulders. He felt rooted to the spot unable to move, even to speak. As usual it was she who moved the situation on. She took two steps towards him and grasped both his hands tightly in hers.

'Louis, my dearest. We've had an adventure over these last week or two and we have done things together that many would never understand. I have found the whole thing almost impossible to understand myself even as it was actually happening. Even now much of what had happened to me is a mystery. But one thing I do understand and that is for this first time in my life I have found myself falling in love. I am sure that most of my friends and colleagues would council against it. We do after all, operate on very different sides of the law and of life. But from the first time we met I sensed that you are not just a different and extraordinary policeman, but you are and extraordinary man. So, Chief Inspector, I think I am in love with you.'

She paused as if uncertain what to say next. She probably felt that there was nothing else to say. So, she just stood quite still, holding his hands and waited. He looked down into her eyes and saw there both bravery and uncertainty. In an instant he was sure as well. He gently drew her to him and wrapped his arms around her, whispering:

'And I with you, my dearest Angèle. And I with you. I have no doubt about that at all.'

Their kiss was long and passionate and when it finally ended, typically it was Angèle who took charge.

'If that is the case, my dear, then I suggest that you take me to bed immediately and we find out what those wonderful words actually mean.'

She kept hold of one of his hands and drew him gently towards the bedroom.

Chapter 17: Sunday 17th April   Scene 1: The Morning at St. Gervaise

The night had been tender and passionate and short. So, it was with something of a jolt that Drangnet woke from a sleep that he seemed only recently to have achieved. Angèle lay silently beside him, her head resting on his shoulder, long dark hair spilling all over the pillow. Very gradually he turned his head to see the time on the mantlepiece clock, trying not to disturb her. In the half light of an early morning he was relieved to see that it was still only just before seven. He had not completely forgotten that he was due to sing in the ten o'clock Mass at St Gervais. For a second, he wondered about giving it a miss. It wouldn't be the first time. But she had said that she wanted to come, and he wanted to sing for her.

He lay there trying not to think of the last few hours. To think about it would be to analyse it and, for the moment at least, he wanted only to remember the feeling; to lie suffused in the contentment. She had been right. He was in love and now it was obvious that he had been for some time. Obsession was perhaps too strong a word, but he had felt drawn into her net almost from the beginning. It now seemed that she too had felt the same. As it turned out that was just as well. Without her he would be dead. There is no debt greater than that.

His reverie was interrupted quite suddenly and in a tone of voice that was far from the soft murmurings that had accompanied his night's rest.

'Right, my dearest', exclaimed a thoroughly business-like voice. 'We must get up and you have a full day of singing and tennis in front of you and I shall be both listening and watching. But before any of that happens, I need a good breakfast.'

The best he could summon was a rather plaintive 'Yes, dear.'

'What time is it?' she asked.

'Er, about seven o'clock.'

'And the service at St Gervaise starts at..?'

'Ten.'

There was a silence, and nothing moved for a moment. Madame was obviously doing some calculations. Then without a sound and with a liquid grace she moved over and lay on top of him.

'Then, we'll have to be quick.'

Breakfast was taken at one of Drangnet's regular cafés on the *Rue de Rivoli*. Given that she wasn't going to get much of a lunch, Angèle went for an omelette with herbs and tomatoes and polished it off with two croissants, butter and apricot jam and copious quantities of coffee. Drangnet stuck to his usual coffee and a quarter of a *ficelle*. He had almost to fight her for a small share of her jam. They sat together and talked about the choir of St Gervais and about the game of tennis later in the day. They talked about her house on the *Île St. Louis*. He father had won it in a game of poker. The man who owned it also possessed most of the houses around that end terrace of the *Île* and was so incensed by the loss that he tried to win the place back. That only resulted in his losing the ones of either side as well. When it was all over the man then tried to get them back by going to court on the grounds that the game had been fixed in some way. He failed. But that probably had something to do with the fact that the two others who made up the four were a prominent judge and the then sub-prefect of Paris.

They both laughed as it was an excellent story; more so because, in all probability, it was true. They saw that time was drawing on, so they finished up and walked the short distance to the church.

The service was short and simple. Many of the currently practiced catholic masses that had survived the revolution and the upheavals of the commune when, amongst others, Georges Darboy, the Archbishop of Paris was executed by the communards, had been simplified and were less ornate than before. Some had even dispensed with the Tridentine Latin mass. St Gervaise had followed suit but still hung tenaciously on to their musical traditions so even a service like this one had its full set of sung responses as well, of course, as sung hymns and psalms. There was no sung anthem. But it did give the organist a chance to show off and the congregation left the church with the sound of a Bach Passacaglia played slightly too loudly ringing in their ears.

The clock was sounding 11:30 as they left the church and stood together on the top step of St Gervais, her arm looped into his.

'You were in good voice, my dear – as were the whole choir, I thought.' She smiled mischievously. 'Not at all tired sounding.'

He refused to get into that.

'Right. I have to be on court at three but Dr. Raspail is coming about an hour earlier. Do you want to have lunch somewhere?'

'What would you do if I wasn't here? This is important afternoon for you and I want you to be at your best. Would you normally have lunch before a match like this?'

'Well, to be honest, I wouldn't normally have any lunch especially after taking breakfast. I would get to the tennis club at about two, have a hit on court to get loose and then just chat with the members or watch the end of the third-place match that starts at noon. Maybe sit in an armchair reading the newspaper until it was time to start. Nothing special really. Jules should at about two but that is uncertain as he will always have something important to do even on a Sunday.'

'Why don't we go for a short walk together,' offered Angèle, 'then take my cab home to pick up your equipment. Then I will drop you at the tennis club at half past one. Madame Ferry is taking me under her wing for the rest of the day. I will pick her up and come to watch the match with her then afterwards, we'll go home with her to get changed for the evening party. I hope that's all right?'

Drangnet smiled broadly.

'My darling that's an excellent set of suggestions. I'm also highly amused that having been seen very publicly at the opera last night with me, a senior police official, you are now to be seen keeping company with the wife of the Prime Minister of the Republic. A lot of tongues will start wagging.'

She just shrugged.

'I've never bothered much about what people think of me. My father was a market porter with nothing. With his help but without anyone else's, I have become something different. I am now a woman in love and there really aren't any rules for that. I don't care about any of the rest.'

Drangnet turned to her and kissed her full on the lips. A number of people coming in and out of the church looked rather shocked.

'Nor do I, my love. Nor do I.

Chapter 17: Sunday 17th April   Scene 2: The Final of the Tennis Doubles

Having collected their various bits of luggage, Angèle dropped him off at the Tennis Club at one thirty. The place was relatively empty. The third and fourth place match had been concluded in very short order and many of the spectators had left to get a quick lunch to returning to reserve their places for the main event. One of the junior stewards was giving the court a good sweep and Biboche himself was inspecting the new set of balls for the match. As usual they had been sewn by one of the junior professionals. The master himself was well past doing that sort of manual chore.

'Chief Inspector. Good afternoon.' Biboche greeted him as he walked into the club. 'You're nice and early.'

'Good afternoon, *maître.*' he replied. 'All well?'

'Of course, sir. We should have a good turnout to see the reigning champions defend their title for, what is it, the sixth time in a row? There'll be some good money on you two this afternoon.'

Drangnet kept silent. It was a moot point whether laying bets on the outcome of the match was strictly legal. It was certainly dubious especially as the man keeping the book was also the man who would be marking the match: *Maître Paumier* Biboche himself. He changed the subject.

'I know that Madame Ferry will be here this afternoon. I also have a lady friend coming to watch. Also, a doctor friend, a Doctor Raspail. I'm not sure if he's been here before but I believe he plays on the *Île St. Louis.*'

'Ah,' replied Biboche. 'I think I know him. He's played here as a guest from time to time. Quite a decent player. Not up to your standard, of course. But very competent.'

Very competent was high praise coming from the *maître*'

'I think you'll find he's already arrived. Said he was free and was quite happy to wait and have a drink with us. I think you'll find him in the changing room.'

'Good. Please seat my two guests with Madame Ferry.'

'Of course, sir. I'll leave instructions with the steward. As you're good and early, do you want one of the boys to give you a hit to get your eye in? Not that you need it, mind you. But I know you quite like it. Strictly between us it's your partner who would benefit more than you.'

Drangnet pretended to be shocked.

'You should show a little more respect of our Head of Government, *maître*.'

'Ah Chief Inspector. As well you know, this is my particular kingdom. But he will almost certainly be late as usual and therefore won't have the time to warm up properly. If you have a hit early, you'll be able to have a look at your opponents when they do the same.'

'Perhaps your right, *maître*. I'll just go and change.'

He was not completely surprised when he found Doctor Raspail calmly sitting in the changing room reading the newspaper.

'Ah. Chief Inspector. How are you feeling?'

'Well Doctor, to be honest I have very little discomfort from it. It is aching a bit, obviously but I can move without it hurting too much and seem to have good mobility in it.'

'Excellent. I'm pleased to hear it. If you get your shirt off so I can have a good look and then we can decide what to do; if anything.'

Having taken the dressing off he spent a certain amount of time pushing and prodding the wound. He then took Drangnet's left hand and started moving it about quite violently. Enough to make him wince, at least.

'Well that's fine. I'm doing to re-dress it and bind it somewhat more tightly that before, primarily so that the dressing doesn't slip while you're playing. I'm also going to give you a little injection on the top of your arm. It's a sort of local anaesthetic that acts on the skin rather than getting into your blood stream. This is just in case you hit it against something. I can't imagine you will, but we'd better be safe.

It won't affect your movement, or your balance at all. With any luck you'll feel perfectly normal and not feel at all inhibited.'

He did the necessary quickly and left Drangnet to finish getting changed and to make his way onto the court for a hit with one of the young assistant professionals. As he left, the doctor turned back to Drangnet.

'I fully intent to recoup my fees from your exploits this afternoon. Chief Inspector. I'm told on good authority that you are a good bet to win.'

Drangnet laughed.

'I'm not sure that is a particularly sensible thing to do doctor.'

'Ah ha.' he smiled. 'I did say it was a good bet not a safe one. Good luck.'

The match started with the well-ritualized formalities. Biboche himself would do the marking as usual. This was something of a mixed blessing. Maître Biboche was as idiosyncratic in his marking of a tennis game as he was in the rest of his life. While an important part of the marker's job was mark the chases, Biboche's verdicts were sometimes tainted by the quality of the strokes being played. Thus, a chase that resulted from a particularly skilful shot was often marked slightly to that player's advantage. The marker himself was, of course, never questioned.

Biboche announced the match and the players to the assembled crowd that now included Eugénie Ferry and Angèle as well as Doctor Raspail. It was to be best of five six game sets, no deuces to be played. A racquet was spun, the players took their chosen ends and the match began. It was always going to be a contest between youth and experience yet again. Drangnet and Ferry served first and started slowly and carefully, taking time to get the feel of the court and the specially made match balls. Biboche had instructed how the balls would be made and they were not quite as hard, it seemed to Drangnet, as the usual ones that were made to withstand much more use every day. These were a fraction softer and would take a little more spin and linger slightly longer on the walls and floor. They also wouldn't bounce quite so high as the harder balls that were in use every day. The difference was infinitesimal, but an experienced player would know. Of course, they were playing with a full set of balls, A unused Royal Set of nine dozen. Their opponents, being both younger and less experienced took a more aggressive approach and started forcing for the dedans immediately, concentrating on outright winning shots rather than on laying chases to win the service end. It was a high-risk strategy, especially against opponents whose experiences had taught them when the leave the ball rather than try to play it.

Drangnet and Ferry ran out winners of the first set, six games to two without ever seeming to get into trouble. Their opponents forcing play was just off the mark and their chases were relatively simple to attack. They remained unruffled under pressure and held everything under control, helped by their opponents' inaccuracies and misjudgements. They seemed particularly prone to try to return very difficult shots sent with much cut into the service end corner as opposed to leaving the ball and fighting the point again when they changed end and replayed the chases.

The second set was less successful for the holders. Their opponents' power plays started hitting the target more often and, by small degrees, as often happens in such matches, without the other side playing noticeable badly, the set slipped away from them. One set all after forty-five minutes and the packed crown was beginning to settle into a long match. The spectators, silent, of course, while play was going on, now regularly started to shout encouragement to one side of the other between rests. Most of the crowd had made wagers on the game; substantial ones in some cases.

'Well?' muttered Ferry clearly frustrated as they prepared to serve at the beginning of the third set. Drangnet had always been the calmer of the two under pressure for as long as they had been playing together.

'Stay steady, Jules. Just carry on as we have been. Keep the ball in play and don't try to return the unreturnable. They are hitting their targets now, but it won't last. No-one can play the forcing game for a complete match, especially a pair that has as little technique as they. Stick to our plan. Run them around and get them tired. Their accuracy will fall off when that happens. Slow the game down. We lost that last set because we followed them too much and tried to out-hit them.'

Sure enough the third set was a repeat of the first with play now slowed down by the elder pair keeping the ball in play even when relatively easy winning opportunities arose. They were playing precisely the right sort of psychological game that would leave their young opponents frustrated and therefore vulnerable. They gave away very few points with mistakes and again their opponents frustration showing in an ever increasing error count. Ferry patrolled the service end base line returning everything as their opponent's forces for the dedans became increasingly erratic and their already limited ability to cut chases into the corners diminished ever further. As a consequence, they increasingly tried to win lesser chases by aiming for the service end galleries.

Standing well up the court, Drangnet's defence of the galleries was exemplary, picking off shots intended for the galleries with accurate volleys, many of which he directed at the base of the tambour, the buttress at the hazard end of the court, making the shot almost impossible to return. Hitting the base of the tambour was a well-established tactic as the angle of the wall that stood out at an angle resulted in the ball taking a violent change of direction often laterally across almost at floor level. It was a speciality of Drangnet's but it required him to take up a position well up the court defending the service end galleries, almost opposite the first gallery perilously near the net. It was a position only used in doubled as the whole of the rest of their end had to be left for his partner to defend. It was a very dangerous place as he was very near their opponent's forces and his reactions had to be very quick and his courage constant. More than once he heard Angèle gasp as the solid ball was driven directly at his head at full pace from a distance of less than five yards. He seemed completely unperturbed by the barrage and stood unmoved. His great strength was that he was calm under fire. It was his intransigence more than his skill that annoyed his opponents more and their play became more erratic as a result. That, of course, was the whole object of the exercise. His position so near the net also made the grill a much easier winning target too. Soon they found that they were denying their opponents the service end for long periods of time. Again, they ran out winners of the third set by six games to two.

As they started the fourth set, there was a good deal of satisfaction in the crowd. Many of them knew that the great game *Jeu de Paume* had always rewarded experience over enthusiastic youth, subtlety and touch over force and bluster. They had put their money on that judgement and, after the slight concern of the second set, they were now confident that their money would be safe.

So it proved. The champions took the fourth and deciding set with an outstanding performance of craft and skill. They were happy to concede the service end from time to time, confident that Drangnet's shots would be cut with increasing ferocity into the corners resulting in chases that were seldom worse that two yards and usually better than that. Ferry even indulged himself occasionally in the delights of stealing a leaf from the young men's game with forces for the dedans, many of which were successful as they were so completely out of character. By the time they won the set without conceding a single game, their opponents were both demoralised and demolished. It was a bravura performance and the whole crown, many of whom had just won a considerable sum of money, stood in prolonged applause. Even Biboche came onto his beloved court and led the applause, an almost unheard-of event.

'Messieurs,' he said offering a bow. 'That was one of the best and most emphatic performances I have ever seen on my court. It was a privilege to see it.'

The great and the good were led from the seats in the dedans and the galleries to assemble on court as well to add their congratulations.

'Well played, my darling,' Angele whispered into his ear as she planted a chaste public kiss on his sweaty cheek. Raspail shook his hand too.

'Thank you, Monsieur. I think that you can regard my fee as being paid in full.'

Drangnet was astonished to see Gant coming towards him. He must have been watching from one of the side galleries. He had never come to watch before.

'Well done, Boss.' he said as he shook his hand. 'Very impressive.'

The assembled company broke up quite quickly. The court had to be prepared for the evening's festivities that were to start at eight. Ferry and Drangnet went to change. It was then that Ferry say the strapping on Drangnet's shoulder.

'What on earth is that all about? You didn't tell me that you were injured.'

'Oh, it's nothing very much.'

'What do you mean, it's not very much. It certainly looks like something to me all right.'

At that moment Drangnet was saved from further interrogation by the arrival of their opponents to get changed. So Drangnet just contented himself with a quiet 'I'll tell you about it when we get home, Jules.'

It didn't take them long to change and they soon left with their partners left for Ferry's house on the *Rue Bayard* to relax further and change for the evening. They had arranged for Drangnet's evening clothes to be picked up from the *Place des Vosges* by Angèle's driver. Drangnet thought somewhat sourly that if this great adventure was to continue, he was going to have to give up a considerable amount of the personal independence that hitherto he had valued so much. However, such ignoble thoughts were quickly banished from his mind as they got into her cab to follow the Ferry's home. Angèle immediately snuggled up to him and put her arm around his waist.

'You were magnificent, my darling. I was very proud of you.'

Drangnet's reply was just to tilt her head up towards him and plant a very long and lingering kiss on her lips.

'Do you think that our hosts would be shocked if we asked for the use of one of their beds for an hour or so?' she asked mischievously. 'Or are you too tired for that sort of thing?'

'I thought you ladies required for ever to get ready.'

'That only goes to show how little you know about women, my dear.'

In fact, by the time they arrived at the *Rue Bayard* they found that both Drangnet's evening clothes had already arrived as well as Angèle's maid with her outfit. There was to be no opportunity for anything more than getting changed and a preliminary glass of something before they left again back to the centre of town. Somewhat to Angèle's disappointment they were shown to separate rooms as Madame Ferry continued to take charge of proceedings.

'Perhaps we can reconvene in the drawing room at seven? We are due back at the club at eight for our grand entry.'

'Six thirty.' Ferry muttered in Drangnet's ear as he passed.

Chapter 17: Sunday 17th April   Scene 3: Party on Court and After

By the time Drangnet had changed and had returned to the drawing room, his host was already there. He had poured a whisky for both on them. They sat either side of the fire each with a whisky in hand. But the conversation wasn't about the tennis. There would be time enough for that later.

'Well. Tell me. What's this all about? How come you come to today's game with a bloody great wound in your shoulder. Your entire arm is black and blue as if you've been beaten with a tennis racquet not just been playing with one.'

Drangnet just handed across the folder in which he had brought the copy of his report to his Superintendent.

'I think, Jules, it would be easier if you just read that. Save a lot of explanation.'

There was a silence while the great man took out his reading glasses from his top pocket and set to read. Drangnet just say there sipping at his drink, wondering what the reaction would be. It wasn't the most conventional report of an equally unconventional police investigation. This was going to test their friendship. His only hope was that Ferry, like all politicians was essentially a pragmatist. He looked primarily for solutions and as long as there were available, he could put up with a bit of a mess. Ferry, well used to reading large amounts of official paper, didn't take long to finish a short report that was distinguished more by what it omitted than what it said. Ferry would see that easily. He would be much less concerned than Dancart with the legal niceties of the whole thing. He just wanted the whole thing to go away quietly. His first reaction was one of exasperation as much as anything.

'Good God, Louis. It really is difficult enough to build a new democratic state from the ashes of defeat at war, revolutions on the street and a totalitarian monarchy without all this. I won't insult you and ask if all this is true. It obviously is. You, above all, don't make things like this up. I don't think you or anyone else could.'

He stopped to re-fill their glasses and took his seat again.

'So, do you think that this unfortunate business of the prostitute murders is at an end, old friend?'

Drangnet felt a sense of relief. As he assumed would happen, Ferry had seen through the fog of it all and had, to use an expression that derived from the game they had just been playing, cut to the chase.

'Only partially, Jules. We rounded up some of the less important member of this rather sinister conspiracy and this policeman Cordiez has, er, been removed from the picture, but the whole thing goes much deeper than that, I think.'

'How deep?' Ferry was looking uncomfortable.

'A conspiracy like this must have had sanction from the top, Jules, and the report given the names of the ones we know about. We mopped up some minor masons with a bee in their bonnets about women. But the whole thing smacks of something much bigger. Cordiez seems to be to have been a sort of link. That's all. Part of the club, of course, – the masonic club, that is - but, at a fairly low level. He was the man who organized the troops to carry out their orders. But these were orders issued from much higher up. We may have put a stop to the killings for the time being, but I wouldn't be at all surprised to see it starting again sometime unless we get to these three senators that, at least, we now about. These men are fanatics and that sort isn't usually put off so easily.'

Ferry looked troubled.

'You mean we have some sort of conspiracy here that is larger than just the people you've uncovered?'

'Yes, we do. And I suspect it is one that won't go away and more than the Masons themselves will.'

'You're pretty sure that the Masons are behind this in some way, Louis.'

'Yes. At the level I have uncovered it. I don't think it is a general masonic conspiracy by any means. But I'm pretty sure that this is a little group of fanatics that grew out of the freemason movement. After all, the use of the masonic symbol and the number in the tattoo is pretty clear. Fanatics like these don't try to offload the responsibility onto someone else. They are usually pretty proud of what they are doing, however secret.'

Ferry was about to object to this until he remembered that he was indeed in a much better position to ferret out those senior masons responsible that his policeman friend. In an effort to change tack, he asked rather gruffly:

'And what about the murder of the murderers. How is that investigation going?'

Drangnet just smiled. This may have been the day of their great triumph on the tennis court, but he wasn't going to let his friend get away with that jibe so easily. His reply was all forced innocence.

'And are you asking, Sir, in your capacity as Head of State, one of those ultimately responsible for the administration of justice in the Republic of France or as freemason responsible for protecting the secrecy of your members?'

Ferry just frowned. It was a good enough question and he knew it. It was also blackmail of a sort. Silence was the best option.

'Well, *Monsieur le President*, I would probably make the same reply however you answered my question. Every policeman has to prioritise his time. From where I'm standing, I can see a number of seemingly deranged young men who are members of a legal but very secret society going around killing young women who are residents of Paris and thus who have a right to expect as much protection from me and my department as anyone else, including officers of state. These people are being in killed in turn by person or persons unknown. In my personal opinion someone is doing the state's job for it and I should feel grateful rather than angry. So unless I receive instructions from my own boss, who probably feels as relieved about finding an explanation about all this as I do, or from the current Prefect of Police of Paris who is, as a senior Freemason, is very high on my list of suspects for the whole conspiracy, I intend to let that matter lie for the moment. It will join the list of our unsolved crimes, and there are plenty of those.'

Ferry's frown deepened as he heard a reply that he didn't like. He was a man used to getting his own way, but he also knew that the man in front of him was not a man to be turned or pushed around.

'You know, Louis, that Prefect Andrieux could be a powerful enemy.'

Drangnet shook his head.

'I really don't care. In any case he is soon to be replaced by your friend Jean-Louis Camescasse and, at least, he's not a freemason.'

Ferry was clearly astonished.

'How, the hell do you know that, Louis? I haven't even told him that yet.'

'Ah, my friend,' replied Drangnet with a slight smile on his face, 'Perhaps it is as well to remember that a good senior policeman should always stand one foot in the *Palais Garnier* with the cream of society but with the other in the gutters of Paris with thieves and prostitutes. A policeman gets his information from a variety of places.'

Ferry nodded glumly as Drangnet went on.

'There is one thing you can help me with though. I can't touch these three senators legally. As you've seen I have absolutely no proof against them although they won't necessarily know that. They might well be sufficiently scared to assume that I know much more than I do and might have at least some evidence against them. But I would very much like to put the fear of God into them. I want to talk to them in private. I want them to know that they have been found out. Not only does the *Sûreté* know about them but that you do too. I want to get them together for a meeting early next week and I want half an hour alone with them. You shouldn't be there, of course, but I want them to be aware that you know about them and leave it to their imagination to guess who else might.'

Ferry didn't have to think for very long. In fact, he seemed somewhat enthusiastic about the idea. It certainly shifted the problem if not actually off his desk for good, then at least well to one side of it.

'Yes, my friend. I think that sounds like a splendid idea. Where would you like this meeting to take place?'

Drangnet thought for a moment. Then a smile crossed his face.

'Let's see if we can frighten them. I suggest I'll get them picked them up from their houses very early one morning next week and take them to the Roquette prison. I'll have my conversation with them in the condemned cells very close to the yard in which Madame Guillotine lives before chucking them back out onto the streets of the *onzième*.

'Right. I rather think that'll do very nicely.' Ferry sounding rather entertained by the whole idea. He then became slightly more thoughtful but still retained a slight twinkle in his eye.

'You seem to have picked up a new companion who is not only charming, intelligent and beautiful but powerful, dangerous and obviously capable of killing people. Just your sort of girlfriend, I would imagine.'

To Drangnet's slight relief, they were interrupted by the arrival of the ladies. Both, of course, looked superb. They were dressed slightly less exotically that for the previous night at the Opera but nevertheless they would ensure that many heads would be turned in their direction tonight. Madame Ferry looks suitably regal in dark maroon silk while Angèle had chosen a slim fitting gown in deepest royal blue. She had again piled her dark hair on top of her head, this time in full Provençale style complete with complex double chignon around a small headdress of interlaced black velvet ribbon. Drangnet immediately remembered his mother and grandmother wearing their hair in a similar way. He looked at it and gave her a radiant smile of thanks; a smile that she instantly understood.

By the time they arrived back at the tennis club the company was assembled. The court had been cleared, the net and net posts removed and the netting that protected the galleries had been dismounted. A long table had been erected along the full length of the main wall of the court and six subsidiary tables at right angles distributed along its length across the court. The tables were covered in white linen and the club silver was out in force with the place of honour given to the magnificent silver trophy. The court was suffused with a gentle, flickering light from the many five-branched candelabra that were spaced along the tables.

The club members and their guests were all there and standing behind their chairs. There was an old and honoured ritual to be observed. The club president and his wife were at the centre of the long table with four empty seats on either side of them. The rest of the members and their wives had been placed, with the unaccompanied bachelors relegated to the ends of the cross tables. In all, slightly more than a hundred people filled the court number one. The traditional applause started as the runners-up entered with their wives and took their places split either side on the vacant chairs furthest away from the centre on the presidents left. The applause then swelled noticeably as Drangnet and Ferry escorted their partners made their way around to the remaining seats. All eight took a little time to be seated and the applause continued until the whole assembly sat at a signal from the president and dinner commenced.

Conversation flowed and there was a generally high-spirited atmosphere. The food was excellent as the service staff and the cooks had been sourced from local restaurants and, by tradition, the club held a substantial collection of some of the finest vintages that France had produced. Drangnet was seated between the chairman's wife and Angèle and they were faced across the table by the Chairman of the tennis club at Versailles who was always invited to this annual occasion. other guest were scattered around amongst their hosts.

After an hour or two, the meal was brought to an abrupt end as the Chairman rang for silence with his knife against his wine glass and rose to his feet to make the presentation of the trophy. Ferry and Drangnet rose and took hold of it and not without some twinging from Drangnet's shoulder, held it aloft as the assembled company then took to their feet to toast the new champions. By club tradition there were no speeches which came as a relief to Drangnet who hated public speaking and a disappointment to Ferry who loved it. That done, the company remained standing while the champions took their partners and processed out of the court, followed by the rest.

'Whatever next?' Angèle whispered into Drangnet's ear as they walked.

'Why, my dear. Now we dance, of course,' after a while adding 'we must start and you should be warned that we change partners half way through.'

The train led out of the first court and entered the second court which had been decorated out as a ballroom. As they entered, a small string ensemble at one end struck up a waltz tune and the two men led their partners to stand into the middle of the floor while the rest of the members and guests distributed themselves around the walls clapping rhythmically in time to the music. When they were all assembled, the champions started their dance, still to the applause of the crowd. After a minute the two pairs came twirling together and in an elegant moment the ladies were handed off to their opposite partners. After a while the rest of the guests joined in and the ball began.

For different reasons, both Ferry and Drangnet were reluctant to stay too long. This particular party had the reputation of lasting most of the night, but the two main protagonists lasted for about an hour and then made their apologies. Ferry had a full day in the legislature the next day and his working day usually started at about six in the morning. Louis just wanted to spend time alone with Angèle. So, he followed Ferry's lead and took the opportunity to rescue Angèle from an ever-increasing line of men wished to add their names to her dance card. Having thanked the club president and the various member of staff, they both piled quickly into her waiting carriage which set off eastwards along the *Quai des Tuileries* on the right bank of the Seine past the *Palais du Louvre* and on towards the *Place des Vosges*. It was only when they drew parallel to the relatively new *Pont Neuf Louis Phillippe*, that they suddenly turned right and crossed to the *Île St Louis*. His companion had long since seemed to snooze quietly against his shoulder, held tightly by his encompassing arm. He decided to say nothing, and it was after a few moments that they halted in front of No 38 on the *Quai d'Orleans* that she seemed to wake and

357

jumped out of the carriage, dragging him out after her. The carriage left and she led him inside. After climbing the stairs as he had done before only a week or so ago they reached her drawing room with the magnificent moonlit view to the west towards the great cathedral.

They stood in silence together his arms around her and looked over the thin strip of water between the two islands in the Seine. Notre Dame was a dark shape outlined against the dim glow of the city, surrounded by a pale necklace of the moonlit water that was flowing very slow around the sides of the island and the yellow lights from surrounding gas lamps.

'Is it over?' she whispered.

He sighed.

'Perhaps, for the moment at least, my love. But in the longer term, I don't really think so. We've broken the chain of command with Cordiez and some of the foot soldiers have been removed but those at the top of this madness are still there, protected by their positions and their masonic secrecy. They are fanatics and fanatics are always the most difficult to stop. And there will always be thugs willing to so the killings for money.'

'Can we really not do anything, Louis.'

'Other than take what precautions we can, it is hard to think of much more for the moment.'

They continued to stand silently together for a while. Each with their own thoughts until she took him firmly by the hand and led him away from the window. Within a very few moments they were lying together in Angèle's bed wrapped in each other's arms. The curtained room was dark except for a small candle on a table beside the bed. She drew back slightly and held his face in her hands.

'And us, my dearest Louis? What is there for us? Do we continue this romance of ours or do we go our separate ways?'

Drangnet was appalled. The possibility of finishing their affair hadn't even occurred to him.

'No, my dearest. I think we are at the very start of something, something very precious and more than anything I want it to continue. You?'

By way of reply she just held him even more tightly and gave him yet another long and adoring kiss. After a while he came up for air.'In any case after the last two weeks and especially the last two days, everyone in Paris knows by now. We have no choice but to continue. Reputations depend on it.'

After a pause, she continued.

'It's going to be difficult, my love, given what we both, er, do for a living, as it were.'

'There's no denying that' he agreed.

'Perhaps, my dear,' she murmured. 'It would be best if we both neither asked each other awkward questions nor told each other difficult lies. It might be a good start.'

He just nodded. There was a slightly longer pause after which she whispered.

'And are you really very tired, my great tennis player, after your exertions of this afternoon and all that dancing?'

His reply came back in an insouciant tone.'

'No, not really very tired.'

'And your shoulder. Is it not very painful?'

'No, not really very painful.'

She reached out and snuffed the candle.

'Good.' she said.

Printed in Great Britain
by Amazon